AFTER HOURS ATTRACTION

KIANNA ALEXANDER

HIS PERFECT FAKE ENGAGEMENT

SHANNON MCKENNA

MILLS & BOON

First Published in Great Britain 2021
by Mills & Boon, an imprint of HarperCollins*Publishers* Ltd,
1 London Bridge Street, London, SE1 9GF

www.harpercollins.co.uk

HarperCollins*Publishers*
1st Floor, Watermarque Building,
Ringsend Road, Dublin 4, Ireland

After Hours Attraction © 2021 Eboni Manning
His Perfect Fake Engagement © 2021 Shannon McKenna

ISBN: 978-0-263-28285-6

0221

MIX
Paper from
responsible sources
FSC™ C007454

Printed and bound in Spain
by CPI, Barcelona

AFTER HOURS ATTRACTION

KIANNA ALEXANDER

To Atlanta, With Love

One

Tapping her fingers on the steering wheel in time with the Migos track flowing through her speakers, Ainsley Voss pulled up to the curb at Carter G. Woodson Academy, joining the long line of cars in the pickup lane. It was just before four thirty on a Friday afternoon, and she expected her eleven-year-old son, Cooper, to appear at any moment. Baseball practice always let out on time because Coach Tyler Rigsby was a stickler, with a family of his own to get home to.

A few minutes later, a stream of students who participated in various after-school enrichment activities offered at the academy began to stream out through the glass-paneled double doors. She scanned the crowd, smiling when her gaze landed on Cooper. His dirt-streaked baseball uniform looked like ten or twelve other kids', but his sideways cap and the bright orange backpack slung over his shoulder made him stand out among his peers. He was chatting with two of his teammates and didn't seem aware of her presence. She started to honk the horn but refrained when she remembered his whining the last time.

As the two other boys split off in different directions, Cooper looked her way. As he walked up and got into the car, she looked at him in the rearview. "Hey, honey."

"Hey, Ma." He threw his backpack onto the seat next to him and buckled his seat belt. "Practice was cool. I know you're gonna ask me that."

She chuckled. "Okay. What about the school day before that?"

"It was okay, too. I was bored out of my mind in Social Studies, but other than that…" He shrugged in that aloof adolescent way.

"Gotcha." She pulled away from the curb, inching along as the line of cars snaked toward the exit. Mindful of the signals from the crossing guard, she asked, "Anything else you want to tell me?"

After a few moments of silence, he said, "Yeah, actually. I need some stuff."

Ainsley wanted to sigh but held back. Whenever Cooper uttered the phrase *I need some stuff*, she knew she'd be bidding a sad farewell to a wad of cash. "Okay, I'm listening."

"Well, first, Coach says I need to replace my cleats ASAP since the soles are starting to come off. Then we have that field trip to DC to go to the Smithsonian in like two weeks. Did you forget?"

Making the left turn into city traffic, she cringed. "Sorry, Coop. I did forget. How much is it again?"

"It's like two hundred since we're staying overnight. And the money and the form were supposed to be turned in today, but Mrs. Rush gave me until Monday."

Damn. There goes girls' night out. "Is there anything else? Or is it just the cleats and the trip?" *Lord, please let that be it. My wallet is crying real tears.*

"It's only one more thing. Can you put some money on my streaming account? So I can download that new Lil Boosie? I promise I'll get the edited version."

Now, sitting in the thick of Atlanta traffic and mentally calculating how much of her hard-earned money she would soon part with, Ainsley felt the subtle throb begin in her right temple. "I guess I can put a few dollars on there, but that's really all I can spare, Coop."

"Oh yeah. Bryce asked if I could go to the movies tonight with him. Can I?"

Bryce Redford, son of her neighbors Fitz and Bebe Redford, was Cooper's best friend. The two boys were thick as thieves, studying together, playing sports together, and whiling away the hours with comic books and *Minecraft* marathons. She rubbed her temple, careful to keep her other hand on the wheel and her eyes on the road. "Yikes, Coop. I just dropped a stack on your semester tuition, plus those class valentines. I'm not made of money, sweetheart."

"I know, Mama. I'm sorry I need so much stuff." His tone sounded contrite.

Guilt squeezed her heart. "Don't worry about it, honey. I think you can go, but I'm not sure I can give you snack money."

"That's okay. Bryce is using his birthday money for snacks."

She sighed, unable to hold it back any longer. Sure, some of these things were wants, not needs, but she had no desire to get into that with him right now. Honestly, Cooper didn't ask for much. And he was a good kid. He studied hard, made good grades and stayed out of trouble—with the exception of the occasional youthful lapse in judgment. Southwest Atlanta held all kinds of trouble for a young boy his age to get into, and yet, despite his lack of a male figure in his life, he kept his nose clean. She was proud of him, and the whole reason she worked as hard as she did at 404 Sound recording studio was to make a good life for him.

By the time they got home, she was in full-blown headache mode. She entered the house and headed straight upstairs to the medicine cabinet for ibuprofen. Popping two of the pills with a handful of water from the sink, she flipped off the light and walked to her room to change. Once there, she kicked off her black suede pumps, then got out of the lavender button-down blouse and black pencil skirt. Donning a pair of leggings and an oversize Disturbing Tha Peace sweatshirt, she tucked her feet into a pair of bunny slippers and headed downstairs to make dinner.

She was at the stove, setting the oven to preheat, when Cooper bopped in, his white buds in his ears. She had no idea what he was listening to since he tended to silently mouth the lyrics rather than singing or rapping aloud. Walking toward her, he popped one bud out. "Are you cooking?"

"I was about to put in a pizza. I thought we'd have some salad on the side."

"It's cool, Ma. Ms. Bebe's gonna get us burgers on the way to the movie."

She reached into her waistband pocket. "Here's ten for your ticket."

He took the folded bill. "Thanks, Ma. I'm gonna go ahead over there." He gave her a dutiful hug and kiss on the cheek, popped his earbud back in and danced his way out the back door.

Ainsley put the pizza in the oven and dropped into a seat at the kitchen table. While the pizza cooked, she opened the budgeting app on her phone, adjusting for all the things Cooper had added to her plate today. The results were not good, and she could feel a frown creasing her face. *At this rate, I'll be selling one of my kidneys online.* It only served as another reminder that it was time for her to move up at work. She'd been executive assistant to Gage Woodson, chief operations officer at the fabled 404 Sound recording studio, for the last five and a half years. She knew the company like the back of her hand, and that's why she had her eye on a management position in human resources. If she could snag the job, it would come with her own office, parking spot and a sizable raise. The raise was the most enticing thing, based on her current situation.

I love my son—I swear I do. But the boy is costing me a mint!

She knew she was more than qualified for the position. But there was one problem: Gage. Her handsome yet incredibly closed-off boss. She'd been taking care of his demands for so long, she didn't know if anyone else could, or would, put up with him. Deep down, she felt a sense of loyalty to him, one that was likely tied to her raging crush on him. Yes, she'd been lusting after her boss pretty much since she'd accepted the position. So far, though, practicality and his tendency to stay locked in his office had kept her from acting on her feelings. How would he feel about her leaving her job as his assistant? Knowing Gage, he'd be annoyed at her for the inconvenience of having to replace her. Still, her dedication to Cooper trumped everything. If she got the job, she'd take it…and Gage would just have to figure it out.

* * *

Gage Woodson stifled a yawn as he flipped on the lights in his home gym at promptly six fifteen Saturday morning. While he did his best to stick to his workout routine, he didn't know if he'd ever think of himself as a morning person. Dressed in gray sweats and neon-green sneakers, he headed straight for the elliptical machine. Putting in his headphones and turning on his workout mix, he started pedaling.

He'd been on the machine about ten minutes when his baby brother, Miles, strolled in. Dressed in a black-and-white-striped tracksuit, he was sipping green juice from a plastic cup through a straw. "Morning, bro."

"Late as always," Gage quipped, raising the difficulty level on the machine just until the point his thigh muscles started to feel it. Keeping up with the pace of the classic Goodie Mob song in his ears helped him make the most of his workout. "What the hell are you drinking?"

Miles chuckled. "Power smoothie with liquid aminos. Gotta make it count, you know?" He climbed onto the recumbent bike next to him and started it up.

After thirty minutes, the two of them switched machines. Gage pedaled the bike a bit slower than the elliptical now that his thighs were protesting in earnest. Once they'd completed an hour of cardio, they headed to the weights.

Gage lay on his back on the bench while Miles set the weights on the bar. "You sure you can press 250, bro? That's your body weight plus like fifty mo'."

Gage rolled his eyes at his brother's teasing. "Just set me up, Miles. Not everybody's arms are weak and spindly like yours."

Miles shook his head but did as he asked. As Gage

lifted, Miles spotted him, and after twenty reps, Gage set the bar back in the bracket. "Any further questions?"

"Nah, you made your point." Miles traded positions with him. "But I'm not like you. So you can go ahead and bust that weight down to 180. I know my limits."

After they finished working out, the two brothers sat on Gage's screened back porch, protein shakes in hand. Mopping the sweat from his brow, Gage took a long drink from his shake. "Who wrote up the preliminary report on quarterly spending?"

"My lead accountant. You know, Kali Ramirez." Miles looked his way. "I signed off on it, though. Why do you ask?"

"I just can't get over that ten-thousand-dollar loss we took based on my actions."

Miles rolled his eyes. "Nobody blames you for that. At least, nobody in finance." As a chief financial officer, Miles managed the budget for the entire company. "It's not your fault, man."

"Yes, it is. I was stupid." He'd never forgive himself for trusting his ex-girlfriend the way he had and still felt responsible for replacing the funds she'd embezzled. "Why'd you list the loss as discretionary?"

"Kali did that. I approved it because it didn't fall into a cut-and-dried category like accounts payable or receivable." Miles waved him off. "We're just splitting hairs here, Gage. It's all semantics."

"I know, but…"

"Nah, bro. No buts. It's Saturday. Can you just stop talking about work for like five minutes?"

Gage cringed. "Sorry."

"I know it's not your fault you're so uptight. I guess you get it from Dad. But the least you can do is try not to give in to it. It's the weekend, nice weather and everything, and your ass is wound up tighter than the security lines at Hartsfield–Jackson."

As much as he hated to admit it, his brother was right. He'd always had a hard time disconnecting from work. His job as chief operations officer came with a high level of responsibility to his family, his employees and the shareholders, and he didn't take that lightly.

"Listen, though. I got a Tinder tale for you."

Gage shook his head. "Don't tell me you put your profile back up. I thought you said all you get are gold diggers?"

"That was before. This time I put up a picture in silhouette and gave a very vague description of myself and my work." Miles rubbed his hands together. "I had six hits in two hours. Went out with this fine, thick shawty last night."

Gage listened to his brother spin a story about drinking at a bar before heading to one of the downtown Atlanta hotels with his "thick shawty," but his mind kept wandering back to work. Or more specifically, back to his gorgeous and extremely efficient executive assistant, Ainsley Voss. She had a body built for pleasure, a beautifully symmetrical face and silky dark hair. Yet, in the five-plus years he'd worked with her, he'd never approached her that way. She was just too good at her job, and he couldn't risk ruining it by asking her out on a date. His embezzling ex had also been a 404 Sound employee, and in the three years they'd dated, he told himself it was fine since she worked in another department. Well, that had blown up in his face in a spectacular way, and now, he was simply too skittish to make that mistake again.

Still, that didn't stop him from fantasizing about Ainsley. She kept her hair up in a bun on top of her head most of the time, with a sharp-line bang straight across her forehead, grazing her perfectly arched brows. In his fantasies, he'd undo that bun and let the dark riches of her hair fall around her shoulders. He'd run his fingers through it, inhaling the scent of fresh flowers that always seemed to follow her. Then he'd graze his fingertips along the hem of that fitted pencil skirt and...

"Gage!" Miles snapped his fingers. "Did you hear what I said, man?"

He shook his head, reluctantly returning to reality. "No, sorry. What?"

"I said, she had triple Ds, bro. *Triple. Ds.*" He made a juggling motion with his hands.

Gage laughed. "Miles, you're a hot-ass mess. And what happens now that you've met her and she knows who you are?"

He shrugged. "I don't know. I'll probably see her again, just based on the strength of that rack." He laughed. "Nah, I'm kidding. She seems like a sweet girl, and I'll text her in a few days to see if she wants to get together again."

Shaking his head at his brother's antics, Gage finished off his shake and set the cup on the wicker coffee table in front of him. He remembered the requisition forms he'd left on the corner of his desk and cursed under his breath.

Miles frowned. "What's wrong with you?"

Knowing how his brother would react if he brought up work again, he shrugged it off. "Nothing. Just remembered something, but it can wait."

"Cool. Listen, you wanna hit up that pancake place for breakfast?"

"Yeah, we can do that." They did this almost every

weekend—work out, then pig out. "But first I'm about to hit up the shower. Can't be going out all sweaty."

"Of course not. Ain't no Woodson man ever going out like that." Miles stood, stretching. "I'll use the downstairs while you use your master, then we'll change and head out."

Gage followed his brother back inside. "Sounds like a plan."

Two

When Ainsley walked into the 404 operations suite late Monday morning, she was met with the usual subdued silence. The suite, which occupied the eastern half of the second floor, contained Gage's office, the offices of two other operations staffers, a small conference room and a lobby area.

The lobby area featured soft gray walls and framed black-and-white photographs of artists who'd recorded at 404. One accent wall, painted a deep shade of red, held a framed poster-size photo of company owner Caleb Woodson with Todd "Speech" Thomas, lead vocalist and producer for the legendary Afrocentric hip-hop group Arrested Development.

Moving to her desk in the center of the lobby area, she tucked her purse into the top drawer. With her company tablet and stylus in hand, she walked down the corridor, past the three closed office doors, to the conference room at the end.

As usual, she was the first to arrive for the department's monthly meeting. Inside the empty conference room, she flipped the switch, flooding the room with soft LED lighting. The polished black lacquer table, with six matching upholstered chairs pulled up to it, showed a reflection of the chandelier above.

Opening the blinds, she set up a pitcher of water and glasses in the center of the table, then took her seat to the right of the seat at the head. While waiting for the others, she used her tablet to peruse the *Greater Fulton Business Journal*'s article on Shana Dresden. After more than twenty years as 404's manager of human resources, Mrs. Dresden would retire in early spring. *And with any luck, I'll be the one to fill her position. I spent the start of my career in HR and I know this company like the back of my hand— I'm perfect for this job.*

Production manager Kelly Ross was first to arrive, with marketing manager Duval Anderson close behind her. After the two management staffers took their seats, the three of them exchanged morning pleasantries while Ainsley closed the article and opened her notes app in anticipation of Gage's arrival.

He strode in a few minutes later, commanding her attention as he did every time he entered a room. He wore a charcoal-gray suit, bright red shirt and a black-and-gray-striped tie. His tall crown of curls and full beard were impeccably groomed, and as he set his tablet down on the table, his arresting brown eyes swept over the room. "Good morning, all." As his gaze met hers, it lingered for a few long moments.

She swallowed. *Why does he have to be so fine?* While her insides melted, outwardly she offered a small smile and nod of greeting.

His answering smile only melted her further.

He took his seat, then clapped his hands together. "Let's get started, shall we? Duval, what's happening in marketing?"

Duval cleared his throat and ran a hand over his close-trimmed fade. "We're testing a new layout for the website to improve ease of use. We also updated the forms for artists and managers to book private studio tours or for them to book studio time."

"Great. And what did you come up with for artist outreach?" Gage leaned forward in his seat.

"I'm running ads on SoundCloud, with several versions to test for efficacy. The purpose is to show artists the benefits of recording with us."

While they talked, Ainsley used her stylus to jot down notes on what was said.

"Sounds good. Kelly, what can you report on the production front?"

Kelly pulled out a pencil she'd tucked into her reddish-brown curls and began tapping the small yellow legal pad as she rattled off the information. "We had four albums produced at 404 in January. Of the four, one went over the predetermined recording time and that artist paid for an additional twenty hours of billable time."

Gage's smile brightened. "Sucks for them, but I'm sure that padded the bottom line nicely. What about this month?"

"We're on track for five albums this month, with a total of 370 projected billable hours…assuming all goes well with the new sound equipment for Studio 1A."

Gage scratched his chin, and once again, his gaze swung toward her. "Ainsley, do we have a status update on the equipment?"

Switching apps on her tablet, Ainsley ran a check on the tracking number for the shipment. Her brow furrowed as the results appeared. *Oh shit.* "It says... shipment lost."

Gage's eyes flashed. "What?" She was sure he'd heard her the first time; he just hadn't liked the answer.

"It says, 'shipment lost.'"

Kelly whistled. Duval cringed.

Gage sighed aloud. "We don't have time for this. We need the studio ready when Organized Noize brings in The Visionary." He ran a hand over his face. "It's been, what, ten years since they debuted a new artist? We can't lose this contract."

She scrolled down, looking for the contact information. "I'll get to the bottom of it. I'm calling the shipper's customer service line."

"Thank you. In the meantime, the meeting's dismissed." Gage stood. "Try to keep everything else running while we deal with this equipment mess."

After Kelly and Duval packed up and left, Ainsley called the shipper's eight-hundred number and waited on hold. While she drummed her fingertips on the tabletop, her boss watched her with an intense, expectant gaze. She could feel the tension rolling off him like a heavy fog over a lake. There wasn't anything she could do but wait for the moment, and under his scrutiny, the waiting seemed to drag on forever. She purposely leaned back in her chair and kept her gaze fixed on the ceiling, knowing that if she looked at him, she'd find only those intoxicating brown eyes. Hell, she couldn't even hazard a glance at the table because the surface was far too reflective.

Finally, a voice came on the line. "How can I help you?"

Ainsley immediately gave her name, stated her problem and rattled off the tracking number for the studio equipment. After a few moments of listening to the rep's typing in the background, she confirmed that the crates holding the equipment were indeed lost. "How? And what is your company planning to do to locate our items or to remedy this?"

The rep rattled off a scripted dialogue about an account credit for future shipping and advised her that a refund for the items would be processed in six to eight weeks after some paperwork. Hanging up, she looked to Gage. "I'm sorry, Gage. It looks like the equipment is legit lost."

"Well, fuck." Gage ran a hand over his face. "I can't let this happen. I've got to get in contact with Marshall Harcroft, now." He came around to her seat, leaning over her shoulder. "Pull up the number, please."

As he moved closer to her, the spicy scent of his Dior cologne invaded her nostrils. The heat of his nearness washed over her, raising her body temperature so much that she could feel the beads of sweat forming around her hairline. He smelled heavenly, and she could feel her brain turning to mush. *Nothing turns me on like a well-groomed, good-smelling man. How am I supposed to focus on work with him this close?*

She did as he asked, immediately locating the number for Harcroft Sound Limited. "Do you want me to call?"

He shook his head, leaning over her shoulder to see the number on her tablet. "I'll do it."

His forearm brushed her shoulder, and she saw stars. Swallowing hard, she said. "Okay, whatever you think is best."

He'd already dialed the number and had his phone against his ear. "Come into my office, Ainsley. We need to talk."

Gage ceased his pacing when Ainsley entered his office. He allowed himself a brief perusal of her beauty. The sunlight flowing through his office window cast an almost ethereal glow on her golden skin. She wore a navy pencil skirt, yellow button-down blouse and yellow pumps. Her hair was on top of her head in that tight little bun she favored, and gold hoops sparkled in her lobes. His eyes connected with hers, and the sparkle he saw there threatened to stop his heart. *Why must she be so stunning?*

"I'm guessing you're still on hold."

He swallowed, trying to focus on her words and not the glossy lips they'd passed through. "I am. I just don't understand how they could have lost such a valuable shipment."

She shrugged. "Who knows? But it doesn't look like we'll get much help from the shipper, so Harcroft is our best hope." She pushed an errant curl away from her face.

He rubbed his hand over his eyes. "Good thinking. Once someone actually picks up, I'll find out everything I can." Harcroft Sound Limited, a boutique company located in San Leandro, California, made all the soundboards and equipment used in 404's studios. Harcroft engineers built each system by hand, directly to the specifications of the person who placed the order. Their skilled craftsmanship of the equipment was what gave 404 the unique, high-quality sound people had come to associate with the company. "The equipment in Studio 1 is dying fast. After twenty years in service, we can't really be mad about it. But the last thing I need right now is a mishap."

"Agreed." She shifted her weight from side to side, clutching her trusty tablet in the crook of her arm. "Is there anything else you need from me right now?"

He gestured to his guest chair. "Have a seat. When they come on the line, I'll put them on speaker, and you make a note of everything they say."

"Yes, sir." She sat, crossing her legs demurely, the tablet resting on her knee.

He pressed the speakerphone button, filling the room with the sounds of the hold music. It was a track by Herb Alpert & the Tijuana Brass, a sultry Latin tune. Looking across the desk at Ainsley, who busied herself by twirling her stylus like a tiny baton between her fingers, he couldn't help thinking how the music matched his perceptions of her. She was beautiful, inviting, smooth and silky with a little kick.

She glanced up at him then, as if suddenly aware of his attention.

Their gazes locked for a moment.

Her lips puckered, slowly, almost imperceptibly.

He swallowed. *Are those lips as soft as they look?* Heaven help him, he wanted to know. And there was only one way to find out. He eased to the edge of his chair, leaning forward.

The music stopped, and a female voice announced, "Harcroft Sound Limited, how can I help you?"

Clearing his throat, Gage sat back in his chair. "Good morning. This is Gage Woodson at 404 Sound out of Atlanta. I need to speak with Marshall."

"Mr. Harcroft has a full day of meetings, and…"

He tamped down his frustration, knowing the receptionist didn't deserve to bear the brunt of it. "Listen, I don't want to sound rude. But I know Marshall is at his desk every morning by seven. We're missing a large, expensive order. And since 404 spends hundreds of thousands of dollars with your company, I'm going to need you to get Mr. Harcroft on the phone."

"Give me just a moment, Mr. Woodson."

"Thank you." He sighed as the hold music returned, though this time it was a jazz composition featuring Ella and Louis on vocals.

"At least their hold music isn't too bad," Ainsley remarked with a half smirk. "Place I called last week had me listening to an acoustic version of a Snoop Doggy Dogg song."

"Yikes." Despite himself, he felt a smile tug his lips. That's how she was. Even in the most stressful of situations, she always seemed to know when to infuse a little humor in the situation.

"Hello, Gage?"

"Marshall, good morning. Ainsley is here with me, too." Gage tented his fingers, turning his attention back to the matter at hand. "I'm calling because our equipment seems to have gone missing."

"I'm sorry to hear that, Gage. Any details from the shipper?"

"Not many," Ainsley volunteered. "There was some sort of malfunction with the tracking system, and the equipment went off the radar somewhere between Oakland and Vegas."

"Sheesh." Marshall's tone conveyed a mixture of frustration and embarrassment. "I'd give it until the end of the day, just to see if it turns up, either at your door or in their tracking system."

"Fair enough, but what if it doesn't appear by then?"

Gage could feel the knot of tension tightening the area between his shoulder blades.

"Unfortunately, you'll have to reorder. At no additional cost, of course."

Gage cringed. "That's good to know, Marshall. But the money's not the issue here so much as time." That wasn't entirely true, especially not if Miles were consulted. Gage knew his number-crunching, budget-minded younger brother would freak if they had to dip into the company coffers to pay for another custom-built studio set. "I know that what you all do at Harcroft is a very delicate operation."

"You're right. If need be, we can put a rush on the order. You know, have a few extra hands working on it." Marshall sighed. "Let's hope it doesn't come to that."

Gage ran a hand over his face. "Okay. Thanks for your help, Marshall."

"No problem. Let me know by 5:00 p.m. Pacific Time if you need to reorder."

After ending the call, he looked over at Ainsley, who'd been busily jotting on the tablet. "Did you get all that?"

She nodded. "I did."

He blew out a breath. "Thanks. Keep an eye on the tracking throughout the day. If you don't have any updates by four thirty, let me know so I can get Marshall and his crew back on the job."

"Yes, sir." She tucked her stylus behind her ear. "Anything else?"

He scratched his chin, watching her. For some reason, he didn't want her to return to her desk just yet. His mind ran through a series of tasks he could give her to keep her in the office with him. Looking into those rich, honey-brown eyes, he found it harder and harder to concentrate. *This is why I avoid working alone with her as much as possible. She's the most pleasant distraction I've ever had to overcome.* Finally, he shook his head. "No. You're free to go."

She stood then. "I'll be at my desk if you need me." Turning away, she strolled out of the office, taking the sweet, floral aroma of her presence with her. The moment she was gone, the office felt somewhat empty.

What was it about Ainsley Voss that seemed to be his undoing? He considered himself a man of poise and control. Yet, whenever she entered his personal space, he felt like a young boy fawning over his first crush. After more than five years of working with her, of trying to deny or avoid the way she made him feel, his fascination with her remained just as strong as ever.

If his hunch was right, she had feelings for him as well. But he knew better than to approach her. The dynamic that existed between them as boss and employee meant that coming on to her was out of the question. His foolish heart had already led him to one workplace disaster, and he didn't need another. Beyond that, he'd never want to make Ainsley uncomfortable.

No, if things move forward between us, it has to be on her terms.

Ainsley returned to her desk and sat down. Drawing a deep breath, she cracked her knuckles and nudged her mouse to awaken the computer from its slumber. *If this shipment really is lost, Gage is going to panic, big-time.*

Everyone in operations knew how much was riding on the safe and timely arrival of the new studio equipment, and no one bore more responsibility for that than her boss. Anticipating the coming storm, she set about doing the work to prepare for it.

Grabbing her phone, she placed a quick call to Mike, one of the interns who worked on their floor, and asked him to run an errand for her around four fifteen. That done, she opened her top drawer and searched through her collection of essential oils for the ones she needed. Locating the tiny vials, she tucked them into a drawstring bag and set them on the corner of her desk.

She opened the folder titled "404-411" that she kept in her cloud, then opened her internet browser. Accessing the company server, she read the most recent company newsletter. Using her stylus, she highlighted items of importance as she read. When she finished with the newsletter, she pulled every single internal memo, regardless of department, that had been published during the last week. Each memo received the same read-and-highlight treatment as the newsletter.

She got up for a quick stretch and grabbed two bottles of water from the break-room fridge. Knowing Gage's tendency to forget to drink water when he got wrapped up in his work, she placed a bottle on the corner of his desk. He glanced up from his tablet, gave a nod of appreciation and grabbed the water. When she saw him unscrew the cap and take a long draw, she left, taking the other bottle back to her desk.

After reading all six memos, she dragged them, as well as the newsletter file, into her cloud folder. This was a weekly routine for her, something she'd done ever since she joined the company. It kept her informed on all the moving parts that made 404 tick. Tracking these things served a dual purpose for her: satisfying her curiosity about the inner workings of the company and making her more efficient at her job.

At twenty minutes past four, an email arrived in her inbox from the shipping company. Opening it, she read it silently. She could feel her eyes widening as she read about the fate of their equipment. When she closed the email, she drew a deep, cleansing breath. Gathering the drawstring bag, her portable diffuser and her wits, she went to Gage's office to deliver the news.

She found him leaning back in his chair, reading something off his tablet. He looked up when she entered the room, setting the tablet aside. "Did we get word on the equipment?"

"Yes." Before saying anything else, she set the battery-powered diffuser on the corner of his desk. After adding a few drops of lavender and clary sage oils to the dispenser, she turned the device on, silently watching as the cool mist began to fill the air.

Gage looked at the diffuser, then up at her. "Oh no. You bringing that thing in here means it's bad news."

She swallowed. "I just got an email. According to the shipper, the equipment was stolen off a truck sometime after it left Cali. They just located it in Reno."

He cringed. "I'm gonna go out on a limb here and say it's not in usable condition anymore."

She shook her head. "Somebody smashed the crate and grabbed most of the components." She sighed. "Nothing left but a tangle of loose wires and some plastic housings."

He slammed his hand on the desk. "Damn." His eyes flashed. "I don't believe this. After all these years of using that same equipment, we finally upgrade and this happens? Unbelievable."

"Gage, I know this is stressful." She leaned against the edge of the desk.

"Stressful is an understatement." He stood, started pacing the floor. "We've got five albums coming up this month. What the hell are the artists supposed to use? The old equipment just isn't going to produce the high-quality sound we're known for. Not anymore. It's obsolete. We can't just…"

"Okay, okay. I get it, you're upset. But this isn't productive." She placed a hand on his shoulder, trying to ignore the charge she got from feeling his muscle flex beneath her hand. Guiding him back to his seat, she gave a gentle nudge to get him to sit. "You know the drill. Take deep breaths."

He frowned. "Oh, come on. I don't…"

She tilted her head to the side, held his gaze so he would know she was serious. "Deep breaths, Gage."

He relented, settling back in his seat. He inhaled, slow and deep, then blew the breath out through his mouth, the way she'd trained him to do in situations like this.

She observed, watching the rise of his shoulders as he took in air and hearing the whoosh as he released the air through his full lips.

A knock at the office door drew her attention. Turning toward the door, she smiled. "Thanks, Mike. You're right on time." Walking toward the young intern, she took the clear plastic cup from his hand. After Mike left, she handed the chilled cup over to Gage.

He accepted it, his jaw visibly relaxing. "A peanut butter protein shake from the Powerhouse. When did you order this?"

"Hours ago. Just in case things went to the left."

A ghost of a smile came over his face as he took his first sip. "You know me too well, Ainsley."

She shrugged. "Just doing my job." There was more to it than that, but she had no plans to tell him how she felt. It would only complicate things between them if he knew she thought the world of him.

He set the cup down and sighed. "Looks like I'm reordering that equipment. And this time, it absolutely has to get here in one piece."

"I've been thinking about that." She sat in the chair opposite him. "And I've got an idea…"

Three

Tuesday morning, Ainsley fought her way through Atlanta traffic to make it to work on time. As she inched her way down I-20, her phone rang, the sound cutting through her music as it filled the car's cabin. Engaging her hands-free calling, she answered. "Hello?"

"Hey, coz. What's up?"

She smiled at the sound of Eden's voice. "Hey! You know what's up here. It's Atlanta at rush hour, and I-20 is a cross between a parking lot and a racetrack."

Eden laughed. "Every hour is rush hour in the ATL. And I gotta say, I don't miss it."

"Must be nice getting chauffeured around New York, huh?"

"It is, I'm not gonna lie." She said something to someone in the background, the sound muffled. "I've mostly been at the studio with Chanel, though. Not too much sightseeing."

She sighed as she reached a stoplight just as it

turned red. "What's it like working with Chanel the Titan?"

"Lots of late nights. Just coming off an all-nighter, actually." She yawned.

"So that explains why you're up so early. You never went to bed." Ainsley chuckled as she finally got within a few miles of 404's headquarters. "Make sure you get some rest."

"You don't have to tell me twice. As soon as I leave here, I'm going back to my hotel room and climbing straight into bed." She yawned again. "What's going on at work?"

Ainsley rolled her eyes. "Pandemonium. That big studio equipment order got lost during shipping."

"Oh shit."

"*Oh shit* is right. We waited until the end of the day yesterday to see if it would turn up in the shipper's system."

"They never found it?"

"That's just it. They did find it. Or what was left of it."

Eden whistled. "That doesn't sound good."

"You're telling me." She briefly recapped what had happened to their order.

"I'm gonna guess Gage didn't take the news well."

She shook her head, recalling yesterday's events. "He took it better than I'd expect, but I know he was freaking out on the inside. I suggested Gage fly out and personally escort the reordered equipment back to Atlanta, and he nearly chewed my head off. I'm not looking forward to what's gonna happen today." She thought back to the tight set of his jaw as he'd gone on and on about how he couldn't afford to be away from the office at a time like this when everything at 404 Sound was in flux. Still, she knew she'd given him a solid idea. It was up to him whether he took her advice or not.

"Whew. Hang in there, Ains. I'm sure he'll come around."

"If he wants Studio 1 up and running for that new artist, he doesn't have a choice."

"That reminds me. I saw a social media post about Shana in HR retiring. You should apply."

She hesitated. "I was thinking about it, but I haven't made up my mind…"

"Ainsley." Eden's stern tone almost sounded like her mother's. "You worked in HR in two different companies for years before working for Gage. Do it. You know 404 Sound likes to hire from within, and who knows how things work around there better than you? No one. Get on it today."

"Hold on, don't jump down my throat. There's still plenty of time. I just need to tweak my résumé a bit, and then I'm on it."

"Okay. But make sure you get it done before the week is out. We both know you're ready to move up into management. Gage will probably be lost without you, but that's his problem."

Ainsley agreed. "You're right. And don't worry, I'll take care of that application."

"Good. Well, enough work talk. How's Coop?"

"He's doing fine. My pockets are crying, though." She shook her head, thinking of all the recent expenses he'd brought to her attention. "I feel like he's got me by the ankles, shaking me for spare change at this point."

"I sent you a little something."

She sighed. "Eden, you don't have to do that."

"I know I don't. But I want to. Remember what I said when Cooper needed that surgery?"

"Yeah, I remember. You said we're in this together."

"Right. And that hasn't changed just because I'm in New York." She paused. "So, no more arguments because it's already done." A notification from her Money Pop app sounded, and she fought back the tears welling in her eyes. "I love you, Eden."

"Love you, too, Ains. I'll talk to you later."

Focusing back on the road, Ainsley stopped off at the Bodacious Bean to grab Gage's morning coffee. She picked up this same order every morning, so when she walked in, the barista handed her the order before could even finish saying *good morning*. Leaving a tip in the fishbowl on the counter, she returned to her car.

When she arrived at the office, she knocked on his closed door. Moments later, he swung it open.

Gage Woodson. Mr. Take Charge. Groomed from his youth to step into leadership at the company, and that preparation was always on display. From his tailored suits to his commanding presence, everything about him fairly screamed, "I run this."

Today's charcoal suit, paired with a royal blue shirt and silver tie, was no exception. His lips tilted into a slight smile. "Good morning, Ainsley."

"Good morning." She handed over the coffee and the paper bag holding his Tuesday pastry—a slice of banana bread. With a nod, she turned and started to walk away.

"Hold on."

At the sound of his request, she stopped and faced him again. "Yes?"

"I...just wanted to apologize for the way I acted yesterday afternoon." He rested his shoulder against the door frame, placing one hand over his chest.

Her brow hitched. *I don't know if I ever heard him*

apologize before. Still, he looked pretty contrite at the moment. "Okay."

"What I did yesterday wasn't okay. I snapped at you because I was under a lot of stress about the equipment, but that's no excuse."

She nodded slowly. "I understand. And consider it water under the bridge."

"I appreciate that." He cleared his throat. "Also, I wanted to let you know that I'm going to take your advice. If I weren't in such a funk yesterday, I would have taken it then."

She swallowed. "I...um... I'm glad you found my suggestion helpful."

"I did. I just wish I'd been able to see it sooner." His gaze intensified. "You're an invaluable asset to this company, Ainsley. And to me."

She felt her heart pounding in her ears. "Thank you."

"No, thank you." He reached for her hand, gave it a squeeze. "I'm meeting with my mother and sister at lunch today, and we're going to discuss the best way to put your brilliant plan in motion."

"Sounds good. Do you need me to attend?"

He shook his head. "No. I'll fill you in on all the details when I get back." He paused, his gaze dropping slightly.

She squirmed inwardly. *If I didn't know better, I'd say he was staring at my lips.* She could feel that familiar heat building inside, the same heat she felt whenever they occupied the same space for too long. "Great. So... if you don't need anything else, I'm just gonna head over to my desk."

Their eyes met again, and she thought she saw a twinkle of mischief. He released her hand, though he seemed somewhat reluctant to do so. "You're good to go. I just wanted to thank you."

As she turned and walked away, she could feel his gaze on her back. Determined not to let him see her sweat, she headed down the corridor and back to her desk as fast as her pumps would carry her.

Seated, she booted up her computer in an attempt at productivity. But in the back of her mind, the question loomed larger than anything else.

Was Gage Woodson flirting with me? After all these years, he's chosen now *to flirt? Just when I'm about to apply for the HR position? Did I make a wrong turn and walk into the damn Twilight Zone or what?*

Sitting in the homey, familiar atmosphere of Mary Mac's Tea Room, Gage perused the menu. The place was an institution, a jewel of downtown Atlanta since 1945. Once, there'd been a total of sixteen similar establishments in the city. Today, only Mary Mac's remained, as both a nostalgic reminder of the genteel glamour of early-twentieth-century Atlanta and a respite from the fast-paced, tech-driven world outside its doors. He'd eaten here more times than he could count over the years, and the food and service never disappointed. *My only real worry is that I'll eat so well, I'll be too sleepy to go on with the rest of the workday.*

"This is my favorite place to come for lunch," Addison remarked from her seat next to him. "It's such a nice escape from whatever's going on at the office."

"True indeed, Mama." Nia, seated across from them, flipped her menu over to look at the desserts. "Besides, getting in here around dinnertime is damn near impossible."

He chuckled. Most ATLiens knew that if they were

craving Mary Mac's delicacies after work, they had better be prepared for a long wait. "How are things on the third floor, Mom?"

Addison shrugged. "Fine, for the most part." Her role as company vice president was largely ceremonial, yet his sister Nia always consulted their parents on any major business decision, out of an abundance of love and respect.

His brow cocked because something in her tone gave him pause. "Something bothering you?"

"I just know it's time for me to start planning our thirtieth-anniversary celebration, and part of me is dreading all the work it's going to take." She released a small sigh.

"It's such an exciting milestone to reach. It's still a few months away. You know you have all of us to help you if it gets to be too much." Nia sipped from her glass of sweet tea. "This is a family business, so planning the celebration will be a family affair."

Addison's expression softened a bit in response to her daughter's declaration. "Thanks for the reminder, Nia."

The server came to take their orders. Nia ordered smothered chicken and a side of turnip greens. Addison got a baked sweet potato with okra and tomatoes, as well as spiced apples.

Mom's still vegan, I see. He had no such aspirations to cut meat from his diet. Since this was his once-weekly cheat meal, he asked for the half slab of barbecued ribs with a side of mac and cheese.

After the server left, Gage rested his forearms on the table, lacing his fingers together. "So, I'm gonna guess you already heard about what happened to our new studio equipment?"

Nia blew out a breath. "We have. I got an interoffice memo from Miles."

"What a mess. And what in the world are those people intending to do with the parts?" Addison shook her head.

"Who knows?" He couldn't imagine another use for the parts. "It doesn't really matter what they plan on doing with them. We're just going to have to replace that equipment, and the sooner, the better."

"Right." Nia's face morphed into that serious expression she always wore when she was thinking about business matters. She tilted her head slightly to the right, sucking in her bottom lip. "I can't say I have any faith in that shipping company. Frankly, their security and tracking are terrible."

"We never should have switched shippers," Gage admitted, his eyes on the white tablecloth. "That's on me. I wanted to give a small shipping outfit a chance with us and save a little money on shipping costs while I was at it." That had backfired, big-time.

Addison waved him off. "There was no way you could have anticipated a mess like this. Don't worry about it."

Oh, I'm plenty worried about it. But he saw no need to verbalize that. "As I see it, we're just going to have to make sure the reordered equipment makes it here, intact and on time."

His sister nodded. "I agree. So, what's the plan? Are we going back to our old reliable shipping company?"

He shook his head. "Even better. I'm going to pick up the equipment myself, in person."

Their plates came, and as they each dug into the delectable offerings, conversation at the table ceased, replaced by the clinking sound of their silverware striking the china plates.

Gage quipped, "Ever notice how quiet it gets when Black people are eating?"

Nia giggled. "Only if the food is good."

With a shake of her head, their mother asked, "Now, what were you saying about picking up the equipment, Gage?" She forked up a bit of sweet potato.

"Oh yeah. I'm just going to go and get it myself. The only way I can be sure it gets here is to personally escort it."

Nia chewed a piece of chicken, her expression thoughtful. "Makes sense to me. It's a long haul to California, though."

"I know. Besides that, I'll need room for the equipment." Gage swiped a napkin over his mouth. "That's why I was going to ask for use of the company jet."

"I don't think it will be a problem."

"Great." Gage leaned back in his chair.

Another period of quiet descended as they enjoyed their lunch.

"Max is back from vacation." Addison polished off her spiced apples. "I'm sure she's ready to get back in the air."

Gage nodded. Maxine Kidder had been the company pilot for the last ten years and was as professional as they came. Flying with her was always a pleasure. "Sounds good."

"When do you want to fly out?" Nia posed the question as she finished off her greens.

"Monday. That's when Marshall promised the new order will be ready." He pushed away his empty plate. "The plan is to fly out Monday morning and be back in town that night. If all goes well, everything will be installed, up and running by Wednesday."

"And when was The Visionary supposed to start using his studio time?" Nia ran a hand over her short curls, then raised it for the check.

"The following Monday. We're cutting it a lot closer than I would prefer, but it is what it is." *The situation isn't ideal, but I figure we're good as long as we can get Studio 1 back in working shape before our artist shows up to record.* "I'm not about to miss out on this. Having Organized Noize in our studio is a hell of a big deal."

"Absolutely." Nia accepted the check from the server and flipped the leather folder open. "It's not just the revenue, it's the notoriety that comes from working with such a legendary production team." After placing her credit card in the folder, she said, "Just have Ainsley fill out the electronic requisition, and I'll have Ariel reach out to Max to get everything organized."

"Okay." Hearing Ainsley's name brought a vision of her into his head. She was the picture of beauty and poise, always carrying that tablet and stylus, always listening and taking notes. Still, her particular brand of witty commentary was a bright spot in his day and had kept him alert during many a dull meeting. And lately he noticed the aroma that followed her, hanging around her like a cloud. He couldn't for the life of him figure out what it was—maybe a new perfume, or lotion, or whatever hair products she used to make her curls shine. The scent was an intoxicating blend of florals, and he found himself inhaling deeply whenever she left the room, just so he could enjoy the remnants that lingered in her wake.

"It was a great idea to go get the equipment in person, son." Addison smiled at him.

"Thanks, Mom." He thought about Ainsley and how she'd been the one to mention that. But he'd already thanked her and saw no need to make the conversation awkward by bringing that up. But he did have another idea, one that would benefit them both.

Ainsley should come with me to California.

On her way back from her lunch break, Ainsley took the elevator down to the basement. Once there, she pushed through the glass doors into the company mailroom, heading straight for the pickup desk.

Mallory Evans, head mail clerk, looked up and smiled as she approached. "Hey, Ainsley. How are you?"

"We've had a little drama in operations, but I can't complain." Picking up a pen from the cup on the desk, she signed the logbook in the proper place.

Mallory whistled. "Oh, I've heard. The CEO's secretary was in here right before lunch. What a shame about the equipment, but at least your boss is going to use the company jet to retrieve the new set himself." She shuffled through the files on her desk, pulling out the familiar blue folder. "Here's the letters for your department. Hang tight for a minute. I've got a couple of boxes in the back for you."

Ainsley watched with a smile as Mallory quickly crossed the mailroom. She knew she would hear the latest info on company happenings whenever she stopped by the mailroom, and Mallory's info had proven valuable to her on more than one occasion. Today's tidbit served as proof that Gage had taken her advice and would be picking up the new sound equipment in person.

After getting the rest of the mail, she returned to the office on the third floor. When she walked in, she was surprised to find Gage standing by her desk. "Hi, Gage. Do you need something?"

He turned her way, his dark eyes connecting with hers. "Yes, actually. I wanted to let you know I'm making arrangements to go to California."

"So you're putting my idea in motion, then?"

"I am. I told you I would. Why wouldn't I? It's a great idea." He paused. "I also wanted to ask you if you'd consider coming with me."

She stopped short, one of the packages falling out of her hands and hitting the floor with a thump. "Really?"

"Yes." He walked over, retrieving the fallen item. "I think the whole process will go much smoother if you're there with me."

She swallowed. Her heart fluttered at the idea of being in the close confines of the company jet with her handsome boss. Yet the logical side of her wouldn't allow her too much excitement. Would she be able to keep herself from doing or saying anything that would make things awkward between them? Something that would alter their relationship forever, something she couldn't take back?

"Ainsley?"

Aware of his scrutiny, she stammered a reply. "I... yes, I guess."

His brow hitched. "I need to know if you're going so I can tell Max to prepare for two passengers."

"When?"

"Monday." He read the label on the package he'd picked up, then tucked it beneath his arm. "This whole situation with the first order has put us off schedule, so I need to get the equipment here as quickly as possible. We need Studio 1 up and running."

She drew a deep breath, moving to her desk to put the mail down. "How long would we be gone?"

"Only a day. My plan is to fly there, do the paperwork, secure the equipment and fly back that same day."

She paused for a moment. "I just need to ask Bebe to look after Cooper when he gets out of school, then. As long as she can do that, I should be able to go."

He smiled. "Great. Can you let me know for sure by the end of the day?"

She nodded. "Just let me text Bebe."

His smile broadened. "Sounds good. I'm really looking forward to this." He gestured at the pile of mail she'd brought in. "Is any of the rest of that mine?"

She flipped through the stack of envelopes and handed three of them to him. "Just these."

"Thanks, Ainsley. You're the best." With a wink, he disappeared around the corner into the corridor.

Is it just me, or is he being overly charming?

She flopped into her chair and willed her pulse to slow. There was something about him, something she'd been aware of since her first day on the job but still couldn't quite name. The longer she looked into his eyes, the more it affected her...whatever it was.

She sent a quick text to Bebe. Leaning against her backrest, she took a moment to think about their conversation. Did he really need her along to help with the business of getting the equipment back to the studio? Or did he just want to spend time with her?

She'd been on company trips before on the jet, with Gage, other members of the executive team and their respective assistants. This would be the first time she traveled alone with him. He'd always been a gentleman, so she had no worries about his behavior. It was her own possible actions that had her concerned.

None of this was of any consequence now. After all, she'd basically agreed to go with him.

Bebe's reply came—she had no problem watching Cooper for a few hours after school.

Dismissing the message, Ainsley drew another deep breath and went to Gage's office to let him know that she would be traveling with him.

Four

Thursday afternoon, Ainsley was back in Gage's office, jotting down notes on her tablet as he rattled off instructions for their upcoming trip to California. *I wasn't really surprised when he asked me to come along.* It had been ages since she'd been on a vacation, and she wasn't one to turn down a free cross-country flight, on a private jet no less.

At the moment, he was on the phone with Max, the longtime company pilot, chatting about the flight. "Well, Max, I'm glad to hear your schedule's clear next week. We'll only need you for Monday, though. How does a quick run to Cali and back sound?"

The sound of Max's laugh came over the speakerphone before she spoke. "I wouldn't call it a quick run, Gage. It's a little over four hours each way. But it sounds great."

"Excellent. Once we make it to Harcroft and properly

pack up our equipment, we can head home. I see no reason we won't be back by that night."

"I got you. What time do you want to push off?"

His eyes shifted to her. "Ainsley, can you be ready to leave by eight thirty?"

She nodded. "That's fine." *Cooper's bus leaves at 7:10 a.m.*

"Can we say eight thirty for takeoff?" Gage asked.

Max replied, "I'll put it in my logbook. Anything else?"

"No."

"Cool. See you Monday." Max disconnected the call. "Great. Now, with that set up—" he turned his gaze on her "—I'll need you to make sure the plane is stocked with these items."

She nodded, taking down his words. The list mostly consisted of his protein shakes, muscle-building snack bars, fresh fruit and bottles of spring water. *He's all about maintaining his physique. Can't say I blame him.* Dragging her gaze over his body, she thought it was definitely something worth preserving.

"I'm just going to double-check with Marshall at Harcroft." He picked up his desk phone and dialed the number. "Before we get too deep into trip planning, I need to make sure the reorder will actually be ready in time."

She waited while he had a brief conversation with Marshall. All the while she tried not to imagine him working out. The struggle was all too real. In her mind's eye, she could see him running on a treadmill, shirtless, with rivulets of sweat running down his muscled back…

"Ainsley?"

His voice calling her name snapped her back to reality. "I'm sorry, what was that?"

"I asked how old your son is now. Will he be okay on his own on Monday?"

She cleared her throat, a bit taken aback by his question. Gage seldom asked about her child. "Oh. Yes. Cooper's eleven. My neighbor will watch him until I get home."

He nodded. "What's that like? Having an eleven-year-old? I don't have much experience with kids."

She shrugged. "It's an adventure. He's old enough to do a lot for himself but young enough to still be needy at times."

He leaned forward. "For example?"

"He has a key to the house, but he forgets it at least once a week. That sort of thing."

"I see." He chuckled. "Well, my hat's off to you. I don't know how parents do it. Just seems like an awful lot of work to not get paid for."

He's not wrong. Parenting involved a lot of unpaid labor. Still, something about the way he said it just… didn't sit right. "Thanks… I guess."

"Trust me, it's a compliment. I mean, my siblings still manage to get on our parents' nerves, and we're all grown." He shook his head. "I guess it's unpaid work you never get to retire from."

"Speaking of children, you know those kids from Keystone Middle are touring the building today, right?" She watched him, gauging his reaction.

He swallowed. "Damn, is that today?"

She nodded. "It was on the calendar. I sent you a reminder a week ago. And yesterday. And this morning." *Does he bother to check the notifications I send to his phone?*

"I forgot. I've been so wrapped up in the equipment drama I hadn't even thought about it." He ran a hand over his dark curls. "I don't have to make a speech or anything, do I?"

"No. The kids will only be here for an hour or two, touring the building and seeing how things work at a recording studio, both in the booth and in the offices." She'd been looking forward to the school visit. She loved kids, and their presence would be a nice change of pace to the sometimes stale, too-serious vibe of the office. "They'll only swing by here briefly."

"I hope we'll get a warning before they show up." Gage stood, straightening the lapels of his sport coat. "I want a little heads-up before they come up here destroying anything."

She frowned, aware of the dismissiveness in his tone. *What's his problem?* Yes, they were children, but these were older kids. Middle schoolers, so around Cooper's age. They tended to be much more mature and far less accident-prone than their younger counterparts. "I'll let Kim at the front desk know to give me a call when the students are on their way upstairs. Do you need anything else from me at the moment?"

He shook his head. "No. You can go on back to your desk." He gave her a crooked half smile. "Just warn me before the youngsters descend on us, okay?"

"I will." She stood, taking her tablet and stylus with her down the short corridor and back to her desk.

She was in the thick of her work when she got a call around three that the students from Keystone were on their way up. She knocked softly on Gage's door, and when he opened it, she met him with a smile. "The kids are coming."

He took a deep breath, checked his watch. "Okay. I can only spare a few minutes before I have to leave to meet my dad for dinner. With traffic being what it is, I need to get outta here by four."

Wondering why her boss looked so nervous at the prospect of entertaining a few twelve-year-olds, she walked to the suite door and waited.

They arrived a few minutes later, a group of about ten middle-schoolers and their accompanying adult. According to the interoffice memo, the students were members of Keystone's entrepreneurship club. Opening the door, she welcomed them and their chaperone inside. "I'm Ainsley Voss. Welcome to 404 Sound."

The lone adult, a raven-haired woman with fair skin and bright red lipstick, reached for her hand. "I'm Ms. Madison, their advisor. Thanks for having us."

After a brief conversation with Ms. Madison, Ainsley led her and her students around the operations suite, letting them ask questions about what they saw. The students briefly interacted with Duval and Kelly before she took them back to the lobby to await their audience with Gage.

When he appeared, he wore his sunglasses on top of his head and carried his briefcase and keys. "Good afternoon. I'm Gage Woodson, chief operations officer of 404 Sound." He waited for a beat as if expecting the kids to applaud or cheer. When they didn't, he spoke again, his tone somewhat annoyed. "Do any of you have any specific questions about what I do here?"

"Aren't you the founder's son?" a boy with blond-tipped dreadlocks asked.

Gage nodded. "404 is a family business. All the execs are my siblings."

"Then you probably don't do much. Since you can't get fired or nothing." The boy chuckled at his own cleverness.

Ms. Madison's reprimand was swift. "Andrew! That's rude and unacceptable behavior."

Gage made a face. Adjusting his sunglasses, he said, "I've got a pressing engagement. Nice to meet you. Stay in school and all that." With his jaw tighter than piano wire, he strode past everyone and left.

Ainsley, left in his wake, shook her head. *I don't believe he acted like that. They're just kids.*

Every time she started thinking Gage was perfect, he reminded her that he wasn't. She couldn't go on pining after a man who couldn't be bothered to engage with children. Because at the end of the day, it wasn't just about her. She had Cooper to think about.

Standing in line at the counter of Chef Rob's Caribbean Cafe and Upscale Lounge, Gage perused the menu in his hands. The restaurant's festive walls, painted in oranges and reds, hosted a collection of unique Jamaican-themed art. His father, Caleb, standing next to him, was engaged in the same hard process of choosing a meal from Chef Rob's many delicious offerings. There were quite a few people in line behind them, and Gage didn't want to hold them up. His father's voice cut into his thoughts. "Thanks for meeting me here, son."

"It's not a problem. I never pass up a chance to come down here and get some of those jerk egg rolls." He rubbed his stomach as an emphasis on the last few words. "Can't get them anywhere else."

Laughing to himself, Caleb returned his attention to his menu.

After they ordered, they seated themselves in one of the black leather–upholstered booths with their drinks. Gage set his phone to vibrate and laid it facedown on the table, as his father usually demanded. "So, what's the occasion, Dad?"

"Just checking in with you. I know you're headed to Cali in a few days to rendezvous with our equipment for Studio 1."

"Yep. I'm not taking any more chances that it will make it here safely." He sipped from his cup of lemonade. "I plan on spending that whole day making sure we're set for The Visionary's session."

"Excellent. I'm glad to see you're taking this seriously, Gage." Caleb rested his hands on the table, clasping his fingers. "Because we can't really afford any more mistakes."

He cringed because the words stung. But he brushed it off just as quickly as he felt it. "You're right, and I don't plan on making any more. That's why Ainsley and I are just making it a day trip. Fly there, get the equipment, be home by dark."

Caleb's brow hitched. "Ainsley?"

"Yeah, she's going with me. Everything pertaining to operations at 404 lives on her tablet. Taking her with me means all the electronic forms can be filled out that much faster, as well as the arrangements that need to be made for getting the equipment set up and operational in the studio."

"I'm not sure she absolutely needs to go with you."

"No, Dad, she doesn't absolutely need to. It will just make the process smoother and faster if she does." He frowned, wondering why his father was suddenly so concerned about the way he chose to run his department. "Is there a problem?"

Caleb sighed, but before he could open his mouth to say anything, their food was delivered. As the waitress set the Rasta Pasta in front of him, he smiled and offered her a polite thanks.

Gage did the same as he looked over his jerk egg rolls with shrimp and steamed red snapper. When the waitress was gone, he picked up his fork but continued to watch his father as he took his first few bites.

"Son, I know you don't like to talk about what happened between you and Tara…"

He felt his jaw tighten. "Then why bring it up? Unless you have news about the case."

"Because it's relevant to what we're talking about." Caleb took several bites of his pasta.

"I don't see how." *You're right, I don't want to talk about Tara.* The one time he'd broken his personal rule of not dating anyone who worked for the company, it had failed spectacularly.

"You let yourself get closer to her than you should have, and it backfired, big-time." Caleb paused. "Normally I wouldn't come down on you about it, but since the company took a financial hit because of your actions, I can't overlook it."

He scoffed. *I got close to her. I loved her. Or at least, I thought I did.* She'd been duplicitous, conniving. She'd used his affections against him. "What does that have to do with the price of tea in China? There's nothing like that going on between Ainsley and me."

"For now." Caleb continued eating, with that same knowing, fatherly look on his face that he always had when he just knew he was right about something.

Gage sighed. "Look. I'll admit that Ainsley is attractive." *Gorgeous, if I'm being honest. No need to tell him that.* "But I've got more self-control than that. Besides, it's just a quick day trip."

Caleb shrugged. "That's what you have planned. But

in all my years of living, I've learned things rarely go according to our plans, son."

Shaking his head, he decided to concentrate on his food rather than continue this fruitless conversation. He kept quiet until he'd cleaned his plate and finished his drink.

"You can't ignore the truth in what I'm saying, Gage. I know you don't like to hear it, but I tell you these things for your own good. Any father worth his salt would."

"I understand your concerns. But, as I said, there's absolutely nothing between us."

Caleb cocked his head to the right. "You're honestly going to sit here and say that, as if I've never seen the way you look at her?"

He frowned. "What? When?"

"Company-wide meetings. On more than one occasion, I've seen you watching her."

"Yikes. That's what you're doing during those meetings?"

His father shrugged. "What can I say? After all these years, meetings aren't terribly exciting anymore, so I take my entertainment where I can get it."

"Really, Dad?" He tossed a balled-up paper napkin at his old man.

Batting the crumpled paper away, Caleb laughed. "In all seriousness, it's hard not to notice. And I've seen her looking at you as well."

That gave him pause. *Is he telling the truth, or is he just heaping on in an attempt to prove that he's right?*

"All I'm saying is, be careful. Try not to let this business trip turn into something more complex between the two of you."

"I hear you."

"I hope so."

Gage thought of Ainsley and couldn't help smiling. She was professional, efficient and gorgeous. Beyond that, she had a magical way of cracking a joke at just the right moment to keep him from going off the deep end. Everyone who crossed her path loved her—she was definitely the glue that held his department together. *No, I know better than to start anything with her.* "Listen, since you brought up Tara, where are we with the case? Do you have news?"

"I do. Our investigator located Tara just outside Cleveland, but she claims to have spent the money on medical treatments for her nephew."

He cursed. "What now? Do we sue her? Will she go to jail?"

Caleb shook his head. "Your mother and I, along with Nia, decided to drop the charges."

"What? Why?"

"Her sister is a single mother of a young child who has a lot of health problems." Caleb ran a hand over his face. "I'm not saying that justifies what Tara did. But our attorney said the likelihood of us ever getting any restitution from Tara was slim to none."

"I don't care. I'll bring my own case against her. She has to face some kind of consequences." His ex-girlfriend had run off with ten stacks of company funds, and he wouldn't let her get away with it. The only thing she'd lost was her job in the finance department. Meanwhile, he'd suffered a much greater loss: he'd lost his father's faith in him. He wouldn't let that happen again.

No. There's no way I can get involved with Ainsley. I know she's not the same as Tara but dating someone at work just isn't going to go well. He just couldn't take the chance. Not now, and not ever again.

Five

Just after seven Monday morning, Ainsley watched over Cooper as he made his last-minute preparations for the school day. "Come on, son. You should be headed to the bus stop."

"I know, I know." He dashed up the stairs.

"Grab a jacket while you're up there!" She waited at the bottom of the stairs for him to return, all the while with the front door propped open. If the bus pulled up before he returned, she could flag down the driver and signal him that they needed a minute.

He jogged back down the stairs then, with his book bag strap in one hand and a jacket slung over the arm.

She furrowed her brow. "Cooper, it's chilly out. Put the jacket *on*."

"You said to grab a jacket," he groused. "Can't I just take it with me?"

She sighed. Many of the mothers with sons on the baseball team often commiserated about their kids' apparent allergy to outerwear. *What is it with boys and not wanting to wear jackets? Why do they insist on being cold needlessly?* "It's not gonna do you any good to carry it, child. Put the jacket on. You can take it off once you're inside the school."

He frowned, his small lips pursed tight, but slipped into the jacket anyway.

"Thank you." She leaned down and kissed his forehead. "I'll see you when I get back from California this evening, okay? Make sure you do as Bebe says while I'm gone."

"I got it, Mom." He slipped his book bag straps over his shoulders, mumbling something.

She knew what he'd said, but she couldn't resist teasing him just a little bit. "What was that?" She cupped her hand around her ear.

"Love you," he repeated as he ran out the front door.

"Love you, too," she called after him. He reached the curb just as the bus pulled up. She watched him get on, then watched the bus pull away.

Closing the door, she climbed the stairs. In her bedroom, she touched up her makeup and shrugged into a tan cardigan over the simple burgundy midi dress she wore. Back downstairs, she grabbed her purse and keys, along with the bag of supplies she'd packed up for the trip, and left. Tucking her things into her car, she walked across her driveway and over to Bebe's house next door.

The Redfords had been her neighbors for seven years, since she and Eden first bought the house. Bebe was short for Beatrice. She ran a marketing company from home, while her husband, Fitz, worked at a car dealership in the city.

Bebe answered after the second knock. She was petite and fair-skinned, with close-trimmed red hair. Clad in gray leggings, a green tunic and dinosaur-feet slippers, she had a steaming mug of coffee in one hand. "Morning, Ainsley. Ready for your trip?"

She nodded. "I think so. As long as my boss doesn't make any last-minute demands, I should be good."

"Great. Do you wanna come in, have a cup of coffee?"

"I can't. We're supposed to be wheels up in less than an hour, and I still have to make it to the airport." She reached out, giving Bebe a quick hug around the shoulders. "Thanks again for looking after Cooper for me."

"No problem, honey. Have a safe trip." With a wink and a smile, Bebe shut her door.

Hopping in her car, Ainsley made her way across town to DeKalb-Peachtree Airport. The route took her east on I-20 then northeast on I-85, cutting right through the heart of downtown Atlanta. As she braved the morning traffic, she watched the beautiful scenery of her hometown passing by her windows. *Even though the commute's a killer, I still love this place.* She couldn't imagine living anywhere else.

When she finally arrived at the private airstrip used by 404, she pulled her car into one of the five parking spots and got out. There was only one other car there, and it wasn't Gage's. Assuming it was the pilot's, she got her things out of the car and headed for the plane. Impressed with the design of the company's recently upgraded jet, she admired the brightly colored logo paint job on the fuselage. The door was open, and the stairs were in place, so she boarded.

She gasped as she entered. The interior was even more impressive than the exterior. Four spacious leather seats were placed on either side of the aisle. In the rear, a minibar and a booth-like conferencing area had been set up. There were two flat-screen televisions, one in the front and one in the rear. Moving to the minibar, she opened the cabinet and fridge, placing Gage's snacks and drinks in their appropriate places.

"Ainsley. It's been a long time since I've seen you."

Turning toward the sound of the familiar female voice, Ainsley smiled when she saw Max coming out of the cockpit. "Hey, Max. How have you been?"

"Can't complain. Especially since the Woodsons upgraded me to this swanky bird. She's a beauty, isn't she?"

"Definitely." She chuckled.

"I call her the Swingin' Ms. D." Max rubbed her hands together.

"Oh, after Dinah Washington."

Max looked impressed. "I see you know your jazz greats. Yeah, she's just like Dinah. Curvy and sophisticated and moves like a dream." With a smile, she disappeared back into her domain at the controls.

Taking the front window seat on the right side of the jet, Ainsley settled in and fastened her seat belt. A quick glance at her phone showed the time. *Where's Gage? He's the one who suggested this eight thirty departure time.* She thought about calling him but decided not to. *He's grown, and he knows where he's supposed to be.*

Pulling her tablet from her purse, she opened the file with the urban fantasy novel she'd been reading. She had a four-and-a-half-hour flight ahead of her, and if she kept reading, she expected to finish the book by the time they got to California.

She'd just flipped the page when Gage rushed onto the plane, carrying his small attaché. He'd dressed in a tan suit with a crisp white shirt beneath and no tie. His sunglasses were nestled in his riotous curls. "Morning, Ainsley. I see you beat me here."

"I didn't want to hold you up."

"I appreciate that. I trust all my supplies are here?"

"Already put away in the minibar."

"Thanks." He tossed his case into the seat across the aisle from her and walked back to the minibar.

She followed his movement, her eyes resting on his firm-looking backside and powerful thighs. She swallowed, her throat suddenly dry. "Would you pass me a bottle of water, please?"

"Sure." He handed her the water as he returned to his seat with one of his coffee-infused smoothies and a protein bar. Twisting off the cap, he raised the bottle in her direction. "Here's to a great flight."

She lifted her water bottle. "Cheers." That said, she broke the seal, tossed the cap aside and took a healthy swig. She always felt like this whenever she and Gage were in an enclosed space together. That was why she avoided this scenario whenever possible. Within the confines of the private jet, though, there was nowhere to hide from his intoxicating presence.

She shook her head, returning her attention to her book. *The best thing I can do is just read the whole way. I'll start the next book in the series on the flight back.* For a few moments, she had herself convinced that she'd give her full attention to the book for the duration of the flight.

By the time they were in the air, though, she couldn't ignore him anymore.

She hazarded a glance in his direction...

And found him watching her.

I should really be doing some work. So why can't I focus?

Gage already knew the answer to that. His proximity to Ainsley made concentration damn near impossible. If they had to share a workspace this size in the 404 building, he'd probably be way less productive.

Gage spent a few more seconds staring at Ainsley. She was wearing a burgundy dress with a pair of matching heels. Her hair was up in a high bun atop her head, and her trusty stylus was nestled in her hair. Cradling her tablet on her lap, her eyes scanned the pages of the book she read.

Suddenly she looked up.

Yikes. Caught. There was no way he could hide the fact that he'd been watching her, so he didn't try. "Sorry," he murmured.

"It's fine. Is there something you need?"

He shook his head. "No."

She returned her attention to the book, and he pulled his laptop out of his attaché case. Opening it up, he turned it on and pulled up the word processor file he'd been using to write his speech for the company's thirtieth anniversary. While he still had time, he didn't want to wait until the last minute to come up with something.

Max's voice came over the intercom. "Buckle up, folks. We may be hitting some turbulence in the next few minutes."

He tightened his belt in response to Max's advice, then went back to his document. Reading over the few paragraphs he'd written so far, he scratched his chin. His parents were expecting each sibling to give a five-minute speech at the upcoming anniversary gala, and he was having a hard time deciding what he wanted to say.

I suppose it's less about what I want to say than it is what's appropriate to say. He wanted his speech to be profound yet entertaining, a look at the company's history as well as its future. *I bet Nia's speech has been done for ages. She always knows what to say at these events.* His eldest sister, CEO of the company and apple of her parents' eyes, never missed an opportunity to make them proud.

He stared at the words on the page for several minutes, making tweaks here and there until the words started to blur together. The plane shook then as they hit a pocket of rough air, and the computer rattled on the tray table. He steadied it, then shut it down and stowed it safely in his bag. *Better to put it away now than risk having to replace it.*

Ainsley kept reading, seemingly unfazed.

Things evened out again, and he settled his back against his seat and pulled out his phone. Even with it in airplane mode, there were still a few odds and ends he could tie up. So he opened his notes app and started typing into it.

He'd typed barely four words before the plane began shaking again, this time much harder than before. He gripped the phone a bit tighter. He glanced across the aisle at Ainsley. She was wide-eyed, clutching her tablet to her chest.

It subsided a few minutes later. When the aircraft ceased its trembling, he asked, "You okay over there?"

She nodded. "Fine. Just…not a fan of turbulence."

He chuckled. "I don't think anybody enjoys being rattled around in their seat like that."

Her answering laugh sounded nervous. "Fair enough."

He tucked his phone away for the same reason he'd put away his computer. It was almost as if the universe were advising him to set work aside for now. "Do you want me to come over and sit with you? You know, in case the turbulence happens again. We can help guard each other's electronics."

She laughed again, the sound a little less strained. She moved her purse from the seat next to her and set it on the floor. "Sure, that's fine."

Securing his attaché case inside the under-seat storage drawer, he moved over to sit in the aisle seat next to her. After he buckled up and settled in, he asked, "Ever been to Cali before?"

She shook her head. "No. Never been any farther west than Las Vegas."

"I see. It's been about a year since I went the last time." He gestured to the tablet, still pinned to her chest by her crossed arms. "I think you can put that down now."

She closed the cover over her tablet and laid it across her lap, resting her arm on it. She opened her mouth, but before she could speak, a loud boom of thunder sounded.

"Oh boy." He felt the tension gathering in his shoulders. This trip had a tight turnaround, and he didn't have time for any delays. "I'm gonna need this weather to calm down so we can get this equipment back to Atlanta on time."

A familiar, steady sound filled the cabin.

She turned away to slide up the plastic shade covering the window. Fat droplets of rain pelted the window, and a flash of lightning illuminated the cloud-shrouded sky. "Looks like Mother Nature might have other plans."

"Well, that sucks." He felt his brow furrowing as the familiar frustration sank its fingers into his flesh.

"When it rains like this, I remember how obsessed Cooper was with jumping in rain puddles when he was younger." She laughed softly. "Regular rain boots wouldn't work for him because he always went for the deepest puddles he could find. Do you know how hard it was to find kid-size hip waders for my little munchkin?"

"I can't imagine." And he couldn't. He could count on one hand the number of times he'd interacted with a small child, and he didn't feel deprived of anything because of it.

Max's voice came over the intercom again. "I'm sorry to report, the storm has suddenly switched course. I don't have enough fuel payload to go around it, so we're going to have to make a surprise landing."

He blew out a breath. "Perfect."

"Maybe we won't have to stay too long." Ainsley crossed, then uncrossed her legs. "We can just pop into town, grab a bite, then be back in the air."

He knew she was trying to lighten the mood, and he appreciated that. But he wasn't sure anything could improve his mood in the face of this unexpected delay.

"Okay, last announcement. We'll be landing in about twenty minutes in a little town called Summer Village, Louisiana." Maxine paused. "Right on the Louisiana and Arkansas border."

He sighed. Not only were they making a landing, but it also seemed they were going to be way off the beaten path. "Ever heard of this place, Ainsley?"

She shook her head.

"Neither have I. I'm guessing it's not that big of a place."

As the plane went into the descent, he leaned back in his seat. She did the same, her hand gripping the armrest between them. Seeing the white in her knuckles, he quietly laid his hand atop hers.

She gasped softly, but he could feel her tension subsiding under his touch.

Neither of them said a word, but their eyes remained locked.

The interaction was totally innocent, but he felt the tingle moving through him as he touched her. He'd merely sought to comfort her and had managed to re-awaken his desire for her in the process.

I could be the one who does this for her. I could be the one who comforts her when she's upset or afraid. Where did that thought come from? *This is a business trip. Business only.*

Six

Ainsley watched out the window as their plane taxied down the remote airstrip. There wasn't much in the way of scenery, just the sheets of rain, the gray skies and a few distant trees.

As they neared a large, barnlike structure, a man in overalls appeared, opening the doors wide. She undid her seat belt as the jet slowly rolled inside the cavernous building.

Next to her, Gage got to his feet. He was getting his things from beneath the seat when they came to a stop.

Inside the hangar, the sounds of the rain and thunder became somewhat muffled.

Max opened the cabin door and stood in the center of the aisle. "Well, we made it to Summer Village. I'm sorry. I thought we'd be ahead of the storm, but it turned at the last minute. We hit the outer edge."

"That's the outer edge? I'd hate to hit it full-on." Ainsley's eyes widened at the thought.

"The real question is, how long are we going to be here?" Gage gripped the strap of his attaché case.

"Depends on the weather." Max ran a hand over her chin. "At least overnight, based on what I know right now. Hopefully, the storm lets up so we can get underway tomorrow."

"Yikes." Ainsley reached for her phone. "I have to call Bebe and let her know I won't be home tonight." Holding her phone up, she started to make the call, then frowned. "Crap. No signal."

Max chuckled. "We're inside a barn in the middle of nowhere, and there's like a hundred percent cloud cover. You're gonna have to hold off on the call."

Ainsley sighed.

Gage scowled. "Damn. Looks like we'll be needing lodging for the night, then."

Ainsley watched his expression and could tell he was annoyed by the inconvenience. *At least he's doing a decent job of controlling it.* She knew no one else understood his moods the way she did.

"Let me get the stairs down and you two can get off." Maxine walked past them to the rear of the aisle, behind where Gage had originally been sitting.

Ainsley's brow furrowed. "'You two'? What about you, Max?"

"I'm staying with my baby," she remarked as she opened the doors and prepared their exit route. "I'll be fine on the jet until we can get underway again. Besides, I need to secure her and supervise her refueling."

"You folks coming out?" A man's voice called.

The three of them deplaned, meeting the man in overalls who'd opened the doors at the foot of the stairs.

"Hey, y'all." The man, with his ruddy complexion,

shaggy brown hair and blue eyes offered them a friendly smile. "Hugh Delmar, at your service."

"Kidder, pilot." Max shook Hugh's hand. "Thanks for letting me in here."

"This storm hit fast and out of nowhere. It ain't fit weather out there for man nor beast, so you're welcome to this old barn as long as you need it. When I heard you over the radio, I knew this was your only good place to land." Hugh turned toward Gage. "And you are…"

"Gage Woodson, chief operations officer at 404 Sound in Atlanta. And this is my assistant, Ainsley."

"Whew, boy. You said a mouthful. Pleased to meet ya, Mr. Woodson." Hugh chuckled softly, then looked to her. "And you too, Miss Ainsley."

"Likewise, Mr. Delmar."

"Welcome to Summer Village, folks." He tipped his ratty old baseball cap in their direction.

"Thanks. Could you point us toward a local hotel?" She watched him expectantly. "Preferably one with a shuttle."

"Oh, there's no hotels here. Not for a good fifty miles or so. The only place to stay is the Duchess Bed and Breakfast."

Gage frowned. "Really?"

"'Fraid so." Hugh started walking toward the open doors. "I can carry you over there if you want, though I can only fit two of you in my truck."

Max waved him off, already going back up the stairs. "No problem. I'm staying with my jet."

"All right. If you need anything, you can use the old landline phone in my office over there. I still do woodwork out of this barn from time to time." As Max disappeared into the jet, Hugh said, "Ready, folks?"

Shielding herself with her tote bag, Ainsley dashed

out into the rain behind the two men. Once she was loaded into the cab of Hugh's old pickup truck, seated between the two of them, she settled in for the ride.

The two men talked over her the whole time, with Hugh asking questions and Gage answering in the same clipped tone he always used when he was upset about something. She opted out of any questions directed at her by shrugging. Gage cut his eyes at her a few times, but she ignored him.

About twenty minutes later, they rolled past a sign announcing their arrival in town. The cluster of businesses along both sides of the main street, along with the old-fashioned streetlights that resembled old gas lamps, could only be described as charming. The relentless rain continued to fall.

The truck turned down a rutted road and drove about a mile before coming to a stop in front of a two-story house. The white structure, with its bright green shutters and the rockers sitting on the wide wraparound porch, resembled an old plantation house.

They got out and ran up on the porch, struggling to dodge the rain. Inside the open door, they approached the tall desk where a woman stood.

Hugh greeted the woman. "How's it going, Mary?"

"Can't complain." The woman tucked a lock of her blond hair behind her ear. "Brought me some guests?"

"Sure did. They stashed their plane in my barn. Got a room for them?"

"Last one." Mary fished around beneath her desk and pulled out a key with a bright pink tag labeled with the number four. "It's your lucky night, folks."

"We're gonna need two rooms," Gage interjected.

Mary cringed. "Oh, honey. We only have the one real room."

Ainsley asked, "What do you mean by that?"

"I mean we've got a single bed set up in the basement, but we only rent that out in emergencies."

Gage pulled out his wallet. "I'll take the basement."

"You sure? It's nothing fancy, and it can get a little damp and drafty down there. That's why we don't rent it out much." Mary watched Gage's face.

"I'm sure it'll be fine. I'll take the basement room." He slid his gold card across the desk.

Mary smiled, a knowing look on her face. "Whatever you say." She retrieved a second key, this one with a green tag attached. "Breakfast is from seven to nine. Miss, your room's upstairs, first door on the right." She passed the pink key to Ainsley, and the green one to Gage. "I'll show you downstairs to yours."

"Gotcha." He pocketed the key. "So, what's the Wi-Fi password here? I'd like to finish up some work, and all my stuff is in the cloud."

Her brow hitched, Mary replied, "There's a computer in the corner of the breakfast room you can use. It's wired for the internet. No Wi-Fi. Sorry, sugar."

Gage sighed. "Thanks for your help."

Watching for a moment as Mary led him away, Ainsley trudged up the stately stairs with her tote bag tucked under her arm.

With his attaché case in hand, Gage followed Mary through the lobby, past the dining room and through the farmhouse kitchen. The kitchen, with its cream wallpaper printed with cherries, reminded him of his great-grandmother's home down in Shreveport. Reaching a door set in the rearmost wall, she gestured to it. "Here it is." Inserting the key into the lock, Gage opened the door to the room. Glancing around, he sighed. A darkness-shrouded staircase lay before him, and to his mind, it looked like the descent into a cave.

"Hold on, hon. Let me get the light." Mary reached around him and flipped a switch.

A dim, yellowish light illuminated the staircase, which descended for several steps before the next landing, where it veered off to the right.

"Watch your step. The stairs are a little crooked in places." Mary walked ahead of him.

The two of them walked down slowly, and he detected the aroma of damp earth filling his nostrils. When they reached the landing, Mary stopped short.

He walked into her. "Sorry."

"Well, fiddlesticks." Mary shook her head. "Looks like this terrible weather has done us in."

Looking down the next flight of stairs, he saw what she was referring to. The entire basement was flooded, and from his position, he couldn't determine the depth of standing water. Only three steps below where they stood were above water, the rest of the space resembling a man-made lake.

"Yikes." Looking to his left, he could see the rectangular glass window around which the water continued to stream in.

"Dang it. I thought we'd sealed up that window leak." Mary whistled. "Well, unless you've got a wet suit and scuba gear in that bag, I don't think you'll be able to sleep down here, Mr. Woodsby."

"Woodson," he corrected. "And no, I don't." He watched a few tools and knickknacks float by before turning and going back up the stairs and through the kitchen.

Mary met him at the front desk. "Sorry about that. You probably wouldn't have been too comfortable in the basement anyway, but I apologize for the inconvenience."

He shrugged. "It couldn't be helped." *I guess I'll be headed back to the barn to crash on the jet. Hopefully, Max won't mind the company.* "Where's Ainsley's room again? I need to let her know what happened."

"She's in room four. It's right by the stairs—you can't miss it." Mary winked.

Unsure of what the innkeeper was getting at, he turned and headed up the stairs. Knocking on the door, he waited.

She opened it a few seconds later. "Gage? I thought you were taking the basement room?"

He shook his head. "The place is more suited for swimming than sleeping right now. It's flooded."

"Oh crap." Her brow furrowed, her expression concerned. "What are you going to do?"

"Head back over to the barn and crash on the jet with Max. I just came up here to let you know."

She shook her head. "No. You shouldn't have to go back out in this awful weather. Why don't you just share this room with me?"

He swallowed, thinking about what she'd offered him.

"I mean, I'm sure the front desk has a rollaway bed or a cot or something."

"I hadn't thought about that, but I guess we can check." He scratched his chin.

She stepped back. "Come on in. You can use the phone to call the desk so you don't have to go back down."

He entered the room and looked around while she closed the door behind him. The accommodations were nowhere near as posh as he usually preferred, but he supposed that was to be expected in middle-of-nowhere,

Louisiana. Moving inside the room, he shrugged out of his damp sport coat. "Whew, that's better. I was roasting."

"If the room had two doubles, it wouldn't be an issue. Unfortunately, there's only one bed," Ainsley remarked, pointing.

He looked where she indicated, well aware of the sarcasm in her tone. Sure enough, the room had one queen-size bed, dressed in an extremely floral bedding ensemble. "Looks that way." One corner of the room held two plush-looking armchairs and a coffee table, situated around a small fireplace. He went to the bedside table and picked up the phone, dialing zero for the front desk. "Hi, Mary. This is Gage Woodson. Would you happen to have any rollaway beds?"

"Sure, we've got one. I'll have someone bring it up to you this evening."

"Thanks." He hung up. "Someone will bring a rollaway up later."

She shook her head as she walked past him, dropping her purse on the coffee table. "I hope it's a decent-size one. It'd take some origami-level folding for you to sleep in one of those little beds."

"So...you're offering to sleep in the rollaway, then?"

She shrugged. "We can decide when they bring it up."

He tossed his attaché case on the bed. "What are we going to do now? Without Wi-Fi, the choices are pretty limited." Heavy rain still fell outside, and the sound, which usually soothed him, didn't seem to be working this time around.

She shrugged. "My first priority right now is getting in contact with Bebe. She needs to know I won't be home tonight since she's looking after Cooper." Slipping out of her shoes, she flopped down in one of the chairs and pulled out her phone.

He groaned inwardly. This entire trip had gone way off the rails. He'd been so determined to make this process quick and seamless. Get on the plane, get to Cali, grab the equipment and get it back to the studio. Now, thanks to Mother Nature, an industrial-size wrench had been thrown in his plans.

And then there was Ainsley. After spending so long trying his best to keep his distance, now he'd be forced to share this tiny room with her. How was he supposed to focus? She was so beautiful; it made his eyes hurt to look at her sometimes. Still, he couldn't help admiring her. So, he stood there, watching her, unable to look away.

Finally, she looked up from her phone. "Um, didn't you have some work to do?"

The question made him cringe, because it felt like outright dismissal. "I did."

"Looks like you get to avail yourself of the inn's 'state-of-the-art' business center, then." She winked.

He cut his eyes at her, not amused at her little quip. "I'll be back."

"Cool. I'll hang out here reading my book, hoping the weather changes." She went back to her phone call.

Stretching his arms above his head to release some of the tension in his shoulders, he picked up his attaché case from the bed and left the room.

Back downstairs, he found Mary seated behind the desk, flipping through a magazine. She looked up as he approached. "Something you need, Mr. Woodsby?"

"That's Woodson," he corrected her. "And yes. I'm going to need to use the computer."

Her brow furrowed. "Might want to make it quick, sugar. The weather report says the storm's bound to intensify, and if it starts lightning and thundering again, I'm gonna have to shut that thing off."

"I'm sorry, what?"

"We don't run unnecessary electronics when it's storming, sugar." She watched him with a curious expression. "Where'd you say you're from?"

"I didn't, but I'm from Atlanta."

She chuckled. "Ain't you ever had a granny? You should know the drill."

He smiled despite his annoyance, because her words reminded him of his paternal grandmother's insistence on total darkness and silence in her house during a thunderstorm.

She gestured to her right. "The computer's in that back corner, right next to the window seat."

"Thanks." He walked through the breakfast area, with its striped wallpaper, dark wood tables and chairs, and aged mauve carpet, until he reached the large picture window that took up the majority of the rear wall. A window seat, complete with a floral cushion, was positioned just beneath it.

The window, dressed in gauzy, sheer white curtains, gave a view of the grassy knoll behind the inn, as well as the dense forest beyond. He imagined the window provided a lot of sunlight to the space on a nice day. Today, though, there was only the gray skies, the rain hitting the glass pane and the trees swaying in the wind.

To the right of the window sat a small writing desk, upon which a less-than-current desktop computer sat. He pulled out the chair, setting his case on the window seat as he sat in the chair by the desk. Pressing the power button, he watched as the aged machine roared to life, with fans whirring. Finally, it booted up fully, and he opened the internet browser to access his personal document cloud.

When he'd finished going through reports and inter-office memos, he shut the computer down and tucked his handwritten notes back into his case. As he passed the desk, he nodded to Mary before heading up the stairs.

Approaching their door, he could hear Ainsley talking. He paused.

"No, he went to use the computer. He's too work-obsessed to just chill for a minute, you know what I mean?" She paused, then laughed.

He felt his jaw tighten. *She doesn't even know me well enough to say something like that. She sees me working because that's the only place she sees me—at the office.* And why should he be blamed for being competent and hardworking anyway? Somebody had to make sure things got done. He rolled his eyes.

"Well, I'm not gonna keep you on the line all day. Since you've got Cooper's key, you can get into the house if he needs anything. Okay, girl. I'll talk to you later."

If only I could shake these pesky feelings for her. Then I wouldn't care what she thought of me.

He wanted her, and it seemed the more he tried to deny his feelings, the more they rose to the surface. Logic and common sense told him time and again that he simply couldn't risk being in another relationship right now, especially one with a coworker.

My ex accused me of being too work focused. Repeatedly. Oddly enough, she'd leveraged that insult to get him to drop his guard so she could swindle the company. He shook his head. Nope. He wasn't going to let his feelings get the better of him. Not this time.

Seven

Ainsley had just pocketed her phone when Gage walked in. Looking his way, she asked, "Did you finish your work?"

"Yeah." His answer was curt, gruff.

She frowned. *What's the matter with him?* Deciding not to engage with his bad mood, she fished her tablet out of her purse. "It's a little after one our time. Do you want me to get lunch now, or should we get an early dinner in a few hours? Because I'm going to take a nap."

"Early dinner after a nap." She watched him kick off his shoes, drop his attaché on the nightstand and fall onto the bed face-first. Shrugging, she went back to the book she'd been trying to read on the plane.

The story, set on a distant planet and featuring some pretty cool fantasy elements, held her attention pretty well under most circumstances. But, with her handsome boss lying just feet away from her, snoring softly, she found herself distracted from the tale. She kept looking up, stealing glances at his sleeping form. Her eyes raked over his body, noting the way the fabric of his dress shirt stretched over the muscles of his arms, the way his back rose and fell in time with his breaths, even the way his slacks clung to his backside.

She swallowed. *Have mercy.*

Tearing her eyes away, she went back to her book. Two hours later, she'd had it. There was simply no good way to focus on reading with a man that fine so close by. So she grabbed her cardigan, which had dried somewhat since they arrived, and slipped it on along with her shoes. Grabbing her purse, she quietly left the room, so as not to wake him as she exited.

Once downstairs, she called Max to get an update on the weather. Although it had slowed here, it was raging along their flight path. They were definitely staying put for the night. Max was safe in the barn with the jet. Ainsley told her to help herself to any of the food in the little fridge.

At the desk, Ainsley spoke briefly with the innkeeper so she could borrow an umbrella. She remembered having seen a diner among the businesses they'd passed, so with the borrowed umbrella and the bright yellow poncho Mary had insisted she use, she made her way outside and started walking. The rain was steady but not as bad as before. If she was going to make a run for food, now was the time.

It took less than ten minutes to make it to the main road, and that was only because she took care to avoid puddles and patches of slick mud. When she stepped onto the sidewalk on Main Street, she made a beeline for the blue-and-white-striped awning she'd seen earlier.

She let down her umbrella beneath the awning, then

opened the door to the Blue Rose Diner. Inside, she left the umbrella near the door and took a good look around. The cream-colored wallpaper was emblazoned with the diner's namesake flower, and the chairs at the small round tables all had blue cushions.

Walking up to the counter, she smiled at the two people she saw behind it. There was a man and a woman, both dressed in blue with black aprons. "Hey, there."

"Welcome to the Blue Rose, little lady." The man, tall and dark-skinned, wore a cook's cap that matched his apron. Touching a long-handled spatula to the edge of his cap in salute, he said, "I'm Bud. This is my wife, Rose. She'll get your order."

Rose, a petite, caramel-skinned lady whose dark hair was streaked with gray, smiled in her direction. "Need a minute to look over the menu, honey?"

"Yes, thanks." She looked up at the menu board above the counter. It was an old-fashioned board, with black plastic letters and numbers stuck to a ridged surface to spell out the place's offerings and prices. It took her a few minutes to find something she thought Gage would eat, and once she settled on that, she ordered. "I'll be taking this to-go. Let me get the grilled chicken salad, no dairy, no carbs, with fat-free dressing on the side."

"Goodness. That's pretty much just lettuce, tomato and cucumber, honey. Are you sure that's all you want?"

She held back a laugh. "Oh, that's not for me, that's for my boss. He's very health-conscious."

"I see." Rose punched the order into the register. "What are you gonna have?"

"Let me get a bacon cheeseburger, well-done, with fries. And two drinks."

"A woman after my own heart." Rose grinned as she entered the rest of the order and gave her the total.

Handing over the cash plus an extra five, Ainsley said, "Keep the change." She walked to the tall, glass-front refrigerator next to the counter and chose a cola for herself and a bottle of water for Gage. Moving to one of the tables by the front windows, she sat down to wait for the food. While she waited, she pulled out her phone. The signal wasn't great, but it was enough for her to do a bit of scrolling down her social media feeds.

"Your food's ready, honey." Rose's voice cut into her thoughts.

Putting her phone away, she returned to the counter to get the large plastic bag containing her order.

"Napkins and everything are already in there." Rose held out the bag. "You enjoy, and come back and see us, okay?"

"Thanks." Tucking the drinks inside, she accepted the bag. With the food in hand, and her purse slung over her shoulder, she grabbed the borrowed umbrella, opening it as she stepped back outside. The chill in the air touched her right away, and she hustled back to the hotel as quickly as she could while avoiding the pitfalls of the wet terrain. The last thing she wanted to do was take a fall and ruin their meal before they even got a chance to enjoy it. *Though I don't know how much enjoyment Gage is gonna get out of this plain-ass salad anyway.* Giggling to herself, she climbed onto the inn's porch.

Inside, she returned the umbrella and the poncho to Mary, then climbed the stairs. When she opened the door, she found Gage sitting on the edge of the bed, flipping channels on the television. "Oh, there you are. I was going to call you."

"While the rain slowed, I thought I'd grab us an early dinner." She closed the door behind her and sat the bag of food down on the bed.

"Where'd you end up going?"

"We passed a diner on the way in, and I grabbed us food from there."

He looked skeptical.

She rolled her eyes. "I know what you eat and what you don't, Gage. Remember, I've been ordering your lunches for years now." She checked the foam trays, removing his and handing it over. "I got you a grilled chicken salad. Fat-free dressing on the side."

"No dairy and no carbs?" he asked as he took the tray.

"And no flavor," she added wryly, handing over his bottled water.

"Very funny." He opened the tray and inspected the contents. "Thanks, Ainsley."

"I'd say it was my pleasure, but I don't typically enjoy running around in the rain." As she took out her own tray and walked over to her chair, it occurred to her that if she didn't care about Gage, she wouldn't have subjected herself to the monsoon outside just to get him something to eat. That wasn't a thought she wanted to dwell on, so she decided to focus on her burger and fries instead.

They ate in relative silence while a home-improvement program played on the television. The burger, well-seasoned and cooked just right, tasted amazing, as did the crisp fries. By the time she finished her food and most of her drink, she berated herself for not having a nap earlier. Stifling a yawn, she got up and started collecting her trash, stuffing it back into the plastic bag. "You done?"

"Yes, thanks." Barely taking his attention off the television, he handed her his trash.

She opened the door and set the bag of trash in the

hallway before closing it again. Walking to the window, she looked out at the stormy sky and wondered what the night ahead might hold.

Gage reclined on the bed, half watching the home improvement show on the television. While the host went on about shiplap and concrete countertops, he was busy stealing glances at Ainsley.

She'd taken out her tablet and was now engrossed in the story she was reading. Artfully arranged in the armchair, she had her legs draped over an arm, with her bare feet dangling side to side while she read. She looked so sexy, he had to look away, so he directed his gaze to the window instead.

Outside, the rain continued to fall at an increasing pace. He could hear the droplets hitting the roof, and it took him a minute to realize that the insistent thudding sound wasn't just rain. He got up, walking past Ainsley to the window. Looking outside, he could see the quarter-size pellets of hail whizzing by, along with the sheets of rain.

"Yikes. First the storm, now hail." He shook his head.

She glanced up from her tablet. "Let's hope it doesn't last. There's no way Max can get us out of here in a hailstorm."

He sighed. His grand plan of getting everything with the equipment settled in one day had effectively been flushed down the toilet. He'd been holding off on calling Harcroft, hoping that somehow this crazy weather would resolve in time for them to make it to California today. Resigned, he grabbed his phone and called them.

"I totally understand, Gage. However, I must advise

that if you don't pick up your custom order within three business days, it will be placed up for sale."

Gage bristled. "You're kidding me, right?"

"Sorry, Gage. We have two additional custom orders that have come in, so we'll just divert our resources where they're needed."

By the time he hung up the phone, Gage was more frustrated than before. *Now I have to rush over there before they sell my equipment. What a colossal mess.*

He thrived on being in control, on having it all together. Yet everything about this situation had taken that power away from him. He dragged his open hand across his face, feeling the tension building in his neck and shoulders as he stood there.

"You okay, boss man?" Ainsley's voice cut through his thoughts.

He turned her way. "We've got a couple of days to get to Cali or Harcroft is going to sell our equipment and we'll be back at square one."

She cringed. "Oh crap."

"Yeah." He ran a hand over his hair. "I'm just stressed."

"I get it. But try not to let it get to you." She gestured toward the window. "It's the weather, something none of us have any control over. So, try not to beat yourself up about it."

He blew out a breath.

"Besides, I can't remember the last time I was out overnight. The circumstances aren't ideal, but at least I'm getting a break from mommy duties." She wiped the back of her hand across her brow, feigning exhaustion.

He chuckled. "Been that long, eh?" He couldn't even imagine the amount of work that went into raising a kid, let alone as a single parent with a demanding career.

She nodded. "I haven't been away from Cooper for more than a few hours since he was in like third grade." She shook her head. "My social life is barely viable."

"Technically it's still dead in the water." He winked. "Even though we're stranded, it's still a work trip."

She pursed her lips and blew a raspberry in his direction. "Thanks for the reminder, Mr. Killjoy."

He returned to the bed, grabbing the remote. "I suppose we might as well make the best of it. Redeem the time, as my granny used to say."

She closed the cover over her tablet. "How are we gonna do that? Do you have some kind of grand plan to bring my social life back from the dead?"

"Not in this weather. But we can at least watch a movie or two." He gestured toward the television screen. "The inn's cable provider has some pretty recent releases available on demand."

Before she could respond, a knock sounded on the door. Opening it, Ainsley stepped aside so a young man could roll in the folded bed. A clear plastic bag containing bed linens sat atop it. Once it was in place between the queen bed and the window, the young man excused himself.

Tucking away her tablet, she joined Gage, sitting next to him on the foot of the bed. "Let's look through and see what they have."

They perused the selection of movies for a few minutes, each choosing a movie. Ainsley picked a gritty thriller with a sci-fi twist, one that left them both scratching their heads. Gage chose next, settling on a recent buddy-cop dramedy. The film was just as funny as the reviews suggested, and by the time it ended, they were both lying across the bed, laughing out loud.

He turned toward her, watching the way amusement softened her expression. "That was hilarious."

"You're telling me." Still laughing, she wiped the tears from her eyes. "I can't believe how raunchy it was."

He had to agree. There'd been more than a few off-color jokes and plenty of innuendos. "Good thing we're both mature adults."

"That depends on the day." She sat up then, tossing one long leg over the other. Stifling a yawn, she announced, "I'm tired."

He stood. "I can take a cue. Time for me to set up the rollaway." He walked over, unfolded the metal frame and used the linen in the bag to make up the bed. With that done, he looked it over. "It's not fancy, but at least it's big enough. I should be able to fit in it just fine."

She nodded. "Looks like it."

He eased out of his shirt then, revealing the white tank beneath. Once he was down to the tank and his boxers, he lay across the bed. Taking a moment to adjust his positioning, he found that no matter what he did, his feet dangled off the end just a bit. *No big deal.* The bed was comfortable, though it felt a bit on the lumpy side. He eyed the flat pillow, shaking his head. Picking it up, he manipulated it in his hands to redistribute the fibers inside. "If you're tired, I won't keep you up. Good night, Ainsley."

She offered a soft smile. "'Night, Gage."

"Shit."

The softly uttered curse woke Ainsley, and she sat up in bed. Years of motherhood had trained her to be a light sleeper, just in case Cooper needed something in the middle of the night.

The next sound she heard in the inky darkness was a sharp inhale, the sound of air being sucked in through clenched teeth. Blinking against the blackness, she said, "Gage? Are you all right?"

"I think I might be bleeding." His reply was tinged with pain.

"Bleeding?" Reaching for the bedside lamp, she clicked it on. In the yellow glow, she looked toward Gage, and found him sitting up on the edge of the rollaway bed. "Where?"

He cringed. "My back." He turned at the waist.

Her eyes widened as she saw the rather large snag, as well as the red stain on the back of his tank top. "You are bleeding. What happened?"

He pulled back the sheets and found a matching stain on the bed. Something silver jutted through a hole in the sheet. "A freaking spring from this bed stabbed me in the back, apparently."

"Ouch. Let me see if there are any first aid supplies in the medicine cabinet." Ainsley slid off the bed and went to the bathroom. Inside the cabinet above the sink, she found a mini first aid kit. Carrying it back to the room, she gestured for him to join her on the bed. "Come here. I'll try my best to patch you up."

"Thanks." He stood and removed his shirt.

His muscular chest came into view, and her mouth watered. His chiseled physique revealed his dedication to healthy eating and exercise, and he exuded a physical strength that captivated her. She imagined what it would be like to have him lift her into those strong arms, press her back against the nearest wall and make love to her until she lost her senses. Her naughty thoughts made her pulse quicken, so she did her best to push them away and focus on the task at hand.

As he sat on the bed, with his back to her, the sight of his wound dragged her back from fantasy to reality. A small, jagged gouge, about an inch long, lay just beneath his right shoulder blade. "Yikes."

"It hurts like hell." He groaned. "I knew the bed was a little lumpy, but I didn't know it was this serious."

She searched through the first aid kit and found an iodine wipe. Tearing open the foil packet, she applied the iodine to his wound as gently as she could.

He winced but otherwise kept his composure.

She dumped out the kit on the bed, separating the contents to find the ones she wanted. "I've cleaned it up. Now I'm gonna put some gauze and tape on it." Hoping to add a little humor to the situation, she added, "I'm sure Mary wouldn't want you ruining any more of her bed linens."

He chuckled. "I'm over here in pain and you're making it about Mary? Why do I put up with you?" His voice was tinged with mirth.

Working to tear off a small piece of medical tape, she placed it along the edge of the gauze square. "Face it, you need me. I keep you balanced." With the makeshift bandage secured, she patted it once more. "There. I'm done."

He turned to face her. "Thanks. And you're right, you do keep me balanced."

She winked. "I'm glad you can acknowledge the truth of things."

He straightened, looking her in the eye. "This little disaster means we need to revisit this whole 'one bed' thing."

She sucked in her lower lip. "I don't really want to

sleep in the chair, and you aren't going to fit in the chair."

"I'm not about to be the one who makes the decision here, because above all else I want to make sure you feel comfortable."

She contemplated his words. She trusted him—that wasn't an issue. And she couldn't say parts of her weren't intrigued by the idea of sleeping in the same bed with him. "Let's just both sleep in the bed. Like you said, we're both mature adults, right?"

He watched her intently. "Right."

"And I'm too tired to be a troublemaker right now anyway." She yawned again. "Just pick a side and stay there, and I'll do the same. It'll be fine, right?"

"Yeah, yeah. It's no big deal."

She swallowed. He wasn't a creeper; he could keep to his side of the bed. What she'd be thinking about while he kept his distance from her…well, that was another matter entirely.

Once she was under the covers, leaving a wide berth between them, she whispered, "Good night, Gage."

"Good night."

She reached to the nightstand and switched off the lamp.

Eight

Ainsley awoke Tuesday morning feeling groggy and out of sorts. Blinking her eyes a few times as she came to full awareness, she shifted a bit then stopped as she realized where she was.

In the inn. In the bed. With Gage. And that would have been awkward enough…but she was also lying across his chest.

She turned her head slowly, her eyes widening as his chest hairs ticked her cheek. He was splayed out on his back, one hand behind his head and the other hand stroking her hair.

She squeezed her eyes shut, hoping she was dreaming.

But when she opened them again, the predicament remained.

Shit.

He stirred, and a moment later, his eyes popped open. "Good morning."

"Yeah, uh, good morning." She swallowed.

"Don't you look cozy?" He winked, fingers still entwined in her curls.

She jerked away from him. "Oh. I'm...so sorry. I must have been doing a lot of moving around. I sleep kinda wild."

He waved her off. "No need to apologize. It's not a problem."

She watched the expression playing over his face and thought she saw a hint of mischief in his eyes. Choosing not to dwell on it, she scooted away and got out of bed.

She found her bag kicked beneath the chair where she'd left it and pulled out the black three-quarter-sleeve tunic and charcoal-gray leggings she'd packed, along with underclothes.

Watching her from the bed, he asked, "You brought a change of clothes on a day trip?"

She nodded. "I always bring a change of clothes. I'm a klutz, and it's pretty likely I'm gonna spill something on myself, so I try to be prepared."

He chuckled. "If only I thought like you."

She grinned. "I'm one of a kind. The world couldn't handle another person who thought like me." Tucking the clothes under her arm, she went to the bathroom and closed the door behind her.

Fresh from the shower, she emerged twenty or so minutes later to find Gage up and sitting in one of the armchairs, checking his voice mail. He had put his sleeveless undershirt back on, and she couldn't help dragging her gaze over his powerful biceps.

She passed him, going to the window to look outside. The skies were still gray, and the rain was coming down in buckets, but at least the hail seemed to have stopped. "After breakfast I'm going to head into town and see what stores are open."

He looked up from his phone. "In this weather? What, getting dinner yesterday wasn't enough of an adventure?"

She chuckled. "If I can find a clothing store, I can grab you a change of clothes." She grabbed her purse. "You're a thirty-eight waist and a nineteen shirt collar, right?"

"Right." A ghost of a smile crossed over his face. "Nothing too brightly colored, please."

Headed for the door, she tossed back, "I know you better than that, boss man. Come on downstairs. I can smell coffee."

After a delicious breakfast, Ainsley walked to the front desk, while Gage headed for the computer. Turning down the umbrella at the desk in favor of keeping her hands free, she donned a plastic poncho and left the inn. The short walk to town took her past groves of tall conifers encased in kudzu before the grass gave way to the concrete sidewalk and the forest to buildings of varying heights and sizes.

Looking down the road, she was again struck by the picturesque charm of Summer Village. Having lived in Atlanta her entire life, she couldn't imagine living in a place so small, without most of the amenities she'd become accustomed to. Still, there was something refreshing about the one-and two-story buildings, the hand-painted signs on businesses, and the old-fashioned feel the town evoked.

A short search led her to Kramer and Sons, a two-story menswear store. Once inside, she greeted the shopkeepers as she shook off her drenched poncho and left it by the door.

"I'm Ted, and this is my son, Teddy." The man, wearing a pair of khakis and a red polo, had a pair of copper-rimmed reading glasses perched atop his graying head.

"Nice to meet you both." She smiled. "I'm Ainsley."

Teddy, who was dressed identically to his father except that his polo was blue, asked, "What can I help you find, Miss Ainsley?"

She put in a request for Gage's size in shirts and slacks, and twenty minutes later, she left with a bag containing a pair of black slacks and a hunter green button-down. As she stepped outside, she stopped short, realizing he'd probably need boxers as well. *Good thing I've got the corporate credit card and a can-do spirit.* She chuckled as she went back inside.

She thought back to that morning, when she'd awakened sprawled across his chest, her eyes just inches away from the waistband of his boxers. She sucked her bottom lip into her mouth at the memory, then let herself follow that thread for just a minute before she shook it off.

She left the store a short while later with her purchases. The rain continued crashing down, but since she was soaked anyway, she decided instead of heading straight back to the inn, she'd look around. A few other rain-soaked people passed her on the sidewalk, and every one of them took the time to wave or say hello.

When the wind started blowing the rain sideways, she quickly ducked into the doorway of a small, one-story brick structure. *Glow Apothecary.* The window display included plenty of artfully arranged miniature Mason jars filled with all kinds of goodies for the hair, skin and body.

She entered the shop to the sound of the tinkling bell above the door.

A tall, slender Black woman with a glorious Afro waved at her from behind the counter. She wore a white top and matching slacks with a black apron over her clothes. "Come in, come in. Get out of this terrible weather. Welcome to my shop."

"Hi. I'm Ainsley." She removed her wet poncho before approaching the counter and set her bag down. "Nice place."

"Thanks for the compliment. I'm Candace, by the way." She stuck out her hand.

Ainsley shook it. "Is it okay if I leave my bag with you while I take a look around?"

"Sure thing."

She started walking the aisles, taking in the shelves lined with artfully arranged jars, bottles and tins. She unscrewed the lid off a small jar of grapefruit body scrub and inhaled deeply. She sighed as the invigorating scent of tart citrus flooded her nostrils. "This smells amazing, Candace."

"Thanks." She walked over to where Ainsley stood. "The citrus line is actually our most popular."

"How do you get it to smell like that? I feel like I just cut into a red grapefruit." She inhaled again and smiled. "I can almost taste it."

"Actually, I make all these products myself, with a little help from two of my cousins. We zest grapefruits, dry the little shreds of the rind and add them to the mixture. That increases the scent and adds to the exfoliating power."

"Wow." She couldn't help being impressed with Candace's artistry. As the conversation continued, she noticed the way Candace's face lit up as she spoke about her products. It occurred to her that her job as Gage's assistant didn't inspire anywhere near that level of excitement.

She belonged in human resources, where she could really use her skills to help everyone who worked for 404. That was where she truly felt her life's work lay.

While Candace chattered on about her lemon verbena body butter, Ainsley's eyes widened as the realization of something hit her.

It wasn't passion for her job that had kept her in the same position for five years.

It was passion for her *boss*.

She swallowed. After last night, when she'd lay over his body in her sleep as if it were the natural thing to do, she didn't think she could go back to pretending the attraction didn't exist.

Gage stood by the window, looking outside. The almost-black skies and torrential rain were starting to affect his mood in a major way, and he didn't think being in the room alone was helping matters any.

Summer Village seems like a nice enough place, but we've got to get the hell out of here.

Grabbing his cell phone, he called Max, praying she was somewhere near enough to civilization that she could get a signal.

She picked up on the third ring. "Morning, Gage. Before you ask, no, nothing has changed since you called me two hours ago."

"Damn. I'm just trapped in the inn with this terrible weather and no Wi-Fi. I'm going crazy." He sighed. "Where are you?"

"I'm in town at a little coffee shop. Mr. Delmar gave me a ride."

"What's going on with the plane, Max? Please tell me we can get back in the air today."

"That's not likely."

He groaned. "Why? It's not a mechanical problem, right?"

"No, not at all." Max chuckled. "It's a brand-new plane, remember? This is just an issue of fueling her up."

Gage ran a hand over his head. "Let me guess. Jet fuel isn't easy to come by way out here, is it?"

"Ding, ding, ding." She paused. "I'm actually gonna have to go to this tiny little airport up in Arkansas to get her refueled."

"If you can fly there then why can't we just load up, stop in for a fill-up and head to Cali? I need to get this equipment before Harcroft resells it."

"That's the plan, but we can't do it today. Visibility is less than ten percent, and unless this next line of storms moves really quickly, we're grounded for probably another eighteen hours. I'm so sorry, Gage. Even I can't fight Mother Nature."

His brow creased. "Did you say the next line of storms? Another one is coming?"

"Yes. It's all over the news. This line is just as strong as the last one but is moving a little slower. It's supposed to hit within the next two hours and last the rest of the day. We can't even get through it to fly above it."

"Shit." A curse was all he had at the moment. "Listen, will you let me know as soon as we're clear to leave?"

"Sure thing."

After he ended the call, he checked the time. It was a good two or more hours since Ainsley had left. Curiosity about what she was up to had started to get the better of him. *What's she doing out there? It's been a while.*

The thought of looking for her crossed his mind, but he dismissed it. After all, she was an adult, and not his responsibility. If she got into some kind of trouble, she could handle it on her own. He'd always known Ainsley to be a very capable person.

His stomach growled loudly. He'd eaten a huge breakfast, but since it was nearly lunchtime, he was hungry again. *Looks like I'm going out.*

He went to the bathroom and got cleaned up. Then he got his slacks from the back of the chair where he'd draped them, shaking out the rumples before slipping them on. Once he was fully dressed, he got a rain poncho from Mary and ventured out of the inn.

The air was thick with humidity and held a slight chill. The rain hitting his face felt like being splashed with a cold beverage, so he walked quickly toward the town's Main Street.

When he came across the coffee shop, he went inside. Glancing around the interior for Max, he realized he must have missed her. The only other person inside was the barista behind the counter. "Hi. Can I have an almond-milk latte with stevia and sugar-free hazelnut?"

The barista smiled but looked slightly confused. "I can make you a latte, sir, but we don't have sugar-free syrups. Or almond milk. Or what was that other thing?"

"Stevia. It's a sweetener."

The barista shrugged. "Sorry. We do have the stuff in the pink packets if you want that instead."

The idea of the pink stuff in his coffee was an immediate turnoff, so he just shook his head. "Never mind. I think I'll just grab lunch instead."

He left the coffee shop and, dodging the rain as much as possible, ran across the street to the Blue Rose Diner.

He assumed it was the same place from yesterday, because he doubted a town this small had very many restaurants.

When he stepped inside, he found Ainsley at the counter chatting, her back to him. She clutched a paper shopping bag with twine handles in one hand. The shapely outline of her hips and thighs in the close-fitting tunic and leggings made his pulse quicken.

She turned around, her smile brightening his mood. "Oh, hey, Gage. Leave your poncho next to mine at the door, then come on and meet Rose and Bud."

He couldn't help chuckling. "Wow. Those your real names?"

"My name's Buford. Bud's a nickname." The man in the apron looked less than amused. "But Rose is my wife's given name."

"Sorry." He swallowed, sensing he'd offended Bud. "I wasn't poking fun." And he wasn't. "I've just never encountered a couple with such complimentary names."

"Whatever you say." Bud moved away from the counter and went to the flat-top grill.

Rose interjected, "Don't mind my husband—he's saltier than brine at times. Welcome to the Blue Rose. What can I get you?"

"I'm going to confer with Ainsley before I decide," Gage answered, throwing Ainsley a grin.

Ainsley shook her head. "Really?"

"Absolutely." They stepped away from the counter, and he leaned close to her ear. "Do you want to eat here? I'm in no hurry to get back out in the rain."

"Sounds good." She paused, held up the shopping bag. "I managed to snag you a shirt and slacks."

He took the bag from her and glanced inside at the

neatly folded—and dry—clothes. "Ainsley, you're a lifesaver."

She grinned. "I do my best." She tapped her chin, looking toward the menu board. "That bacon cheeseburger was awesome, but I feel like I should try something else. What are you gonna get?"

He shrugged. "Probably the same thing you brought me yesterday. I don't know if much else on the menu will work with my diet."

"True." She squinted. "Hmm. I think I'll try the chicken club this time. Can't go wrong with bacon and cheese, right?" She winked.

He shook his head. "I think I hear your arteries crying."

"Nope. That's the sound of my stomach singing in anticipation." Laughing, she left him standing there as she walked back toward the counter to order.

Watching her hips sway, he couldn't help smiling. He'd been so frustrated since they landed in Summer Village because he hated having his plans altered. Aside from that, there was a lot at stake here for the company. But when he looked at her, heard her witty repartee and the tinkling of her laughter, everything suddenly seemed right.

She's really something special.

And I want her. Not just as my assistant, but as my woman.

Nine

Back at the counter, Ainsley placed her order. When she finished, Gage stepped up. "We'll be on the same ticket."

Ainsley balked. "You don't have to do that."

"I know, but I insist." Gage turned his attention back to Rose. "Let me have your grilled chicken salad, no dairy, no carbs and fat-free dressing on the side, please. And I'll be drinking water."

"No problem, honey." Rose typed in the order.

As he took out his wallet to pay, Bud appeared behind his wife again. "You know, the little lady ordered the exact same thing yesterday. Said it was for her boss."

Gage nodded. "Yeah, that's me."

Bud snickered. "I thought for sure she worked for another woman. But I see you're just a pampered city-boy type instead." He looked him up and down with thinly veiled disdain.

Gage's jaw tightened, and Ainsley noticed the irritation clouding his face. She'd never understood the pissing contests men seemed to love having with each other. *Bud doesn't know Gage from a can of paint. He's in no position to be passing judgment on him.*

"Bud!" Rose spun on him. "Get back to your grill and keep your smart mouth shut before I box your ears!" Turning back to them, she gave them foam cups with the diner's logo printed on them.

Bud backed up a step. "Now, Rose, I was just—"

"You were just what? Insulting a paying customer?" Ainsley knew her tone was sharp, but she thought it appropriate for the situation. "I like you, Bud. You're a straight shooter, and I can respect that. But I'm telling you right now, nobody talks trash about my boss but me."

A perturbed-looking Gage eyed Ainsley. "Say what now?"

"Don't worry. Just enough trash talk to keep you humble." She nodded.

He shook his head but still let a smile tilt his full lips.

Bud threw up his hands. "I'm going back to my kitchen."

After they filled their cups at the drink machine, Gage walked behind Ainsley, following her to the booth she chose near the back. Once they were seated across from each other, she asked, "What made you decide to leave the room?"

I missed you. He didn't know how that would go over if he said it aloud. "Stir-crazy, I guess. It's crappy weather, but it was still high time I got out of there."

"Fair enough." She sipped her soda through the striped straw.

"Listen. I just wanted to say thanks for coming to my defense."

She waved him off. "It's nothing."

"Still. I appreciate you speaking on my behalf." He looked into her eyes. "I know you didn't have to do that."

"You're welcome." She let her gaze drop, a bit overwhelmed by the intensity in his eyes.

"You do so much that makes things easier for me, and I really haven't been as appreciative as I should have. That's going to change from now on."

"Wow, Gage." She stirred her drink around a few times, needing the distraction. "I don't know what to say."

"You don't have to say anything. I'm going to show you how much you mean to me."

She looked up from her cup and found him watching her. There was something in his eyes this time, something quite different. He'd made some strong declarations, and at first, she'd thought he was talking about work. Now it seemed to go much deeper than that.

Could this be it? Could this be the moment he realized how much she wanted to be with him, that they were meant for each other? After so many years of pining for him, it all seemed too much to hope for.

Rose appeared next to the table with the bright red trays holding their food. "You two enjoy."

After she walked away, Ainsley dug into her sandwich. She needed time to analyze and process what was happening right now. Her heart was on the line here, and she didn't want to risk misreading anything and making a dumb mistake that would leave her brokenhearted and looking foolish.

"Any word from Max on when we can leave?" She

needed to change the subject before things got any more intense.

"Eager to get home, huh?" He blessed her with a megawatt smile.

"Honestly, yes. I miss Cooper. And besides that, I'm worried he may be eating my neighbors out of house and home." She chuckled, though she'd only been half joking. Her son could put away food like a human garbage disposal.

"Max is hoping we can get off the ground tomorrow. There's a second wave to the storms, and she said visibility is almost nonexistent for now." He forked up some of his salad.

She sighed. "I'm sorry, Gage. I know how you like keeping to a tight schedule, so I know this little unexpected detour must be driving you bonkers."

He chewed, looking thoughtful, then swallowed. "You know what? It was bugging me. But I'm beginning to embrace what's happening."

She frowned, confused. *That doesn't sound like the regimented man I've known for all this time.* "Why's that?"

"For two reasons. One, we have to make safety our absolute first priority. If it's not safe to fly, then we need to stay put."

"I agree. What's the other reason?" She put a fry in her mouth.

"You. I couldn't ask for better company. And even though we aren't supposed to be here, I'm enjoying spending time with you, away from the office."

Her eyes widened, and she had to snatch up her cup and quickly wash the wayward fry down before she succumbed to a coughing fit.

"You okay?" He stood up.

"I'm fine, I'm fine." She took a deep breath, then one more sip of soda. "Just…uh…a little surprised to hear you talking like this."

"I have to admit, I didn't intend on saying all that out loud." He sat back down. "But I'm glad I did. It's high time we're honest with each other about how we feel."

She gave him a sidelong glance. "We? Oh, you speak French now?"

"Don't try to play me like that. You know what I'm talking about."

"I just think it's mighty cocky of you to say it that way. As if you're so sure I have feelings for you. You ain't all that, Gage Woodson." She couldn't resist teasing him some more. Not only did it amuse her, but it helped to defuse some of the rising romantic tension she sensed between them.

He simply shook his head. "Nice try. But you can't deny it, Ainsley. I feel it, you feel it. It's been there for a long, long time."

She looked out the window, knowing that if she made eye contact with him, it was over for her.

They finished their food, and she avoided his gaze the entire time. When she got up to discard their trash, he called after her.

"You're going to have to look at me sometime, Ainsley."

It was all she could do to get the emptied trays into the slot on top of the trash can. As she walked back to the table, he stepped in front of her. With a gentle hand beneath her chin, he tilted her head, effectively forcing her to look up.

"What do you need, Ainsley? Is there something you want?"

Oh, you have no idea. "There's some pricey body scrub at the apothecary I had my eye on."

"Take me there, and it's yours." He held her gaze for a moment, then let his hand fall away.

Walking with him out of the diner, she couldn't help noticing the knowing looks on Rose and Bud's faces.

Despite being back outside in the dreary weather, Gage felt his mood lighten considerably because now, Ainsley walked by his side. Their meal together had turned into something of a confessional for him. He typically avoided any conversations about emotions and feelings, and he still wasn't quite sure what had come over him. All he knew was that he cared about Ainsley, and that he wanted a much deeper connection with her than just their working relationship.

The ball was in her court, though. What he wanted in no way superseded her autonomy. His mother, Addison, had raised all her children as womanists, and those teachings were deeply ingrained in his mind. He'd never disrespect Ainsley or do anything to make her feel uncomfortable. So now that the truth was out, he'd simply have to follow her cues, whatever that might lead to.

He watched her as she walked beside him. Even in the rain-dappled poncho and sensible outfit, she radiated beauty. Her gaze rested on the scenery as they passed, and he wondered if she were avoiding his eyes again. He smiled. Suddenly, his effervescent assistant had become somewhat shy, a quality he'd never known her to exhibit before.

"Here's the place." She grasped the door handle at Glow Apothecary.

"Allow me." He reached to open the door, and their

hands grazed momentarily, sending a charge of magic up his arm. He held open the door for her to walk in, then followed her inside.

The interior was small, but the setup showed creative use of the space. The displays were both aesthetic and practical, and the whole place smelled like warm sugar cookies. It was, hands down, the most inviting place in Summer Village. He heard a familiar beat, playing softly from a hidden speaker. Listening intently, he tilted his head and stood near the middle of the store until he identified the song. "'Good Lovin'? Classic Atlanta hip-hop. That song doesn't get enough love."

"Thanks. Not everyone around here appreciates my taste in music." The Black woman behind the counter, who introduced herself as Candace, offered a bright grin before turning her attention to Ainsley. "Good to see you back so soon!" It was obvious she and Ainsley had a certain rapport. He could feel himself smiling. There was something about watching Black women chatting, laughing and enjoying each other's company that always warmed his heart. While he was eager to spoil Ainsley a little, he hung back and let them talk.

After a few minutes, Ainsley turned his way. "So, the stuff I wanted is over here."

Candace's expression brightened. "Oh, honey. You didn't tell me earlier you were here on a little romantic getaway." She winked.

Ainsley's wide-eyed expression, a mixture of embarrassment and humor, was priceless. She swallowed visibly but didn't say anything.

Under normal circumstances, he would have corrected Candace. But considering all he'd said a short time ago, he simply slipped his arm around Ainsley's shoulders and said, "Show me what you want."

"I'll leave you two to your shopping. Let me know if you need any help." A still-grinning Candace returned to her post behind the counter.

Ainsley led him to a section where baskets of wax fruit adorned the displays and showed him Glow's grapefruit and shea collection. Grabbing a tin of body scrub from the shelf, she twisted off the cap and held it up to his nose. "You have to smell this. It's amazing."

He inhaled, and the fresh, bright aroma washed over him. "Wow. That does smell good."

"I know, right?" She screwed the lid back on. "They have so much good stuff in this scent." She gestured to the shelf as she spoke. "There's handmade soap, body butter…"

She kept listing products, but most of it went underwater as he fixated on the phrase *handmade soap*. His mind flashed to an image of her, reclining in the old claw-foot tub in their room, gliding a soapy cloth over her beautiful dark skin as steam rose around her like a fog.

The proprietor's voice cut into his fantasy. "If you buy the collection, you get a free Glow Apothecary silk robe."

They both turned toward the counter.

Candace chuckled. "Just letting y'all know."

He returned his attention to Ainsley. "Can't knock the hustle, right?"

"Yeah, right." She giggled. "But I don't expect you to buy me all of this stuff."

"I'm going to buy it all." He kept his gaze fixed on her.

Her eyes widened again. "But Gage. That's almost…"

"I'm in operations. I'm good at math, and I know how much it's gonna cost." He started gathering the various jars and bottles of each product. "It's still not a bad deal. Remember, you're getting a free robe."

She blinked. "Wait. You can't…"

"Can't what? I'm going to buy this for you, Ainsley. When's the last time you bought something for yourself anyway?"

She looked thoughtful for a long moment. "It's been forever since I brought something this frivolous. Most of my money either goes to Cooper's basic needs, his extracurricular activities or his college fund. The rest is eaten up on living expenses."

"Let me ask you something." He held the items from the collection in the crook of his arm. "Is this bath stuff gonna make you feel relaxed and calm?"

She nodded.

"Then don't call it frivolous." He started walking toward the counter. "Candace, can you total this up for us? And let her pick out her free robe."

"Gladly." Candace took the items and began ringing them into the register. After that, she gestured to the rainbow of silk robes hanging on the wall behind her. "What color and size, sweetie?"

"Let me get the lavender one. Size large." Ainsley still looked a bit taken aback by what was happening, but at least she seemed to understand now that he wasn't going to be dissuaded from making the purchase.

"Sure thing." Candace added a new, plastic-wrapped robe to the bag and quoted a total to Gage. He paid with his credit card, and soon they were on their way again, each carrying shopping bags. She was quiet for the rest of the walk, and he didn't press her since she seemed to be thinking about something.

They arrived at the inn thoroughly damp, and he

could feel the chill starting to get to him as he stepped up on the porch.

They stopped there, neither of them reaching for the door.

"Thank you, Gage." Her voice was soft.

Facing her, he stroked her jawline. "You're welcome." Tilting her chin, he asked, "Can I kiss you?" Without waiting for a response, he pressed his lips against hers as the rain battered the roof.

Ten

Upstairs in their room, Ainsley felt her cheeks warm as Gage watched her carry her bag of body products to the bathroom door. The afternoon was now turning darker as more storm clouds rolled in. She'd done a lot of walking today. *Better to take care of it now than be sore tomorrow.* "I think I'm going to take a hot bath."

"Be my guest." He smiled at her as she shut the bathroom door behind her.

The bathroom, with its pink, ivy-print wallpaper, pink toilet and pedestal sink, and pictures of roses on the wall, reflected a taste in home decor she certainly didn't share. She did, however, approve of the deep, welcoming-looking bathtub that centered the space. It was painted the same shade of pink as the other fixtures, but the overall shape and design of the tub made it the showpiece of the room. A short-legged wooden stool had been placed next to the tub.

While she unloaded the bag onto the small wall shelf

next to the sink, she reflected on the kiss they'd just shared on the front porch of the inn. Of all the things she'd thought might happen today, getting kissed by her boss hadn't even been in the realm of possibility. Now, she knew that nothing would ever be the same between them. Whether that was a good or a bad thing remained to be seen.

She moved over to the old claw-foot tub. It took some maneuvering to get the hot water handle to turn, but when she finally did, a torrent of water rushed forth, so loud it almost drowned out the sounds of the falling rain. Passing her hand under the water, she waited for it to get nice and hot before inserting the rubber stopper into the drain. As the tub began to fill, she unscrewed the lid to the bubbling bath salts and used the small enclosed scooper to add some to the water. The sweet, fresh aroma of citrus filled the room, and she sighed.

There are so many things going through my head. In a way, I don't know how I should feel.

But right now, with the slight tingle in her lips and the memory of Gage's kiss lingering in her mind, she felt pretty damn good about it. She'd carried this torch for him for five years, watching and waiting for any sign that he felt the same way. There had been glimmers of hope along the way, but no proof as solid as his behavior today.

Apparently, my patience has finally paid off. While the tub filled, she stripped off her clothes, folding the items neatly and placing them on the stool with her phone on top. When she shut off the water, the room was filled with steam, just the way she liked it when she decided to have a good soak. With a soft washcloth and her soap in hand, she stepped into the tub.

A sigh of pleasure escaped her lips as the hot water

enveloped her. The tub was deep enough that the water came up to her shoulder blades, and she could feel the tension in her muscles melting away on the spot. This little pit stop in Louisiana hadn't been on the agenda when they'd left Atlanta, but this steamy bath, and the peace and quiet surrounding her, were almost enough to make this little detour worth the trouble.

There was a tub in her master bathroom back home. Though it wasn't as nice as this one, she tried to use it as often as she could. A lot of factors had to align for that to happen—the plumbing and water pressure had to cooperate, Cooper had to be occupied or out of the house, and she had to be alert enough that she didn't fear falling asleep while she was in there.

She wondered what her son was up to, and if he were getting on Bebe's nerves. Reaching for her phone, she texted her neighbor to check in on him. A response came in a few seconds later.

Cooper is fine. Fate has given you a break. Enjoy it.

She chuckled. Old straight-talking Bebe. She'd been a lifeline to her, especially since her cousin and former roommate Eden had moved out and gotten married.

She used her music subscription service to start up a soft contemporary jazz station, then set the phone aside. Since she stayed busy with Cooper, tied up with work or household stuff, tired, or all of the above most of the time, she was accustomed to taking quick showers most days. A bath seemed like decadence, a rare luxury. She scooted down until the water rose up to her neck, determined to enjoy this to the fullest.

With the relaxing music filling the room, she let her eyes close and her mind wander. A few random ideations passed through, but they were soon replaced by her thoughts of Gage. What they'd shared today…she couldn't get the memory of his kiss out of her head. And she didn't want to.

What's going to happen between us now? Are we gonna be an item? Will things get super weird at work? She couldn't answer any of those questions. All she knew was that she'd been enamored with him since the first time she laid eyes on him, and whatever the consequences might be, she just couldn't pass up this chance to find out what could develop between them.

She touched her lips, sending a few droplets of water running down her chin. Kissing him, after wanting to for só long, had felt like something special. The charge that went through her body effectively changed her, removing any notion that they could remain strictly colleagues. And honestly, she felt like that had been Gage's intent. A lot could be communicated through a kiss, and that kiss seemed to say, "I want you."

She sucked in her bottom lip, realizing that while she soaked, he was right outside the door. She hadn't heard him moving around and assumed he was keeping quiet for her benefit.

Here they were, in this room in the middle of nowhere, where they barely knew a soul. In this room with just one bed. She wasn't terribly religious, but she did believe that the universe put us in the place we were meant to be, at the time we were meant to be there. This little side trip was almost a cosmic setup, an insistence that they explore their attractions.

She imagined him in the room with her. In her mind's eye, she saw him approach the tub, his shirtless torso revealing his hard-earned strength. Kneeling beside the tub, he took the cloth from her trembling hand and soaped it. He mouthed the words, *Want me to wash your back?* It was all she could do to nod. He smiled, then began sliding the sudsy cloth over her skin...

A sudden thud snapped her back to reality. She sat up, water sloshing around her, and looked for the source of the sound. Seeing that her phone had slipped off the stool onto the floor, she blew out a breath. Cooper had texted her a good-night message, and the vibration must have sent the device crashing to the floor. The water was starting to cool, so she picked up the soap and bathed, all the while daydreaming it was Gage moving the cloth.

Once she was clean, she drained the water. Using some of the body butter from the apothecary, she moisturized her skin before slipping into her new robe. Gathering everything back into the shopping bag, including her clothes and phone, she gripped the handle of the bathroom door.

Gage was sitting on the bed when Ainsley walked out of the bathroom, clad in the silken robe they'd purchased earlier. He swallowed, his mouth watering as he surmised her nudity beneath.

The television was still on, a remnant of his attempt to stop thinking about her bathing. He'd done his best to focus on the cable news station, but the scent of her bath products and steam wafting from the bathroom had completely killed his interest in anything else but her.

With the shopping bag in hand and the bundle of her clothes tucked beneath her arm, she walked past him and deposited everything beside the chair she'd been favoring since they arrived. Turning back his way, she watched him for a moment. "Gage? Are you okay?"

"I'm fine," he insisted, his tone gruffer than he'd meant it to be.

"Just making sure, because you look like you swallowed a bug."

He laughed. She always knew when to crack a corny joke. She wasn't a comedian per se, but she had excellent comedic timing. "Damn, Ainsley."

She shrugged, feigning innocence. "What? I mean if you swallowed a foreign object, you may need medical intervention."

His laughter only increased as she went on joking about this supposed bug he'd swallowed. Every time he stopped laughing for a minute, he'd look at her, see that deadpan expression, and he'd start up all over again.

Soon she broke and started laughing along with him.

When he finally calmed down and got his breath, he said, "Thanks. I needed that laugh." It had given him the mental space to think more clearly about his feelings.

"I know you did." She gave his hand a small squeeze. "My particular brand of goofy has its benefits."

Something came over him in that moment, and he grasped her hand a little tighter. "Did you...enjoy your bath?"

She sucked in her bottom lip. "I did. Thanks again for all the fancy bath stuff."

"You're welcome." He gazed into the shimmering depths of her brown eyes. "It's the least I could do, considering everything you do for me."

"Oh, come on. Not that again." She shrugged, her gaze dropping as if she were suddenly becoming shy. "I always try to be the best assistant I can."

"You have to know by now that you're so much more than an assistant to me, Ainsley." He tugged her a bit closer to him and used his fingertip to trace slow circles over her jawline. "Or did I not make that clear earlier when I kissed you?"

She stared up at him, her eyes wide.

"Thank you, Ainsley, for everything you do that makes my life better."

She swallowed, nodded. "You…uh…you're welcome."

There was silence between them for a few long seconds.

Then he spoke. If he didn't lay his cards out now, who knew when he'd get another chance?

But before he could open his mouth, she spoke.

"This may be off base, and please tell me if it is, but…" She touched his arm, slowly moving her hand until it was over his heart. "I think we should… I mean…do you want to just…you know…do it?"

His brow hitched, his heart pounding. "I need you to be specific."

"Make love."

"Is that what you want?" He picked up her hand from his chest, kissed it.

Her answering sigh was followed by, "Oh yes."

"Absolutely." He led her by the hand to the armchair. Taking a seat, he pulled her into his lap. A moment later, she leaned in for his kiss.

He groaned as their lips met, tasting the remnants of her lip gloss. Her lips were soft, yielding, intoxicating. Holding her body close to his, he licked her lips and she opened to him, letting his tongue delve into the sweetness of her mouth.

She shifted in his lap, and he could feel her tugging at his shirt buttons as they continued to kiss. Breaking the contact, he unbuttoned his own shirt while holding her gaze.

Her tongue darted out, sliding across the fullness of

4

her bottom lip. "I want you so bad." The words were barely a whisper, a quiet declaration in the darkness-shrouded room.

"Don't worry. You got me." He stood then, lifting her with him, and carried her the short distance to the bed.

There, he quickly stripped her of her robe. Leaving her briefly to grab the small packet of condoms he kept in his attaché case, he returned and tucked one beneath a pillow. Stripping down to his boxers, he joined her on the bed. Hearing her sigh when their bodies touched, he pulled her into his arms and began kissing her again.

With the rain falling from the cloud-shrouded sky, and the dim light coming from the streetlamp outside, he moved his kisses slowly down her body. First, the sweet-swelling curve of her neck and shoulders. Then, he drew each dark nipple into his mouth, sucking and licking until she whimpered. He placed a series of lei-surely kisses between the full globes of her breasts, down her stomach, until he settled his face between her thighs.

"Gage…"

Before she could utter another word, he'd placed her legs over his shoulders. Leaning into her mound, he buried his face there, his tongue finding her swollen bud right away. Circling it, teasing it, he listened to the sounds she made and observed the movements of her body to learn what pleased her. She was sweet, hot and flowing, her sex glistening from arousal. He found the pattern that made her moan and made her back arch, then kept that cadence as he slipped a finger inside her. When he crooked his finger gently, she screamed, and he could feel the wetness flowing down his hand in the darkness.

Satisfied that she'd gotten that first orgasm, he

crawled up beside her for a kiss. She moaned into his mouth and suddenly gave him an insistent shove, rolling him onto his back. Straddling him, she asked, "Protection?"

He swallowed, getting the condom from where he'd put it and handing it to her. While he watched, she tore open the packet and held his gaze as she covered his hardness. It was one of the most erotic sights he'd ever seen. No sooner had she protected them than she positioned herself and lowered her body onto his.

He gasped as her tightness enveloped him, consuming his entire being. Her motions were skillful and slow as she rose and fell, softly purring with pleasure. The subtle bounce of her breasts enraptured him, and he reached up to touch them, palming and squeezing the firm globes. Then he slid his hands down and gripped her sides as she rode him, and his vision swam as pleasure made his eyes roll back in his head.

She was magnificent. Better than any lover before, and far above any fantasy his mind had ever created. The way her body moved, the way she gripped him so perfectly as if their bodies were made to fit together. The sounds she made with each roll of her hips. Nothing compared to her, to this moment and the fire spreading through his very soul.

"Oh shit." She whispered the words as her head lolled back, and she increased the pace of her ride.

He slid his hands over her sweat-dampened skin, cupping her ass in his hands. Moments later, she was coming, her inner muscles flexing around him.

He lost all control and growled as his own release tore through him. She collapsed on top of him, and he held her close, letting his heavy eyes drift closed.

Eleven

Ainsley awakened in the morning darkness to the feeling of Gage's lips brushing over the plane of her stomach. She shifted a bit, feeling the smile tipping her lips. "And just what are you doing down there, sir?"

"What do you think?" His reply was tinged with mischief as he continued to move his warm lips over her sensitive flesh.

The trembling set in again as his actions reminded her of their lovemaking, of the passion he'd awakened in her. A soft moan escaped her lips.

"That's the spirit." His voice had taken on a downright wicked edge, and she didn't fight him when he eased her thighs apart and slipped between them.

After he'd reduced her to screams again, she came back to herself and turned the tables on him. Getting him onto his back, she murmured, "Turnabout is fair play." A breath later, she took his dick into her mouth.

She gave as good as she received, letting her desire show through in the way she worked her mouth over his hard flesh. Before long he was pushing her away. With a groan, he positioned her on her hands and knees, entering her from behind.

Later, she lay in his arms, feeling safer than she'd felt in years. Being with him like this all night, while new and somewhat unfamiliar, felt right. She had no idea what time it was, but as the colors of dawn began to splash across the sky, she lay there listening to him tell stories from his childhood. He'd never been one to disclose much about his personal life, so she let him talk.

She rested her back against the pile of pillows, with him lying on his back between her legs, staring up at the ceiling as he spoke. "I remember all kinds of shenanigans my siblings and I pulled when we were younger. It's a miracle our parents didn't put us in a box and ship us off to our family up in Jersey."

"That bad, huh?"

"Think about it. It was a literal house full of kids. Three boys and two girls. Nia, being the oldest, did her best to help wrangle the rest of us—I think that's why she's so serious. But a lot of the time, we still got into trouble."

She chuckled. "Tell me about it."

"For example, Teagan used to be obsessed with rabbits. I mean high-key obsessed. One time, when she and Miles were about three years old, she wandered off from our backyard following a bunny. It took two hours of searching before we found her, curled up asleep under a tree about a quarter-mile beyond the property line." He shook his head. "I think my mom got her first patch of gray hairs that day."

"Yikes." She cringed. "I know what that's like. I

think most parents do. Cooper wandered off from me in the mall when he was about that age. I freaked out for ten minutes before I found him hiding behind one of those big planters near the food court. He was laughing so hard because he thought it was just another game of hide-and-seek. And there I was, crying and on the verge of a breakdown."

"Wow." He shook his head. "Then there was the time Blaine and I were roughhousing, and I ended up having to go to the hospital because I cracked my head on a door frame. I think I was like twelve or thirteen when that happened." He scratched his chin. "Or when Miles tripped over a cord and landed on a crossfader Dad had been setting up in the studio and shattered the damn thing."

"Crossfader. The thing on the soundboard?"

"Yep. Dad had to replace it, to the tune of thousands of dollars." He could still see the look on his father's face, a mixture of frustration and anger. "He barred all the kids from the studio for like a year, and made Miles work off the cost of the equipment by doing odd jobs around the house."

"Y'all certainly did cause your parents a lot of grief, huh?" She laughed. "But there have to be some good memories, too, right?"

"Oh sure. For us, as the kids, there are plenty of those. Sleepovers. Birthday parties. Cookouts. Family vacations." He smiled, but it didn't quite reach his eyes. "I don't think my parents have as many happy memories, though."

She frowned. "What makes you say that?"

"Raising us cost them so much. Not just in money, but in time. In the ability to do the things they wanted to do for themselves. In disappointment and frustration." The smile faded away. "That's what parenting is. A long road paved with sacrifices and unpaid labor."

She didn't know how to respond to that, because there was definitely some truth in what he'd said. She'd fallen into bed many a night both physically and emotionally drained by mothering. She'd cried over missed opportunities and gatherings she couldn't attend because she didn't have a sitter. Despite it all, though, she couldn't imagine her life without her son.

"I just don't think I'm cut out for fatherhood, you know?" He sighed. "Maybe I'm too selfish. But I just can't see myself sacrificing on that level for so many years. It just seems like too much."

She swallowed. *So that's his view of parenting? That it's this horrible slog through life, where your child acts as a weight dragging you down into the abyss?* She'd dated a few men who expressed doubts or downright refused to engage with the idea of raising a child. Yet she'd never encountered someone who seemed to genuinely disdain children. Looking back on his interaction with the middle schoolers who had visited the office, and some of the remarks she'd heard him make in passing over the past five years, she supposed she should have picked up on this attitude earlier.

His phone rang, bringing an end to the awkward silence between them. He glanced at the screen before answering it in a hushed tone. "Hello?"

She watched as he scrambled from the bed, hastily pulling on his pants and shirt. "I need to step out to take this," he whispered, his hand over the mic.

"Okay." A bit confused, she watched him slip from the room, shutting the door behind him.

What was that all about? She decided not to dwell on it, because even though they'd just slept together, she knew that didn't entitle her to know every single detail of his personal life. Grabbing the remote, she switched on the television to catch one of the national morning news shows.

While the anchor delivered a news story about the line of storms that had trapped them here in the first place finally beginning to move toward the coast, she sighed. *I should be listening to this, but I can't stop thinking about what Gage just said. He seemed to genuinely dislike the idea of raising a child.* But if they were to have any shot at a relationship, he'd have to be able to love and guide Cooper until he reached adulthood, and that was a nonnegotiable fact. She refused to be romantically involved with a man who couldn't tolerate her child, no matter how handsome that man might be.

She got up long enough to slip on her clothes, so he wouldn't think she'd be up for another round of lovemaking when he returned from his top-secret call. Then she sat down in her armchair, trying not to look at the rumpled bed.

"Good morning, Miles." Gage walked downstairs and into the breakfast room. The sunlight streaming through the windows gave the place a soft glow, and he felt thankful for a break in the weather. The air held the scent of bacon, and as he passed the counter where the food was laid out, he noted the scrambled eggs, English muffins and fresh fruit accompanying his favorite source of protein.

"Good morning yourself," Miles snapped.

"Somebody's grumpy." Spotting the coffee bar, he fixed himself a mug, nodding to a few others seated in the room before finding his own table. Settled into the chair, he said, "What's the matter? Woke up on the wrong side of a hookup?"

"Shut up, Gage." Miles yawned. "I'm only talking to you right now so Mom won't take me into the kickboxing ring."

"What's up?"

"Seriously, bruh? You were supposed to be back in town with the equipment two days ago! You didn't call anyone here to let them know there was a problem. And now you're surprised to hear from me?"

He chuckled. "I guess not. We had a little weather-related snafu."

"Well, that's nice to know. When you didn't come back Monday, we assumed it was just a delay. But yesterday, Mom got worried. So, she called Max and discovered you're in Louisiana, cold chillin'?"

"I wouldn't say that." He rubbed a hand over his face. "Listen. I'm sorry I didn't call. But I did check in with Harcroft to let them know we were delayed."

"Wonderful. Check in with them but just forget about your family." Miles didn't bother hiding the irritation in his voice. "Mom was worried."

"You already said that." *What you mean is you were worried.* Gage sighed, knowing his baby brother would never admit to being concerned for his safety. "Look, I know I should have called, and I already said I'm sorry. But the weather's improved, so hopefully, we can get in the air and out of Podunk today. So, can you chill?"

"Normally, I would absolutely be chill. But there have been some developments here while you've been enjoying the quaint scenery of an idyllic town in the Deep South, Gage."

He rolled his eyes. "Miles, what are you flapping your gums about now?"

"The Visionary had some kind of epiphany, a fit of artistic inspiration."

"That's great." That meant they could expect some stellar tracks from the album, the publicity from which could only draw even more high-profile clients to the studio to record.

"Yeah, but I'm not finished. Apparently, he sat down and wrote the lyrics for an entire album over the last few days. Yesterday, the producers got in contact with Teagan about coming in sooner to record his album. *Sooner.*" He emphasized the last word.

Gage felt his throat tighten. "How soon?"

"Friday."

"As in, two days from now?"

"Well, look at that. You *do* have a sense of time."

"Watch it, Miles."

"Whatever. You'd better get your asses back here with that equipment, quick, fast and in a hurry," Miles groused. "As head of finance, I don't even want to think about the kind of money we'd lose if The Visionary takes his album elsewhere to record."

Gage cringed. Even though Miles hadn't said it, he could tell that his brother still held some resentment against him for Tara's embezzlement. *This is my chance to help us make up that shortfall.* "Listen. I'm gonna do my best to get the equipment back there, ASAP."

"We really need you to come through on this, Gage. So cut your little impromptu vacation short, please."

"I assure you, I'm not on vacation. As for enjoying this town, I'd say it's quite the opposite. The whole place is about the size of a postage stamp, and it lacks so many things. I've been called a city boy just because I enjoy certain conveniences. There isn't even wireless internet where we're staying."

"Where are you even staying there?" Miles's footsteps could be heard as he walked around. "I was curious, so I looked it up online, and there aren't any hotels near that place."

Gage shook his head. His brother had been nosy—under the guise of being "curious"—ever since they were kids. "We lucked out. Found a little bed-and-breakfast."

"And Max stayed on the plane. She told Mom that much." There was a pause. "Gage, how big is this bed-and-breakfast you're staying at?"

"Not very."

Another pause. "So…in this 'not very big' place… did you and Ainsley get separate rooms?"

He swallowed. "What kind of question is that?"

"Oh shit."

Gage frowned. "Miles, don't start with me."

"Y'all sharing a room." He stated it rather than asking. "Oh shit!"

"Damn, Miles. Can you relax?"

"No, I can't relax. Your voice went up half an octave, and it always does that when you're hiding something. You definitely slept with her, and I—"

The call-waiting alert went off in his ear. Talk about saved by the bell. "I gotta go, Miles. Max is calling me."

"Yeah, whatever. But this conversation ain't over, bruh."

It gave him great pleasure to hang up on his brother and accept Max's call instead. "What's up, Max?"

"Hi, Gage. The weather's finally broken and visibility is crystal clear, so we can get out of here this morning. But just to be sure we can avoid any more weather, I'd like to be wheels up in an hour. Can you two make it back to the airstrip by then?"

"Yeah. We'll figure it out." No way was he about to stay here any longer than necessary, especially not with what he now knew about The Visionary. "See you soon."

Hanging up, he looked at the food and realized they hadn't had breakfast here yet. Draining his coffee, he pocketed his phone and jogged back upstairs to let Ainsley know of these new developments.

He found her in the chair, her attention focused on her tablet.

"Hey, Max says we can leave, but we need to get to the airstrip in an hour."

"Okay." She closed the cover over her tablet, got up, and started packing her bag. During this whole series of actions, she never once made eye contact with him.

He frowned. *What's the matter with her?* "The breakfast down there looks surprisingly good. Do you want to grab some on the way out?"

"Sure." Again, she spoke without looking in his direction. Unsure of what to make of her attitude, he went to gather his things so they could go.

With their bags in hand, they went downstairs and ate a silent meal together. Ainsley barely looked up from her plate. *What's with her? Does she not want to leave, or is it something else?*

At the desk, they had a brief chat with Mary, the innkeeper, and secured a ride to the airstrip with Hugh Delmar, the man who'd brought them to town on Monday.

They rode to entire way to the airstrip with only Hugh talking. While he chattered on about being relieved that the sun had finally returned to Summer Village, Ainsley stared out the window and Gage only nodded in response to Hugh's words. Her silence had soured his mood, and he didn't want to make things even worse by saying something wrong. Sure, he'd had some concern that making love to her might make their relationship awkward, but he certainly hadn't expected this.

The barn came into view. *At least we won't be so close to each other once we're back on the plane.* Right now, she seemed to be pressing herself against Hugh to avoid touching thighs with him, and he just couldn't figure her out.

Twelve

Strapped into her seat on the plane, Ainsley sighed when Gage sat down in the seat next to her. While he buckled himself in, she focused on her tablet screen. She was less than a hundred pages from the end of the first book in the series she'd been reading, and she wanted to finish it before they landed in California. Aside from that, she had nothing to say to him right now.

"Aren't you glad to be leaving this one-horse town? Maybe now I can finally get a decent latte."

She leaned toward the window, hoping her body language would convey her disinterest. He'd spent all that time talking about how awful children were, and now he'd moved on to insulting an entire town and its residents. She would have told him to shut up, that the people there were perfectly nice and that not everyone felt the need to be so anal about their diet. But she didn't because that would involve talking to him.

He watched her for a moment, then slipped his arm around her shoulders. "After we get the equipment squared away, our next stop should be Starbucks. There's one not too far from Harcroft."

Her annoyance rumbled through her just like the plane's engine vibrating the floor beneath her feet. "Look, I really want to finish this book. Can you just… give me some space?"

"That's funny. You didn't seem to want any space last night."

Ugh. Is he really going to be that guy? The one who acts like sex with him is so life-changing you'll never be the same? She stared at him, wishing the heat in her glare could singe that smirk right off his face. "Gage, get away from me."

He looked as if he took offense, but he unbuckled his belt and did as she asked, moving his handsome, infuriating self and his case across the aisle. As they finally took off, she started reading her book again, determined that she would ignore his presence for the entirety of the flight.

After a quick refueling stop in Arkansas, the plane landed at Oakland International Airport around ten o'clock local time. As soon as they came to a stop, Ainsley gathered her things and headed for the exit door.

"Damn, Ainsley. Where's the fire?" Gage followed close behind. "And you don't need to take your stuff with you, we'll be back…"

She spun on him. "When we got waylaid, all you did was complain about being held up. Now you want to slow down?" Seeing the surprised expression on his face, she rolled her eyes, turned away and descended the stairs to the tarmac.

While Max again remained with the plane, a chauffeured car took them on the short ride from the airport to Harcroft headquarters in nearby San Leandro. There, she got out of the car, again carrying her tote with her.

Harcroft's headquarters was a modern structure, a marvel of steel and glass that stood out among all the other cinder-block buildings in the tech district. Entering through the front doors, whose handles were steel bass clefs, they were greeted by a friendly receptionist who was seated behind the tall, silver welcome desk. On either side of the desk, wide corridors led deeper into the building. The walls, painted a soft yellow, were accentuated by a continuous black print of horizontal lines and musical notes that made the walls look like sheet music.

Marshall Harcroft came out to greet them as they stood by the desk. Right away, Ainsley noticed the striking blue of his eyes. Wearing dark slacks, a red button-down and black loafers, he had brown hair grazing the back of his neck tucked beneath a fedora. He stuck out his hand as he walked toward them. "Glad you folks finally made it."

Gage eyed him. "Just show us the merchandise, Marshall, and we'll be out of your hair."

"Come this way." He started walking down one of the corridors. "I think you'll be very impressed with the finished product."

They followed him down the corridor and into a room on the left side. The brightly lit room held a seating area with a small, round table and four chairs sitting around it.

Marshall remarked, "Hang tight here at the table with me for a minute, and the guys will bring your equipment for you to inspect."

The three of them took seats around the table, and

she made sure they ended up with Marshall sitting between them. A few minutes passed before two men rolled in a dolly with the equipment on it. After parking the dolly next to the table, the two men accepted thanks from Marshall before disappearing the way they'd come. Gage stood, circling the soundboard as he took a closer look at it. "I see you were able to incorporate a crossfader near the center like I asked."

Marshall nodded. "What can I say? Our engineers love a challenge, and you always give them one."

Ainsley watched as the two men paced around the equipment, talking about its various features. Even though she'd worked at the recording studio for five years, she couldn't say she'd developed much of an interest in the inner workings and finer points of studio equipment. She simply took notes, as she was expected to do, by using her stylus to enter what was said into the document open on her tablet. When Gage's back was turned to her, she found herself admiring the hard lines of his buttocks and thighs beneath his slacks, and she silently cursed. *I know he's no good for me. He can't seem to tolerate children, and I have a son. I would never dream of putting a man before Cooper. If I keep staring like this, it will only make it harder to get over him.* The ringing of her phone brought her back to reality. Checking the display and seeing Bebe's name, she stood. "I have to take this. I'll go out in the hallway so I won't disturb you."

Gage nodded, barely acknowledging her exit as he and Marshall talked shop.

In the hallway, she swiped her screen. "Hey, Bebe. What's going on?"

"Not much. Cooper says he has a stomachache, so he stayed home with me today."

She frowned. "Oh no. Has he had dairy? Is there a bug going around the school?"

"Look at you, already in troubleshooting mode. He did have ice cream last night. Two bowls, if memory serves."

Ainsley rolled her eyes. "I don't know how many times he has to be laid up with the tummy ache from Hades before he realizes that his lactose intolerance is a real thing." As much as she loved Cooper, she could do without the stubborn streak he seemed to have acquired over the last few years. "Take his key, go in the medicine cabinet in the downstairs bathroom and you'll see a bottle of the pink stuff he usually takes for this."

"Roger that. I'll pop over and get it for him after we get off the phone." Bebe paused. "So, listen. I don't want to pry, but what's going on with you? I know the weather screwed up your trip plans, but what's happening now?"

She gave her neighbor a brief recap of the last thirty-six hours, leaving out that she'd slept with her boss. *No need to give up the whole operation.* "So, we finally made it here, and my boss is inspecting the equipment right now."

"Well, you don't have to rush home. Cooper's no trouble at all. Though, if I'm being honest—" she dropped her voice into a whisper, as if she didn't want to be overheard "—I think your son misses you."

A smile tipped Ainsley's lips. "Aw. I miss my little monster, too."

"I'm really impressed with this soundboard, Marshall." Gage circled the equipment one last time, stopping at the front. "Can you break down the changes and updates you've made to it?"

"We've gone digital since 404 purchased their last

soundboard system from us in the early 2000s." Marshall pointed at the large device, which would easily take up a third of the floor space in the sound booth of Studio 1. "This is our top-of-the-line, custom Harcroft Diamond Edition Digital Audio Workstation."

Gage tilted his head. "It's got a big, fancy name. I hope it has capabilities to match." He really wanted to wow The Visionary and his production team when they came in to start recording.

Marshall's grin only broadened in response to the challenge in his voice. "Oh, this thing is a music-making powerhouse. You've got three monitors, our proprietary software installed to give you nearly endless sound generation possibilities, cloud-based file storage so you never run out of space to store tracks, sound effects, whatever you need. Along with that, you've got video capability, integrated editing and playback functions, and smart encryption to make it impenetrable to hackers."

"The producers will like that. Nothing spoils the buildup to an album release like leaked tracks." He scratched his chin. "Sounds like she does a lot."

"This baby will do everything except your taxes." Marshall chuckled. "That's the one feature my tech guys just couldn't figure out."

Gage laughed. "No worries. My brother Miles and his team handle all that financial stuff." A text message came through, the vibration of his phone grabbing his attention.

The message, from Nia, simply read, We have a problem. Call me.

Damn. His sister loved to pull this stunt, telling people just enough information to worry them so they'd do what she wanted. Having no idea of the nature of this problem, of course he was going to call. "Give me a sec, Marshall. Something I gotta handle right quick."

"Take your time." Marshall returned to his seat at the table as he left the room.

He passed Ainsley in the hallway, and she seemed to be on her way back to the room they'd just left. Seeing her tight expression, he asked, "Everything okay?"

She gave him a curt nod before passing by him without a word.

Shaking his head, he went to the lobby and sat down to call his older sister. When she answered, he blurted, "What is it now, Nia?"

She scoffed. "Nice greeting, little brother."

"You're the one who insisted there was a problem. So, what is it?"

She blew out a breath. "You won't believe the shit that's happened here today while you're off gallivanting."

"Sis, you are tripping. I'm not gallivanting. I'm personally escorting our business-essential equipment to its destination." He rolled his eyes, knowing she couldn't see him. "Look, why don't you just tell me what's up?"

"The Hamilton twins, that's what's up. They were here today with their mother's checkbook and an offer to buy 404 Sound."

"Pierce and London were both at our building?" Gage blinked several times, both shocked and incensed at what he'd heard. "You can't be serious."

"I wish I weren't. They really did come in here with Everly Hamilton's checkbook, asking to meet with Mom and Dad to discuss a purchase price."

Holy crap. "I leave town for a few days and this is what goes down in my absence?" He rubbed his palm over his face. "Well, what did Mom and Dad do? I know they didn't take the meeting."

"Hell, no! Mom had security escort them off the premises." Nia laughed, the tone bitter. "But if I know the Hamiltons, this isn't over. They're not going to give up."

"You're probably right. Pierce already tried this with Dad several months back." He raked his hand through his hair. "Shit. I need to get back there."

"You're damn straight, and sooner is better. Dad is sullen and Mom is pissed. Odds are we're going to be called to some kind of meeting to discuss next steps in shaking off Hamilton House and their takeover attempts."

That's exactly what this is, a takeover attempt. He didn't know if their tactics qualified as hostile, but they sure as hell seemed determined to take ownership of the Woodson family's legacy. "Okay. I need to wrap things up here by signing off on the equipment and getting it back to the private jet. Hopefully, I'll be back in Atlanta before nine." He knew they'd lose three hours in the air traveling from west to east.

"Fine. Just text me when you land. See you later, Gage."

"Bye, sis." After he disconnected the call, he stood and walked back down the corridor, returning to the room with Marshall, Ainsley and his shiny new soundboard.

"I've briefed your assistant on all the details." Marshall clapped his hands together. "So, I'm ready to move forward with paperwork whenever you are."

Gage looked at Ainsley, seated at the table with her tablet in front of her and the stylus in hand.

Without looking up from her screen, she said, "I've taken detailed notes on all the pertinent information, sir."

He frowned. *Sir? When did we get back on such*

formal terms? After the passion they'd shared, he would never have imagined she'd be back to referring to him that way. But he didn't want to cause a scene by asking her about it now. They were working, and there was no reason Marshall should be privy to their private affairs. So instead, he simply nodded. "Thank you."

"Well, I'm going to pop over to my office for the tablet so you can digitally sign the forms and take delivery." Marshall walked toward the door. "Feel free to play with the controls until I get back. Just don't do anything crazy or you'll void the warranty." With a grin, he disappeared through the door.

Alone with Ainsley, Gage could no longer hold back his curiosity. "Ainsley, why are you back to calling me *sir*?"

She shrugged. "We're working, aren't we? I'm just focused on the job right now."

"Oh, that's nice. But it doesn't explain why you were so snappy toward me on the plane." He watched her expectantly, awaiting her answer.

She groaned. "I'm not going to talk about this with you right now, Gage."

He walked closer to her, placing a gentle hand on her forearm. "But, baby…"

She drew away from him. "Don't call me that, Gage." Her eyes flashed, but behind the anger, he could see hints of pain.

"What's going on with you? Is it something I did? Or something I said? Because…"

"Save it." She shook her head. "I can't believe you don't know what the problem is."

He cringed. Apparently, she found him not only annoying but dense at this juncture. "Just tell me what I did so I can at least try to fix it."

She turned her back to him. "As I said, we're not talking about this right now."

He stood there watching her, not knowing what else to say. Their night together had been special…at least to him. Had it all been some kind of game to her? He'd taken a chance and now she was making a fool of him.

Just like Tara had.

Thirteen

"So, does the equipment meet your standards?" Marshall returned to the room, a large tablet tucked under his arm.

Gage took a huge step back, turning his attention away from Ainsley to respond to the question. "Yeah, everything looks great. We just need to get it loaded onto a truck and taken to the airport so we can get it on the jet and back to Atlanta."

"It's already arranged." Marshall turned on the tablet, the screen illuminating as he pulled a stylus from his pocket. "As soon as we're done with the forms, I'll just put in a quick call for my staff to bring the truck around, and you can ride to the airport with them if you like."

"Thanks." Gage scratched his chin. "You know if you had sold the equipment from under me, this would have been a totally different kind of meeting."

Marshall chuckled. "Well, I did promise you I'd hold it for three days, and I'm a man of my word."

From observing their interactions after years of overhearing their phone calls, Ainsley could see that Marshall and Gage had a strange sort of kinship. As two men in adjacent fields, they didn't need to compete with each other. But that didn't stop them from ribbing each other whenever they had the chance.

She watched in silence as Marshall walked Gage through the electronic forms, having him sign and initial in all the proper places. With that done, the truck was summoned.

The truck pulled around to the front of the building about a half hour after Gage had begun filling out the forms. A crew of three men helped to wrap and secure the equipment for shipment and, using a ramp, loaded it onto the back of the box truck and shut the door. Ainsley watched all this from a safe distance, wondering how to say what she had to say to Gage.

"I'm going to text Max and let her know we're on our way back to the plane." As the men loaded the equipment, Gage headed for the cab, typing on his phone as he walked. "Ainsley, you don't mind catching a ride with the truck driver, do you?"

She took a deep breath. "No." She had so many things she wanted to get off her chest. But standing in the parking lot of their equipment supplier, she knew better than to get into all that with him. It wasn't the time or the place.

They got into the cab of the truck, with her sitting in the middle, just as she had in Hugh Delmar's truck, and rode to the airport. She was thankful that the drive was less than ten minutes, because she didn't want the awkward silence hanging between her and Gage to stretch on for any longer than necessary. *That's why I can't get back on the company jet with him.*

As the truck rolled onto the tarmac, she could see Max, waving to them from her spot near the plane. The pilot's all-black uniform and red-and-black bow tie were immaculate as always, and her braids were pulled back into a neat bun. Ainsley sighed. *As much as I like Max, I'm not excited about this trip.*

Ainsley did her part to make sure the equipment was safely loaded and properly secured on the plane, clutching her tote bag the entire time. Once the job was done, Gage started walking up the steps to board the jet. He glanced back at her, still standing on the ground. "Come on, Ainsley, get the lead out. We need to get back."

She swallowed. *I wish I could afford to fly commercial. The last thing I want right now is to be trapped with him for four hours.* Alas, her wallet wept at the thought of paying the price of a last-minute plane ticket, so she finally got her feet moving and climbed the stairs.

Once they were back in the air, she found herself staring out the window, at the ceiling, the floor—anything to avoid looking at Gage.

From his seat across the aisle, he said, "I spoke to Nia earlier. She said the Hamilton twins came by today and tried to buy the company."

Even though her interest was minimal, she knew any sale of the business could possibly affect her current job or her ability to make the move into human resources. So, she engaged, despite the fact she didn't want to talk to him. "Oh, really?"

She half listened while he talked about the Hamilton family's attempts to take ownership of 404 Sound. Mostly, she found herself staring at his lips, the same full lips that had kissed her in her most intimate places just last night.

"From listening to Nia, I can't tell if she's more upset

about the whole takeover thing, or the fact they just skipped over her to ask for Mom and Dad. Nia is the CEO, and it's not like a deal could go down without her."

"Yeah." She watched him gesture with his hands, the hands that had gripped her hips as he took her to paradise. She cursed her hormones for trying to override her good sense and went back to looking out the window.

"I…uh…feel like I'm losing you, Ainsley."

"No," she insisted, still staring into the endless blue void. "I'm still listening."

"That's not what I meant."

The tone of his voice made her turn back to look at his face again. The moment their eyes met, she regretted her decision but found she couldn't look away.

"I feel like I've really put myself on the line here, Ainsley." He rubbed his hands together as he spoke. "I've broken my own personal pledge not to get romantically involved with a colleague. And for a while there, I thought it had all been worth it."

She swallowed, feeling the irritation rise within her. *There he goes again, martyring himself, talking about what he's been inconvenienced with. He's so selfish sometimes. He never thinks of the consequences of his words.* "You aren't the only one taking a risk here, Gage."

"It certainly feels that way. I mean, you haven't even expressed your feelings to me." He paused, a small but wicked grin tilting the corner of his mouth. "Well, at least not with words."

She could feel her lips tightening. *He thinks awfully highly of himself, though that's nothing new.*

"Either way, I'd rather have you tell me than to assume." He cracked his knuckles, one by one, as he continued. "Just be honest with me, Ainsley. Tell me what's on your mind."

She narrowed her eyes, feeling the southwest Atlanta fire rising within her. "Oh, trust me. You're about to get every bit of this smoke."

Gage felt his shoulders tense up in response to Ainsley's terse words. "What?"

"You wanna know how I feel, right? Then you better guard your grill, because it ain't nothing nice." She folded her arms over her chest and glared at him.

He was used to Ainsley speaking to him in such professional tones that hearing her talk this way took him by surprise. "Are you serious right now, Ainsley? After the ordeal we went through just trying to get here, you're going to hit me with this. Now? When we're finally almost home?"

"The timing may not be the best, but it is what it is, Gage."

"Okay, I don't like the sound of that, but I do want to know what's going on. What is your problem? You've been acting strangely all day."

"What you see as me acting strangely is simply self-preservation."

Gage pressed his fingertips to his temple. "I don't mean to sound dismissive, but that makes literally no sense at all."

"Really, Gage?" She rolled her eyes. "You spent the entire time in Summer Village looking down on the people there."

He frowned. "No, I didn't. I barely interacted with them."

"I know. And that was by design. At the times when you did interact with them, I saw your attitude. You were so annoyed that this charming little town didn't have your soy lattes and Wi-Fi."

He sighed. "I'll admit that. I'm a city boy to the core, and I—"

"Nah. It's more than that. I grew up in the city, too, but only one of us grew up spoiled, having their every whim catered to."

That remark hit him right in the chest, and if the smug look on her face were any indication, that had been her intention. "That's not fair, Ainsley. My parents worked extremely hard to build 404 and give us a decent life."

"Which is why you should have a better attitude." With her upper body turned toward him, she leaned in, her glare slicing through him even from across the aisle. "But you know what's worse than your attitude?"

"No, but I'm sure you're gonna tell me." He let his head drop back against his seat.

"Your absolute intolerance of children. Why do you dislike them so much?"

"I never said that."

"You didn't have to. It was written all over your face every time you spoke about children." She shook her head. "Remember, I was there last week when those schoolkids came to visit the office. You were cordial at first, but the minute one of them said something you didn't like, your whole demeanor changed. It seemed like you couldn't get out of there fast enough."

That was true, but not for the reasons she thought. "Listen, I'll admit I'm not comfortable around kids. But I don't—"

She cut him off. "And then this morning, while we're supposed to be enjoying the afterglow of lovemaking, you start to get chatty. And since I want to know about your childhood, and you've never opened up to me like this, I let you talk. And what do you do? You go on and on about the misery you must have caused your parents, simply by existing."

He swallowed, his throat dry. "I didn't mean it like that. I just…"

"I know you're about to give me some lame excuse, but don't bother. I'm a single mother, Gage. And while my son exhausts both my energy and my finances, he's been an absolute joy to raise."

He held up his hand. "Wait, Ainsley. You can't think I was talking about Cooper. I wasn't. I was only speaking in general."

"It doesn't matter. It's not about the words so much as the attitude behind them." She shook her head, feeling the tears spring to her eyes. "To think I let myself get wrapped up with you like this. I can't believe I let you get so close, knowing how you felt about children." The tears welled in her eyes. "I can't do this, Gage. I can't risk my heart for someone who wouldn't accept my son."

He closed his eyes, his sadness morphing into frustration. "You know what, Ainsley? You're being unreasonable."

Her eyes flashed, and she pointed to herself. "Oh, *I'm* unreasonable, huh? Me. I'm the one that's out of step here."

He could hear his tone changing to match the darkness of his mood, but he no longer cared. "Absolutely. You're entirely too sensitive. You take everything I say in passing and twist it around to fit your little agenda, to make me out to be the bad guy."

"Oh, and why is that? Since you suddenly know everything about the way I think and operate." She tilted her head until it almost touched her shoulder, staring at him, her lips pursed.

He shook his head, chuckling bitterly. "You're not trying to hear it."

"Nah, don't stop now. You're on a roll." She clapped her hands together. "Enlighten me, Gage. Why am I acting so sensitive? Tell me more about my li'l agenda."

If the situation weren't so tense, he'd be amused at the lengths she took to goad him into answering. "You really wanna know?"

"Hell, yeah, Gage. I *really* wanna know."

He inhaled. "You're scared. You can't commit, and you're using your kid as an easy excuse to avoid letting me into your life." He paused. "You've probably been doing it for years. I can't be the first one who's tried to love you." The minute he'd finished, he realized how harsh his words must have sounded. "Look, I didn't..."

"Don't." She closed her eyes for several long moments. When she opened them again, the fire was gone, replaced with a coldness that nearly made him shiver. "You know what, Gage? I'm gonna put on my headphones now. And it would be wise if you didn't say another single word to me for the rest of this flight."

"Baby, listen. I just..."

She held up her finger. "Don't you dare 'baby' me. Whatever happened between us in Summer Village can stay there. It's strictly business from now on. Now please, just leave me alone." She popped in her earbuds, plugged them into her phone and rested her head against her seat, her gazed focused out the window.

He sighed. He'd thought they were finally getting somewhere, that he could finally share his affection with someone. But it seemed fate enjoyed making a fool of him, again and again. Not even the luxurious surroundings of the private jet could remove the awkwardness and tension hanging in the air. But he knew better than to try to engage her again, so he simply closed his eyes and tried to sleep for the remainder of the flight.

I thought we had something special. Now it's over before it even began.

Fourteen

Friday afternoon, Ainsley sat on the bleachers at Carter G. Woodson's baseball field, watching the game. Her son and the rest of the Roaring Lions were up against the Fulton Leadership Bears, their old rival. The orange-and-blue uniforms worn by the home team were already streaked with soil and grass stains, as were the red-and-white uniforms of the opposition. The young men played hard. It was as if they were all bucking for a place in the major leagues. As they headed into the seventh inning, Ainsley stifled a yawn.

Bebe, sitting next to her, gave her a soft poke in the shoulder. "Wake up, Ainsley. Game's not over yet."

Ainsley gave her a little half smile. "I'll try. But to tell you the truth, I'm exhausted."

"I noticed. Ever since you came back from your work trip, you've seemed a little down." Bebe gave her shoulder a squeeze. "I'm not one to pry, as you know. But if you decide you want someone to talk to, I'm here. I know it's probably been hard on you since your cousin moved out."

"Thanks, Bebe." Ainsley inhaled deeply, taking in the scents of grass, dirt and two dozen sweaty preteens. Bebe was right on both counts. She had been down since she got back from California, and she missed Eden terribly. Still, she wouldn't begrudge her cousin the happiness she'd found when she married Gage's brother Blaine.

She hadn't had a decent night's sleep since her return, and having to go to work and see Gage every day, knowing what they'd shared and what they could never have, was exhausting mentally and emotionally. The lack of sleep, coupled with her usual activity level, had drained her physically. Basically, she was tired in all the ways a person could be tired. Putting on her best fake smile in case Cooper looked at her, she directed her attention back to the game.

The Lions were ahead, and she joined the other families in cheering them on. She fought off the urge to wave at Cooper or make any kind of spectacle of herself, knowing he was in the thick of the "everything my mom does is embarrassing" phase. Aside from that, she knew she probably looked a hot mess. She'd thrown on an old pair of medium-wash jeans and a Carter G. Woodson Academy PTA sweatshirt. Her hair was in a haphazard knot low on her neck, and she'd crammed her feet into a pair of old sneakers as she rushed out the door, bent on getting Cooper to the field in time. Their coach demanded that they arrive thirty minutes prior to all games or spend the game guarding the dugout. Today, she'd just barely gotten him there on time.

"Look at Bryce! That's the second run he's scored tonight!" Bebe stood, clapping furiously for her son.

Ainsley shook her head. While she was proud of Cooper's athletic accomplishments, his academic ones held much more weight in her mind. Still, her son didn't want her cheering for him at debate meets, either. So, she'd learned to hold on to the praise she wanted to heap on him until they were alone at home. That way she could hug him, and maybe even give him a peck on the cheek, without him making too much of a fuss about it.

In the end, the Lions trounced the Bears, and the parents joined Coach Rigsby and the team on the field for a congratulatory pep talk. When the coach released them, Bebe announced that they were headed out for a celebratory pizza party. Ainsley smiled and cheered along with everyone else, though inside, she wanted nothing more than to go home, burrow under her covers and sleep until Monday.

At the pizza place, Ainsley sat at one end of the table with Bebe and another team mom. The three of them were tasked with chaperoning the fourteen adolescents as they gorged on pizza and soda and, later, making sure all of them made it home safely. She ate her own slice of pepperoni slowly, thinking as she chewed. While her eyes rested on the boys, who were currently huddled around one teammate's phone watching goofy videos on the internet, her mind was elsewhere. She kept replaying the argument she'd had with Gage. She remembered how angry she'd been, and how that anger had melted into total awkwardness as she spent the rest of the flight trying to pretend he didn't even exist. Being trapped with him on the plane had made the whole conversation all the more difficult to have.

In a way, she was glad it had happened, or so she

told herself. By giving him a huge piece of her mind, she'd saved herself further heartache down the line. She couldn't imagine how much worse it would have been for her if she waited, fell deeper in love and really let him in, only to have him disappoint her.

Her heart clenched. She missed his touch, and it was driving her nuts. It made no sense. They'd shared several steamy hours in bed in a tiny town down South, and now she just couldn't go back to the way things were. She'd still see him at work every day, and she didn't see that changing unless she got the HR manager job. That's what had prompted her to apply first thing Thursday morning. No more excuses. She needed this change.

Feeling the tears welling up in her eyes, she excused herself and went to the restroom. *If Bebe sees me crying, she'll start asking questions, and she won't stop badgering me until she gets to the bottom of it.*

In the privacy of a stall, she leaned against the wall and let the tears flow. Keeping her sobs quiet in case someone walked in, she pressed a ball of tissue to her face. *I'm so pitiful. Here I am, locked in a bathroom stall, crying like a high schooler.*

Blowing out a breath, she left the stall.

And almost ran into Bebe.

She closed her eyes. "Bebe, please. Don't ask."

Bebe nodded. "All right." She stepped aside and let Ainsley pass.

At the sink, she washed her face and hands, then held a cool, damp paper towel to her eyes in an attempt to reduce the puffiness. Then, with Bebe still watching her warily, she exited the restroom and returned to the table.

Later, as she leaned over Cooper's bed to kiss him good-night, he called her. "Mom?"

"What is it, sweetie?"

"Are you okay?" He watched her, concern filling his dark eyes.

"What makes you ask that?"

He shrugged. "I don't know. You just seem...sad." He paused, his expression turning serious. "Did somebody do something to you? Do I need to beat somebody up?"

She felt the smile stretch her lips. *My baby.* "No, Cooper. While I love that you want to protect me, I don't need you to beat anyone up. I'm just working through some complex adult feelings, but I'll be fine once I get it figured out."

His tone earnest, he asked, "Promise?"

She nodded. "I promise." She leaned down and gave him a second peck on the cheek. "Good night, Coop."

"'Night, Mom." He snuggled down under the covers.

Turning out the light, she left his room, closing the door behind her. As she sought her own bed, she couldn't help thinking that everyone around her seemed to be able to tell she was upset.

Get it together, girl. She'd gotten to enjoy the fantasy of Gage as her boyfriend for a little while. Now it was time to abandon that fallacy and go back to thinking of him as her boss.

Stifling a yawn, she crawled into bed.

Gage sat at the table in 404's main conference room Friday evening, drumming his fingers on the table. It was already after six, and it was rare for the executive team to even be at work this late, let alone sitting in an emergency meeting.

Around the table, the entire Woodson family was assembled. Nia sat at the head, with their parents flanking her. Miles and Teagan were sitting on Dad's side, while Blaine and Gage were on Mom's side.

The other end of the table was occupied by the enigmatic, rarely-seen-in-public Everly Hamilton.

What Gage knew about the older woman could fit into a bottle cap. He knew that his parents had known Everly for years and had even considered her and her late husband good friends. He also knew that she'd become something of a recluse over the last decade, preferring to send her children or her assistants out in public to do her bidding.

Gage couldn't help staring at her, but at least he tried to keep his attention discreet. She wore a black dress beneath a huge white fur coat. Her short-cropped hair, dyed platinum blond, was swept dramatically across her forehead and teased at the crown. She was somewhat fair in complexion, but very obviously African American. Huge designer sunglasses obscured much of her face, until she reached up, her red manicured nails grasping the arm. She pulled them off, revealing two penetrating gray eyes. "Woodson family. How nice of you to take time out of your busy schedules to meet with me."

Gage was taken aback by the depth of her voice; it didn't seem to match her appearance. He could only attribute the tone to years of smoking.

Addison scoffed. "You're a real piece of work, Everly."

"I'll take that as a compliment coming from you, *old* friend." She leaned forward as she placed emphasis on the word *old*.

Addison's eyes flashed.

Caleb grabbed his wife's hand. "Look, we didn't come here for any immature foolishness. We're tired of you sending your little lackeys here to do your dirty work."

"You mean the twins? How dare you refer to my babies that way." Everly slapped the table.

"Oh please. They're both adults," Nia interjected. "Though I'm not sure they know much about anything, beyond parroting your words."

Everly laughed, a sort of croaking sound. "Whatever. I think it's high time you kids had a little history lesson." She locked eyes with Caleb. "Don't you think so, Caleb?"

Gage watched his father's jaw tighten.

"Don't act as if my opinion matters," Caleb groused. "You're just going to do what you want anyway."

"How astute of you." Everly cleared her throat, settling back in her chair. "Let's take a little trip down memory lane. Years back, before any of you were born, your father and my boyfriend Philip were the best of friends. Their friendship created one between Addy and me, since we were dating the boys at the time, and we were together pretty much all the time."

Teagan tilted her head. "Phil. I've heard that name before."

Everly continued. "Over the years, our bond deepened, and Addy and I were privy to the boys' dream. They talked about wanting to build the best, most state-of-the-art recording studio in Atlanta. The city was experiencing a creative boom, and it seemed new hip-hop and R & B artists were coming out of every neighborhood. Phil and Caleb worked on their plan together for several years, through our college career and the beginning of our marriages."

Gage scratched his chin. He followed the story, but what he didn't understand was what any of this had to do with Everly's attempts to take over the business. His mind wandered then, back to the same subject it had been wandering to since he'd gotten back from California.

Ainsley. He missed her. The past two days in the office hadn't been the same. Things had definitely changed between them, and he knew they couldn't go back to the working relationship they had before. He was fine with that, but what bothered him was the idea that he'd never get to see what it was like to be her man. They'd danced around their attraction for so long, and when they'd finally connected romantically, he'd managed to screw it up. He wanted to kick himself. Shaking off the thoughts as best he could, he tried to refocus on Everly's story.

"Then, I got pregnant." Everly's tone darkened. "It threw a wrench in the plan. We needed money, and Phil vowed to do right by me and take care of our babies. And so he set his dream aside, placing it in Caleb's hands while he joined up with the marines." She paused, touching her hand to her chest. "He only served eight months before he was killed in a training exercise at Camp Mayfield."

Miles shifted in his seat. "I'm sorry for your loss, Mrs. Hamilton."

Everyone around the table added their condolences, though Caleb was oddly silent.

"Thank you, all of you. But that's not where the story ends." Everly brushed away a tear. "Did your father ever tell you where half his start-up capital came from? The money he used to purchase the first studio?"

Nia shook her head. "No, and to be honest, I never thought to ask."

Everly inhaled deeply. "Philip. He willed that a portion of his death benefit be paid to Caleb if anything should happen to him."

All eyes in the room turned toward Caleb, who looked as if he wanted a trapdoor to open in the floor and consume him.

Tears welled in Addison's eyes. "How could you keep that from me, Caleb?"

Everly's perfectly sculpted brow rose. "You didn't know?"

Addison shook her head. "I had no idea. But that explains why you've been so interested in the company."

"Maybe now you understand where I'm coming from." Everly raked a hand through her hair. "I lost my husband, but I had two things to keep his spirit with me—our babies and his dream. I'll admit I've taken too strong an approach, but all I really want is to be a part of the thing he was so passionate about."

Caleb sighed. "I'm sorry, Addy. I should have told you. But at the time, I just wanted to be the hero. I needed you to think I'd done this on my own."

Gage blinked. *This is wild.* He would never have expected his father to pull something like this. Glancing at his siblings' faces around the table, he could see that they all looked similarly shocked.

Caleb continued. "And Everly, I'm sorry I dishonored Philip's legacy by not including you and the twins." He looked genuinely contrite. "I'm still not going to sell you the company. But I'm willing to sell you a stake."

"Majority?" Everly tilted her head.

"Don't push it, Ev." Caleb shook his head. "How does thirty percent sound?"

Everly appeared to think it over for a few moments. Everyone waited in silence for her response.

Finally, she countered, "Thirty-five."

"Thirty-two." That came from Addison, who eyed Everly intently.

"Deal."

Both women rose from their seats and met near the center of the table, sealing the deal with a handshake.

"One more thing, Everly." Addison still clutched her hand. "We'd really like it if you, Pierce and London would take part in the anniversary celebration we're having later this year."

Everly appeared genuinely touched. "Do you mean it, Addy?"

Addison nodded. "Absolutely. It's only right."

"Then we'll be there." Everly gave her hand a squeeze.

Gage blew out a breath, relieved that this meeting had gone in a positive direction. Seeing the way things had unfolded made him think.

If these three can heal from a decades-old mistake, maybe there's still hope for Ainsley and me.

Fifteen

Ainsley trudged to the kitchen table Saturday morning, clutching her favorite mug filled with coffee. Clad in an old pair of leggings, an oversize T-shirt and bunny slippers, she rubbed her eyes with her free hand as she walked. Pulling out her chair, she sat down and took in the scene.

Cooper, wearing an old T-shirt and basketball shorts, walked over with a bowl of cereal and a glass of orange juice. "Here you go, Mom."

She smiled. "Thank you, baby." To her mind, this was better than a fancy breakfast at a five-star restaurant. Her son had made it for her, and she knew he'd done so with love.

"I made toast, too. Let me go get it." He dashed off, returning with a piece of wheat toast on a small saucer. "I buttered it for you." He sat down across from her with his own food.

"I really appreciate this." She marveled at her child's

thoughtfulness as she ate. Though he had his moments where her affection embarrassed him, deep down, he still wanted to take care of his mother. *I must've done something right with his raising.*

When they'd finished, he cleared away the dishes. "Ready to get started?"

"Sure." She got up and went to fix herself a second cup of coffee.

Cooper moved back and forth across the room until he'd placed everything he needed on the table. The supplies for his school project were spread across the tabletop. There was water, flour, salt, paint, brushes and a large foam-core poster board.

"Do you have the paper with the instructions on it?" She stifled a yawn.

"Right here, Mom." He held up a white sheet with typed instructions on it. He began reading aloud. "'Students are to create a full-color salt dough map of a fictional country that includes the following landforms: river, lake, ocean, mountain, valley, plateau, island and beach.'"

"That's a lot of landforms." She took a long swig from her coffee cup. "Have you drawn a diagram yet?"

He shook his head. "No. Do I need one?"

"I think you do." She stretched. "Salt dough dries fast. So, by the time you start, you already need to know everything you're doing and how it's going to be laid out." She gestured to his notebook, lying on the counter. "Go get some paper, draw out the whole surface of your country and mark where all your landforms are going to be. That's gonna help out a lot when you get ready to sculpt."

He got up to get his notebook, and she drained a considerable portion of her coffee. *Come on, caffeine.*

Don't fail me now. She'd slept slightly better last night than the previous two nights, but that wasn't saying much. And having to get up early this morning to fulfill her promise to help Cooper with his project meant she couldn't linger in bed.

An image of Gage came into her mind, and she pushed it away. She'd spent enough time thinking about him. Now she needed to focus on Cooper and his project. Her son deserved her full attention, and she planned to give it to him.

She stood behind Cooper's chair, providing guidance as he used a pencil to sketch out his fictional country. "It looks really good so far, Cooper. What are you going to call your country?"

"Hmm. I don't know yet." He kept sketching, adding in the small details to the larger shape he'd drawn. "I probably won't know till I'm finished and I get a good look at it, ya know?"

"Fair enough." She finished her coffee and went to put the mug in the sink.

"You know what Bryce is calling his country?"

"No, what?"

"New Redford."

She chuckled, wondering if Bebe had helped her son name his country. While she washed up the breakfast dishes, he worked quietly at the table, finishing up the diagram of his fictional land. He held it up for her to see as she returned to the table. "What do you think, Mom?"

"Looks good. Let me see that paper." She took his instruction sheet, comparing the list of required landforms to the ones depicted on his drawing. "Awesome. You've included all eight landforms. I think we're good to go on mixing the dough."

"Cool." He slid the bowls of flour and salt closer to him. "Do we need to measure this out?"

"We could, but I did this same project as a kid." She picked up the pitcher of water. "I think we're good to just eyeball it. First, dump that little bowl of salt in with the flour." Cooper did as she asked, and she handed him a rubber spatula. "Okay. Now you stir while I add the water."

She added water slowly, watching him mix, until the consistency of the mix looked about right to her. Setting the pitcher aside, she said, "Now, here's the messy part. Get in there with your hands and work it into a dough ball."

She watched Cooper do just that until he was left with a pretty sizable lump of dough. "How's this?"

"Great. Now we'll start sculpting." Using the poster board as a base, they spread out the dough, forming and shaping it to be as close a match as possible to the diagram he'd drawn.

He placed the small island off the coast and flattened it out, stepping back from their creation. "How long will it take to dry?"

A knock at the door interrupted her before she could answer. "I'll be right back." Going to the front door, she checked the peephole. Smiling, she opened the door. "Eden! It's good to see you, cousin."

Eden, dressed in dark skinny jeans and a sunny yellow tunic, stepped inside, immediately engulfing Ainsley in a hug. "I missed y'all, so I decided to come hang for a while."

"Come on in the kitchen. We're working on a school project."

In the kitchen, Ainsley watched as Cooper ran to hug his favorite cousin. "What do you think of my project?"

Eden eyed the board, confused. "It's great. Now... what is it supposed to be?"

Cooper laughed. "It's a country. It'll look better after I paint it."

"Sounds good." She squeezed his shoulder. "Listen. Why don't you take a break while this dries so your mom and I can chat?"

Ainsley interjected, "Yeah. I think that's a good idea. Go on next door and see what Bryce is up to, but be back in an hour."

After Cooper left, the two of them sat on the couch, drinking iced tea. Eden set her glass down and faced Ainsley. "Okay. I can tell something's bothering you, so spill it."

Taking a deep breath, Ainsley recounted what had transpired between her and Gage, including their argument on the flight back from California. "And just like that, it was over. I barely got to enjoy the high of being with him before reality hit, hard."

Eden sighed. "Oh, honey. I feel your pain here, and I hate to see you hurt. Do you want my advice, or did you just want me to listen?"

"If you have advice, I'll take it." She welcomed a solution to her Gage problem since she couldn't seem to come up with one on her own.

"Let him be the bigger person. You're right to be cautious about whom you bring around your son, and if he can't see that, then he's not the man for you."

"That sounds so sensible."

"Because it is."

Ainsley chuckled. "Remember all those months back, when you pointed out my crush on him and told me to do something about it?"

Eden nodded. "I remember. But trust me, this isn't how I anticipated it turning out."

With a deep sigh, Ainsley admitted, "Looks like time has made fools of us all."

"Well, that was dramatic." Eden grabbed her hand, squeezing it. "Either he'll come to his senses and apologize, or he won't, and you'll know it's not meant to be."

She let her head drop onto Eden's shoulder. "Thanks for the advice, E."

"Anytime, honey."

Saturday afternoon, Gage jogged the trail at Piedmont Park, doing his best to keep up with his brother Blaine. Despite the way he'd been feeling the past few days, he was determined to keep up his fitness routine. The first half of the week was still wearing on him, affecting his sleep and his ability to concentrate. Now more than ever, he needed the endorphins to boost his mood.

Blaine, a longtime runner, seemed to be taking great pleasure in leaving him behind. His long strides carried him over the bumpy terrain of the trail with ease, like a gazelle crossing the savannah.

Gage panted, knowing he probably looked more like a giraffe loping through the forest. "I said we were jogging, Blaine," he called out. "Not running."

"Can't keep up, bro?" he called over his shoulder.

"Isn't that obvious? Now slow down!" Gage stopped, placing his palm against a tree trunk to grab a few moments of rest.

Blaine finally slowed, then turned around and jogged back to the tree where Gage stood. "You all right?"

He shook his head. "We talked about this, dude. I'm

not a runner. Listen, can we just walk the rest of the trail?"

Blaine eyed him for a moment before relenting. "Sure, that's fine. I don't wanna have to take you to the ER."

"Angel of mercy." Gage took a few more deep breaths, then the two of them started walking the trail.

They walked a short distance in silence, and Gage finally got a moment to enjoy the scenery. A squirrel scurried across the path, leaving a trail of acorn shells in his wake. The thick canopy of trees shaded them from the sunlit sky above, the air heavy with the scent. There were magnolias, dogwoods, mimosa. Piedmont Park was home to around 115 species of trees, and a seasonably warm, blue-sky day like this was the perfect day to take in the sights.

Still, he couldn't enjoy it the way he normally would. Though surrounded by natural beauty of all kinds, he saw Ainsley's face everywhere he looked. He heard her voice on the wind, whispering his name. To say he missed her would be a gross understatement. Seeing her at work just wasn't the same. He wanted to be more than her boss, more than just a friend she knew from work.

Fat chance of that now that I've screwed up so royally. He sighed.

Blaine looked his way. "Man, what's the matter with you?"

"What makes you think something is wrong?"

"Are you kidding? You just literally deep sighed. Aside from that, last night, while we were all learning an epic secret about the beginnings of our family's company, you looked completely spaced out." Blaine poked him in the shoulder. "We grew up together, and you think I can't tell when you're upset?"

Gage sighed again. He and Blaine were the closest in age, the middle sons who often played together, went to school together and got into trouble together. "If I tell you, you have to promise not to be judgmental about it."

"Whew. That bad, huh?" He pointed at a bench up ahead. "Maybe we'd better sit down for this one, then."

When they reached the bench and sat down, Blaine said, "I'm listening."

"Tell me how you and Eden are doing first."

A broad grin spread across his face at the mention of his wife's name. "We're amazing. She's amazing. Waking up with her every morning makes my life so much better. I mean, she has this little thing she does when she's asleep and…"

Gage held up his hand. "Okay, a little of that goes a long way. Much more and I'm gonna barf." Teasing was his only recourse here. He loved knowing that his brother was so happy, but he couldn't help feeling a twinge of jealousy as well. "So, let's pivot to my problem now."

"All right, all right." Blaine feigned offense. "Go ahead."

"So, it's about this trip I took with my assistant to pick up the equipment…"

"C'mon, man. You say 'my assistant' as if Ainsley and I don't go way back." Blaine shook his head. "Man. I wonder if I could ever get her back in the studio. Not many girls who are so confident singing alto." He paused, tilted his head, and stared at him. "Wait a minute."

Gage swallowed.

Blaine's eyes grew wide. "Oh shit. Y'all didn't…"

Gage closed his eyes against his brother's accusing

stare. He knew what Blaine had been about to say, so he responded in kind. "Yeah, we did."

"Oh wow." Blaine shook his head. "Man. I know you had a thing for her for a while, but…"

"Wait. How did you know about that?"

"Bro, we all know." Blaine scoffed. "I mean, all your siblings know. I don't think Mom and Dad are around the offices enough to be aware, but we all know."

"How?" He knew that his father knew. He didn't want to think his attractions were on display at such a level that everybody else could see them.

"Easy. Anybody who's spent more than ten minutes in the room with the two of you can see it. I mean, she likes you back, so…" He stopped. "So y'all finally sealed the deal. I'd think you'd both be happy. So, what happened?"

He recapped the argument they'd had. "She was high-key pissed at me, and she told me that any chance of a romantic relationship between us was dead."

Blaine scratched his chin. "Hmm. Let's just take a look at what she said. She thinks you hate children."

"Basically. I tried to tell her that's not true, but she wasn't hearing none of it."

"Well, I mean…" Blaine twisted his lips.

"What? Don't tell me you think I hate kids, too."

"Nah. I think it's more like a phobia."

Gage glared.

Blaine laughed. "Sorry, sorry. Anyway, what I mean is you just don't seem to know what to do when you're around kids, so you default to this kind of grouchy personality."

He ran a hand over his head. "So, you're saying there's some truth in what she said."

"There is. The question is, what are you gonna do about it?"

Gage inhaled deeply, thinking about it. "I don't really know. I guess my first step is to get to the root of it, because I can't really give a reason why being around kids makes me so nervous."

Blaine nodded approvingly. "Now we're getting somewhere. Self-reflection is always a good thing."

He made a mental note to start looking for a therapist when he got back home. "That's one step that will help me. I still need to figure out what I can do to get Ainsley to give me another chance, though."

Blaine released a wry chuckle. "Oh, I've got some experience with being in the wrong. My advice is to start with a sincere apology. Then let her know that you're working through your issues around children and parenthood."

"That sounds like a levelheaded approach. What happens if she still won't hear me out?"

He shrugged. "I guess you'll just have to accept that it wasn't meant to be. I don't think it'll come to that, though. From what I know of Ainsley, she'll probably give you a shot."

"I hope you're right, B. I really hope you're right."

A few minutes later, they got to their feet and continued down the trail.

Sixteen

Ainsley rolled out of bed Sunday morning around ten. It was the first time she'd slept for more than three hours, and she felt surprisingly good—physically anyway. She checked on Cooper and found him lying in bed playing a game on his e-reader. Satisfied that he was occupied for the time being, she returned to her room and took a hot shower.

Refreshed and clean, she dressed in a pair of clean black leggings and her black Pretty Girls Like Trap Music sweatshirt that she'd bought from the merch table at a 2 Chainz concert. Tying an old pink bandanna over her hair, she stepped into her bunny slippers and headed downstairs for her usual Sunday routine: cleaning and lounging. On the way down, she stopped by her son's room again and peeked inside.

Without looking up from his game, he said, "I know, Mom. Change my sheets, clean my room and clean the upstairs bathroom."

She smiled. In spite of the slight annoyance in his tone, at least he knew what his responsibilities were. "Good boy. I'll come up and check on you in a couple of hours."

She had a bagel and a cup of coffee for breakfast. A glance in the sink let her know that Cooper had already had cereal, so she didn't need to interrupt his gaming to offer him food. After she'd eaten, she pulled her cleaning caddy out from under the cabinet and set it on the counter. Setting her small wireless speaker to stream a classic soul station from her phone, she started clearing the clutter from her counters and table.

By the time she wiped down the counters, she was dancing with the broom to the tune of an old Barry White song. Something about her Sunday cleaning ritual made her feel renewed, and today was no different. She'd rid the house of the grime accumulated during the past week and, hopefully, do the same for her mind.

After mopping the kitchen floor, she grabbed her caddy and her speaker, carrying them with her into the living room. Setting everything down on the coffee table, she began by picking up the random trash scattered around the room.

She was carrying a handful of Cooper's discarded snack wrappers to the trash can when she heard a pounding sound. At first, she thought it was the bass line of the New Birth song playing on her speaker, but when she stopped and listened, she realized someone was knocking at the front door. Assuming it was Bebe coming over for a gab session, she strode over and opened the door.

Her mouth fell open when she saw Gage standing on her doorstep. His expression contrite, he held a bouquet of pink roses in his arms. "Hi, Ainsley."

She swallowed. "Uh, hi, Gage." Suddenly aware of her cleaning-day attire, her hand flew to snatch the bandanna off her hair. "Sorry. It's cleaning day and I wasn't expecting company."

"Don't worry about it. Besides, you always look beautiful to me." A small smile tilted his lips.

She gave him a sidelong glance. "Was that an attempt to get me to let you in?"

He shook his head. "No. Just the truth. Whether you let me in or not is up to you." He pointed past her. "If it were up to your neighbor there, I think she'd prefer we stay outside anyway."

Ainsley turned, and sure enough, Bebe was sitting on her porch, pretending to read a magazine. When Bebe saw Ainsley looking, she at least had the decency to raise the magazine higher, as if that's where she'd been looking all along. Ainsley rolled her eyes as she turned back toward Gage. "I love Bebe. She's a great neighbor, but the woman lives for gossip. So, come on inside."

"Thank God for nosy neighbors," Gage remarked as he entered the house.

She shut the door behind him. Gesturing toward the blooms in his arms, she asked, "Are those for me, or do you want me to call Cooper down?"

He laughed. "Guess I'm nervous. These are definitely for you." He handed them over.

"Thanks. I'll put them in the fridge until I can find a vase." She walked away to do that, then returned. "So, other than awkwardly giving me flowers, what brings you here?"

"Can we sit down and talk for a bit?"

She eyed him warily.

"I know I don't deserve it, but all I ask is that you give me a few minutes. Hear me out, and if at any time you get tired of listening, you can kick me out and I'll leave. No questions asked."

Her brain told her to tell him to kick rocks, but her heart was moved by the sincerity on his face. "Fair enough. Let's sit on the sofa."

They both sat, and she made sure to leave a good amount of space between them.

"I want to start by apologizing. I had no right to make judgments about your dating life or how you parent. And I'm sorry my attitude about children and fatherhood is so off-putting."

Wow. She'd never expected this level of self-awareness, and she had to admit it was refreshing. "Okay, I accept your apology."

"Great. I also need you to know that I'm seeking help. I don't really know why children make me uncomfortable, and I'm going to talk to a therapist about it so I can find out how to move forward in changing my attitudes."

"That's wonderful, Gage. It's also very evolved, because a lot of Black folks don't trust the validity of therapy." She watched him, saw the determination in his eyes. "You must really want to get to the bottom of this."

"I do." He reached for her hand, touching her gently. "I never took the time to really examine my feelings on fatherhood before, because I never had a strong enough reason. But now I do."

She frowned. "What's the reason?"

"You and Cooper." He squeezed her hand. "Ainsley, I want you in my life. Not as my assistant, but as my girlfriend. My lover. My confidante."

She felt the tears spring to her eyes. "Really?"

"Would I have made arrangements for 404 Sound

to sponsor Cooper's baseball team if I wasn't serious about this?"

"Oh my gosh." She could already imagine how amped Coach Rigsby and the rest of the team would be to hear that.

"And would I have paid for three nonrefundable, all-inclusive tickets to Disney World for spring break?"

She pressed her palm to her chest. It was a lot to take in. "Oh wow. Those tickets cost a mint." Cooper had been asking her to go for a long time, and while she'd been saving up, it would have probably been another six or eight months before she had enough for a grand trip. Wiping the tears from her eyes, she asked, "What would you have done if I had turned you down?"

He shrugged. "I guess I would have taken Teagan and Miles, since they're basically kids. Wouldn't have been as much fun, though." He winked.

She blinked away a fresh set of tears. "I love you, Gage."

"I love you. And I promise to spend the rest of my life showing you it's real."

Gage pulled Ainsley into his arms, feeling a sweet relief spread through his body as he held her close. When he'd come here, he knew things could have gone either way. But he thanked his lucky stars that she'd been willing to listen and had been receptive to what he'd said.

He nudged her chin up, kissing her deeply. Their tongues mated and tangled for a few humid moments before she pulled back. "What's the matter? Shouldn't we be making up right now?"

"Absolutely. But remember, my child is right upstairs."

"Okay, so we'll kiss quietly." He drew her mouth

back to his again. As the kiss deepened, she leaned into him, and he held her tight against his heart.

He heard the sound of footsteps on the stairs and abruptly ended the kiss. They both turned their heads and saw an amused Cooper standing there on the last step, watching them.

"Hi, Cooper." Gage waved.

"Hi, Mr. Woodson." The youngster gave him a crooked half smile.

"You can call me Gage."

"Cool." Cooper turned his gaze to his mother. "Hey, Mom, does this mean you're not going to be looking sad anymore?"

Gage's eyes widened.

Ainsley, who'd turned five shades of red, smiled. "Yes, son. I'll be fine."

"Good." Cooper walked into the kitchen.

Ainsley looked at Gage and burst out laughing. Soon enough, he was laughing right along with her.

Cooper emerged from the kitchen and headed back up the steps, carrying a glass of water and an apple.

"Hey, Coop," Gage called out to him.

Cooper stopped. "What's up?"

"You seem like the type that looks out for his mom. That's a good thing. So, I'm giving you permission right now to beat me up if I ever make your mom cry again, okay?"

Cooper stared at him for a moment before saying, "You got it." Then he went upstairs and disappeared around the corner.

Ainsley punched Gage in the shoulder. "Laying it on mighty thick, eh, Mr. Woodson?"

"Whatever I gotta do to keep you happy, I'm willing to do." He smiled. "It never hurts to have a contingency plan. If ever I think about stepping out of line, I'll just remember the beatdown I'm gonna catch from our kid."

Her big brown eyes grew even larger. "*Our* kid?"

He nodded. "You two are a package deal, as I understand it."

Her hands flew to her face.

He gently tugged her wrists. "Ainsley, I'll admit I don't know what I'm doing when it comes to kids. But what I do know is you've already given Cooper such a solid foundation. He's a good kid. Between working it out in therapy and watching you, I'm sure I can figure out how to be there for him, in whatever way you both need me to be."

Tears standing in her eyes, she looked wistfully at the top of the stairs. "He is a good kid. I'm so, so proud of him."

"And I'd be honored to be a part of his life." He squeezed her hands. "I know it's going to take time and effort, but I'm willing to put in the work."

She blew out a breath. "I really appreciate that, Gage."

"So...does this mean I'm forgiven, and we're a couple now?"

She laughed, nodding. "Oh yeah. You're stuck with us."

"Sounds great." He kissed each of her hands in turn. "I need to ask you something. It's still months away, but I don't want to wait till it's too late."

"What is it?"

"Will you be my date for the thirty-year anniversary gala? It's not until the fall."

She cringed. "Isn't it black-tie? I hate dressing up."

"I know. But it's only one night."

"Can I wear a nice pantsuit instead of some big poufy gown?"

"Sure." He knew his mom felt similarly about formal attire. "As a matter of fact, you're my mom's kindred spirit. She usually wears a tailored pantsuit. Says she hates being trapped in what she refers to as a 'taffeta prison.'"

She giggled. "Does your mom still do Krav Maga?"

"She does kickboxing now. She already got her green belt in Krav Maga."

"Your mom is my kindred spirit."

He smiled because seeing her this happy made him happy. "Since I'm here, and I'm interrupting your Sunday plans, why don't I help you clean?" He gestured to his jeans and short-sleeved blue polo. "I'm dressed for it."

"You don't have to ask twice. I never turn down housework help." She got up, handing him a microfiber cloth and a can of dusting spray. "You can start by dusting. Make sure you get the electronics, the windowsills and all the little collectibles on the mantelpiece."

Taking the items, he gave her a mock salute. "I'll get right on it, ma'am."

Shaking her head, she opened up the closet beneath the stairway and dragged out a huge vacuum cleaner.

Well into the afternoon, he helped her restore the house to neatness. They moved from the living room to the guest bedroom and half bath, then upstairs to the laundry room.

The last space they cleaned was her bedroom, and as they worked there, she showed him the family pictures she had on her wall of her mother and her favorite aunt, Eden's mother, Miriam.

"I don't know if it's okay to ask, but…"

"Where's my father? It's fine. He ran off when I was about three." She threw the last decorator pillow onto her freshly changed bed. "Cooper's father repeated the same behavior, so I guess now you can see why I'm cautious about who I date."

He nodded. "I understand, and you don't have to worry about that kind of bullshit from me."

Ainsley walked down the hall and into Cooper's room, with Gage close behind. "Looks clean in here. I think we're done. The whole place is spotless."

Back downstairs, the three of them had turkey sandwiches and chips for lunch, then piled on the couch to watch as Cooper played a fighting game on his console. Gage tried his hand at the game and promptly had his ass handed to him. What made it so bad was that while Gage frantically pressed buttons, trying to figure out how to land a hit or at least dodge the barrage of blows the kid dealt out, Cooper appeared as cool as the proverbial cucumber.

Cooper grinned. "Remember what you said earlier. Just know that if I come after you over Mom, it's not gonna be a game."

"I'm fully aware." Gage gave the kid a fist bump. "You're a fierce competitor, Coop."

"Usually only Mom and my friends call me that."

Gage cringed. *Is the kid about to lambaste me? Hasn't my ego suffered enough?*

Cooper laughed. "No worries. You can call me Coop."

And with that small acknowledgment, Gage felt like he'd taken his first big step in discovering the many facets of parenthood for himself.

Ainsley tapped her son on the shoulder. "Cooper, don't you have that book report to finish?"

He cringed, then nodded. "Yeah. It is due tomorrow."

"I've got an idea. Why don't you take your book

and your notebook next door and let Bryce help you finish it up?"

Cooper looked thoughtful. "He did already finish his. And I think it will go faster if two of us work on it."

"Great." Ainsley pulled out her phone and texted Bebe. When Bebe responded a minute later, giving her permission for the boys to work together, she said, "Bebe's on board. Go ahead and gather up everything you need."

Under her watchful eye, Cooper gathered what he'd need into his book bag.

"After you finish your work, you can hang out for a while," Ainsley said as he headed for the door. "But you need to be back by six for dinner, okay?"

"Okay, Mom." With his book bag strap slung over one shoulder, Cooper left, closing the front door behind him.

Turning toward Gage, still seated on the couch, she said, "I seem to be child-free for a few hours."

Setting the remote aside, he met her gaze. "Then this seems like prime time for us to make up."

Laughing, she jogged up the stairs.

Gage gave chase and caught her in the doorway of her bedroom. Pulling her into his arms, he kissed her deeply. When they separated, he said, "You know I'm never letting you go again, right?"

"You won't be able to get rid of me." She tweaked his nose, then slid her hand down to his shirt collar, tugging him into her bedroom.

At the foot of the bed, she kicked off her bunny slippers and undid the three buttons at the collar of his polo. She stepped back, letting him take the shirt off while she tossed her own sweatshirt aside. They alternated between fevered kisses and removing articles of clothing until they were both nude. Then she let herself be pulled into his embrace. His muscled arms engulfed her, making her feel safe, loved.

Taking a step back, she sat on the bed. When he joined her, she straddled his lap, the mattress giving beneath their weight. He kissed her eyes, her cheeks, her lips. Then he slid his attentions to the hollow of her throat, the expert movements of his mouth making her head drop back from the heady pleasure.

He whispered into her neck, his breath warm against her damp skin. "Ride me, baby."

She raised herself and, with his large hands guiding her hips, sank onto his dick, purring as he filled her.

With a growl of his own, he moved his hands around to cup her ass.

She moved in slow, deliberate ways, rising and falling on his hardness in time with the passion glowing inside her. While her hips rocked, she pressed her lips against his, seeking the comfort of his kiss, a safe harbor in the raging storm.

He gripped her tighter and began lifting his hips to meet her stroke for stroke. Her core was on fire, ecstasy spreading from low in her belly until it reached the tips of her fingers and toes.

Ragged little cries escaped her throat as she got closer and closer to orgasm.

As if he could sense her state of mind, he wove his fingers into her curls and tugged her head until her ear was next to his mouth. "Come for me, baby. Let me hear you scream."

Moments later, she did just that. Her body flexed around his, her legs trembling with the force of the pleasure crashing over her.

He continued to pump until his own orgasm tore a growl from his lips.

Seventeen

Ainsley used her key tag to unlock the door to the resort suite, then held it open so Cooper could enter. She followed him in, with Gage close behind. They'd had an amazing, fun-filled day at Epcot, and while she was utterly exhausted, she was also smiling from ear to ear.

While Cooper ran off to use the bathroom, she flopped onto the sofa in the main part of their two-bedroom suite. "I don't know about you, but I'm beat."

Gage blew out a breath as he sat down next to her. "Same. Where do kids get all that energy from?"

She shrugged. "Some of it came from sugar. As for the rest, I wish I knew. If I could harness it, I wouldn't need coffee anymore." She heard the sound of the toilet flushing, then water running.

Cooper appeared a few moments later. "Mom, can I—"

"Oh, honey. Please don't tell me you want another snack. Or that you want to go anywhere else tonight."

He shook his head. "No. I know we usually play board games in the evening, but I was gonna ask if I could just go to bed. I'm really tired."

Her brow hitched. "Oh. Well, that's fine. Just come over and kiss me good-night first."

"Aw, Mom." He trudged over to her, leaned down and gave her a peck on the cheek. "Love you, Mom."

"I love you, too."

Turning to Gage, he gave him a double fist bump, which had become their customary greeting over the last several weeks. "Good night, Gage."

Gage winked at him. "'Night, champ."

Cooper went to his bedroom and closed the door behind him. She could hear him moving around inside the room for a few minutes, probably changing into his pajamas. Soon, though, the light flipped off and the room went silent.

"Hey. Let's go sit out on the balcony for a little bit." Gage squeezed her shoulder, brushing his lips against her cheek.

"Sounds nice. I'll grab us a couple of glasses of wine."

Soon, they were seated on the cushioned wicker love seat on the room's balcony, enjoying the warm night air and the view. From their tenth-floor room, they had a great view of the dimly lit, manicured landscaping around the resort. Their room also offered a view of the nearby lagoon, and while she sipped from her glass of merlot, Ainsley watched a flock of geese gliding over the glassy surface of the water.

"It's beautiful out here."

"You're right about that." He raised his arm, placing it around her shoulders. "Gorgeous scenery, gorgeous company."

She smiled. "Very sly, Gage."

He took her glass, setting it down on the glass-topped table next to the love seat along with his own. "I meant every word, and you know it."

She gave him a peck on the cheek. "I know."

"I have something important I want to say."

She looked into his eyes, feeling herself drown in the liquid brown pools. "I'm listening."

"Ainsley, spending all this time with you has been amazing. But to tell you the truth, I expected that. What I didn't expect was how much I'd come to care about Cooper."

She felt herself grinning. "You two have really been getting along well. When you're not around, he talks about you. I know he really likes you."

"I'm glad to hear that. I feel like Cooper and I have bonded." He swatted a mosquito about to make a meal of his forearm. "Dr. Vance has really helped me work through a lot of my issues pertaining to children, and he says that my budding relationship with Cooper is helping my progress immensely."

"That's great. I'm so glad to hear it's going well." She took a deep breath. "Because I have something to tell you."

"And I'd love to hear it. Just let me say this first. I could tell Cooper was a good kid. But the more I get to know him, the more I want to be a part of his life. As he gets older, he'll need some male guidance, and I want to be there for him." He squeezed her hand. "Now, what were you going to tell me?"

She chewed her lip for a moment. "Remember the day you showed up with those flowers, and we went upstairs to make love?"

He chuckled. "Of course, I remember."

"Well, do you remember that we were so hot for each other that we didn't use protection?"

He paused. "Wait a minute." His eyes darted from her eyes to her belly, then back again. "Are you...could you be..."

"Pregnant?" She teased, finishing his sentence. "Very."

His grin seemed to show every last one of his permanent teeth. "Ainsley. Baby, that's amazing. You're amazing." He laid his palm over her belly, which barely showed any evidence of the life growing inside her. "I'm gonna take such good care of you. I promise."

"You're not nervous?" She hadn't known how he'd react to the news, especially considering the way he'd struggled around children in the past.

"Not at all. I'm working through the things I need to work through so I can be a great father. Not only to Cooper, but to our baby as well."

He looks so damn earnest. She could feel her eyes welling up. "Damn it, Gage. Why do you have to be so wonderful?"

"You ain't seen nothing yet, baby." He reached into the pocket of his short-sleeved button-down shirt and pulled out a small black box. Dropping to one knee in front of her, he said, "This isn't just about Cooper. It's about you, and all the ways you make my life better. I've loved you for so long, and when you finally gave me a chance, I almost ruined everything." He flipped open the box, showing her the two-carat princess-cut solitaire inside. "Now that I've got you back, I don't ever want to be without you again. Ainsley Elaine Voss, will you marry me?"

A sob broke forth from her lips, tears coursing down her face. She wanted to say yes, but she couldn't talk and sob at the same time, so she stuck out her hand and nodded furiously.

"Is that a yes? I need to hear it from you."

Taking a few deep, steadying breaths, she finally found her voice and shouted, "Yes!"

Grinning, he placed the ring on her finger and tossed the box aside.

She leaned in for his kiss, and the moment their lips connected, she felt her heart swell with affection. He made her feel alive in a way no one else ever had. In the last two months, he'd shown her a love she never would have expected to find, especially not after motherhood began to dominate her life.

A loud popping sound scared her, causing her to break the kiss. Looking to the sky, she saw the source of the sound as thousands of sparkly, multicolored points of light painted the sky. It was one of the park's famous nightly fireworks shows, and it was beautiful.

But as far as Ainsley was concerned, nothing could match the fireworks she felt inside.

Sitting at his desk, Gage stifled a yawn as he looked over the previous month's operations report. It was a Monday, and he'd just come back from an amazing vacation with Ainsley and Cooper. It was the least motivated he'd felt to be at work in a long time, but there were still things to be done, so he pressed on.

He took a sip from his now tepid coffee as he flipped the page on the report. A soft tapping sound drew his attention, and he looked up to see Ainsley standing in his office door. She wore a black knee-length shirt-dress that showed off the length of her honey-brown legs. "Can I come in?"

"By all means." He slid his chair back from the desk, inviting her to sit on his lap.

She giggled. "Now, Mr. Woodson, we're at work. That wouldn't be appropriate professional behavior, would it?"

"We're engaged, baby." He rolled his eyes but didn't lose his smile. "You're gonna get enough of teasing me about that one day."

She sidled around his desk and sat on his lap. "Okay. I just wanted to stop by before I left for the meeting and get a good-luck kiss."

He wrapped his arms around her, happy to oblige her request. When she broke the kiss a few minutes later, she said, "I'll have to redo my lipstick, since you're wearing it all now."

Grabbing a napkin from the top drawer of his desk, he wiped his mouth. "You look beautiful, as always. Now go over there and see what they have to say. You said your first two interviews went well."

She got up, straightening the hem of her dress. "They did, and I have a good feeling. But there's a lot of competition for the HR position. You know, if I get the job, you're going to have to replace me as your assistant."

"You're a tough act to follow, babe. But I've got my eye on a few candidates from the intern pool downstairs." He shooed her out. "Don't worry about that. Just go and be amazing."

She blew him a kiss as she headed out. "I love you."

"I love you, too, sugar."

While she was gone, he went about his workday. He finished going over the operations report, signed off on it and emailed it to Nia's assistant to be archived. With that done, he left his office and went down to the first floor to check in on the recording session in Studio 1.

Inside the control room, he sat next to Teagan, who was working the Digital Audio Workstation. The baby of the family and younger twin to his brother Miles, Teagan's official title was chief technology officer. In her heart, however, she was a sound engineer. On any given workday, she was far more likely to be found in the studio than in her office on the fourth floor.

Putting the final touches on his album, The Visionary was in the booth, sitting on a stool jotting notes on a pad, but already wearing headphones.

"Where's the production team?"

"They were here Friday and said they'd drop back by at the end of this week to check on his progress." Teagan gestured to the artist. "He's a pretty independent worker, and he writes on his feet. All I've really been doing is giving him playback to riff on."

"Good." He spent a few more moments watching the artist as he wrote, then asked, "So, sis. After two months, do you still like the new equipment?"

Teagan's grin broadened. "Gage, this workstation is awesome. I'm discovering new things every day. The features on this thing are great, and it's making my job a whole lot easier." She rested her cheek on the surface of the workstation. "I've named her Fancy."

Gage laughed. "Jeez, Teagan. You're such a nerd."

"I know, but in my line of work it comes in handy." She winked. "Now, get out of my studio. I don't want you making our artist nervous."

Standing, Gage glanced at The Visionary, thinking he should stop in and say hello. But seeing how deep the lyricist was in his writing process, he decided not to bother him. Tipping an imaginary hat toward his baby sister, he returned to his office to get some more work done.

Just before lunch, Ainsley returned, and when he looked up and saw the broad grin on her face, he knew what she was about to say. He stood up. "You got the job?"

"Yes!" She nearly screamed the answer, her excitement apparent. "I start as human resources manager next Monday. I'll have my own office, and get this, I get an assistant, too!"

He pulled her into his arms. "Congratulations, baby! I'm so proud of you."

"Thank you." She pecked him on the lips. "Now, I have to ask. You didn't interfere in the process, right?"

He shook his head. "Absolutely not. You forbade me to get involved, and I don't want to end up on your bad side. Cooper will end me."

She laughed. "Well, I'm happy to know you followed my wishes."

"How about a celebratory lunch?"

"Sounds wonderful."

He grabbed his wallet and keys and followed his beautiful bride-to-be out the door.

Eighteen

When the plane had raised its wheels and carried her away from Summer Village, Louisiana, four months back, Ainsley had no reason to believe she'd ever return to the quaint little town. Yet today, it seemed only right that she and Gage return to the place where they'd finally succumbed to their feelings for each other.

Standing by the mirror in a downstairs room of the inn, she checked her appearance one more time. She smoothed her hands over the flowing skirt of the knee-length white sundress she'd chosen for this occasion. The skirt left plenty of room for her expanding waistline, without sacrificing style. The halter neck was accentuated by tiny embroidered pink rosettes, and she'd swept her hair up into a messy bun.

Eden appeared then, tucking a fresh pink rose and a sprig of baby's breath into her cousin's hair. "You look beautiful, Ainsley."

"Thanks, E." With one final glance in the mirror, she said, "I think I'm ready."

"Then let's get you married."

Riding with Eden in the rented sedan, she held her sequined white clutch and watched the scenery passing by. The familiarity of the place touched her, and she knew then that returning to this place for their special day had been the right choice. *Maybe we should come here for our anniversary every few years.*

They arrived at Simmons Lake Park, and as Eden parked the car, Ainsley took in the sight of the gathering with a smile. Down by the lake, an old gazebo stood, which was now festooned with crepe paper wedding bells and streamers. She crossed the grass, her arm linked with Eden's. Inside the gazebo stood the local justice of the peace, and Gage stood next to him. The sight of her husband-to-be made the tears start gathering in her eyes. Gage looked handsome in his white shirt, tan slacks and brown loafers. Next to him stood Cooper, in a matching outfit. A pink rose boutonniere was pinned to each of their collars.

A grouping of about twenty chairs was set up, and as Ainsley walked down the white runner aisle, she glanced around at the faces of the Redford family, the Woodsons and a few of their colleagues from work. She felt her smile growing wider.

Beneath the gazebo and the canopy of trees, she and Gage exchanged their vows. Her hands trembled as he placed the white-gold band on her finger. And when the justice of the peace pronounced them married, Gage pulled her into his arms, leaned her back and kissed her as if no one were watching.

After the ceremony, they convened at the Blue Rose for refreshments. Sitting on Gage's lap at their table in the center of the diner, Ainsley said, "This day has been perfect in every way."

"I'm glad to hear that."

"I love it here." She sighed contentedly.

"Oh, so would you rather I cancel those tickets to Egypt and we can just spend our honeymoon here instead?"

She cut her eyes at him. "Nah. I need to see the pyramids."

His eyes took on a wicked gleam. "And I need to see how many ways I can make you scream on another continent."

She punched him in the shoulder. "You're too much, Gage."

"But I'm just right for you." He gave her hip an affectionate squeeze. "I love you, Ainsley Voss-Woodson."

She responded with all the love she felt inside. "And I love you, Gage."

* * * * *

HIS PERFECT FAKE ENGAGEMENT

SHANNON MCKENNA

One

"I was set up."

Experience had taught Drew Maddox to keep his voice even and calm when dealing with his volatile uncle, but nothing was going to help his cause today.

"The damage is the same!" Malcolm Maddox flung the crumpled handful of cheap tabloid magazines he'd been clutching in his fist onto the conference room table. "For anyone who looks at this, you're just a coke-sniffing scoundrel with a taste for eighteen-year-olds! Why in God's name were you at a party at that lowlife degenerate's house in the first place? What in holy hell were you thinking?"

Drew let out a breath, counting down slowly. The photos in the tabloids were of him, sprawled on a couch, shirt ripped open, looking clouded and disoriented, while a young woman in a leather miniskirt, large breasts popping out of her skin-tight silver top, sat astride him.

"I was trying to help a friend," Drew repeated. "She found out that her younger sister was at that party. She couldn't get in herself, but she knew that I used to run with that guy years ago, so she asked me to check up on her sister."

"We were supposed have dinner with Hendrick and Bev tonight," Uncle Malcolm said furiously. "Did that even cross your mind before you got into this mess?"

"I do remember the dinner, yes," Drew said. Hendrick Hill was Malcolm's longtime partner and cofounder of their architecture firm, Maddox Hill. Drew had always liked the guy, uptight and humorless though he usually was.

"Then Bev reads about your drunken orgy at Arnold Sobel's house at her hairdresser's!" Malcolm stabbed the tabloids with his finger. "She sees the CEO of her husband's company in these pornographic pictures. She was horrified, Drew."

"It wasn't a drunken orgy, Uncle, and I never—"

"Sanctimonious bastard," Malcolm growled. "He had nerve, sputtering at me about morals and appearances. As far as Hendrick is concerned, it doesn't matter how many architectural prizes and honors you've won if you can't keep your pants zipped. He thinks you're a liability now, and if he persuades the rest of the board, he has the votes to oust you, no matter what I say."

"I know," Drew said. "But I was set up at that party. Someone played their cards carefully."

Malcolm let out a savage grunt. "You're the one who's playing, from what I can see. And if the board fires you, all of our clients will smell blood in the water. It's humiliating!"

I was set up. He had to stop repeating it. Uncle Malcolm didn't want to hear it, so at this point he'd be better off just keeping his mouth shut.

PR disaster or not, he couldn't have done anything differently. When his friend Raisa found out someone brought her sister Leticia to one of Arnold Sobel's famously depraved parties, she'd been terrified that the younger woman would fall prey to a house full of drunken, drugged-up playboys.

Then Leticia had stopped answering her phone, and Raisa had completely freaked out. If Drew hadn't intervened, she would have forced her way through Arnold's security and into Sobel's party by herself—with a gun.

It would have ended badly. Certainly for Raisa. Maybe for everyone.

Drew couldn't let that happen.

Of course, as he discovered afterward, Leticia had never been at the party at all. He and Raisa had been played. The target had been Drew all along.

But Uncle Malcolm didn't want to hear it.

"I was set up." He knew the words wouldn't help, but he couldn't stop repeating them. "They staged those pictures. The photographer was lying in wait."

"If there's one thing I hate more than a spoiled ass who thinks the world only exists for his pleasure, it's a whiner," his uncle snarled. "Set up, my ass. You're a Marine, for God's sake! Taken down by a pack of half-dressed show-girls?"

Ava, his younger sister, jumped in. "Uncle Malcolm, think about it," she coaxed. "Drew's not a whiner. A rebel and a screwup, maybe, but he always owned it. And this is so deliberate. The way those girls ambushed him—"

"Doesn't look like an ambush to me. It looks like a damn orgy!"

"Someone's telling you a story, Uncle," Ava insisted. "Don't be a sucker."

"Ha. All I see is that your brother couldn't care less about the reputation and the future of the company I spent my life building! If Hendrick uses his muscle to get the board to remove you as CEO, I can't stop him. So start brushing up your resume. As of today, you're job hunting. Face Hendrick tonight like a man. He can tell you his decision then. But as for myself, I'm done, boy. Done with your crap."

Uncle Malcolm stomped out of the room, cane thudding. He tried to slam the door for effect, but the expensive hydraulic hinge made it sigh gently closed after him with a delicate click.

Drew leaned forward, rubbing his aching temples. "I'll

skip the dinner with Hendrick," he said wearily. "No one needs me there to make that announcement. I've reached my humiliation quota for the day."

"No, don't. That looks like an admission of guilt," Ava said thoughtfully. "You need to come to dinner, Drew. I have an idea."

Drew gave his sister a wary look. "If anything could make me feel worse right now, it's those four words coming out of your mouth."

"Don't be a wuss," Ava scolded. "This place needs you here as CEO. You're the new face of Maddox Hill. Hell, you're the new face of architecture. Nobody else has what it takes to head up all those big carbon sink building projects you got going. You're the one who won the Global Award for Sustainable Architecture, and the AIA COTE Award—"

"You don't need to flog my résumé to me, Av. I know what's on it."

"And the Green Academy competition, and that's just the eco stuff," Ava persisted. "You're, like, Mr. Cross-Laminated-Sustainable-Timber-Is-Our-Future. Maddox Hill can't stay relevant without you. Everyone will line up to thank me eventually. You'll see."

It didn't surprise him that she would think so. His sister had curly blond hair, huge cobalt blue eyes, a drop-dead figure, charisma to burn and a very, very high opinion of herself. She could bend people effortlessly to her will, especially men. He was the only one who could resist her. She was his little sister, after all.

The whole thing was still sinking in. How much he stood to lose today, in one fell swoop. Control of all his design projects, many of which had been years in the making. Most of all, he hated the thought of losing the Beyond Earth Project. He'd put that together with the collaboration of the robotics research arm of the Maddox Hill Foundation, opening up the field to young architects and engineers to problem-solve the obstacles to human habitation on the moon and Mars.

That project would have just rung all of their late father's bells. Dad had been a dreamer.

"I'm not proposing that you charm Hendrick, or even Uncle Malcolm," Ava said. "That's a woman's job. Your fiancée will do the heavy lifting. You just smile and nod."

"What fiancée?" Drew asked, baffled. "I have to find a fiancée before dinner tonight? That's setting the bar high, Av, even for a wild, carousing playboy like me."

"No, big brother, the finding's done for you already. It came to me like a beautiful brain-flash while Uncle Malcolm was ranting. We need to fight this false story, and I have the perfect counter-story. And she happens to be right nearby today, coincidentally!"

"What the hell are you talking about? Who's here?"

"Your future bride," Ava announced.

Drew was struck silent, appalled. "Av, you're joking, right?"

"Nope! A temporary engagement, of course. Just a few months, to get you over the hump. You met her once, when you were on leave from Iraq, remember? You stopped to visit me at my dorm in Seattle. Remember Jenna, my roommate?"

"The little red-blonde with the glasses? The one who dumped a pitcher of sangria all over me?"

"That's the girl. I was supposed to meet up with her for coffee before her Wexler presentation over at the Curtis Pavilion this afternoon, but Uncle Malcolm was in such a tizzy, I had to reschedule so I could calm him down. Not that it helped much."

"What presentation?"

"Jenna's a biomechanical engineer, and she started her own bionics company a few years ago. She designs prosthetic mechanical limbs. Brain activated, artificial nerves, sensory feedback. Real space-age stuff. I have been doing their PR, and she's up for the Wexler Prize for Excellence in Biomedical Engineering. She gave her introductory presentation to the committee today. Her mission is to make affordable, high-functioning mechanical arms available to everyone who needs one. She's brilliant, she's focused, she cares…in short, she's perfect."

"But why?" He shook his head, baffled. "Why would she do this for me? And why would anyone buy it? And what the hell is the point?"

"They will buy it, and they will love it," Ava said. "Underestimate me at your peril, bro. I am a genius."

"I don't want to tell a pack of lies," Drew said. "It makes me tense."

"You have to fight fire with fire," Ava told him sternly. "You'd rather just give in and torpedo Uncle Malcolm's company rather than try something bold and risky? Someone is pushing a fake story about you. That you're a spoiled, entitled asshat who uses and discards vulnerable young women. Ouch. My story is much better. Handsome bad boy, redeemed by love, his social conscience shocked to life—"

"I have a social conscience already," he growled. "I'm not a complete tool."

"Shh, I'm just brainstorming. The cynical rogue with the secret hunger in his heart who falls for the smart girl in glasses. Humbled by the power of love. Oh, yeah."

"Secret hunger in my heart?" Drew tilted an eyebrow. "Really, Av?"

"Just roll with it, bro. This woman is making artificial arms for people so they can hug their kids again. See where I'm going? Pathos. Warmth. Connection. We all crave it."

"I get it just fine, and you're still nuts," Drew said.

Ava picked her tablet up from the table and tapped the screen a few times, passing it to Drew. "This is Jenna. I had my assistant go over to the Curtis to record her presentation to the Wexler Prize committee, and he already sent me the video. Take a look."

In the video, a young woman was spotlighted on the circular stage at the Curtis Pavilion, one of the newest high-profile Seattle skyscrapers that Drew had designed. She wore a microphone headset. A sleek fitted short gray dress. She had nice legs. Her strawberry blond ringlets were twisted up into an explosive messy bun, ringlets sproinging out in every direction. She still wore glasses, but now they were cat-eye style, the frames a bright neon green.

Drew held up the tablet. The camera zoomed in on her face. The pointed chin, the tilted hazel eyes. A sprinkle of freckles. Her mouth was full, with a sexy dip in the pillowy softness of her lower lip. Painted hot, glossy red. He tapped the tablet for the sound.

"…new nerve connections, opening the doorways to actual sensations," she was saying, in a low, musical voice. "Holding a paintbrush. Braiding a child's hair. Dribbling a basketball. We take these things for granted, and don't see them for the daily miracles that they are. I want these daily miracles in arm's reach for everyone. Thank you."

There was enthusiastic applause. He muted it. Ava took her tablet back.

"Her company is called Arm's Reach," Ava said. "She's won a bunch of awards already. Most recently the AI and Robotics International Award. That one was a million bucks. But she needs more, to develop ways for people to access the specialized nerve surgery that goes with some of her tech." Ava paused. "She's cute, too. Though I'm sure you noticed."

"Av, I'm sure this woman is too busy helping people with real problems to participate in your little theater project to solve mine," Drew said absently, still gazing down at the tablet. "Send me that video."

"Sure thing." A smile curved Ava's mouth as she swiped

and tapped the screen. "Done." She picked up the phone on the table. "Mrs. Crane?" she said. "Is Ms. Somers there? Excellent. Yes, bring her in. Thanks so much."

"Jenna Somers is here, now?" Drew was alarmed. "Ava, I never agreed to—"

"Don't be silly. She's here right now, Drew. What's the point of wasting any time? Hers or ours?" A knock sounded on the door. "Come in!" Ava sang out.

It was too late to answer Ava's question the way it deserved to be answered.

The door was already opening.

Two

Jenna followed the white-haired receptionist along a suspended walkway over a huge open-plan workspace. A wall of glass three stories high highlighted the Seattle cityscape. From there, they turned into a starkly minimalist corridor, paneled with gleaming wood, lit by slanted skylight windows. She'd been wanting to check out the famous new Maddox Hill building in downtown Seattle, made completely out of eco-friendly sustainable wooden building materials, for some time now. Unsurprisingly, it was gorgeous, inside and out. The wood gave it an earthy and welcoming warmth that steel and concrete could never match. A glimpse inside an open office door showed floor-to-ceiling windows and a stunning view of the rapidly transforming city skyline. Just what she'd expect of a world-famous architecture firm.

It was all very elegant, but she wished Ava had kept their original date hours ago at the coffee shop near the Curtis Pavilion, and not strong-armed Jenna into coming up here. She'd hoped for a chance to rehearse the main points of her intro presentation with her friend before she had to give the speech. Ava had a keen ear for anything flat, boring or repetitive.

But whatever. She'd gotten through it okay, even without the dry run, and it was out of her hands now. Fingers and toes crossed. The Wexler Prize was a juicy one. Half a million dollars would kick her research forward and turbocharge all her hopes and plans.

Maybe Ava had just wanted to show off the new Maddox Hill headquarters building, and if so, she was suitably impressed. Her uncle Malcolm Maddox was the firm's cofounder, and the building itself had been recently designed by Ava's sexy brother, Drew, the infamous bad boy of modern architecture.

The receptionist stopped in front of a mahogany door, and knocked.

"Come in!" Ava's voice called.

This room, like the corner office Jenna had glimpsed, was large and featured big slanted windows, and a breathtaking view. The sun glowed low on the horizon, painting the clouds pink. Ava gave her a welcoming smile, and then the man at the table stood up and turned around. Jenna stopped short—and stopped breathing.

Drew Maddox himself, in the flesh. Ava's big brother and architect of the superrich: the tech tycoons, oil sheikhs and Hollywood royalty. Currently the focus of a fresh sex scandal.

And also, incidentally, of her most feverish and longstanding girlish crush. Because of course, she had such impeccable taste in men. Ha ha.

She hadn't seen Drew Maddox since the sangria episode in college. She'd fled the scene in a state of utter mortification, and hadn't come back with a bucket and mop to clean up the mess until he was safely gone. He'd roared off on his motorcycle into the sunset and straight into her wildest sexual fantasies.

Where he proceeded to take up permanent residence. He was her go-to. Always.

He was just as gorgeous now as he ever had been. No, even more so. Eleven years had rendered him denser. More solid and seasoned. Even bigger than she remembered. He was so tall. Broad shouldered, with that tapered waist. Hard muscular thighs. On Drew Maddox, a pair of dress pants, a crisp white shirt and a silk tie looked almost dangerous.

His face was so beautiful. Golden olive skin. Dark hair. Deep-set, tilted green eyes. Lashes longer and darker than any man needed them to be. Sharp cheekbones, a strong, chiseled jaw and full, sensual lips. The dramatic slash of his dark eyebrows was mesmerizing. He was so fine, no wonder women flung themselves at him, at least according to this morning's tabloids. She didn't blame them.

Ava looked discreetly amused when Jenna finally dragged her gaze away.

Damn. Caught gawking. And of course, now her face was red. It was the cross she had to bear, with her pale, red-headed complexion. Freckles and blushing.

"You remember my brother, Drew?" Ava said.

"Of course." Jenna tried to smile. "Our dorm room, back in college. I believe I dumped a pitcher of sangria all over you."

"I remember that." His voice was so deep and resonant. "It was sticky."

"I was telling Drew about your presentation," Ava said. "I sent him the video Ernest made for me."

Yikes. Fresh insecurity rocked her. Drew, watching her speak? She could have had lipstick on her teeth for all she knew.

"Come in, come in," Ava urged. "Shall I ask Mrs. Crane to bring you coffee, tea, a soft drink? A fresh-pressed juice? We have a juice bar."

"No, thanks. I don't need anything."

"Sit down, Jenna. There's something we needed to ask you."

"Go ahead." Jenna settled herself in a chair, tingling with

nerves. Drew stood with his back to them, gazing out the window at the fading sunset colors glowing on the horizon.

Jenna wrenched her gaze away from his perfect, fabulously muscular butt with great force of will. "What is it you want to know?"

"Um… This is kind of awkward." Ava's eyes flicked over to Drew, then back to her. "But we appear to be in some PR trouble. I don't suppose you saw the tabloids today."

"I noticed a couple of silly headlines online this morning," she admitted. "But I didn't read the articles. Nobody pays attention to those rags anyhow."

Total lie. She'd read through all four articles. Every word. In fact, she'd stared avidly at the pictures until her coffee was cold wondering what a guy like Drew Maddox saw in those pumped-full-of-silicone party girls. Men. She would never understand.

"Triple Towers Starchitect Caught with His Hand in the Cookie Jar!" read one headline. A photo of Drew's Hollywood starlet girlfriend's scowling face was captioned: "Bonita Furious! Bad Boy Drew Maddox strays…again!"

Drew turned around, his mouth grim. "Uncle Malcolm is pissed. But his partner, Hendrick Hill, is the real problem. Hendrick wants me out as CEO on moral grounds. My uncle owns forty percent of the controlling shares, Hendrick has forty, and the other twenty percent are controlled by the rest of the board. With those pictures, Hendrick will be able to persuade over half of them that I'm a liability. And I'll be fired."

"Oh," Jenna murmured, dismayed. "That's terrible. I mean, I'm sure you'll be fine eventually. You're a brilliant architect. Nobody questions your talent. But still. It's awful."

"It is, particularly since those pictures were staged," Ava told her. "He was set up."

Drew made a pained sound. "Ava, do we have to go into the gory details?"

"She needs to know the situation. Be clear. You were lured into that place on false pretenses and ambushed. Those girls jumped on you and posed you for those photographs. We don't know who organized it, but they've gone to a lot of trouble to mess with you, and their plan seems to be working. That's where you come in, Jenna."

"Me?" Jenna looked from Ava to Drew, confused. "How me?"

"Well…we were just thinking—"

"*You* were thinking, Av," Drew said. "Own it."

"Okay, fine. I, Ava Maddox, was thinking, because I am a freaking genius, that a whirlwind engagement would help the optics of the situation. You know, to draw attention away from those pictures. To counter Drew's soulless playboy image."

"Whirlwind engagement with…who?" Jenna's voice trailed off. Heat rushed into her face afresh. "Wait. You can't possibly mean…"

"Yes, exactly! You! Of course you." Her friend's face was bright with enthusiasm. "You're perfect. Smart. Pretty. Respected in your field. You're out there walking the walk, helping people in ways that are concrete and personal. Your social cred would help Drew right now. Plus, Hendrick's a sucker for a romantic story. Uncle Malcolm once told me that Hendrick was quite the naughty bad boy himself, back before he met Bev. He shaped right up when he snagged her. Hendrick and Bev are the real challenge, but I think you could charm them into submission if we moved fast, with assurance. You know, if you guys act as if this were an absolutely done deal, and had been for a while."

Jenna could think of absolutely nothing to say. She forced her mouth to close.

"Of course, we're talking a temporary arrangement,"

Ava went on. "Just until the fuss blows over and Hendrick calms down. I wouldn't ask if I didn't know for a fact that you're single at the moment."

"Right," she muttered. "No conflicts there at all." Now the heat in her face was in full flower. The humiliation caused by her ex-fiancé Rupert's betrayal was still unpleasantly fresh. Being jilted for Rupert's curvaceous blonde intern had been a nasty blow to her heart and her pride.

"And also, as a bonus… It would not suck to be engaged yourself while that pig-dog Rupert is getting married, right?" Ava pointed out. "Just for a few months."

"Maybe not," Jenna said cautiously. "I guess."

"Be Drew's arm candy," Ava urged. "Attend swanky parties, dressed to kill. Make contacts, rub elbows. This place is crawling with people who have more money than they know how to spend. Teach them to spend it on your research. It's a win-win for everyone. This romance is going to be the magic touch that will shoot the profile of Arm's Reach up into the stratosphere. More than any of my other efforts so far. Brilliant though they are."

Jenna shook her head. "I'm honored to be asked, but I don't think it will work."

"I'd understand if you didn't want your organization associated with this mess," Drew said, gesturing at the pile of tabloids.

"Oh, no," she said hastily. "That's not what I'm saying. Um… The thing is, I just don't think that it would be, you know. Believable. Him and me."

"Why not?" Ava asked. "You two would look adorable together. You'll be the ultimate power couple. Each with his or her own personal superpower."

"Av, get real!" she blurted. "I'm not his type!"

"Type?" Drew frowned at her. "What the hell? What type is that? I don't have a type."

"You are your own individual type, Jenn," Ava soothed.

"You're utterly unique. Come on. What do you think? Will you give it a shot? For me?"

"Ah…" Jenna's voice trailed off. "I don't think this makes sense."

"Back off," Drew said sternly to Ava. "You're bulldozing."

"Of course I am!" Ava protested. "Because I'm right! It would be beneficial to both of you. My spin-doctor instincts are right on the money, every time."

Drew pulled a chair up and sat down near her. So close, she could smell his cologne. A deep, piney, spicy, musky whiff of masculine yum, overwhelming her senses as he gazed searchingly into her face.

He glanced back at Ava. "You really think it will be worth her while? Taking on my bad reputation?"

"Once I get to work on this story? You better believe it'll be worth it." Ava's voice rang with utter conviction. "It'll send her profile through the roof."

Drew turned his gaze back onto Jenna. "I don't like to misrepresent myself," he said. "But if it genuinely makes sense for you, too, I'd be willing to give it a shot."

Make sense for her? She couldn't make sense of a damn thing while she was staring into Drew Maddox's face. *Damn, Jenna. Sharpen up.*

"How about this," Drew went on. "We can give it a trial run tonight. Ava and I were supposed to have dinner with Uncle Malcolm, our cousin Harold, Hendrick and his wife, Beverly. Come with us, just as my date, not my fiancée. We'll see how it feels. See if Hendrick and Bev buy into it. See if it makes you too uncomfortable. If it does, just say no after dinner. No harm, no foul. I will absolutely understand."

"Really? Wouldn't that be, you know…really awkward?"

His smile was so gorgeous. Subtle dimples carved deep

into his lean cheeks, bracketing his sexy mouth. His hyp-notically beautiful, long-lashed eyes studied her intently.

"Of course it would be awkward," he said softly. "Wel-come to my world."

Ooh. Those words sent inappropriate shivers rushing down her spine.

Drew Maddox waited, eyes fixed on her. After a mo-ment, one of those black winged eyebrows tilted upwards.

She didn't want to imagine the dazzled, starry-eyed look that must be on her face right now.

Just like old times. Ava had dragged her into lots of trouble back in their college days. But this time, it was just playacting, right? In the interests of securing more funding for Arm's Reach. Her cause was a good one. It was worth it.

And what was the harm, really? She wasn't lying to any-one but the predatory gossip rags and this tight-assed part-ner, Hendrick Hill. And it wasn't a lie that would damage anyone, or take anything from anyone.

Plus, she wasn't locked into it. She could bail tonight if they crashed and burned.

"Okay," Jenna said slowly. "I suppose we could give dinner a try."

Ava's delighted hand-clapping startled Jenna, causing her to sit bolt upright in her chair. "Excellent!" her friend said briskly. "You have just enough time to get home and dress for dinner. You came here in a cab, right?"

"Ah, yes, but—"

"I'll call a car to take you home, and I—hold on a sec." A guitar riff from a classic rock tune came from a smart-phone on the table. Ava glanced at the display and tapped the screen, holding it to her ear. "Hey, Ernest. Talk to me… really? Three of them? They're hungry today. Okay, I'll tell them to hurry up. Thanks."

She laid down her phone, her eyes sparkling. "You guys! We have an opportunity to launch this right now with a splash. My assistant, Ernest, has identified three celebrity photographers lurking down in the front lobby, waiting for Drew. Jump on it! Use them for once, instead of letting them use you!"

Jenna drew in a sharp breath. "You mean, paparazzi? They follow you?"

Drew's mouth tightened. "They bother me occasionally, yes."

Ava waved her hand. "Ever since that thing he had with that actress who did the last dinosaur flick, what's her name? Bonita Ramon. It's hard to keep your love affairs straight. Anyhow, the tabloid sharks discovered that stories about Drew sell newspapers even without a movie star attached to him. His money, his looks, his sex life—"

"Ava, don't," he said.

Ava rolled her eyes. "Your own fault for being so damn photogenic. You're, like, walking clickbait. So? They're waiting, people! Go get 'em!"

Ouch. Jenna winced inwardly at the thought of being compared to the radiant movie star, Bonita Ramon. This adventure could prove to be more dangerous to her self-esteem than she'd thought. "You mean, just go downstairs right now? Together?"

"Wait, Av," Drew said. "We told her she could bail after dinner. If she goes out with me now in front of the photographers, she'll be in it up to her neck. No going back."

"So decide now! Call it fate, okay?" Ava pleaded. "Walk through the lobby holding hands. Laugh, smile, flirt, improvise. Seize the day! If this is going to work, you can't be tentative or coy. You have to hit it hard and keep on hitting!"

Drew glanced at her, and shrugged. "Your call, Jenna," he said. "Do not let her pressure you."

Ava clasped pleading hands. "C'mon, Jenn," she coaxed. "Don't you trust me? Tell me you do."

"Hush up and let me think," Jenna said distractedly.

Thinking was hard, with her wits compromised by Drew Maddox's proximity, which created a huge racket in both mind and body.

Drew was right. Going out now nixed any chance of changing her mind discreetly.

Ava was also right. Now was the moment to announce their fake romance to the world. If it was the plan, she should just do it. Waffling and pussyfooting was stupid.

Ava had gotten her into plenty of trouble back in the day, true. On the plus side, most of it had been a blast. The most fun she'd ever had. Before or since.

She looked at Drew, who looked back without smiling, arms crossed over his chest, and her ex-fiancé flashed through her mind. Rupert, who was currently planning his honeymoon with Kayleigh, the twenty-three-year-old intern. She of the big blue eyes that went blinkety-blink like an anime waif. Pouty lips always dangling a little bit open.

The hell with it. Her love life was in a shambles anyway. Empty and sterile and stupid. So why not put it at the service of a friend? Besides, she could use a little goddamn distraction right now. And Arm's Reach needed a good push.

"I'm in," she announced. "Let's go downstairs."

"Yessss!" Ava bounded up to her feet, jubilant. "Go, go, go now! I'll call a car to pick you up out front so they'll have time to get some nice shots of you two together. Don't walk too fast across the lobby. And remember to smile. Oh, and be sure to look up into his—"

"You're micromanaging," Drew said. "Back off. We'll take it from here."

Despite her brother's tone, the irrepressible Ava didn't stop beaming as she herded them down the hall and into one of the elevator banks. She waved excitedly as the doors slid shut.

Suddenly Jenna was alone with Drew Maddox, every

angle of his big, stunning self reflected in the gleaming, reflective silver elevator walls, all the way out into infinity.

Whew. That was a whole lot of Drew Maddox to process.

He smelled so good. She was hyperconscious of how well his pants fit. The width of his shoulders. The bulge of his biceps, filling his jacket sleeves, and they weren't even a type of sleeve designed to showcase great biceps.

Say something, Jenna. Speak. "Ah, wow. That was… intense."

"Sure was," he agreed. "Too intense. Ava's classic bull-dozer routine. Sorry."

"I'm familiar with it," she told him.

"Yeah? Has she dragged you into her crazy schemes before?"

"All through college," she admitted. "I was a big nerd, trying to squeeze mechanical and electronic engineering into my head, and Ava wanted to save me from myself. It was her sacred mission to get me into a respectable amount of trouble."

He laughed under his breath. "Respectable?"

"Oh, yeah," she assured him. "Only lame-ass losers never get into any trouble."

His teeth flashed, gorgeously white. "Sounds like something Av would say."

"She likes to challenge me," Jenna said. "Get me out of my comfort zone."

"I imagine that's usually a good thing. But seriously. If this makes you uncomfortable, you don't have to do it. No pressure. Are we clear?"

Aw. How sweet. She nodded.

His smile made her legs wobble. "Good. Door's opening. Last chance to bail."

The decision made itself on some deep, wordless level of her mind, just as the doors started to slide open.

She went up onto her tiptoes, cupped the nape of his neck and pulled him down into a forceful kiss.

Drew stiffened for a fraction of an instant—and then leaned into it.

His lips were so warm. She registered the silken texture of his short hair. Touched his cheek with her other hand, exploring the faint, sandpapery rasp of beard shadow, his warm, smooth, supple skin. She was vaguely aware of flashes of light from the cameras, hoots and whistles. They seemed far away. Irrelevant.

Drew swayed back. "Whoa," he murmured. "You took me by surprise."

"Sorry," she whispered back. "Snap decision."

"Don't apologize. I'm there for it. Anytime."

She waited. "So?" she prompted. "Shall we go out there? Get in their faces?"

Drew stuck his hand in the elevator door as it started to close again and they stepped out, shoulder to shoulder, to the constant flashing of the cameras on every side.

Act confident, silly girl. Smile. Act like Drew Maddox is your boyfriend.

Wow, that was some potent make-believe magic. It made her suddenly three inches taller. Her chest swelled out, her chin went up, her face turned pink.

They wound their arms together and clasped hands. Jenna wasn't sure which of them had initiated the contact. It seemed to happen of its own accord. The building security people finally caught up with the photographers and blocked them from following them out the main entrance, and an older man in a suit hurried out after them, his face clearly anxious. "The car's waiting, Mr. Maddox," he said. "I am so sorry about this. We had no idea they were going to descend on you like that."

"It's okay, Mr. Sykes. Let them take all the pictures they

want from behind the glass but I'd appreciate if you'd keep them in the lobby until Ms. Somers's car is gone."

Drew pulled her toward the big Mercedes SUV idling at the curb. "Here's your ride," he said. "We still on for tonight? I wouldn't blame you if you changed your mind. The paparazzi are a huge pain in the ass. Like a weather condition. Or a zombie horde."

"I'm still game," she said. "Let 'em do their worst."

That got her a smile that touched off fireworks at every level of her consciousness.

For God's sake. Get a grip, girl.

"I'll pick you up at eight fifteen," he said. "Our reservation at Peccati di Gola is at eight forty-five."

"I'll be ready," she promised.

"Can I put my number into your phone, so you can text me your address?"

"Of course." She handed him her phone and waited as he tapped the number into it. He hit Call and waited for the ring.

"There," she said, taking her phone back. "You've got me now."

"Lucky me," he murmured. He glanced back at the photographers, still blocked by three security men at the door, still snapping photos. "You're no delicate flower, are you?"

"By no means," she assured him.

"I like that," he said. He'd already opened the car door for her, but as she was about to get inside, he pulled her swiftly back up again and covered her mouth with his.

His kiss was hotter than the last one. Deliberate, demanding. He pressed her closer, tasting her lips.

Oh. Wow. He tasted amazing. Like fire, like wind. Like sunlight on the ocean. She dug her fingers into the massive bulk of his shoulders, or tried to. He was so thick and solid. Her fingers slid helplessly over the fabric of his jacket. They could get no grip.

His lips parted hers. The tip of his tongue flicked against hers, coaxed her to open, to give herself up. To yield to him. His kiss promised infinite pleasure in return. It demanded surrender on a level so deep and primal, she responded instinctively.

She melted against him with a shudder of emotion that was absolutely unfaked.

Holy *crap*. Panic pierced her as she realized what was happening. He'd kissed her like he meant it, and she'd responded in the same way. Naturally as breathing.

She was so screwed.

Jenna pulled away, shaking. She felt like a mask had been pulled off. That he could see straight into the depths of her most private self.

Drew helped her into the car and gave her a reassuring smile and a friendly wave as the car pulled away, like it was no big deal. As if he hadn't just tongue-kissed her passionately in front of a crowd of photographers and caused an inner earthquake.

Her lips were still glowing. They tingled from the contact.

She couldn't let her mind stray down this path. She was a means to an end.

It was Drew Maddox's nature to be seductive. He was probably that way with every woman he talked to. He probably couldn't help himself. Not even if he tried.

She had to keep that fact firmly in mind.

All. The. Time.

Three

Drew watched Jenna's recorded online speeches for well over an hour. First the Wexler Prize presentation, then the Women in STEM speech that he found online, then a TED talk she'd done a couple of years ago, then a recent podcast on a popular science show.

He listened to the podcast as he drove home. He liked her clear alto voice. The direct, lucid way that she described her techniques. Her intense enthusiasm and drive. He had friends in the service who'd lost limbs in Iraq and Afghanistan. The implications of her work for them were exciting.

He couldn't wait to get home and watch the video, along with the audio. To see the conviction shining out of her eyes. Her complete, passionate investment in what she was doing.

It was sexy to watch.

He set up the tablet in his bedroom while he was changing for dinner and listened to the TED talk again. He liked the way her voice made him feel. Strange, that he hadn't taken much note of her when they first met. But he'd been a different person back then.

Oddly enough, he'd stopped constantly reliving that fiasco at Arnold Sobel's party since meeting with Jenna. Up until that moment, he'd been seeing it over and over, smelling that foul, drugged perfume that had been sprayed into his face. Remembering the moment he woke up naked in that unfamiliar bed, head throbbing, stomach churning. The bodies of strangers pressed up to him.

He'd been violently sick to his stomach. His head had felt like a mallet slammed into it with each heartbeat. He'd felt humiliated, helpless. And so damn stupid for letting that happen to him.

He hadn't told anyone about the drugged perfume or the blackout. The words stopped in his mouth before they could come out. Humiliation, maybe. Or macho embarrassment. Who knew, but he just couldn't talk about it. Not to anyone.

Meeting Jenna had made that shame evaporate like steam. The surprise kiss in the elevator forced him to drape his coat over his erection. He'd kissed her again at the car just to see if his first reaction was a fluke.

It was not. He'd kept that coat right where it was.

Her kisses were burned into his memory. The feeling of her slim body, molding against him, pliant and trusting. The fine, flower petal texture of her skin. The softness of her lips. Her perfume was a warm, teasing hint of honey, oranges. He'd strained for more of it.

One final detail. He pulled the case that held his mother's jewelry out of his wall safe. He'd tried to give it to Ava years ago, but she'd burst into tears and run out of the room. So he'd just put the jewelry box away and never mentioned it to her again.

He pulled out the small black velvet box that held Mom's engagement ring. The kiss in front of the gossip rag photographers had committed them to this charade, so the hell with it. He was all in.

With more time to think, he might have gone out and bought a new ring, but Malcolm would recognize Mom's ring, maybe Hendrick, too. Certainly Hendrick's wife would. Bev had been friends with his mother since before he was born. Nothing got past that woman.

Besides, it felt right. Jenna was the kind of woman to

whom a guy would give his mother's engagement ring. Mom would have liked Jenna.

He put his coat on and stuck the ring in his pocket and headed for the car. Thinking about Mom and her ring had triggered an uncomfortable line of thought.

Namely, that Mom would not have approved of him using Jenna like this. Taking advantage of her hard-won assets for his own agenda.

Using her to clean up his mess, essentially.

That uneasy thought tugged on his mind. He tried to rationalize it in every way he could. He had not gotten into this trouble because of his own depraved behavior. He'd been trying to help a friend. The only thing he was guilty of was being stupid, and not jumping clear before the trap closed. His conscience was clear.

Besides, Jenna had her own fish to fry. This situation was in both of their best interests. No one had been fooled. No one was being coerced. It was completely mutual.

The accident that killed his parents was eighteen long years ago, and yet he could still see so clearly that look Mom gave him when he was less than truthful, or when she'd caught him taking a lazy shortcut. Her tight mouth. The frown between her eyes.

In spite of Mom's disapproving look in his mind's eye, the closer he got to Jenna's place in Greenwood, the more buzzed he felt. He was actually looking forward to this. He couldn't even remember the last time he'd felt that way.

Drew parked on the steep slope in front of an attractive three-story house. Jenna's apartment was on the top floor. An external staircase led him up to a comfortable wrap-around deck furnished with a swing and wicker furniture. He buzzed her doorbell.

It opened after a moment, and Jenna smiled up at him. "Right on time, I see," she said. "I like that in a man. Come on in."

He couldn't think of anything to say for a moment. Sensory overload shorted him out. Her figure-hugging, textured, forest green dress looked amazing. It accentuated her high, full breasts, nipped-in waist and luscious round bottom, and the color was great for her flame-bright hair, which was twisted into an updo like a fiery halo.

Cat-eye glasses again. Amber-tinted tortoiseshell, with glittery stones in their pointy tips, which matched her drop earrings, but her huge smile outshone it all. Ruby-red lipstick. Beautiful white teeth. A gray cat leaped over his feet and darted out the door.

"You look great," he offered. "I like the glitter on your glasses. Hey, your cat just ran outside. Is that a problem?"

She beckoned him in. "Not at all. He has his own cat door. Plus, he wants dinner, so he'll be back soon. My rhinestone-studded specs only come out for the special occasions, by the way. If the paparazzi show up, I'll blind them with my bling."

"Perfect." He pulled the ring box out. "Speaking of bling, I brought this, if you feel comfortable wearing it. Since you really went for it this afternoon in the lobby."

He opened the box. Jenna blinked, taken aback. "Oh, my gosh. Is that real?"

"Teardrop sapphire with diamond baguettes. It belonged to my mother."

Jenna's eyes went wide and somber behind her glasses. "Um… Are you sure? I mean, since this isn't a real thing, maybe we shouldn't…"

"Malcolm, Hendrick and Bev will all recognize this ring," he told her.

"Oh. Well. In that case, I suppose it makes sense." There was a tiny frown line between her dark eyebrows as he took it out and slid it onto her ring finger.

It fit perfectly. Her cheeks flushed, and her gaze

dropped. "It's beautiful," she murmured. "I'll be careful. I know how precious it is."

On impulse, he lifted her hand to his lips and kissed it.

Jenna froze, the color in her cheeks deepening, and tugged her hand free. "Excuse me. Gotta, um, feed my cat. Before we, um, go." She hurried into the kitchen.

Drew wandered around the open-plan apartment. A sliding picture window opened out onto the deck overlooking the backyard. City lights twinkled below it. The living room was separated by a bar from the kitchen, and a couch and a cushy armchair were angled around a TV. The rest of the room was dominated by a long worktable, lit up by industrial hanging lamps and piled with cables, electronic components and schematics. The walls were paneled with corkboard, and a mosaic of information was attached, as well as dozens of photographs. Jenna with various other people. One was a child with a gap-toothed grin, holding up two prosthetic arms triumphantly high in a double thumbs-up.

Jenna came back into the room buttoning up a long, nipped-in black wool coat.

"Is this where you do your research?" he asked her.

"Most of it I do at the Arm's Reach lab. But I like having a workspace at home. When I get ideas, I like to have everything I need to pin them down fast."

He strolled around, gazing at the schematics tacked to the wall. "Impressive."

"So is the Triple Towers sustainable housing complex in Tokyo," she said. "That's some truly amazing, forward-thinking design. Congratulations for your prize, by the way."

"You heard about that?"

"Read about it online. *Time* magazine, I think. Great profile they wrote about you, too. Fawning, even."

"Was it? I didn't notice."

She smiled at him. There was a moment of odd silence,

and Jenna gestured toward the door. "Smudge can let himself in the cat door whenever he's ready for his dinner, so shall we go? I wouldn't want to be late."

"Right."

Drew got her settled into his car before getting inside himself. As he turned the key in the ignition, the podcast he'd been listening to on the drive over blared out of the speakers, startlingly loud without the car noise to cover them.

"...with artificial sensory nerves, the issues are different," recorded Jenna said to the podcaster. *"We've brought together many different lines of research in the—"*

He switched it off. Damn. That podcast was online, out in the public domain, and yet still he felt as if he'd been caught snooping in her phone.

"Holy cow," Jenna said, startled. "Was that me? The *Outside the Box* podcast?"

"Yeah. Just, you know. Informing myself about who you are. What you do."

"Oh, of course," she said quickly. "That makes sense. I should have done the same. But I probably know more about your business just because Ava keeps me up to date on the big stuff. Prizes, and all that. She's so proud of you. She boasts and gloats nonstop."

They drove in silence for a while, and finally Drew found the nerve to say it. "I saw your Women in STEM talk, too. The TED talk. And your Wexler Prize presentation speech."

She gave him a startled glance. "Good Lord. All that tonight?"

"You're an excellent speaker," he said. "I got sucked in. Didn't want to stop."

Her eyes slid away, but she looked pleased. "It was hard-won," she admitted. "Public speaking terrified me for the longest time. But I just kept at it until I could power through. I can't believe you watched all that stuff in one go."

"It was fascinating," he said. "Clear, convincing, well structured. Funny."

"Oh. Well. Thanks, that's, ah…encouraging." Jenna twisted her hands together, wrapping the strap of her purse around them. Twirling the engagement ring.

"You don't need to be nervous tonight," he said.

She let out an ironic snort. "Are you kidding? How can I not be?"

"After watching those speeches, I think you'll be great."

"At what? Presenting myself as something I'm not?"

"That's not what you're doing. You just need to be yourself. That's why we asked you to do this."

"Oh, yeah. Just act like a woman who's gotten herself engaged to a guy like you. No biggie." She laughed under her breath. "The more I think about it, the less credible it seems."

"Why?" Drew was genuinely baffled. "What do you mean by a guy like me?"

"Please," she scoffed. "Give me a break. You're a world-renowned architect. You run in exalted social circles. You're American royalty. You went out with Bonita Ramon, for God's sake, and then for your next relationship, you hook up with me? Jenna Somers, Super-Nerd? Anything sound weird about that?"

"I don't see anything," he said. "What does Bonita have to do with it? That's over." Not that it ever really began.

Jenna snorted. "If you have to ask, I don't know how to begin to explain it to you."

Drew blew out a frustrated breath. "I met Bonita at a yacht party in Greece. She was on the rebound from some asshat producer. We hung out for a couple of days, and found out fast that we didn't have much to talk about."

Bonita was also a self-absorbed whiner with a huge personality disorder, and she'd bored him practically into a coma by the end of the second day, but he would never say that to anyone. Kissing-and-telling was for losers with no self-discipline or class.

"Wow," she said. "So. Do you often party with movie stars on yachts in Greece?"

He felt defensive. "I was in Crete for work. I got a call from some friends who were vacationing there. I'm not a coked-out party animal stumbling from orgy to orgy."

"Not at all," she soothed. "I didn't mean to offend you."

"No offense taken. But after the past few days…aw, hell. Sorry to bark at you."

"Don't mention it," she said. "Relax. We'll just play our parts and hope for the best. Can't ask for more than that."

He pulled to a stop in front of the hotel that housed the restaurant and got out, giving his keys to the parking attendant. Jenna got out herself before he had a chance to open the door for her. He took her arm, and the light weight of it felt good. Mom's ring glittered on her slender, capable-looking hand. It looked like she'd been born to wear it.

Out of nowhere, he felt irrationally angry. It was humiliating that he had to hustle and con and play games to protect his professional position. To beg and plead for the help of a woman like Jenna to lend him some goddamn credibility, instead of being taken seriously by her. Courting her with class. Blowing her mind properly.

Jenna must have felt his frustration, sensitive as she was, because she shot him a troubled glance. He manufactured a reassuring smile, but she didn't look convinced.

Jenna was playing along with this scheme out of loyalty to Ava. She was sorry for her friend's screwup brother. That poor sorry bastard who couldn't keep his act together.

Play our parts and hope for the best. Can't ask for more than that, she'd said.

Like hell. He did want more than that. He didn't want to make do with crumbs.

He wanted it all, whether he deserved it or not.

Four

Jenna shook hands and smiled until her cheeks ached as Ava and Drew introduced her to the people at the table in the restaurant. Ava looked gorgeous in her skin-tight black lace dress. Ava and Drew's cousin Harold Maddox was there, straitlaced and unsmiling in his dark suit and tie. Harold had the Maddox height and good looks, but he wasn't as striking as Drew and Ava. Drew's Uncle Malcolm she'd already seen in Ava's pictures. He was an older, grimmer version of Drew, shriveled by age and twisted by arthritis. Malcolm's partner, Hendrick Hill, was bone-thin and bald, with sharp cheekbones and sunken cheeks. He studied her doubtfully with deep-set, suspicious eyes beneath thick black-beetled brows. His wife, Beverly, was his polar opposite. Short, round and friendly, she had a blindingly white pixie cut and lots of white gold jewelry dangling over her midnight-blue silk caftan. Her smile froze for only a moment when Drew introduced her as his fiancée, and all eyes fastened instantly on Jenna's hand, which she'd been quick to position so that the stunning engagement ring was visible to all.

"Fiancée?" Malcolm Maddox's bushy gray brows knit together. "What's this? How is it that I've never laid eyes on you before? Where did you come from, girl?"

"Uncle," Ava reproved him. "Manners, please. She's an old friend of mine, and you're meeting her now. Be nice."

"I was just waiting for the right moment to tell you, Uncle," Drew said. "Things got crazy."

"Hmmph," Harold muttered. "I'll just bet they did."

Ava elbowed Harold, but no one else seemed to notice. They were all staring at her. Then Bev's brilliant smile flashed as she made her way around the table to hug and kiss Jenna. "Oh, my goodness! Congratulations! How exciting. I wish you all the best."

The warmth of the older woman's good wishes made Jenna feel guilty. The benevolent older lady reminded her of her own mother, gone six years now.

The meal proceeded pleasantly enough. Jenna had Drew on one side and Bev on the other, and Ava and Bev were both masters of the art of cheerful, entertaining chitchat, to which Jenna did her best to contribute, though it was hard to concentrate with a scowling Uncle Malcolm dissecting her furiously with his eyes from across the table.

Sometime after the appetizers, Bev took her hand and lifted it to examine the sapphire ring. "The sight of that ring really brings me back," she murmured, a catch in her voice. "Diana and I were sorority sisters, back in the day. She was so special. Brilliant, funny. A real beauty. Ava is her living image. I miss her so much, even now."

Jenna smiled into the wet eyes of the other woman, and squeezed her hand. "I wish I could have known her."

"Oh, me, too." Bev dabbed at her eyes with a tissue, sniffing delicately. "So, how did you and Drew meet, anyway?"

Jenna froze, panicked, and Ava piped up. "Oh, that was my doing. I take full credit for that. I am Cupid personified, people. Arrows and all."

"Why am I not surprised," Uncle Malcolm muttered.

"I met him for the first time eleven years ago," Jenna explained. "Back when Ava and I were in college."

"I was on leave," Drew said. "In between tours in Iraq."

"He came to visit me on his way to Canada," Ava said. "He was going to do the Banff-Jasper Highway in the Canadian Rockies on his motorcycle."

"So long ago?" Bev looked bewildered.

"That was long before we got together," Jenna explained. "He was unimpressed with me at the time, particularly after I dumped a pitcher of sangria all over him. Not my finest moment."

"Oh, dear." Bev tittered into her white wine. "How awful."

"It was," Jenna said ruefully. "I wanted to die."

"I'm glad you didn't." Drew lifted her other hand to his lips and pressed a hot, seductive kiss against her fingers that sent shivers rippling through her body. "My shoes stuck to the floor when I walked for days afterward. But it was worth it in the end. Baptized by Gallo port and peach nectar."

His smile made her go molten inside. Oh, he was good. She knew it was for show, and even so it made her feel like she was the only woman in the world. And now she was staring back at him, starry-eyed, mouth slightly open, having completely lost her train of thought. The Drew effect. Whoa. Debilitating.

The waiter arrived and began serving the entrees. Bev patted her hand and waited, clearly amused, while Jenna struggled to orient herself in the conversation.

"So, when did you and Drew reconnect?" Bev asked, gently nudging her back on track.

Another split-second-panicked pause, and once again Ava jumped to the rescue.

"Actually, that was my fault, too," Ava said. "Last spring Jenna asked me to do PR for her Arm's Reach Foundation, so I went down to see the Women in STEM speech in San Francisco to talk strategy. Drew was down there, too, working on the Magnolia Plaza job. The three of us had dinner, and it all came together. Like magic."

Jenna stabbed a couple of penne with vodka sauce on the end of her fork, trying to breathe down the panic. Okay. Thanks to Ava, she and Drew now had an origin story. Yay.

Drew's eyebrow tilted up for an instant, like Ava's did when she was doubtful about something. Then he kissed her hand, going with it. "Changed my life," he murmured.

"Huh. I was down in San Francisco working on Magnolia Plaza, too," Harold said slowly. "Funny that I never ran into Jenna once that entire time. We were there for three months."

Ava shrugged. "Doesn't seem funny to me," she said. "You weren't with us on those nights."

"Evidently," Harold said. "But I did not get the impression that Drew was engaged to anyone during that time." He gave Drew a thin, knowing smile. "On the contrary."

"Women in STEM, did you say?" Bev swooped in to salvage the conversation, sensing tension in the air. "What was it Ava said you did, dear? Some sort of engineer, right?"

"Yes. I design neuro-prosthetic devices," Jenna explained.

Bev blinked. "Ah. I see."

"She designs brain-directed bionic limbs for amputees that give actual sensory feedback," Drew broke in. "It's overly modest to just say, 'I design neuro-prosthetic devices.'"

Jenna laid down her fork. "I didn't think this was the time or place," she told him sternly. "But I do know how to toot my own horn."

"Yes, but this actually is the time and place," Drew said. "Bev works with the Bricker Foundation, so she needs to know about Arm's Reach." He looked at Bev. "I'll send you the link to the Women in STEM speech. You'll be intrigued, considering your work with veterans."

Bev sipped her wine, her eyes sparkling behind her rimless glasses. "Thank you, Drew. By all means, do send me that link."

"The TED talk is fine for a quick overview," Drew went on. "But the Women in STEM speech goes into much more detail."

"And there's the Wexler Prize presentation she gave today at the Curtis." Ava picked up her phone and tapped it. "Forwarding video links right now, Bev."

"I can't wait to see them." Bev smiled, her eyes soft. "I love how he's so proud of you. That's just as it should be."

Another awkward pause. Everyone's eyes on her. She was starting to sweat.

"You certainly have been doing your homework, Drew," Uncle Malcolm said.

"Just admiring my fiancée's accomplishments," Drew said. "It's worth a look. She does groundbreaking work that transforms people's lives."

Malcolm grumbled under his breath. "I'm sure it does. Yours included, eh? So she just pops out of the woodwork, fully formed and already engaged to you?" He scowled in Ava's direction. "You plotting and scheming again, girl? I know your tricks."

Ava batted her big gray eyes at him. "Uncle," she murmured. "You wound me."

"Ha," Malcolm grunted. "Suffer."

Hoo-boy. Jenna did not want to hear them thrash this one out right in front of her. Time out. She jumped to her feet. "Excuse me, everyone. Back in a moment."

She fled toward the ladies' room, grateful for some air and a break from all that intense scrutiny. To say nothing of the mind-jamming effect of Drew's over-the-top hotness. She lingered in one of the stalls, trying to settle herself with deep, slow breaths.

This was trickier than she'd anticipated. She disliked lying on principle, and hated lying to people she liked. And she liked Bev Hill. Hendrick still had that mistrustful pucker to his mouth, and Malcolm Maddox couldn't stop frowning. Both men were hyper-wary of a trap, but not Bev. She was sweet and warm and genuine.

Jenna came out, straightened herself up, washed her hands at the gray marble sink and tried, more or less in vain, to get her hair in order. She was touching up her mascara when Bev came out of one of the bathroom stalls. Bev waited for another couple of women who were there to finish their washing and primping and walk out.

As soon as they did, Bev moved closer and placed her hand on Jenna's shoulder.

"Honey. I have to say something to you," she said earnestly. "I don't have the right to say this yet, since we just met. But you seem like a lovely girl, so I'm going to risk it."

Jenna braced herself. "What is it?"

Bev's eyes were anxious. "How well do you really know Drew Maddox? I mean, beyond the sangria and the meeting in San Francisco. Do you really know him?"

"Ah… I, um…" Jenna stammered, groping for words. "Bev…"

"I know I just met you, and have no right to ask," Bev said swiftly. "And it was clear to everyone that you're madly in love with him, so I'm sorry to cause you any pain."

Jenna tried not to wince. So her crush was really that visible. "Bev, um… I just—"

"He's ridiculously handsome, yes. Far more so than is healthy for him. Brilliant, talented, charming. Naturally seductive. Ava, too. Their parents both were, and Malcolm was, too, back in the day. But Jenna… I don't know how to say this, but—"

"You don't have to," Jenna said. "I know Drew didn't live like a monk before we got together. His love life would be hard not to notice even if you wanted to ignore it."

"Well, thank goodness you're aware of that. But I… I just wanted you to be forewarned of, ah…" Her voice trailed off. She looked pained.

"I assume you're referring to the pictures in the tabloids lately?"

Bev's lips tightened. "I'm glad you know about them. I would hate to be the one to tell you."

"It's not what it seems," Jenna explained. "Drew got ambushed by the photographer and the girls when he got to that party. The whole thing was staged."

"Oh." Bev's lips were still compressed. "Is that a fact?"

"It is," Jenna insisted. "Really. Someone is trying to take him down."

"You truly believe that?"

"One hundred percent," Jenna said firmly. "Not a doubt in my mind."

Bev let out a sharp little sigh. "Well, then. If you're sure, then I suppose there's nothing left to say, honey. Except sorry, for overstepping my bounds."

"I know it came from a good place," Jenna said. "You're very kind. Trying to protect me when you barely even know me."

"That's a generous way for you to look at it, my dear," Bev said. "My husband and I were worried the second he introduced you as his fiancée. We just hate to see a lovely young woman with all that energy and promise running right off a cliff."

"No cliffs, I promise," she assured the other woman. "My heart is safe."

"Good luck with that, honey." Bev patted her shoulder with a smile. "But it's not supposed to be safe, you know. That's not what hearts are for."

Five

Drew gazed after Jenna as she vanished around the corner on her way to the bathroom. Bev got up and excused herself shortly afterward to follow her. Then Hendrick mumbled some inaudible excuse and fled, which surprised no one. Hendrick could tolerate mixed social situations only if Bev was by his side.

That left Ava, his cousin and Uncle Malcolm. All family. No one left at the table to constrain his uncle to basic politeness. He'd been tossed to the wolves.

Uncle Malcolm got to it without losing time, wiping his mouth aggressively with a napkin. "So, then," he growled. "Jenna Somers, eh? Quick and well-timed, wasn't it? Engaged to a scientist philanthropist, out of the blue? She's not your usual type, boy."

"I don't have a type," Drew said.

"I told you," Ava butted in. "Jenna was my college roommate. She's my best friend in the world, and she—"

"I'm not talking to you, girl. I'm talking to your brother. Why don't you run along and powder your nose with the other females?"

Ava's eyes flashed. "I don't need to pee, Uncle," she said through her teeth. "And I don't run from a fight, either. Guess who taught me not to?"

Uncle Malcolm made an impatient sound. "I don't want

to fight with you, girl. I want to talk to him." He jerked his chin toward Drew. "Privately."

"Tough," Ava said. "You want privacy, make a private appointment in your office. Don't banish me from the table at a public restaurant during a dinner party. That's just rude. Jenna is perfect. There is no way that you could object to—"

"Too perfect," Malcolm said grimly. "You don't pull a woman like that out of a hat. You two are cooking up some scheme, and I want to know what's up."

"Nothing is up," Ava said. "No schemes. Just true love. What's the harm?"

"Probably none, for Drew." Harold sounded smug.

"Exactly," Uncle Malcolm said. "The harm will all be to her when she realizes that she's been sold a bill of goods. No nice young lady deserves that."

Drew stared his uncle down. "Thanks for the vote of confidence," he said.

"I'll have confidence in you when you earn it," was Malcolm's curt reply.

At that moment, Jenna and Bev reappeared, engaged in a lively conversation about Jenna's company. Hendrick trailed close behind.

"...to widen my reach," Jenna was saying as the two of them drew nearer. "I would love to meet with them. It sounds like we would be a perfect fit."

"Wonderful," Bev said briskly. "I'll get back to you first thing tomorrow about possible times, as soon as I speak to Jayne and Helen and take a look at their schedules."

"Don't forget that we'll be busy all day tomorrow," Ava reminded her. "My whole crew, along with Drew, are going to be at Arm's Reach, filming a new installment of our video series."

"Me?" Drew said, startled.

"Of course you," Ava said. "Eight thirty on the dot. Ruby's Café is the rendezvous point, on Hatton Street, just a couple of blocks from Jenna's house. My camera crew will meet us there, we'll all grab some breakfast, and off we go to shoot our video."

"What exactly are we shooting? And how long will it take?"

"You'll see," Ava said airily. "Jenna will show us all how the prosthetics function. It'll be fascinating. Don't worry, you can go back to your crazy fourteen-hour workday soon enough. I already talked to both of your assistants. They're on board."

"I can manage my own damn staff, Ava."

She smiled at him, all sweetness. "Just trying to help."

Coffee and dessert arrived, as if Ava had timed it herself, and for a while they were all taken up with sampling tiramisu, panna cotta and the pine-nut cream pastry. Hendrick and Bev said their goodbyes, and Bev gave Jenna a hug, murmuring something into her ear that made Jenna laugh.

Uncle Malcolm shrugged on his coat and made a point of limping around the table and taking Jenna's hand, frowning into her eyes. "I hope you know what you're doing, young lady. You look like a fine girl, but I believe you're in over your head with this one."

"We'll see about that." She leaned close to kiss his leathery cheek. "Don't underestimate me, Mr. Maddox," she murmured. "Or him."

"Hmmph," he muttered. For a fleeting moment, it almost looked as if he were threatening to smile. "Good night. Harold, my cane. See me down to the car, please."

Harold took Uncle Malcolm by the arm, and Drew, Ava and Jenna all watched their cousin help Malcolm down the staircase.

When they were out the door, Ava threw herself at Jenna and hugged her. "Jenna, you were brilliant. They were eating out of your hand. I would never have guessed that you two weren't wildly in love. Bev was charmed to pieces, and Hendrick will follow anywhere Bev leads. Like a lap dog."

Jenna pulled away, looking flustered. "She is a lovely person."

"And so are you! Like recognizes like!" Ava swatted her brother on the chest. "And that bit about her work, how she was underselling it? Genius, bro. Simply inspired."

His sister's words irritated him, obscurely. "I wasn't acting at all. It's just stating the truth as I saw it."

"Right!" Ava crowed. "Perfect! My plan is working. Don't deny it!"

"We're not denying anything," Jenna said. "It's just complicated. It's doesn't feel good, to tell a lie to a person like Bev."

Ava gazed at Jenna with a puzzled frown. "I suppose it's not ideal," she admitted. "But desperate times, desperate measures, right?"

"Let it go, Av," Drew said. "It's been a long day. We're tired, and you're bulldozing again."

Ava took a step back, laughing. "Well, now. Look at the two of you, defending each other. In cahoots against me. That is freaking adorable."

"Av, don't condescend," Jenna said wearily.

Ava backed away. "Okay, okay. See you two lovebirds bright and early at Ruby's. Night!"

Drew and Jenna stood there after Ava disappeared, locked in an embarrassed silence.

"So did Bev corner you in the ladies' room?" he finally asked. "When she excused herself she had the look of a woman on a divine mission."

"She was worried about me," Jenna admitted. "Poor innocent maiden that I am, falling prey to a heartless seducer's honeyed promises."

Drew winced. "I'm sorry she feels that way about me."

"I told her you were set up. I'm not sure if she bought it,

but she feels sorry for me, and she believes that I believe. I guess our performance was, um…convincing." Her eyes slid away. Her face was pink.

"I guess it was." Drew waited for a cue, but she wouldn't meet his eyes, so he had to just throw his invite out there into the cold with no clue how she'd receive it.

"Want to go somewhere else?" he asked her. "We could get a drink. Hash it out."

She looked up and finally gave him what he'd been craving. That nerve-jolting rush from eye contact. Her big hazel eyes. Streaks of green and gold and a border of dark slate, setting all the bright inner colors off.

She caught her full red lower lip between her teeth, her delicate blush deepening. "Actually, it's been a long, weird day, and tomorrow will be another one. We'd better catch some sleep, if we're going to meet up with Ava's crew at eight thirty."

He let out a silent sigh, crestfallen. "Okay. I'll just take you home."

"Oh, no. I can call a car. There's no need for you to—"

"I insist," he said.

There was a brief struggle, but he managed to persuade her. Once she was inside his car, the self-conscious silence between them deepened. He kept sneaking quick glances, catching the curve of her high cheekbone, the glitter on her glasses. The flash of the ring on her finger. He felt as nervous as an adolescent, asking a girl on a date for the first time. Tongue-tied and struggling.

"Usually Ava drives me crazy when she lets her mouth run," he said. "But she saved the day with that dinner–in–San Francisco story. It should have occurred to me to get our stories straight on the ride over here, but I didn't even think of it."

"I forgot, too," Jenna said. "Thank God Ava thinks on

her feet. I'm not much of an improviser. There was no time to think it all through."

"Sorry about that," he said. "We rushed you into this."

"It's okay," she assured him. "I agreed to this freely. No one coerced me."

He pulled up in front of her apartment and killed the engine. "Good. I'm glad you met Bev. She's a good person for you to know. She's connected and extremely committed to her charitable enterprises at the Bricker Foundation. I want this arrangement to be useful for you."

"I'm sure it will be." She smiled at him. "Good night, Drew. Thanks for the ride."

"Let me walk you to your door."

"Oh, no. That's not necessary—"

"Please. I'd prefer to see you safely inside."

Jenna sighed. "Fine. If you insist."

Drew followed her up the stairway and stood at the end of the porch, waiting while she dug in her purse.

"I don't usually fumble for the key, I'll have you know," she told him. "Normally, I'd have it in my hand, ready to jab into an assailant's eyes. I'm a little off my game tonight."

She opened the door, and looked up, opening her mouth to say goodbye, and wild energy suddenly arced between them. The breathless silence felt charged with meaning. Possibility.

Jenna held the door open and shifted back, making room for him to come inside.

She closed the door after he followed her, hung her key ring on the hook on the wall, placed her purse on the shelf and stood there waiting. Seconds passed. They turned into minutes.

"Is there something you wanted to say to me?" Jenna's voice was a soft, throaty whisper.

Yes. But not in words. Words had abandoned him. Something else had taken him over. Something hungry, restless, prowling.

Jenna made a startled sound as he reached out and took her glasses off. He placed them on the shelf by the door, his movements slow and deliberate.

Her hands floated up, but not to push his hands away. He touched her jaw, her cheekbones, with his fingertips. The tender skin at the nape of her neck, behind her ear. The warmth of her hands came to rest on top of his, brushing along his fingers, then pressing his hands against her face.

Every part of her was just as soft and fragrant as he remembered from that astonishing kiss outside the Maddox Hill building.

Her arms wound around his neck. He cupped the back of her head, the thick mass of twisted curls wound up in the back, the ringlets coming loose and twining around his fingers. Breathing in her perfume.

Scolding voices in his head yapped at him. He shouldn't be doing this. It was irresponsible. He was being a self-serving tool. This was going to blow up in his face, and there would be no one to blame but himself.

The voices faded to a background buzz. Distant, irrelevant. And then he was kissing her.

Wildly, like he was starving for her.

Six

It was happening again. He'd bypassed her brain. Just reached past it into something deeper, rawer, truer. A part that didn't care about consequences. It just wanted more of that delicious, virile, wonderful-smelling man who was ravishing her mouth with slow, enthralling skill. *More.*

He lifted her up, and she just clung, like he was her center of gravity, winding her legs around him. He pressed her against the door, letting the hard, unyielding bulge of his erection rock against that tender ache of need between her legs as he kissed her, making her shift and move and moan. She held him tighter, moving over him until he was positioned right where she needed him to be, and then moving again...squeezing. Even through all those layers of cloth, his natural, innate skill was electric, amazing. The way he touched her, as if his hands just sank magically inside her senses, stroking her, changing her. Transforming her.

Jenna pulled him closer, having forgotten completely to be embarrassed about it. He was pulling the stretchy fabric of her bodice down over the low-cut cups of her bra, and she helped him do it, arching her back and holding his head against her chest. His lips felt amazing. Now he was caressing her breasts, circling her nipples through the lace of her bra. Every slow, deliberate caress a delicious lick of flame that sent shivers of anticipation through her body, jacking up the sensations to exquisite madness. She writhed against him, rocking, holding tighter—

And exploded, into pure bliss. Endless pulsing waves of it rushing through her. Sweet, pure, blinding pleasure beyond anything she'd ever felt. Or even imagined.

She came back to herself slowly, feeling so limp and soft, she could barely breathe. She was still pressed to the door, pinned by his body. Her face rested against his big, broad shoulder. Her legs were still wound around his.

She lifted her head. Her face was burning. Good thing his coat was dark, because her eyes were wet, and her mascara was in a highly unstable state.

Drew nuzzled her ear, kissing her throat. Slow, soothing, seductive kisses that promised more, more, more. As much as she could take. For as long as she wanted. His erection still pressed against her, since she was practically astride it. But he wasn't moving or pushing. He was still, waiting for a cue from her.

It took a few panting, shivering minutes to work up the courage to look into his eyes, as reality began to grip her mind again. The hard truth behind this craziness.

This could not happen. Being dumped by Rupert had already left her heart bruised. This was just a game Drew was playing. There was no way it could end up someplace real. She couldn't do this to herself.

She just…didn't…dare.

"Wow," she whispered, licking her trembling lips. "Where did that come from?"

"Let's find out." His voice was a velvety rasp, stroking all her secret senses. "Let's explore it. See how far it goes. How deep. Just say the word."

Before she could stop herself, her mind began to whirl with images of Drew Maddox, naked in her bed. She'd imagined him there often enough. He'd starred in her sexual fantasies ever since she first laid eyes on him.

But Drew always kept it superlight when it came to sex. He was famous for it, while she herself had never been very good at not caring too much when things got intimate. She certainly wouldn't be able to pull it off with a guy she'd had a massive, blazing crush on for over a decade.

Jenna knew how this would go. He'd amuse himself with her, and he'd be great in bed. It would be mind-blowing. Delicious. He would rock her world. Best sex ever.

Then boom, she'd fall for him like a ton of broken rock. He'd be embarrassed by her intensity and pull back fast. She'd be humiliated and hurt, hating herself for being so stupid when she knew the outcome from the start. Why even begin that sad story?

No. She was not going to hurt herself like that. No matter how tempting he was.

She steeled herself. "I think, um…that we've had a miscommunication," she said carefully. "I'm really sorry, but when I agreed to this, I never meant to put sex on the table as part of the bargain. That's just not who I am."

Tension gripped him. He shifted back, and she slid down his legs as he set her gently on her feet. "I never dreamed that you were," he said.

Jenna fumbled with the neckline of her dress, trying to get it up over the cups of her bra. "I'm sorry if I sent mixed messages. Made things more complicated."

"Complicated why? Because I made you come? Don't worry about it. You're so beautiful. It was incredible to watch. I'll dream about it all night long."

"Oh, stop that," she said sharply.

He looked startled. "Stop what?"

"The smooth lover-boy routine that makes all the ladies melt." She backed away from him. "I don't want to join the Drew Maddox fan club. I'd get lost in the crowd."

His face didn't change expression, but she saw startled hurt in his eyes.

"I apologize," he said. "I misread your cues. I'll get out of your way now."

The look on his face made her feel terrible. His only crime was in kissing and caressing her into a fabulous orgasm, and here she was, punishing him for it.

"Damn it, Drew," she said miserably. "I'm sorry. I didn't mean—"

"Excuse me." Drew nudged her to the side. "Scoot over, please. I need to get through the door."

He pulled it open. Jenna followed him out onto the porch. "Look, what I said was unfair," she called after him. "I wish I hadn't said it."

Drew lifted his hand without turning. "Don't sweat it. I appreciate that you're honest. Good night, Jenna."

She watched from the top of the stairs as he got into his car. The lights flicked on, the engine purred to life, and she dug her fingernails into the wooden porch railing, resisting the urge to run down the stairs after him, waving her arms.

Come back. Give me some more of that. I didn't mean it. I'm sorry. Forgive me.

She clamped down on the impulse. Her track record with men so far was spotty, Rupert being her latest disaster. She'd let him use her to further his own career and found herself ignominiously dumped, three months before their planned wedding date.

Odd how it had felt like such a huge disaster at the time, but at the moment, she could hardly remember now how she'd felt about it. All the hurt, mortification and embarrassment had been completely eclipsed by what she was feeling right now. After just a few kisses.

It hurt so badly, to shut Drew out. Like she'd just killed something beautiful and magical, full of unknown, shining possibilities.

But she had to do it. Because it was a trap, damn it. A pretty illusion. She had to be realistic. Drew Maddox would fulfill all her wildest dreams while he was giving her his undivided attention...until suddenly, when she least expected it, and for whatever reason, he no longer did.

At which point, she'd fall right off the edge of the world.

The night was so damn long when he couldn't sleep, which was often. He'd suffered from stress flashbacks for years after his deployment. Even now his sleep was often troubled and fractured by nightmares.

Drew came to a decision in the interminable darkness, as he stared at his bedroom ceiling. It sucked, to be awake in the darkest, deepest part of the night. Stiff as a board, mind racing with every shortcoming, every screwup, every wrong move he'd ever made.

This mess being the latest, and greatest, of many. He'd been insane to let Ava drag him into this. But if he was honest with himself, he had to admit that he'd done it because he was intrigued by Jenna herself. He'd wanted to get closer.

Now her words kept echoing in his head. *Stop the smooth lover-boy routine. I don't want to join the Drew Maddox fan club. I'd get lost in the crowd.*

Lost in the goddamn *crowd*? Seriously?

Man slut. Playboy. User. That was his rep now? Would that be his legacy?

Not all of it was deserved. Only a tiny percentage. He'd had a few talkative, angry drama-queen ex-lovers. After Bonita, he'd attracted the attention of the tabloid press, and this was the result. His current nightmare, Sobel's party being the crowning disaster.

The thought of that night made his gut clench. He was a decorated Marine, and a hundred-and-ten-pound showgirl with glitter on her eyelashes had taken him down with a drugged perfume bottle. It made him sick.

The best trick to beat that nausea was to think about

Jenna. Her softness, her scent, her incendiary kisses, her gorgeous eyes. But that was a pitfall now.

He shouldn't have come on to her but something huge and ruthless had reached inside and grabbed hold of him. Made him do and say things that were head-up-ass stupid.

Screw this. He couldn't go through with it, knowing what Jenna really thought of him. Let the Maddox Hill Board of Directors fire him, if that was what they needed to do. He'd survive. He wouldn't get to helm the Beyond Earth projects, or any of the other large-scale eco-building projects he'd been working toward, but too damn bad. Life wasn't fair.

With his reputation, he'd always find work. He could go someplace far away. New York, Toronto, London, Singapore, South Africa. Sydney, maybe. He'd start fresh. Try the whole damn thing again. From the top.

When the sky had lightened to a sullen charcoal gray, he gave up even trying to sleep. He took a long shower and made coffee, pondering how to inform his sister that her crazy reality show had run its course. The board could vote as they pleased. Uncle Malcolm could rant and rave. Harold could gloat and rub his hands together. Drew would be on a plane, jetting away from it all.

He could open his own company. Maybe get Vann and Zack to come with him. He'd served with them in Iraq, and then convinced them to come to Maddox Hill with him. Vann was chief financial officer, the youngest the firm had ever had, and Zack was chief security officer. Both were excellent at their jobs.

Come to think of it, maybe he should leave his friends' perfectly successful professional careers alone and not appeal to their loyalty and drag them along with him just because he wanted company in exile. *Grow the hell up, Maddox.*

The world had been trying to tell him that for a while. It was time to listen.

Ava would be furious, but Jenna would probably be relieved, after last night's cringe-worthy leave-taking. This whole thing could so easily become a huge embarrassment for her. She had to regret agreeing to it in the first place.

He showered and shaved, and had just enough time to draft a letter of resignation and put it into his briefcase before he got on the road. Traffic was no worse than usual, and he'd left plenty of time to get there. He got lucky with a parking spot, too, so he was right on schedule when he walked into the Ruby Café.

Ava and her crew were there already, occupying two tables in the back. Ava spotted him and jumped up. She was in work mode, in black jeans and a long, tight-fitting red sweater, black combat boots and red lipstick. Her hair was twisted up into a messy bun. She lifted her tablet and waved it at him triumphantly, and his heart sank.

"Good morning, big brother," she sang out. "You hit the jackpot!"

God, no. His jaw clenched until it cramped. "What's the damage?"

"Who said anything about damage? I'm talking priceless free viral publicity! Get that mopey-ass look off your handsome face and sit down. I'll grab you some coffee while you admire my handiwork."

Drew sank down into the chair and glanced at the headlines on the screen. The pictures jolted him. All different angles of the passionate lip-lock with Jenna after escaping from the lobby of the Maddox Hill building. He was looming over her, clutching her like a conquering hero while she arched back in sweet surrender.

Whoa. Hot.

The headlines made him flinch. "Lust-Crazed Architect

Romances Sexy Scientist" was one. Then, "Bad Boy of Architecture Locks Lips with Brainiac Beauty of Biomed." And another gem: "Already? Billionaire Starchitect Frolics with Brand-New Plaything."

Ouch. They'd surpassed themselves this time.

Drew shoved the papers away, dismayed. So Jenna wasn't getting out of this unscathed. At best, she'd look foolish and gullible, and at worst...

Never mind. He'd worry about the worst when it crawled down his throat.

Ava set down a fragrant, steaming mug of coffee in front of him and perched on the table next to him. "So?" she said, eyes expectant.

"So what?" he said sourly. "So Jenna's reputation is rolling downhill right after mine, and picking up speed. You want me to celebrate that?"

Ava rolled her eyes. "You're missing the point. Bev is completely taken with Jenna. Hendrick won't do anything to displease her. The board doesn't meet for another week. If we scramble, that's more than enough time to distract, deflect and dazzle, because Jenna is dazzling, right? Is she not the best?"

"Ava," he began grimly, "I've been thinking about this all night, and I've decided that—"

"Wait! Hold that thought. There she is, the Brainiac Beauty of Biomed herself!" Ava bounced up and was gone.

Drew turned, bracing himself.

Ava had her arms wrapped tightly around Jenna's neck, and was jumping excitedly up and down, which made Jenna's corona of bouncing red-gold ringlets toss and flop. When Jenna finally detached herself, smiling, her hazel eyes flicked over to his.

The buzz of that eye contact brought every detail of yesterday's encounter back to his mind. He could smell her scent, feel her softness. Taste the sweet flavors of her lips, her mouth. The way her hair felt wound around his fingers. The way pleasure made her shudder and gasp and move.

His face got hot. His lower body stirred.

He hung back, not wanting to get in her face if she felt self-conscious about last night, but there was no need. Jenna hung up her coat, ignoring him. She was dressed in a black wool sweater that hugged her curves, and a pencil skirt. A narrow gold belt accented her trim waist. Black tights. Lace-up boots with pointy toes, perfect for kicking a light-weight playboy's ass right into an alternate dimension. Her hair was free, a mane of bouncing curls. No twisting or braiding or bunning today.

"Good morning," he ventured cautiously.

Her eyes flicked to his briefly. "Morning." Her voice was offhand. Remote.

"Sit, sit," Ava urged. "Look at these!" She snatched the tablet away from Drew and presented it to Jenna. "Behold, the magic is happening. Check it out! Superhot, huh? You guys really rocked the method acting. So real! Rawr!"

"Oh, my God." Jenna scrolled through the articles, pausing on each of the pictures. "Wow," she whispered. "That's…really something."

"I know, right?" Ava crowed. "You brainiac beauty, you! Rupert's going to choke on his bran flakes. And only Kay-leigh will be there to perform the Heimlich maneuver on him. The poor guy's done for."

Jenna snorted. "I doubt that Rupert follows these particular news channels."

"Oh, you better believe he has his system set to ping if your name is mentioned, that jealous little user. He's always been jealous that you're a better engineer than he is. He couldn't marry you, Jenn, because he wants to *be* you."

Jenna scanned one of the articles, a frown of concentration between her eyes. "Wow. I've never been described as a plaything before. It's like getting written up on a toilet stall in the guys' bathroom. For a good time, call so-and-so. It's a twisted compliment of sorts, but what do you do with it?"

"Enjoy it," Ava suggested. "Accept it. You might as well. What's the alternative?"

"But how do playthings even dress? Higher heels? Shorter skirts? Longer nails, brighter lipstick? Should I giggle and squeal?"

Ava snorted. "Like Kayleigh, you mean?"

"Who's Kayleigh?" Drew asked.

Jenna's mouth tightened. "My ex's twenty-three-year-old intern," she said. "Now his wife. Currently on a romantic honeymoon on a beach in Bali. I wish them well."

"They deserve each other," Ava said. "Rupert is a big butt-itch, and Kayleigh is a classic plaything. Big empty eyes with nothing behind them. Big oversized boobs."

"Hmm," Jenna said. "So I should stuff my bra? And the glasses have got to go."

"No," Drew blurted out.

Ava and Jenna looked around, startled. "Excuse me?" Jenna said.

"Don't stuff your bra," he said. "You're perfect. And I love the glasses."

Damn. Babbling like an idiot. He had no business weighing in on this. He had a goddamn letter of resignation in his briefcase. "Which brings me to what I wanted to tell the two of you," he said swiftly. "I spent some time last night thinking it over. And I've decided that this whole thing was a big mistake."

Jenna's eyes narrowed behind her glasses. "Oh, really? Why is that?"

Her cool, dispassionate tone confused him. "We don't have time for this crap," he told her. "You, especially. You're doing real work, Jenna. Important work. You've got no business playacting for the paparazzi."

Ava crossed her arms over her chest. "Bite your tongue," she said. "It's working, Drew. It's effortless. I'm pulling all the strings and they're doing all the work. Please remember that it's not all about you. This raises the profile of Arm's Reach, too."

"But is this really the way you want Arm's Reach's profile to be raised?" he asked.

Ava shrugged. "Who cares? You know the old saying 'there is no such thing as bad publicity,' right?"

"Big oversimplification, Av. And you know it, or we wouldn't have this scandal problem to begin with," Drew said. He looked at Jenna. "You're no plaything. Don't bother pretending to be one."

Jenna's eyebrows climbed. "So you're chickening out on me?"

Drew was startled. "Chickening out? What the hell? You mean you actually *want* to continue this farce?"

Jenna shrugged. "Right now, I'm just a sexy plaything to the tabloids. But if you bail on me, I'll be a failed plaything. A loser plaything. One who sucked so badly at playing, she couldn't even keep the bad boy of architecture entertained for one single night. I can see the headlines already. 'Dumped by the Starchitect.' 'Sorry, Geek-Girl, One and Done.' I'll be an object of pity and scorn."

"Jenna—"

"Bev Hill will be too embarrassed by my pathetically bad judgment that she won't even want to look me in the eye, so to hell with any partnership possibilities from the Bricker Foundation," Jenna said. "Of course that won't stop my crusade, but it's still embarrassing." She crossed her arms over her chest. Chin up, staring him down.

Turning him on.

"I just thought, after what you said last night, that you'd be glad to be done with this," he said carefully.

"What?" Ava's gaze sharpened, flicking back and forth between them. "What happened last night?"

"None of your business, Av," he said. "Private conversation."

Ava's eyes widened. "Excuse me? Private conversation? About what? Clue me in, guys. Oh, wait. Am I being a bossy, condescending hag again?"

"Yes, you are, since you asked," Jenna said. "Leave him alone, Ava."

His sister started to laugh. "Oh, man. Again. It's just so cute. I'm dying."

"What's so cute?" Jenna sounded annoyed.

"You two," Ava said. "When you close ranks against me. It's just precious."

His sister kept on talking, but her voice faded into background babble. All he saw was the spark in Jenna's eyes. The jut of her chin, her upright posture. Her tilted eyebrow, silently asking him if he could rise to the challenge.

Oh, hell yeah. He'd already risen, in her honor. In every sense. He let his gaze rove appreciatively over her body. The color deepened in her cheeks, and her gaze slid away.

Good. She was aware of him as a man, no matter how low her opinion of him as a person might be. That was something.

"I give in. I can't bear to see you billed as a failed plaything," he said, leaning over and grabbing one of the breakfast sandwiches. "Let's do this thing."

Jenna pawed through the sandwiches and selected one herself, shooting him a quick, sidelong smile as he took his first bite. Mmm, smoked ham, poached eggs, melted Gruyere cheese on an English muffin. Lots of pepper. The cheese was still hot and gooey.

He suddenly felt like he could eat five of them.

Seven

"I don't understand why I have to wear makeup at all." Michael Wu flinched away from Suzan the makeup artist's bronzer brush. "It tickles, and it smells funny."

"The lights will wash you out, Michael," Jenna explained patiently, for the umpteenth time. "You'll look like a ghost."

"So lemme be a ghost, then. I'm fine with that," Michael shot back, rebellious.

Ava swept in to the rescue, perching on the chair next to him and giving him a coaxing smile. "Come on, Michael," she wheedled. "This video's going to be seen by a lot of people. You've got to look good."

Yay, Ava. Jenna left her to it. Thirteen-year-old Michael had a huge crush on her glamorous friend. It came in handy at times like these.

She glanced back when she heard Michael laughing. He was already getting his cheeks bronzed by Suzan, talking animatedly to Ava. Damn, she loved that kid.

Today, she had her three most experimental cases on display, all of whom had benefited from the expensive preparatory surgeries that had been funded by the AI and Robotics International Award. Michael had lost both arms to meningitis septicemia, one above the elbow and one below, but with the sensory reinnervation surgery, which had rerouted the nerves that had originally run down to his fingers onto the skin above his stumps, Michael now had nervous impulses running both ways. He could command the prostheses at will, and get actual sensory feedback from the sensors. Pressure, texture, grip force, heat and cold. With ferocious practice, he'd achieved remarkable motor control.

Roddy Hepner and Cherise Kurtz were the other two featured in Ava's video. Roddy was a Marine who had lost an arm in an IED blast in Afghanistan. Right now, he was seated on one of the couches by the wall talking with Drew, having already submitted, if reluctantly, to Suzan's bronzing and shading.

Drew was speaking as she approached. "...in Fallujah. First Infantry Battalion. I was the squad leader of an M252 mortar platoon."

Roddy nodded sagely. "You got wounded during Operation Phantom Fury, then?"

"No, that happened later, in Ramadi. I took a couple bullets to the back. One of them fractured my L-5 vertebra and lodged in the spinal canal, so I spent the next few months at Walter Reed. I'm lucky I can walk." Drew paused. "And that I'm alive."

"Me, too. I started out in Landstuhl and then got shipped to San Antonio." Roddy noticed her, and a huge smile split his bushy dark beard. "Hey, Prof! They tell me you're engaged to this dude. Who knew? You're breaking my heart!"

"Sorry about your heart," Jenna told him. "Word travels fast."

"Well, if it can't be me, at least you picked a Marine," Roddy said philosophically. "Way better than that last guy you had. That dude had no discernible balls at all."

She laughed at him. "Did you tell Drew about your music?"

"Yeah, I was telling him how the team here worked out some extra attachments for my arm for the drumsticks, and we're working on more bounce and flex for drumming. I've been practicing like a maniac. My roommates wanna kill me, but I can do crazy polyrhythms now that two-handed drummers can't even dream of doing." His grin flashed again. "First, the Seattle music scene. Then, world domination."

"Roddy writes his own music," Jenna told Drew. "He gave me a demo with some of his original songs, and they're gorgeous."

Roddy's smile faded a notch. "Yeah, well. That demo was recorded back when I could still play bass, guitar and keyboards. I laid down all those tracks myself. But I can still write songs, and sing 'em, even if I can't play the chords. Say, Prof, if you invite me to your wedding, I'll play your favorite song for your first dance. What's the one you liked so much? It was 'Thirsting for You,' right?"

There was a brief, embarrassed silence, during which Jenna couldn't look at Drew.

Roddy chuckled and waved his prosthetic arm at her. "Aw, don't sweat it. Cherise said your guy is, like, a rich famous architect, so it'll probably be a string-quartet-playing-Mozart kind of wedding, right? That's cool. I don't judge you. And I dig Mozart."

By now, Jenna had reordered her wits. "No, Roddy, not at all. There is nothing I would rather have for my first dance than you performing 'Thirsting for You,'" she said, with absolute sincerity. "We're on, buddy. Whenever and wherever it happens."

"Aw, shucks." Roddy grinned, but his gaze flicked speculatively from her to Drew and back again. "Maybe you should play my demo for your guy first," he advised. "He might not groove to my gritty country-rock vibe. It's all good, either way, got it?"

"I like gritty country rock," Drew told them. "I'd love to hear your stuff."

"Awesome, then. Jenna has the audio files," Roddy told him. "She can set you up."

"Great," Drew said. "I'd like to hear you. Do you play anywhere around town?"

Roddy's face fell. "Not yet," he admitted. "Haven't had much luck getting gigs since I came back without my arm. I did better when I could play four different instruments. Now I just got drums and vocals. And with only one arm, well… It's hard. Club owners, well. They don't look past that. I can't catch a break. Not yet."

"Tell me about it, man."

They all turned to see Cherise Kurtz, the third star in Ava's video series. Her makeup was gloriously done, as she was the only one to give Suzan full rein. In the last video, her hair had been teal green. This time, it was shaved tight on the sides with a long forelock dangling over her eye that shaded from pink to a deep purple.

"Love the hair," Roddy said admiringly. "You're the baddest babe, Cher."

"You know it, big guy." They fist-bumped carefully, their prostheses making a clickety sound. Twenty-five-year-old Cherise, an aspiring commercial artist and graphic designer, had lost her right arm to bone cancer. Her goal was to be able to draw again.

Cherise seized Jenna in a tight hug, patting her back with the prosthetic arm. "Hey, Professor! Ava was telling me you're engaged again! Last I heard, you'd just unloaded that useless tool Rupert. Screw that guy. Onward and upward."

"Absolutely. This is, uh, pretty new," Jenna said, flustered. "Cherise, meet Drew."

Cherise gave Drew a long, lingering once-over, and looked back at Jenna, owl-eyed. "You go, girl," she said in hushed tones. "This one is *fine*."

"Don't overdo it, Cherise," Jenna murmured. "It'll go to his head."

"I'll try to contain myself. Ava said to tell you we can get started. I go first today, boys. Before I start sweating under the lights and my mascara starts to run."

They got underway in front of the cameras. Jenna started by filming the process of fitting the sensor map sleeve over Cherise's stump. Then they attached the muscle-reading ring, and fitted the prosthesis directly onto the titanium plug emerging from her stump that she had gotten in the osseointegration surgery. It allowed the prosthesis to attach directly to the bone without stressing her skin. Twist, *click*, and it was in place.

"Flex, and clench," Jenna directed.

Cherise did so smoothly.

"Thumb to every fingertip," Jenna directed.

Cherise did so: *tap, tap, tap, tap*. Then back again, swiftly and smoothly.

"Excellent," Jenna said, delighted. "Your control improves every time."

"You better believe it," Cherise said fervently. "I practice sixteen hours every damn day with this thing. I want my life back."

"What is it that you want to do?" Drew asked.

"I'd just applied to a bunch of graphic design schools last year when I got diagnosed," Cherise told him. "I got distracted. But I'm not giving up. Let me show you this latest thing I've been working on."

They moved closer, along with the cameramen, as Cherise hoisted up a big folder. She laid it on the table, struggling for a few seconds to open it with her prosthetic fingers.

When she finally got it open, she showed them a series of bold-colored drawings of prosthetic arms like her own, with various decorations superimposed on them.

"I have a bunch of ideas," she said, leafing through them. "These are just a few. This is Fairy Kingdom. This is Thunder Dragon. Then there's Skull Snake, Sith Lord, Starsong, Elven Realm, and this is my favorite, Goblin King. You put these on with a light adhesive so they can be switched out easily whenever you need a different look."

"Those are amazing, Cherise," Jenna said. "What a great idea."

"You drew these with your prosthetic hand?" Drew asked.

"Yes. I'm slow, but it's getting better, bit by bit. I'm training my left hand, too." Cherise looked at Jenna. "I want to propose a series of decorations for the prosthesis for your brochure and your online catalog. Amputees need to make fashion statements, too."

"Great idea," Jenna said. "We'll discuss it."

"I also really need for you guys to put some sort of base to apply decorative fingernails to the prosthesis," Cherise said. "A girl needs her fingernails."

"We're on it," Jenna promised.

"Was this project in your design school application portfolio?" Drew asked.

"No, I applied before I started these," she replied. "I've already got a bunch of rejection letters in my collection. You gotta hang on to those, you know? Every good success story has a big fat wad of rejection letters in it."

"A project like this would attract their attention," Drew said. "I bet they don't see this level of dedication and commitment every day."

"Aw." Cherise beamed at him. "Thanks, handsome. You made my day." She looked over at Jenna and mimed fanning herself vigorously. *Lucky girl,* she mouthed.

Jenna felt a clutch in her throat. It felt just as wrong to fake an engagement with Drew in front of Cherise and Roddy as it had in front of Bev. It felt disrespectful to misrepresent something that important to people whom she loved and respected.

But she'd recommitted to this strange charade herself, in the café this morning. And she'd deliberately goaded Drew into recommitting to it, too. All because being the failed plaything had stung her pride. Wow. Talk about shallow. Nothing to do now but grit her teeth and tough it out.

Eight

Drew watched Roddy's segment with intense interest, amazed at the dexterity the other man had developed with the drumsticks.

He was impressed. Not just by the accomplishments of Jenna and her team, but also by his sister. He'd known in a general way what she did for a living, but he'd never seen her actively doing it. Ava had the air of a seasoned professional who knew what she wanted and how to get it, and she was effortlessly authoritative. Her crew snapped to it because they wanted to please her.

He could never let her know this, however. His bratty and annoying little sister was already insufferable and nearly impossible to manage. No need to fan the flames.

He got out of their way while they were setting up for the next segment. At the far end of the crowded, busy room, a skinny adolescent boy with two prosthetic arms sat on one of the couches. His black hair was buzzed off, and he was wearing an oversize *Angel Ascending* T-shirt. Two women flanked him on either side who had to be his mother and grandmother. The women looked like older and younger versions of each other, both short and slight and with long hair pulled back, the mom's into a braid, the grandma's into a bun. The mom's hair was black, the grandma's snow white.

Drew nodded politely at them as he addressed the kid. "You're Michael, right?" He gestured at the T-shirt. "You like *Angel Ascending*?"

The boy's eyes lit up. "Yeah. Cool game."

"Did you see the movie?"

"It was awesome," he said. "Lars Feehan is the bomb."

They were discussing the game they both played, though Michael had made it several levels beyond Drew, despite his prosthetic arms. Jenna appeared beside them and waited, smiling at Michael's enthusiasm.

"You gotta watch the YouTube gamer videos for clues if you want to make progress," Michael instructed him. "That was how I learned about the ancient scroll and the dimensional portal. Oh, hey, Jenna."

"Hey, Michael." She gave Michael's mother and grandmother a smile. "Hi, Joyce. Hello, Mrs. Wu. Michael, how are the flexibility adjustments working out for you? Is the writing and typing going better?"

"Not enough of the writing and typing is going at all, in my opinion." Joyce cast a stern eye at her son. "All he practices is gaming."

Michael rolled his eyes. "Not true, Mom. It's going fine. So far so good."

"Let's go take a look," Jenna said, beckoning.

Drew followed them all back to the spotlighted zone where the cameramen were waiting, hanging back to stay out of the way, but watching in fascination as Jenna and her team did the sequence of preparations on Michael's stumps; adjusting the sensor map sleeve and then snapping on the arms, which were black and chrome-colored.

"Those arms are badass," Drew commented.

Michael shot him a grin. "Yeah. I'm, like, the Terminator."

"Okay, Michael," Jenna said. "Flex…clench…thumb to

each fingertip...very good. I can see you've been working hard. Let's test the sensory pads. Close your eyes."

Michael squeezed his eyes shut. "Ready."

Jenna touched his prosthetic hands lightly in a random pattern with her fingertip, and Michael announced each touch. "Right forefinger. Left pinky. Left wrist. Right heel of the hand. Right middle finger. Left ring finger. Right ring finger. Right wrist. Left heel."

"Excellent," Jenna said. "So much better than the last time, which was already impressive."

"Come try the gaming console," Jenna said. "We got it all set up for you."

Michael settled himself in the chair in front of the monitor, the cameramen shifting unobtrusively into place around him, and woke the screen with a stroke on a touchpad with his prosthetic finger and logged into his account. He grinned over his shoulder at his mother. "I can feel the pad now, Mom! I can tell that it's kinda sticky and soft."

"That's great, baby," Joyce told him.

"I'm going to try to make it through a new portal this time," Michael said to Drew as he picked up the console. "I saved this moment for your video. 'Cause it's, like, dramatic."

"Very generous of you," Ava said.

Michael shot her a mischievous grin over his shoulder as he positioned his mechanical fingers carefully over the buttons. "I know," he said. "Here goes. Wish me luck."

They waited through the logo and opening scenes of *Angel Ascending*. Then Michael's avatar appeared and began to run, bounding like a gazelle across the landscape pictured on the screen, right toward a cliff.

"Okay, here we go," Michael said under his breath. "Full power...and *jump*."

The avatar leaped. Enormous wings unfolded, glinting

silver and billowing like a sail, filling with wind currents. The game had begun.

After several minutes of intense play, Michael deftly steered his avatar through the magical membrane of the portals into a blaze of golden light, whooping with joy. "*Yes!* I made it! I'm in level thirteen, and I got dragon wings now! I am killing it! Did you see me, Mom?"

Joyce Wu burst into tears and covered her face with her hands.

Michael turned around, alarmed. "Mom? What's wrong?"

"Sorry, honey," Joyce said, her voice strangled. "I'm just... I haven't seen you look that happy in a long time."

"Aw, Mom. Don't." Michael launched himself at his mother. He wrapped his prosthetic arms around her, patting her carefully. One of the hands landed on her long braid. He closed his mechanical fingers around it and tugged on it gently.

"I can feel your hair, Mom," he said, in a wondering voice.

That just made her cry harder. Drew had a lump in his own throat. Then he felt something soft bump into him from the side. Thin, wiry arms wound around him.

It was the elderly Mrs. Wu, also weeping. She, too, needed to hug someone, and he was the closest person. Whatever. He wrapped his arms around the old lady, because what else could he do? Over her white hair, he caught Ava's smile as she gestured silently for one of her cameramen to capture the moment.

Then he saw Jenna's face, and promptly forgot everything and everyone else.

She was beaming at him. Her eyes were wet. She took off her glasses, dabbed below her eyes and then sniffed into a tissue.

What a beautiful, radiant smile. It gave him an amazing rush. He could get used to this.

He wanted to chase down smiles like that every day. Endlessly. He could dedicate himself to that project and never get tired of it.

Mrs. Wu didn't let go, but nothing could embarrass him when he was flying so high from Jenna's smile. He embraced the elder Mrs. Wu as carefully as if he were holding a baby bird, and just breathed it all in. Letting himself feel it.

He hadn't felt this good in…well, damn. Maybe never.

Mrs. Wu finally let go of him with a motherly pat on his back. He caught Michael's eyes, which were also suspiciously wet. "You play *Angel Ascending* in online mode, right?" Drew asked, on impulse.

"Yeah, sure," Michael said. "As much as Mom will let me."

"I know I'd have to up my game to play with you, but let's hook up online. I usually play after midnight when I can't sleep, but I could move it up a couple hours."

"More like four hours," Joyce announced. "He has to be in bed by ten thirty."

"Mom!" Michael shot her a mortified look. "As if!"

"Done by ten thirty, always," Drew agreed. "Hey, I play with Lars Feehan sometimes. He's a night owl, too, like me."

Michael's eyes went huge. "No way! Lars Feehan the actor? Who starred in the *Angel Ascending* movie? He games? For real?"

"For real," Drew said. "Whenever he can. He's good, too. Last I checked, he'd just cracked level eight, but that was a while ago. He might have moved up since then."

Jenna's eyes were wide with startled wonder. "You know Lars Feehan?"

"Yeah. I designed his producer's beach house a few years

ago. Maybe we could all three hook up online and play sometime."

"Lars...freaking... Feehan!" Michael repeated, his eyes still dazzled. "The gold angel! That guy is so cool!"

"Yeah, and if you hook him up with Lars, we get to film it, okay?" Ava said pointedly. "The guy has thirty million Twitter followers."

"I'm sure he'll be up for that," Drew said. "He's a great guy."

"You play video games with Lars Feehan?" Jenna said. "The Hollywood A-list hottie and the bad boy of architecture, two of the busiest guys in their respective professions, have time to play video games together in the middle of the night?"

He sure did. It helped during those long and sleepless nights when nightmares and stress flashbacks kicked his ass. But that was nobody's business.

"Video games relax me," he said, defensively. "They're a great de-stressor."

"Dude. Don't even try to make her understand." Michael's voice sounded world-weary. "If she doesn't game herself, she just won't get it. They all just say, 'Oh, you're rotting your brain,' or 'Oh, you're wasting precious time that you'll never, ever get back,' blah-blah-blah."

"True," one of the cameramen agreed wryly. "That's what my wife says."

"Well, people. Be that as it may." Ava clapped her hands. "I think we have what we need for the day. Thanks, everyone. You were beyond fabulous. Until next time."

Then came a big round of emotional hugs, from which Drew was by no means exempt. "I'll look for you online," he told Michael.

"Look for CyborgStrong8878." The teenager gave him a tight, shaking hug and then hurried out with his mom and grandma on either side, chattering excitedly.

Drew figured that he was technically free to go himself, after the Wu family, Cherise and Roddy had all left, but still he lingered watching Ava's crew pack up. He wasn't ready for the whole experience to be over, and Jenna had disappeared from the room a few minutes ago. He didn't want to leave until he said goodbye to her, and maybe got another one of those gorgeous smiles as a farewell gift.

Then Jenna and Ava reappeared. Ava was on her cell phone, and she spotted him and waved him over, still talking as he approached.

"You diabolical schemer, you. A man after my own heart. I'll let them know." She pocketed her phone. "Okay, my lovelies. Time to get back to my workshop and start postproduction. That was Ernest, and he wants you to know that A, he called in some favors to get you two a reservation at Piepoli's for eight, and B, news of this dinner reservation has been discreetly leaked to our favorite paparazzi. A few of them should bite."

"Paparazzi? I don't feel camera ready right now." Jenna looked doubtful.

"Nonsense," Ava said briskly. "You've been thoroughly worked over by Suzan, the makeup goddess, and you look beautiful. Let's keep up the pressure, people."

"Too much pressure," Drew said. "It's been a long day, Av. Let her rest."

"You still have to eat, right?" his sister pointed out. "So multitask."

Drew looked at Jenna. "No pressure," he told her. "At least not from me. I could take you straight home, or to some other restaurant where you could relax in peace and privacy. Your call. No one else's."

Ava sighed sharply. "Don't be difficult, Drew. I'm going to a lot of trouble here."

He kept his eyes on Jenna. "Don't push her around."

His sister snorted. "You know you're just egging me on when you defend her, right?"

"I'm ignoring you," he said calmly. "And Jenna decides on her own dinner plans."

Jenna gave him one of those smiles that blew his mind. "I've heard great things about the lobster ravioli at Piepoli's," she said. "I'm up for some of that."

"Yes!" Ava clapped her friend on the back. "That's the spirit! All you need to do is pretend to enjoy each other's company while eating a fabulous meal. No sweat."

Jenna shrugged, her gaze darting away from his. "I'm, ah, sure we'll manage."

Drew looked at the color blooming on Jenna's cheeks, longing to touch it. Feel the soft heat. She'd made her boundaries plain, but he still wanted more of her attention.

As much of it as he could get.

Nine

Jenna felt like she was floating as she followed the waiter through the bustling restaurant. She'd lived in this town five years and she'd never yet managed to get a table at Piepoli's. But around Drew, all kinds of impossible things became possible.

Effortless, even. He knew Lars Feehan? Seriously?

The day's emotional intensity had left Jenna feeling dangerously unshielded, but for some reason, she'd still jumped on the chance to have dinner with Drew. She didn't care if his sister had maneuvered him into it, or if he was doing it for his own selfish ends. Who cared? Tonight, she just wanted to sit across a candlelit table from Drew Maddox and drink him in. This was her chance to look her fill. Listen to his beautiful, resonant voice.

He'd been so sweet with Michael. She was beyond charmed. She'd melted into sniffling, laughing-through-her-tears goo.

And it was a bad time to lower her guard. She was putting herself in temptation's way. Throwing fuel on the fire. She was a smart woman, and she knew better, but tonight, she just…didn't…care.

The waiter seated them at a table by the window that overlooked the boardwalk outside.

"Don't look now," Drew said. "Our friends are already outside, snapping pictures."

"I guess you must be used to this by now, right?"

"More like indifferent. I barely notice them, unless they're bothering you. Here." He seized her hand. "I'll give them a dose of what they like best."

She gasped and laughed at him as he kissed her knuckles, then turned it over and kissed her palm. Intense awareness of him raced through every part of her body.

"I'm impressed that you can be so relaxed about it." She struggled to keep her voice even.

"There are worse things," he said.

Drew's tone was light, but she knew enough from Ava about what he'd been through in the military to guess what he was thinking. "You mean Iraq?"

He nodded. "I saw things there I won't ever forget. A few times, I thought it was the end of me. Once you've taken enemy fire or had your convoy blown up, people snapping pictures of you no longer registers on your radar as an actual problem."

"Ava told me you'd been wounded," she said. "I overheard you talking to Roddy about it today."

"Yeah. A bullet fractured one of my lumbar vertebrae and lodged next to my spine. That was the end of my time in the Marine Corps. I'm lucky that I can walk, and that I'm alive. I think about that every day."

"I can imagine," Jenna said. "A bullet to the spine? It must have been so painful."

"It was. Three surgeries. Months of recovery. It puts everything else into perspective."

"I bet it does," she murmured.

"I got into video games during my recovery, after I got home," he told her. "My convalescence was long and boring, and it hurt. Video games take your mind off things."

"Did you play that game that Michael showed us during your recovery?"

"Oh, no. *Angel Ascending* is much more recent. Lars sent me that last year after the movie opened, just for laughs. He's a really good guy. I'll introduce you sometime."

She laughed. "Wow, lucky me. Lifestyles of the rich and famous."

"I suppose. We're all the same when it comes to the important stuff. Getting shot in the back teaches you that. No matter how privileged you might be, you're never exempt from pain, or death. Keeps you honest." He paused. "Sorry," he said, self-consciously. "Didn't mean to get all heavy and self-involved on you."

"I don't see it that way at all," she said. "I've worked with veterans."

"I bet you have," he said.

She squeezed his hand, which she was still holding. "You were wonderful with Michael today. Roddy and Cherise, too. Michael was so excited."

"He's a great kid," Drew said. "Entirely apart from how he's overcoming the challenges he faces."

"That he is," she agreed. "I just love him. So funny. He has a great attitude."

"They all impressed me," Drew said reflectively. "The whole damn thing impressed me. Your techniques, your team, your tech, your lab. Even my sister impressed me today. Just don't ever tell her I said so."

Jenna laughed. "I won't. And thanks, that's good to hear. Now I just need to make the techniques affordable for everyone who needs them."

The waiter arrived, and they gave him their order. After the wine had been served, Jenna asked Drew a question she'd wondered about ever since she first met him. "I'm curious about something," she said. "How did you end up joining the Marines? It's not an obvious choice. Being a Maddox and all."

Drew's eyes narrowed thoughtfully as he considered his reply. "Long story."

"We're not in a hurry," she remarked.

He sipped his wine. "I don't know how much Ava told you," he said. "But after my parents were killed in that plane accident, I went sort of wild."

Sort of? Ha. That was a massive understatement.

"Ava did mention that," she murmured.

"That was my way of coping. I was pissed at my folks for dying. I didn't care about consequences. So I got into a lot of trouble. It was lucky I was a juvenile offender, and that I never actually hurt anyone. But Uncle Malcolm was beside himself. You saw how he is. He got in my face, made threats and ultimatums. He got my back up, to the point that I wasn't in the mood to trot off to college like a good boy, study hard and make him proud. I wanted to raise hell. So I joined the Marines. First Division, First Battalion. Ended up in Iraq. I learned some very important things there."

"Such as?"

He was silent for a long moment. "No need to raise hell," he said simply. "I was already there."

Jenna nodded and stayed quiet, waiting for him to go on.

"I saw a lot of bad things," he said slowly. "Things I can't forget. But it's not like it was all a nightmare. I worked hard, grew up, learned a lot. Made good friends in my platoon. Two of them work with me right here at Maddox Hill. Vann's my CFO. He's freakishly good with numbers, and Zack is our CSO. Those guys are solid as a rock. I've trusted them both with my life and they have never let me down. In the end, I'd say it was worth it just to have found them."

"You're fortunate to have friends like that," she said. "So

after you got wounded, you decided to follow the family architecture tradition?"

"I always knew I'd get there eventually," he admitted. "It was destiny. I grew up around architects. My dad was one, and when I was a kid, he always talked like it was a given that I would be, too. Then after I got shot, I had all these long empty hours to think about my future. By the time I recovered and got to architecture school, I was maniacally focused. I made up for all the lost time."

"I bet Uncle Malcolm was relieved," she said.

"He couldn't believe his luck," Drew said. "Back then, anyway. Now he's changed his tune. Decided that I'm more trouble than I'm worth."

Jenna shook her head. "No. This is all just a blip on your screen. It won't hurt you in the long run."

"I hope you're right," he said. "I had some projects in the works that I was really attached to."

"Anything I might have heard of?"

"We haven't landed them yet, but Maddox Hill is in the running for the Beyond Earth project. I thought a lot about Mars when I was in the Al Anbar Province. Lots of time to stare at the rocks and sand and think about the unique problems inherent in building in environments inhospitable to man. It would involve robotics and three-D printing with local building materials. It's a long shot, with lots of competition, but I have my fingers crossed."

"Wow." She was silent for a moment, digesting it. "That's huge."

"Yeah, it is for me. My dad used to read science fiction stories to me to put me to sleep when I was small. We always said we'd build houses on Mars together someday."

That made her throat tighten up. She couldn't reply.

"I'd hate to miss out on that chance," he said. "He would have gotten such a kick out of that. If I ever do manage to pull it off, it'll be in his honor."

Fortunately for her, the lobster ravioli arrived, and food took center stage for a while. The ravioli were tender and plump and fabulous, the wine was excellent, and Drew was great company. By the time dessert and coffee arrived, the elements of the evening had combined into a magical alchemy that made her relaxed and giggly and mellow.

Then Drew glanced outside at the walkway. "Persistent bastards," he murmured. "I was kind of hoping they'd get bored and go home, but there they still are. Hanging in there."

Jenna looked out the window, realizing that she'd completely forgotten about the photographers. Which was to say, she'd forgotten the whole reason they'd come to this restaurant in the first place.

She laughed to cover her embarrassment. "Want me to do something crazy and dramatic to entertain them? I could throw a glass of wine in your face."

He grinned. "It's a little early in our relationship for that."

"I could feed you a bite of my *sporcamuss*," she said, spooning up a bite of the delicious, goopy puff pastry with cream. "That fits the narrative, as Ava would say."

He accepted the bite, and savored it. "Mmm. Wow. Good."

Whew. That smile of sensual promise unraveled something inside her. She felt like she was teetering on the brink of something dangerous and wonderful in equal measures.

Oh, boy. This was bad. She'd been prepared to be dazzled by his looks, impressed by his smarts, wowed by his talent, allured by his seductive charm. Those reactions were all foreseen and adjusted for. She was being smart. Taking care of herself, like a grown-up.

But she hadn't expected to like him this much.

That was a dirty trick.

Ten

No one ever, in the history of dining, had made a cup of espresso last as long as Drew did after they finished their dessert. He didn't want that perfect day to end.

He'd been with a lot of women, in his time, and he'd made it his business to be good at pleasing them, appreciating them, seeing them, knowing them. But apart from the sex, he'd never felt like anyone had ever successfully known him back.

Some women had tried, to their credit. He'd always assumed it was his fault when they failed. A mysterious personality defect on his part. His defenses were too high, he couldn't let anyone inside, yada-yada-yada. Big shame, but what could you do.

But he'd been open to Jenna from the start. Wide open. No choice about it. The intimacy of it stirred him up, made him feel shaky and off balance.

It was strange, how much he liked it.

Drew dealt with the bill, and they went outside and strolled together down to the street. The wind coming off the sound was raw and cold, whipping a hot pink color into her cheeks and tossing her curls wildly.

Then they were holding hands. He didn't remember deciding to do it. It felt as if the natural state of their hands was to be clasped.

She glanced up at him. "Are the photographers still following us?"

"No idea," he said. "Didn't think to look."

"Ah. So you're staying in character just in case?"

That stung, a little. "I suppose," he said. "Didn't really think of it that way."

"Hey, wait," Jenna said. "Drew, wasn't that your car? Back there behind us?"

Drew turned to look. She was right. He'd walked right past it. Lost in space.

He unlocked his black Jag with the key fob and opened the door for her.

Jenna backed away, flustered and smiling and holding her hands up. "Oh, no. That's not necessary. I'll call a car. It'll save you an hour of pointless driving."

"I can't just leave you here," he told her. "Please. Get in. Let me take you home."

She sighed, but got in without further argument, to his immense relief.

Once they were on their way, having his eyes on the road ahead instead of on her made the question he'd been wanting to ask her come out more easily.

"This mission to help amputees get the use of their hands back, it seems like more than a career for you," he commented. "It seems very personal. What's that all about?"

Jenna was quiet for a long moment, so he started looking at her profile, trying to gauge if he'd overstepped some boundary.

"It is personal," she said. "My brother Chris lost an arm to bone cancer, just like Cherise. They amputated his right arm right above the elbow."

"That must have been hard," he said.

"He was only eighteen. I was twelve. He'd just won a big basketball scholarship, right before he was diagnosed. He was a very gifted athlete."

He winced. "Oh, God. That hurts."

"Yeah, it broke everyone's hearts that he had to give up that dream."

"What does he think of your line of work? Does he have one of your magic arms?"

Jenna was silent again. This time for so long that he suddenly guessed, in a flash of total dismay, what she was going to say and cursed himself for being so damn clumsy.

"We lost Chris about a year after that operation," Jenna said. "They didn't catch it in time. They found it in his spine, his liver. He did chemo and all that, but it got him."

He just let that sit for a moment before he said, "I'm so sorry." He wished there was something less trite and shopworn to say, but there never freaking was.

"Thanks," she murmured.

They were silent for a long time, but he finally gathered his courage and gave it another shot. "How about your parents? What's their story?"

She shook her head. "My dad was never in the picture. He left not long after I was born. My mom raised us on her own. But she never quite came back to herself, after losing Chris. She struggled for years. Then she had a heart attack six years ago. So it's just me now." She gave him a brief smile. "Something we have in common. Both orphaned."

He nodded. "That's why you do this work, right? You want to give to all these people what you couldn't give to Chris?"

Jenna gazed down at her hands clasped on her lap. "I suppose," she said. "Hadn't ever thought of it like that. Chris was my North Star, I guess. The whole world needs to be saved, and no one can save it all, since we're not comic book superheroes. But if we all do a little, maybe we have a chance. And this is my bit. Someone else can work on saving the whales and the bees and the ozone and the ocean. I'm doing the arms."

"You make me want to save the world, too," he said. "I feel like such a slacker."

She laughed at him. "Ha! You just keep doing what you're doing. Your buildings are gorgeous. You're helping make sustainable eco-friendly urban planning a reality in cities all over the world. Beautiful things make the whole world better."

He felt both embarrassed and ridiculously pleased. "Thanks."

He parked in front of her apartment and turned off the engine.

Tension gripped them. They were in the danger zone again. Every detail of last night's passionate episode, and its painful aftermath, hung heavy in the air between them.

"I really want to walk upstairs with you and see you safely inside," he said. "But I will not come on to you. I swear it. On my honor."

"That's really not necessary," she murmured.

"What? Walking you upstairs, or swearing sacred vows on my honor?"

"Both. You're being overdramatic. But if it makes you feel better, fine."

He walked her up and stopped when he saw her front door, mindful of his vow.

Jenna drifted reluctantly onward toward her door. "Good night," she said. "Thanks for everything. The ride, dinner. And for making Michael's day. It was so sweet of you."

"Don't thank me," he said. "This was a great day for me. Best day I've had in longer than I can even remember."

I could make it the best night, too.

The unsaid words vibrated between them, because apparently he hadn't learned last night's lesson well enough. The longing to touch her just kept getting stronger.

"It was wonderful for me, too," she admitted.

They gazed at each other. This was his cue, to say something lighthearted. Repeat the good-nights. Turn the hell around. Walk down the damn stairs. Left foot, right foot.

But his voice was locked in his throat. And he made no move to go.

Jenna looked tormented. "Please," she whispered. "Please, Drew. Stop that."

He knew exactly what she meant, but all he could do was play dumb. "I'm not doing or saying anything."

To his dismay, her face crumpled, and she covered it with both her hands, cursing.

He reached out. "Oh, damn. Jenna—"

"No!" She jerked back, out of range, and wiped at her eyes. "No, I'd really better not. Sorry. It's been an emotional day. I'm wrecked."

"I wish I could help," he said.

Jenna looked miserable. "I'm so sorry about what I said last night. The problem is, my reasons for saying it haven't changed." Her voice shook. "I'm extremely attracted to you, as I'm sure you've noticed, and this is hard, and awful. I'm so sorry. But I just…can't."

Ouch. He turned away before she could see the look on his face. "Okay," he said. "I'm gone. I won't put you on the spot like this."

He ran down the stairs. He felt like he'd been punched in the chest as he started up the car.

For God's sake, look at him. So last night's slap-down hadn't been enough punishment for him. He just had to come back for more. He'd practically begged her for it.

Women came on to him all the time. There was an art to steering around them, evading them, letting them down gently. He'd considered himself good at it.

The irony was painful. He'd finally found a woman he wanted to get closer to, and she'd slammed the door on him. She thought he was a train wreck waiting to happen.

It would be almost funny, if it didn't suck so hard.

Eleven

"Stop bugging me, Av," Jenna said testily. "My black-and-white gown will be fine for the presentation dinner. It looks good on me. It was expensive. We do not need to shop for another damn dress. End of story."

Ava picked a hunk of artichoke out of her salad and popped it into her mouth. "Sorry to contradict you, but you are so very wrong."

"Why? Why shell out all this money? My closet is full of nice clothes."

"You're being difficult just to be difficult. That dress is old, and done." Ava rolled her eyes at Drew. "Drew, tell your lovely fiancée that she needs a gorgeous new evening gown for the exhibit dinner at the Whitebriar Club, okay?"

"Of course she needs a new evening gown." Drew's voice was offhand. "And this is a Maddox Hill event, so it's only fair you let me pick up the tab for it. I'll give you my credit card. Knock yourselves out. Send me hot photos from the fitting room."

Jenna tried not to flinch. She stared down at her sea-food salad, which she'd barely touched. Drew had been like that with her all morning. Pleasant. Polite. And completely emotionally absent.

They'd done yet another interview this morning with a podcast whose online audience was growing fast. The latest of many PR events. Too many. Ava's punishing schedule was exhausting her. The idea today had been to grab an early lunch before everyone went back to work, but Drew's friendly, indifferent blandness had killed her appetite.

She just…freaking…hated it. With all of her heart and soul. And she had no one to blame for it but herself.

"I'm putting my foot down," she said through her teeth. "No new dress."

Ava made a frustrated sound.

"Save it, Av." Drew signaled the waiter for the check. "It's not a good time to discuss it. Obviously."

"Oh, whatever." Ava shrugged, her face rebellious. "But hey. Big news." Ava's voice was elaborately casual. "We heard from the producers of *Angel Ascending.*"

Jenna put down her fork, her nerves buzzing with alarm. "You did?"

"Yes. They want to feature Michael in the ad campaign for next year's game."

Jenna sucked in a sharp breath and gazed at Ava's triumphant face, heart thudding hard. "Careful, Av," she said. "I don't want him exploited. He's just a kid."

Ava sighed. "And here I thought you'd be excited at how my hard work is doing marvels for raising your organization's profile to stratospheric heights. Silly me."

"I think you're amazing at what you do, don't ever doubt it," Jenna said. "But you're doing your work too well. And I'm scared for Michael."

"Don't worry," Ava soothed. "Joyce and I will both defend him like a couple of pit bulls. It would be a nice chunk of change for his college fund, right? Stanford, MIT, am I right? This is all good, Jenn. Be excited for him. And for Arm's Reach. This is great for his future, and it's great for you, too. Michael will be fine. He's strong, and smart."

"But I wanted him to get back his normal life," she said.

"Everyday stuff. Not some high-stress, high-visibility situation where people are constantly trying to use him."

"Oh. You mean, like you?" Ava's voice was crisp. "Are you tired of the limelight, Jenn? Do you think we're using you?"

Jenna locked eyes with her friend…and swallowed the sharp reply that Ava did not deserve. She shook her head. "I'm just tired," she said.

"I know, and I'm sorry about that, but buck up. Be strong. Oh, by the way. Speaking of good things. Roddy told me that he has a gig tonight. He's filling in for the Vicious Rumors' drummer down at the Wild Side. All weekend, starting tonight."

"Yes, he texted me about that," Jenna said. "I'm going to try to catch the first set tonight."

"Alone?" Drew's eyes snapped to her. "At the Wild Side? In that part of town?"

"It's fine," she said. "I'm going to the early set. It's a hip, busy neighborhood."

"You can't go down there all alone." He sounded horrified.

"Certainly I can," she told him. "I don't mind going alone, and I'm sure—"

"No way. I'll take you. Want me to get you at the lab, or pick you up at home?"

Jenna just looked at him, bewildered. "Drew. Don't feel like you have to do this. I'm sure you have better things to do with your evening."

"Not really," he said. "I want to see Roddy play."

It was the first time that Drew had looked her straight in the eyes since that disastrous evening last week, and the blazing directness of his gaze was almost jarring.

She let out a careful breath. "Fine," she said. "I'll meet you at the club. I'll be there around nine thirty."

The waiter brought his card back. Drew got up, gave

each of them a businesslike peck on the cheek and left, already focused on whatever came next in his busy day.

Jenna watched him walk away, feeling flat and dull. It had been over a week since that disaster after their dinner date. A stressful, chaotic week jam-packed with activities calculated to jack up Arm's Reach's media profile. She was exhausted, and her work was suffering... But that wasn't the real problem, and she couldn't convince herself that it was.

She'd come to dread seeing Drew. But the problem wasn't because of anything he said. It was what he didn't say. He was unfailingly polite and pleasant. Attentive, thoughtful, gallant. No one could fault him.

He was wearing a perfect-fiancé mask. But now that she'd seen the man beneath, the mask almost offended her. Being kept at arm's length felt like a punishment.

Not that she blamed him. Not in the least. She'd demanded herself that he pull back. And that didn't help worth a damn.

On the contrary, it made things worse.

It had been a long time since Drew had seen the inside of a club, but he paid no attention to the strobing lights, the pounding music or the crush of people. People tried to catch his eye, male and female, and he ignored them, having become a ruthless and single-minded scanning-for-Jenna machine. He roved through the place, sensors tuned to her and only her. Scanning for that mane of bright hair, either floating high in an explosive updo or bouncing in a cloud around her head. Cat-eye glasses. The glint of clear bright hazel eyes. Those high cheekbones. That elegant posture. That perfume.

No way could he hear her sweet-toned, sexy voice in this noise, but his ears still strained for the sound of it.

A different band was playing at the moment, not the

Vicious Rumors. Roddy wasn't onstage yet. The warm-up band was winding up their last big head-banging number. Still no sign of Jenna. He glanced at his phone again. Still no messages from her.

He started another circuit, cruising the place again from the top, room by room.

Yes. A blaze of yellow light had caught her hair, lighting it up like a flame. He fought his way closer. She was wearing a tight, tailored blue coat, a black wool mini-skirt and those ass-kicking boots.

Next to her was a blazing crest of pink and purple. Cherise, talking excitedly. As he approached, Cherise threw her arms around Jenna's neck and hugged her, pounding her with the prosthetic arm. Which was now decorated by long threads of little lights inside flexible plastic tubes wound artistically around it.

Cherise saw him over Jenna's shoulder and waved excitedly, yelling into Jenna's ear. Jenna turned around and caught sight of him.

Bracing himself never worked. He couldn't get used to the rush it gave him to lock eyes with her. The contact seemed to touch him everywhere. Suddenly, he was turned on.

Exactly what she did not want or welcome from him.

"Hey." He greeted them both with a polite nod. From a safe, secure distance.

Cherise was having none of that. She lunged for him and wrapped him in a big hug.

"Drew!" she crowed into his ear. "You are the bomb!"

"I am?" he said, bemused.

"You totally are! You inspired me! I was telling Jenna about my application to the DeLeon Design Institute! They're, like, the hottest program for commercial art, and when I applied last year, they turned me down flat. But I got to thinking about what you said last week, so I applied again, and this time I included my arm decorations in my portfolio. And they called me in for an interview! The director told me that you forwarded the video link from last week's shoot to her!"

Jenna's searching eyes met his. "I had no idea you had these connections," she yelled over the noise.

"Trix DeLeon and I went to high school together," Drew said. "I just sent Trix a link. That's all."

"Aw, don't deny it, buddy. You helped, whether I get in or not. So thanks."

Cherise hugged him again and planted a loud and smacking kiss on his cheek.

"Hey! Drew!" This time it was Roddy who accosted him. He was looking bright-eyed and excited. "I didn't know you and Jenna were coming! Good to see you, man!"

"Yeah, it was a last-minute thing," he said.

"Hey, now's a great time to play that song for you, whaddaya say?"

"What song do you mean?" Drew asked.

"The one for your first dance, at your wedding!" Roddy yelled. "'Thirsting for You,' remember? I got the Rumors to try it out in our rehearsal this afternoon, just in case, and they liked it. I'll make sure it's in the first set!"

"Hey, look at you, Roddy," Cherise called out. "You're using one of my sleeve decorations. Looks supertough. Good choice."

"Yep, I went with Sith Lord tonight. Decided not to use the light strands, though. Didn't want to draw too much attention to the arm. Could look gimmicky."

"Me, I went with Fairy Kingdom today," Cherise said, holding up her own arm.

"Hey, I gotta go. We're about to go on," Roddy said. "Cherise, come on backstage with me and I'll introduce you to Bose, the bass player." He gave them a conspiratorial grin. "She has a crush on him," he added, in a stage whisper that was more like a shout.

"Nah, I'm just a big fan," Cherise protested. "Later, guys!"

Roddy and Cherise plunged into the crowd and were swiftly lost to sight.

Drew and Jenna looked at each other. She leaned forward and yelled into his ear. "Let's go to the room near the front entrance and get a drink. It's quieter out there."

"Sure." Drew slid his arm into hers, and his body got a tingling jolt of Jenna hyperawareness, even through all the layers of fabric.

They found seats at the bar and placed their orders. One of the problems about having to keep his distance emotionally was that he no longer knew how the hell to start a conversation with her.

"I'm sorry that Ava's schedule is stressing you out," he told her. "She just doesn't know when to stop. It's the source of her superpower. It's also a huge pain in the ass."

"I can't deny that it's working," Jenna said. "My team are over the moon at how much attention Arm's Reach is getting. And this thing with Michael and the *Angel Ascending* producers, well. It's incredible, but I'm just not sure how I feel about it."

"I'm glad something useful is coming of it for you," he said. "I was afraid that all my bad press could be damaging to you."

"Not at all. I think it's more like the spice that makes it interesting. You know. The rum in the eggnog. The hot pepper in the salsa."

He snorted. "I'm glad it's good for something."

The bartender delivered their drinks. Jenna sipped her margarita, and turned to him, frowning thoughtfully. "Can I ask you something?"

"Sure."

"The guy who threw that infamous party, the one where you got photographed," she said. "He's made quite a name for himself."

"Arnold Sobel," he said. "Yes, he has. What about him?"

"I was just wondering why you would hang out with a guy like that. He doesn't seem your type. Why go to that party in the first place?"

Just mentioning Sobel's party made tension grip him, as if it had just happened. His stomach heaved nastily. "I knew him way back," he said. "In my crazy partying days, before I joined the service. I only went there as a favor for a friend."

"Ah," she murmured. "Why am I not surprised?"

"Excuse me? What the hell is that supposed to mean?"

"Nothing bad," she assured him. "By no means. It's just that helping people seems to be how you roll. It comes naturally to you."

"My friend Raisa heard that her sister Leticia had gone to that party," he told her. "She's been in some trouble already, and Raisa got nervous. Leticia wasn't answering her phone, and Raisa panicked. She knew I knew Sobel. So she begged me to go to his party and check up on her."

"Did you find Leticia?"

He shook his head.

"Ah." Jenna cocked her head to the side, frowning. "That's strange."

"Yes, it was," he agreed. "The whole thing stank."

"Did you find out if she was ever there?"

"Leticia said afterward that she was somewhere else entirely. She never even knew about that party. Someone was just winding Raisa up. For no reason she can figure out."

"What happened after they took those pictures?" Jenna asked. "You just left?"

He put his beer down, fighting the nausea. That sickening perfume stench filled his nose, even though he knew it was just a memory. Cold sweat broke out on his back. He couldn't seem to breathe. His heart was pounding triple time.

"Could we not talk about this anymore?" he said abruptly. "It wasn't my finest moment."

Jenna looked taken aback. "Sorry. Didn't mean to pry. Won't mention it again."

Damn. He'd screwed up again. "Sorry," he said. "I just—"

From the back room, someone with a mic announced the next set. Drew was grateful for the distraction. "We better get in there."

"Sure, but one second. Let me do something first." Jenna took her cocktail napkin, pressed one of her ice cubes against it and swabbed his cheek gently. "Cherise left a big red lipstick stamp on your cheek when she kissed you. Can't let another woman put her mark on my man."

The Jenna effect zapped through him at her touch, even through the cold, soggy cocktail napkin. "You're just telling me about this lipstick stamp now?" he complained. "You just let me walk around in here like that?"

"Sorry." She looked like she was trying not to smile. "Let's go listen to Roddy, now that you're decent."

Decent, ha. Drew followed her closely through the crowd as they made their way through the various rooms and toward the stage. Little did she know.

In his current state, he felt anything but decent.

Twelve

The room was packed, the band was hot and Roddy was excellent. He had loads of furious, hardcore energy, but he could be low-key and subtle when the music called for it, and he meshed with the seasoned local band as if they'd been playing together for years.

The great music and the margarita had slowly unknotted Jenna's twisted nerves. Her heart was full to overflowing as she watched Roddy play. It was a huge personal victory for her that Roddy had regained enough dexterity and flexibility with his arm to let his musical talent flow through it. That was a kiss of grace from on high. Same with Cherise's promising news about design school. The world was filled with sorrow and disaster and infamy, but tonight, she got to chalk up a few points for the good guys.

Roddy faded out expertly at the end of a song with a shimmery tinkle of the hi-hat, and the lead singer of the band grabbed the mic.

"Boys and girls, I have been informed by our amazing guest drummer, Roddy Hepner, that we have a pair of love-birds in the audience, and he wants to dedicate one of his own original songs to them. You lucky folks are the first to hear the Vicious Rumors perform this song, but you won't be the last. So here it is, folks! 'Thirsting for You,' written and performed by Roddy Hepner! Make space in the middle of the dance floor, everybody, and give it up for our lucky lovers... Jenna...and... Drew!"

People surged and shifted, leaving a big open space around them. They stood together, ringed by a crowd of onlookers, and the light guy trained a rose-tinted spotlight right on them. Their eyes met, as the opening chords of Roddy's beautiful ballad began.

Drew had that look on his face. Like she was the only woman in the world, and he was desperate with longing for her and her alone. His arms encircled her, pulling her close. It felt so right. So natural and inevitable.

Roddy leaned into the mic angled over the drum set and began to sing. His singing voice was wonderful. Deep and slightly rough but beautifully resonant.

The desert dust is in my shoes.
A thread of hope to see me through.
I seek what's good, I seek what's true.
But now I see I thirst for you.

It was too much. She couldn't resist the pulsing music, the intense emotions. Drew's magnetism. The look in his beautiful eyes, deep and endless as the ocean.

She tried to remind herself that she was just a normal woman, not a glammed-up movie star beauty. No way could she hold this guy's interest in the long run, or fit into his jet-setting lifestyle. She was miles out of her league. Cruising for disaster and heartbreak.

And yet, she clung to him. Their bodies had their own merged magnetism. They were one single swaying entity, and they were on the brink of something momentous, and unbearably sweet. Patterns of colored lights swirled and blended over the dance floor like a dreamy kaleidoscope as Roddy sang on, his voice a tender, scratchy croon.

My eyes are burning and my throat is dry.
My thirsty heart's been seeking far and wide.
But shining from your deep and honest eyes.

I find my reason why.

Drew cupped the back of her head in his warm hand, sliding his fingers tenderly into her hair, his gaze still locked with hers. His deep and honest eyes. They made a space just for her. They saw her so clearly. Made her feel so vibrant and alive. So real.

And they were kissing again. Nothing could have stopped it. They were floating in a shining bubble, the rest of the world shut out.

Their kiss was a language in itself, passionate and direct. It spoke of hunger and longing and tenderness, it promised exquisite pleasure, it coaxed and lured and teased.

She couldn't get enough of it. She kissed him back, saying loud and clear with the kiss everything that she'd been trying so hard not to say since the moment she met him.

Yes. God, yes. Please, yes.

She could feel his erection, hot against her belly. She dragged him closer to feel it better, aching for his heat, his strength and energy as the song slowly ended.

The applause was thunderous. Hoots and howls from the crowd finally penetrated their magic bubble as the space around them dissolved.

People flooded back onto the dance floor, crowding in around them.

Jenna stared at Drew, willing her arms to loosen from their desperate, clinging hold, but they were not obeying her commands.

She finally managed it. By force, she pushed herself back, almost stumbling into someone behind her. Drew caught her and steadied her.

Careful. I got you. She saw his lips form the words, but couldn't hear his voice in the noise. Those beautiful lips that had just kissed her into a wanton frenzy of desire right in front of a cheering crowd.

"I have to go," she said inanely, pulling away.

His grip tightened, and his lips moved again in the raucous noise. "Where?"

"Uh…uh…the bathroom. Going to the ladies'. See you in a minute. Bye."

She pulled away again. Drew hung on for a split second, sensing her panic, but then let her go.

Jenna slipped away, weaving swiftly through the crowd and toward the door.

Someone stepped in front of her as she made for it. She ran right into him.

"Sorry, Jenna! Didn't mean to bump you!"

It was Ernest, Ava's eager-beaver young assistant, with his spiky white blond hair and his big round glasses that made him look like a crazed steam-punk aviator.

"Ernest," she said. "What on earth are you doing here?"

"The usual," Ernest said, holding up a tablet. "Recording your love!"

Jenna's insides thudded two stories down. "Oh, God. Ava told you to come here?"

"She wanted me to record Roddy's gig. The romantic dance and that be-still-my-heart steaming-hot kiss was just an awesome bonus. It's gonna totally blow up online!"

"Oh, no, no, no! Ernest, do me a favor. Don't post the dance and the kiss, okay? I understand about filming Roddy, but just leave me and Drew out of it."

Ernest looked bewildered. "Why not? I thought this was the whole point!"

"It's just, um, kind of private."

"Well, duh. Of course. That's why people go for it."

"Just don't, this time," she pleaded. "Just this once. I need a breather."

"Sorry." Ernest looked anything but sorry as he lifted his tablet. "I already uploaded it to your and Drew's YouTube channel—"

"I don't have a YouTube channel!"

"Oh, but you do, and since last week, you two have already racked up twenty-one thousand followers. Let's see, I just uploaded this video of the dance and the kiss five minutes ago, and it's got…lemme see here how many views… ooh! Seven hundred and eighty-five…six…seven… It keeps going up! You guys are a hot property!"

"That's just it," Jenna wailed. "I'm not a property! Or a reality TV star! Sometimes I need to get a drink or go hear some music and have it just be for me, for God's sake!"

Ernest gazed at her, looking blank and very clouded. "Just for you? Like, what does that even mean? What do you care if people like to watch? What does it matter?"

Jenna turned her back and left before she lost her temper and smacked the guy.

The cold wind whipped her hair as she walked down the street. Her eyes stung, and her face felt hot. Her throat was tight, like a cruel little hand was squeezing it.

But she'd signed up for this insanity.

There was a taxi cruising by. She hailed it and got in, then pulled out her phone as soon as she'd given directions to the driver. Her hand was shaking as she pulled up Drew's number and texted him.

had to go. grabbed a cab. on my way home now. sorry.

A few moments later, his response appeared. wtf! seriously?

I needed to be alone. sorry. really.

Another minute passed, and his answer appeared. WHAT DID I DO

She hastened to reply. nothing. you were great. it's me. I need some space.

A long pause. Then his terse reply. understood.

Damn it. Damn this whole thing. sorry, she repeated, digging for a tissue.

me too. he responded, and then after a moment. good night. stay safe.

Great. Now he was making her feel like crap by being courteous and classy and restrained about it. Damn that guy. He made it so…flipping…*hard*.

She had to run away from him, because she knew exactly how the evening would play out if she didn't. Drew would insist on taking her home. He would insist on walking her to the top of her steps to see her to her door. He would smolder at her with those deep, beautiful eyes that promised the moon and the stars and everything between, and she would lose her mind, drag him inside and jump all over him.

If they even made it inside. She might just ravish him right there on the porch.

She was nine-tenths in love with him already. If they went to bed, that would be it.

There would be no walking this back.

Thirteen

Jenna looked spectacularly beautiful when she joined him at the top of the stairs at the Whitebriar Club for their big entrance. It hit him like a blow.

She wore no glasses tonight. He'd barely recognized her for a moment, since her cat-eye specs were such a distinctive part of her look. She was gorgeous without them, too, in sea-foam green silk, with a string of iridescent beads as shoulder straps and shimmering beadwork on the neckline. The silk skimmed her gorgeous figure and showed a tantalizing shadow between her breasts. A hairdresser had tried to tame the curls into a decorous updo, but the efforts were in vain. The curls would not be contained. Some longer ones had sprung free already. Others swung and bounced around her delicate jaw.

She smiled at him, but her gaze dropped, embarrassed, as he took her slender arm.

"You look stunning," he said.

"Thank you."

"This isn't the black-and-white dress you talked about. Did you shop for that gown with Ava? I remember you two arguing about it a few days ago."

"Are you asking if you paid for it?" Her eyes met him with a glint of challenge. "You did not. This is one battle with your sister that I actually won, I'm proud to say. I bought this dress months ago, all by myself at a vintage clothing shop downtown. I had to get the beading restored by a costume expert, but I loved the color."

Her in-your-face tone irked him. "I was not asking if I paid for it," he said tersely. "Not that I would give a damn if I had."

She shot him a repentant look. "Sorry. I guess that sounded snarky."

"Sure as hell did," he agreed.

"I just wanted to emphasize that I am not a billionaire's plaything. Even if I do play one on TV."

"It's crystal clear to me that you're not a plaything. Don't strain yourself."

She laughed under her breath, and gave him an assessing glance. "You look sharp yourself," she said. "Nice tux."

"I do my best," he said. "You look different without your glasses."

She gave him a rueful smile. "I've always had these contacts. I'm just too lazy to use them, and they make my eyes tired and red."

"You look great both ways," he said.

"It's a classic fantasy, you know," she said. "Woman takes off glasses. Man notices for the first time that she's female."

Drew looked her up and down. "I noticed it before."

Her gaze whipped away and her color rose as they started descending the stairs toward the sea of people below. Drew was frustrated and angry with himself. When he spoke to her, every damn thing that came out of his mouth sounded like a come-on.

Solution A: Shut up and ignore her. Solution B: Avoid her altogether. As in, definitively and forever, by getting the hell out of Maddox Hill. Those were his options.

She glowed like a pearl. His arm was buzzing from that

light contact with her hand, even through his tux jacket and shirt.

Enough. This farce ended tonight. It was making him miserable. That night at the Wild Side had been the last straw. Passionately kissing her while slow dancing and then having her run out on him—it was the ultimate slap.

He wasn't coming back for more. He regretted the embarrassment that breaking their false engagement would cause, but at least Jenna wouldn't have to fend off his unwelcome moves. Since he couldn't seem to stop himself from making them.

He'd get through tonight, hopefully without incident, and make the announcement to everyone concerned before he went home, and that would be that. On to the next thing.

He'd met Vann and Zack last night for a beer, to give them a heads-up before he tendered that letter of resignation he was still carrying around. His friends were angry at him. They thought he was bailing on them. He couldn't make them understand that this was a desperate survival move. A last-ditch effort to salvage what was left of his dignity.

Vann looked up from the bottom of the stairs, a frown between his dark eyes, and glanced at Jenna. His brows went up in silent question. Because of *her*?

Drew kept his face stony. As he and Jenna reached the bottom of the stairs, he saw Harold bearing down on them, a woman on his arm. She was a tall brunette with a black sequined gown and glitter spray on her prominent, bulging breasts, and she was staring straight at him.

Wait. Whoa. He knew that woman. That was Lydia, an architect he'd met in San Francisco, while working on the Magnolia Plaza project. They'd had a casual affair, but he hadn't called her since leaving San Francisco six months ago.

Or thought of her at all, to be perfectly honest.

Harold steered his date so that Lydia and he were right in front of Drew and Jenna at the foot of the stairs, blocking any further progress into the room.

Then it hit him, like a freight train. Lydia's perfume. A heavy, reeking cloud of it.

The same heinous stuff that had been squirted into his face at Sobel's party. Drew's stomach turned and he broke out in a cold sweat. Heart racing. Blood pressure dropping.

"Hi, Drew," Lydia cooed. "Looking good, as always. You've been busy, hmm?"

For a moment, Drew couldn't speak, he was fighting so hard for control. "Hello, Lydia," he forced out. "This is Jenna Somers. My fiancée."

"She knows about your fiancée," Harold said. "At least, she sure knows now."

"Yes, it's so funny how I had absolutely no clue that you'd gotten engaged to this woman last spring when you were down in San Francisco," Lydia said, in a voice that carried far and wide. "You didn't act like a man who'd just found the love of his life, as I very clearly recall." She looked Jenna over, and clucked her tongue. "Sneaky Drew."

"Excuse us. We have to go work the crowd." Drew ground the words out, pulling Jenna away from them.

"We'll talk more later! We're seated right next to each other at the banquet," Harold called after them with barely concealed glee. "You and Lydia can catch up on old times! Lydia can get to know Jenna. Won't that be nice?"

Drew pressed on, putting space between them so he could breathe, but now that the memory was activated, that horrific perfume was all he could smell, and the room was wavering in his vision. Sounds seemed distorted, as if he'd been freshly dosed with whatever drug they'd sprayed on him at the party. A stress flashback, right now? God. He was furious at his own brain for betraying him like this. *Breathe deep. Chill. Control.*

"...matter with you? Drew? What is it? Are you sick?"

Jenna was squeezing his arm and frowning. Her eyes looked worried.

"I'm fine." He forced the words out.

"You don't look fine. Your lips are white. What the hell?"

He groped for an explanation. He finally got a whiff of Jenna's scent. Honey, wildflowers. It settled him. He got a deep breath into himself. Then another.

"I think I had some kind of an allergic reaction to Lydia's perfume." He threw out the first excuse that came to his mind, but it was actually kind of true.

"I think I've got you beat there. I had an allergic reaction to Lydia herself," Jenna said with feeling. "She and your cousin are quite the poisonous pair. Better now?"

"Better," he said.

Damn good thing, too, because now they were in the room where the architectural exhibits were displayed, and the crowd closed around them. The work of the evening began; the shaking of hands, hugs and air kisses, pleasantries and chitchat, posing for photos and selfies, speaking authoritatively about the projects he'd designed. Architects and engineers, board members, local politicians and businesspeople, journalists, a stream of people to interact with. He tried to fake normal, and when he faltered, Jenna covered for him as best she could.

It felt like forever, but eventually the crowd started drifting into the stately banquet room where dinner would be served and the endless speechifying would begin. By the time they got to their table, everyone else was seated, and there was no graceful way to switch out their places elsewhere without drawing a great deal of attention to themselves.

Harold and Lydia were lying in wait for them. They both stared at Drew and Jenna from the table with cold, watchful eyes. Lydia's perfume hit his nose like a foul cloud of toxic gas. The place card with his name was right next to Lydia's chair. His guts lurched.

Jenna elbowed him to the other side and sat down next to Lydia herself, giving the other woman a big smile. "Hope you two are having a lovely evening."

"Getting better all the time." Harold's eyes dropped to Jenna's chest, where it stayed like it had been nailed there, all the way through the appetizers and the first course. Drew wanted to smack Harold under the chin until his jaws clacked together to get him to look up into Jenna's eyes when he spoke to her. Disrespectful sleaze.

Drew braved Lydia's perfume and leaned closer, careful not to inhale, to focus on what his cousin was saying.

"…on YouTube. You know, the incendiary kiss. The slow dance at the Wild Side."

"Oh, God." Jenna sounded embarrassed. "That was so silly. Ava's assistant, Ernest, was filming the drummer. We had no idea he was there. So embarrassing."

Harold took a swig of his wine and licked his lips. "So spontaneous," he commented.

"Are you usually such a shameless exhibitionist?" Lydia's eyes glittered. She had a lipstick stain on her teeth. "Does Drew inspire you? I don't blame you. That man is inspiring. No one knows that better than me. He can get a girl to do any wild, crazy thing he wants. Like, anything."

"Excuse me," Jenna said, recoiling slightly. "I'm not sure I understand."

"We just wondered." Harold gave her a lascivious smile. "You know, if the two of you get off on having the whole world watch while you, ah…get busy. Is that your thing?"

Drew shot to his feet, hitting the table. His chair fell backward, silverware rattled, a wineglass toppled. Wine splattered across the table and Lydia jumped up, scooting backward in an attempt to save her dress.

"Clumsy jerk!" she hissed. "Watch it!"

Drew ignored her, addressing his cousin. "What the hell kind of question is that?"

Harold's smile widened. The room fell silent. Everyone was watching and listening.

"I'm surprised you even heard me, you're so zoned out tonight." Harold's voice was clear and carrying. "Go easy on that wine, Drew. Are you on antihistamines? Or maybe something stronger?"

"I heard what you said," Drew said. "Do not speak to her again."

"Just admiring your fiancée," Harold said innocently. "You've smeared your red-hot scorching love affair far and wide all over the internet, so I could hardly avoid admiring her if I wanted to. Don't go all caveman on me now. It's unbecoming."

"Admire someone else. Keep your goddamn opinions to yourself."

"Drew!" Jenna said in a fierce whisper. "Holy crap! Calm down!"

Harold lifted his hands, grinning widely. "Take it easy, big guy."

"What the hell is going on?" Uncle Malcolm's furious voice came from behind him.

"Oh, no biggie." Harold's tone was light. "Just the usual. Drew's had a few too many, and now he's making a public spectacle of himself. Same old same old."

"What's this?" Uncle Malcolm glared at Drew. "What's this? Is this true?"

Drew opened his mouth, but Lydia spoke up first.

"I can't take any more of this," she quavered, clutching the wine-stained napkin she'd used to clean up her dress in her shaking hand. "You lying, cheating son of a bitch. They say you were engaged to this woman last year, when you were in San Francisco!" She pointed at Jenna. "Engaged!

And you never said a word about it, all those times when you were nailing me right on the desk in your office! You filthy, selfish *bastard*!"

Gasps and low murmurs of scandalized conversation followed that outburst. The waiters all around the tables froze in place, terrified, holding their trays of prime rib.

Lydia burst into tears. She hurried out of the room, weaving and bumping between tables. Sobbing, tear-blinded, but taking her toxic cloud of perfume with her, thank God.

When she was out the door, Uncle Malcolm turned back to Drew and cleared his throat. "So. Nephew. Just to be forewarned, for the sake of my heart health, are there any more of your disgruntled chippies roaming around here on the rampage tonight?"

"Not to my knowledge," Drew said.

Uncle Malcolm harrumphed and looked around, scowling. The entire room looked back, waiting for their cue. Malcolm made a disgusted sound and waved his hand. "For God's sake, finish serving the damn meat before it's stone-cold," he snarled at the waiters. He turned to Drew. "You, come with me. I need to speak to you privately. Right now."

Drew let out a slow breath. He'd reached the end of the line.

In some ways, it was for the best. His bridges were burned, so he no longer had to torture himself with doubts or second thoughts. All he could do was move forward.

He should feel relieved, but as he looked into Jenna's worried eyes, he felt like something precious had been ripped from him. Something he'd just learned how to value.

He fixed Harold with a grim stare. "If you slime her again, I will flatten you."

"Come *now*!" his uncle snapped. "You're making a spectacle of yourself!"

"Yeah, that seems to be the general theme of my life

lately." He leaned down and cupped Jenna's face. "I'm sorry," he whispered to her. "Goodbye."

He kissed Jenna, slowly and intensely, with all his pent-up desperation, ignoring the rising hum of excited chatter and his uncle's furious sputtering. Because what the hell.

He had nothing left to lose.

Fourteen

Jenna watched Drew follow his uncle out of the crowded room, head up and shoulders back, like a soldier on the march. Her fingers were pressed to her tingling, just-kissed lips. She was shocked speechless. On the verge of tears.

She jumped up to follow him, and found Harold's hot, damp fingers suddenly clamped around her wrist. "Jenna, no," he murmured. "Let them go. Sit down."

She jerked her wrist away. "With you? Why the hell should I do that?"

"Calm down," Harold said. "I am not the bad guy here."

She laughed right in his face. "You expect me to believe that?"

"This is old stuff, Jenna. Family stuff. A long time coming. Don't mix yourself up in it. You don't know the history."

She stared at Harold. "I don't think I need to. It's very clear to me."

And it was getting clearer all the time, like watching a photograph take form in a bath of darkroom chemicals. She thought of her first flash-assessment of Harold when she met him at the restaurant. Perfectly good-looking in his own right, but he suffered in comparison with Drew.

From what Ava had said, the same held true for Harold's professional life. He was competent and successful in his field, unless Drew was next to him with all of the medals and prizes and honors and high-profile projects. Next to Drew, Harold got bumped several notches down the scale, until he registered as barely higher than average.

She disliked the very thought in itself, because she did not believe in judging people in that way. But the rest of the world did.

Harold had spent his whole life in Drew's shadow and he was sick of it.

"You set him up," she said. "You sneaky bastard. You organized this whole thing."

Harold sipped his wine. "You'd like to have me be the villain so that your perfect, fantasy Drew can be innocent. News flash. He's not. Sorry to break it to you, honey."

"I am not your honey," she said. "You brought that woman up from San Francisco on purpose. I bet you told her to make that big scene as soon as Malcolm was in earshot."

"I didn't have to tell her a thing. Everything she said was literally true. Drew gets into trouble all by himself. He doesn't need help from me or anyone. Like that orgy at the Sobel party. He did that all by himself, and he does it often. That time, he just happened to get busted."

"He was lured into a trap," she said. "He was there to help a friend."

"That's what he told you?" Harold gave her a pitying look. "I checked the dates of your Women in STEM speech in San Francisco last year, when you and Drew hooked up. I know for a fact that Drew was screwing Lydia that whole time, and for months afterward. You were sharing him back then, Jenna. Knowing Drew, you're probably sharing him now. He's a star, and he never denies himself. I'm sorry to hurt you, but it's true. Think long and hard before you get in too deep with him."

Jenna stepped back, whipping her arm away before Harold could grab her wrist again. To hell with this guy. He wasn't worth another moment of her time.

And she had a few choice things she wanted to say to Malcolm Maddox.

She marched through the tables, chin high, ignoring the muttering and the stares, following the path Drew and his uncle had taken. Once outside the ballroom, she homed in on Malcolm's haranguing voice. It came from upstairs, so she followed it up, and down the wide hall until she came to the double doors of the Cedar Salon, a luxurious old-fashioned parlor.

As she threw the doors open, the old man's voice blared even louder.

"...sick of your depraved antics! After all Hendrick's complaining about your behavior, you decide to put on a floor show like that right in front of all of them?"

"Uncle, I didn't plan on that woman showing up to—"

"You think you dodged a bullet when you trotted out your perfect little Miss Butter-Wouldn't-Melt-In-Her-Mouth, eh? You think you can use her like some sort of goddamn human shield. But whatever you think you might have gained by that cheap trick, you just lost ten times over, and I for one am not fooled by your—"

"He is not using me!" Jenna yelled. "If anything, I'm the one using him!"

Malcolm's head whipped around, eyes shocked. "This is a private conversation, Miss Somers!"

"I don't care. If you're trash-talking me, I insist on participating. Miss Butter-Wouldn't-Melt-In-Her-Mouth, my ass! You should be ashamed of yourself!"

Malcolm Maddox stared at her for a moment, mouth open, and cleared his throat. "Well," he said gruffly. "That is a matter of opinion."

"So now you know my opinion!"

"Certainly. At that volume, the whole building knows your opinion."

"I'm fine with that," she said hotly. "I have nothing to hide. Nothing."

"That's not the case for him, unfortunately." Malcolm gestured at Drew. "You heard what that woman said. It's the story of his life! Is that what you want for yourself?"

"He was set up! He goes miles out of his way to help people, time and time again. He took a bullet in Iraq, risking his life for his country. Does none of that count for you?"

"Oh, God." Drew looked pained. "Jenna, I don't need for you to—"

"You just hush up!" She rounded on him furiously. "You've been doing a crap job at defending yourself lately, so step aside and let me handle it this time!"

"I appreciate your zeal, young lady," Malcolm said. "But you're sticking your nose into matters that aren't your business."

"Guilty as charged," she said. "I don't give a damn. Just don't expect me to smile and nod while someone I care about is being put down. I just…won't…do it. Period."

Malcolm Maddox frowned at her for a moment, then his gaze flicked to Drew. "Hmph," he grunted. "Played the wounded soldier card, eh?"

"I play the cards I have," Drew said.

"Don't blame you, to be honest." Malcolm looked her over, his eyes sharp and assessing. "She is something when she gets going, hmm?"

"That she is," Drew agreed.

"Do not talk about me as if I'm not here," Jenna snapped.

Malcolm laughed and gestured toward Jenna with his cane. "Hang on to this one if you can, boy," he said gruffly. "But you know damn well you don't deserve her. You're just a dog on the furniture. Pull yourself together. Try not to make spectacles of yourselves for the rest of the evening, if you can possibly manage it, eh? Both of you."

He turned his back and stumped out, hunched over his cane, still muttering.

Drew and Jenna looked at each other after the door fell to after him. Jenna shook her head, bewildered. "Um... What just happened?"

"Looks like you just charmed Uncle Malcolm," Drew said. "Congratulations."

She stared at him. "Charmed him? By scolding him? *That's* what charms him?"

"We're a contrary bunch." Drew's tone was almost apologetic. "And he favors strong women. With strong opinions."

"Oh, God." Jenna pressed both hands to her hot cheeks. "This is so crazy." She started digging in her evening bag for a tissue, sniffling into it.

"What's wrong?" Drew asked. "Why are you crying?"

"It happens when I lose my temper. Something shorts out in my brain. Don't be alarmed, you don't have to comfort me or anything like that. It'll pass quickly."

Drew still looked worried. "You're sure you're okay?"

"Fine," she assured him. "Really."

He just looked at her, hesitating. "Ah...thanks," he said, awkwardly.

"For what?"

"For coming out swinging like that. For having my back. I know that it was part of the whole being-engaged act, and I think we can hang that masquerade up at this point. But act or no act, it felt really good to hear."

She was horrified by a fresh wave of tears. "Oh, crap," she muttered. "That was not an act, Drew Maddox." There it was. The truth. She'd blurted it out at last.

His eyes sharpened. "Meaning what? You haven't been pretending?"

"Not at all," she admitted. "I've been a goner ever since I dumped that pitcher of sangria on you. I know I shouldn't tell you this, but that's the short circuit in my brain. I cry, and then I blurt out stuff people don't necessarily want to hear. Anyhow. I've done enough damage tonight, so I think I'll just get my coat and get the hell out of—"

She let out a startled squeak as Drew pulled her against himself and kissed her.

It was electrifying. His breathless urgency. His hard body, muscles taut, shaking with emotion. The shining thrill racing through her, the ache of hunger in her body, always a constant smolder, but when he touched her, it flared into a bonfire.

Jenna wrapped her arms around his neck and melted into him. Kissed him back with everything she had. Ravenous for the delicious heat of his mouth as a new world of emotions and sensations opened up inside her.

Drew maneuvered them down onto an antique love seat, pulling her down onto his lap and kissing her bare shoulder with desperate tenderness. The beaded straps of the dress slid down, and the top of the lacy cups of her strapless bra were showing. Drew made a rough, tormented sound in his throat and pressed his face against them. Both of them moaned at the sweetness of it. The warm tenderness of his lips was an intoxicating sensation, kissing her, nuzzling her. His arms were so strong. Everywhere he touched her touched off a rush of delight. He stroked her back.

"Oh, God. So hot and soft," he murmured. "So smooth. You're killing me."

She settled right over that hard, unyielding bulge of his erection and leaned down to kiss him again. The bodice of the dress was slipping down but his hands stroking her bare back felt so good, and his hot kiss was so searching and seductive.

The doors squeaked, and a swell of noise behind them made them both freeze and turn. Drew's body went tense beneath her.

Uncle Malcolm, Hendrick, Bev, Harold, Ava, Ernest,

eyes popping, mouths agape, and a dozen more people stood right behind them, pushing, craning. On tiptoe. A hum of shocked murmurs, embarrassed giggles.

"Oh, my God." Jenna struggled with her neckline, tugging it back up over the cups of her strapless bra before sliding off Drew's lap and onto her feet.

"Out! Everyone get out!" Uncle Malcolm shouted, but there was no possible retreat for the people in the doorway. The crush of gawkers pressing up behind them blocked their escape. Harold's face was a cold mask. Ava's smile was conspiratorial. Like she was in on the joke.

Except it wasn't a joke. It never really had been.

Bev smirked at her husband. "Well, Hendrick, that looks pretty sincere to me, wouldn't you say? I think I won this bet. Better get ready to pay up."

Hendrick just peered at them, his thick eyebrows knitted together like he just couldn't figure out what was going on.

Not that Jenna was doing much better, when it came right down to it.

"Get back!" Malcolm bawled. "All of you! Out! Damn it!"

Jenna finally got her dress straightened and slid her shoe back on. She scooped up her beaded evening bag from where it had fallen on the carpet. "That's my cue," she murmured to Drew. "Time to disappear."

"With me," Drew said swiftly. "Only with me."

She looked into his eyes, and promptly forgot that people were watching them. The longing in his eyes called out to her, a sweet pull so strong, not even public humiliation could quench it. It just raged on and on, wanting what it wanted.

"Yes," she said. "Let's disappear together."

His eyes flashed, and his warm hand closed around hers.

Malcolm overheard them. "That would be best, since neither one of you seems to be capable of any self-control," he snarled. "For the love of God, go! Let me try to salvage what's left of my company's image."

"Don't be grumpy, Uncle." Ava was still trying not to smile. "Everyone loves it, and you know it."

"Enough, Av," Drew said. "Dial it down to zero."

"Me?" Ava's chin rose. "I'm not dialing anything. I'm not doing a damn thing, bro. You two are doing it all on your own. But it would be a shame to stop now when everyone's having so much fun, don't you think?"

"We're out of here." Drew slid his arm around Jenna's waist and made for the crowd of people who blocked the doors. "Make way."

The steely quality in his voice made people actually shuffle backward. Jenna's face burned as they forced their way through, but Harold's cold eyes chilled her as she passed. She could feel the anger emanating from him.

People tried to speak to them, but she couldn't follow what they were saying. Drew ignored them, sweeping them both onward through the press of people and down the stairs, toward the coat check desk. He helped her slip her coat on. "You're shaking," he said as they made their way toward the exit. "Put on my coat. It's heavier."

"Not from the cold. I'm actually kind of hot," she said, as they went out the door.

The cold, damp night air felt good against her feverish face.

"Where's your car?" he asked.

"Didn't bring it," she told him, teeth still chattering. "I used a car service. Didn't want to be bothered with parking or driving."

"Good," he said, as the parking attendant pulled up in his silver Jag.

He opened the door for her, and she got in, waiting while he tipped the attendant and got in himself. Then they sat in stunned silence for a moment.

She laughed shakily. "Holy cow. What a circus."

"Yes it was." He started the engine and pulled out onto the street. "I'm sorry to put you through that."

"It wasn't your fault. I mouthed off to your uncle. I showed my strapless bra to the Board of Directors and God knows who all else. That's going to follow me around until I die."

He laughed. "At least the bra was still on."

"Well, thank God for that," she said. "I can't believe how I just behaved. I can't carry on in public like that. I'm going to lose all my professional credibility."

"I'm sorry if I put you in a compromising position," he said. "The last thing I want is to damage you professionally."

Jenna wound the beaded strap of her purse around her fingers. "I imagine that whole exhibition was kind of a buzzkill for you, right?"

"No." Drew reached across the console and grabbed her hand without taking his eyes off the road.

The contact with his hand flashed up her arm, then raced instantly to deeper, more secret places. "No?" She tried to keep her voice even, but it still quavered, betraying her. "You're not traumatized?"

"I barely noticed them," he admitted. "All I saw in that room was you. Nothing on earth could kill my buzz."

A glow of anticipation was filling her whole body.

"How about you?" he asked. "Are you still with me?"

She squeezed his hand. "Oh, yeah."

He squeezed back. "Can I take you to my house? It's closer. And I want you to see it."

"Yes, please. I'd like that."

Game on. She was done trying to control this.

Whatever he offered, she would take. If it was just his body, that was fine. Just a fling, fine. Just one night, also fine. She wanted this. She was grabbing it with both hands.

She could process the hurt later. There would be plenty of time for that.

Wow. Just look at her. After all her lofty notions and uppity attitude, she'd tumbled into Drew's honeyed trap after all.

She had just officially become a billionaire's plaything.

So be it. It was finally time to play.

Fifteen

Drew was tongue-tied the entire way home. Having Jenna in his car, taking her to his home—it was huge. It filled up his chest until he could barely breathe, let alone speak. He'd never felt this way, even when he was a teenager just learning about sex. He'd started out by faking it. Pretending to be cool and confident and smooth until that became the truth.

But it wasn't his truth anymore. Not with Jenna. He couldn't pretend. All bets were off with her. Nothing could be taken for granted. And the stakes were so damn high.

He kept his grip on her slim, cool hand, when he didn't need his own hand for driving. Whenever he had to let go of her, he promptly reached for her again. Assuring himself that she was real.

But she was also nervous. He could not screw this up.

He pulled into the driveway that led to his property on Lake Washington and parked the car in the garage.

"You designed this house," she said.

"How did you know that?"

"I've seen your buildings. I knew it was yours because it was so different from the lakeside McMansions we passed. Your designs don't fight with their environment. They're harmonious."

He was absurdly pleased that she got it, and that she

liked the house he'd designed for himself. As well as embarrassed. He was showing off to impress her, like a little kid.

"Come on in." He took her hand to lead her down the flagstone path that wound through the trees and landscaped garden of the front lawn to the main entrance. When they went inside, Jenna stood in the middle of the entry hall with its row of skylights, and then strolled into the living room. A long wall of glass overlooked the lake, with lights from the other side of Lake Washington wavering on the water. French doors led out onto the patio. A wooden walkway wound through the grass and trees down to a floating dock, and his boat. Another thing he'd been too busy to use lately.

"I'll give you a tour tomorrow," he offered. "When we have some light."

But not now. I'm dying to touch you.

"Okay," she murmured.

Drew watched her as she wandered around his living room. He tried to remember what common courtesy demanded.

"Can I take your coat?" He slid open the panels in the wall in the entry hall, revealing the deep cedar-lined closet. She moved closer, turning to let him lift the coat from her shoulders. That released an intoxicating waft of sweet fragrance. Her hair had rebelled from its coif, her ringlets floating up free and dangling around her throat. Her skin was so fine. So soft. He wanted to bury his face against it.

He swallowed, hard. "Can I get you a drink? I have whiskey, brandy, or I could open a bottle of wine. Or mix you a drink from the bar. Anything you like."

She peeked over her shoulder, a seductive smile curving the corners of her luscious red lips. "Better not," she murmured. "I'm in an altered state already."

"Want me to build a fire?" he asked.

"When we're already so hot?"

Her light, teasing words made the heat roar through him. His hands flexed, clenched. "You have a point," he said, rigidly controlled.

"I'm too impatient for time-wasting moves like that," she told him. "After weeks of being constantly tantalized."

He let out a harsh crack of laughter. "Me, tantalizing you? Like hell! I've been stretched out at your feet ever since that very first day. I have held nothing back!"

"And this smooth seductive patter of yours? The drink, the fire?" She rolled her eyes at him. "Are you going to show me your etchings now? Your butterfly collection?"

Her voice was playful, but he was so attuned to her now, he could sense she was wound incredibly tight. Trying to keep him at arm's length with her teasing.

The first step was to unwind her. Very...slowly.

He didn't try to reply. Just came up behind her, and leaned down to kiss her shoulder, letting his lips trail up to the nape of her neck. No words. No seductive patter. Just his lips, moving over her skin. A slow, dragging caress, the rasp of his teeth. A delicate nip. Her hair was so soft and fragrant. So warm.

She tilted her head, allowing him more access.

He took advantage of it. Gave himself up to it. Oh, yeah. He could do this all night. Hot, hungry kisses, slowing down time. Exploring every inch of her throat, her shoulders. Getting her to relax and soften in his grasp. He wanted her helpless with pleasure. So aroused, she couldn't even stand up. That was the goal.

Her breath was uneven as he slid his arms around her waist from behind. One hand splayed over her belly, whisper-thin silk separating him from her warm skin. He loved the tremor in her body, the breathless sound in the back of her throat as he slid his hand up, feeling her rib cage. The soft weight of her breasts. The smoothness of her skin above the dress. Her racing pulse.

Jenna placed her hands over his. Not stopping them, just covering them. Pressing them closer to her. He leaned down, kissing her shoulders. Nudging the beaded strap of her gown until it fell off one shoulder. Then the other. He was slow. Persistent.

His pulsing erection was pressed up to her backside, and she leaned back against him, welcoming the contact. Inviting his touch, with that dreamy smile on her face.

It was getting more and more difficult to keep this slow. His hands shook, but he soldiered on. He found a stray hairpin trapped in one of her ringlets during his nuzzling kisses, so he took a moment to sort through her hair and pull out all the pins, setting that halo of wild ringlets loose. "I like it best when it's like this," he said. "Free and wild."

"Getting wilder by the second," she murmured. "The way you kiss me makes me crazy."

"That's how I want you to feel," he said. "I want you primed."

"That's how I want you, too."

"Not an issue. Done deal. I've been in that primed state pretty much since you first kissed me in the elevator."

She looked back at him, the mix of colors in her eyes hypnotically beautiful. Then she straightened up and turned around to face him, shrugging the bodice of her dress down until it was hanging off her hips.

She shook back her hair, holding his gaze with a blaze of sexy challenge in her eyes as she reached behind herself and undid the clasp of her bra.

She let it drop, and stood there, shoulders back. Displaying herself. The color in her cheeks was high. Her lips parted, breath coming fast. But her hands still shook.

Her breasts were so beautiful. High, full and soft, with tight dark pink nipples, and her skin was so fine-grained and smooth and perfect. The chill in his house had given her goose bumps but her chest had a pink blush that matched the one on her cheeks.

He wanted to lunge for her like a ravenous animal. *Easy does it.*

Drew placed his hands on her waist. A tremor went through her at the contact, then another as his hands slid slowly upward, over her rib cage. Under her arms.

He cupped her breasts, almost reverently. "You are spectacular."

"I'm still waiting for the spectacle to begin. You certainly do keep a girl waiting."

"I'm trying not to rush it," he said. "We'll never get this first time back. I want the memory to be perfect."

Her smile sent fire shooting through every part of his body. "Really? Wow. I had no idea you were so sentimental."

"Neither did I," he admitted. "That thought has never passed through my mind before in my life. Only with you."

Her eyebrows went up. "Well, then," she murmured. "I am honored to be the one to have sparked an original thought in your head."

He gave her a narrow look. "I'm not sure quite how to take that."

She laughed at him. "You don't have to take it at all. I'm just messing with you." She reached up to deftly loosen his bow tie, then she started in on the buttons of his shirt, sliding her hand inside to caress his chest. "The way I feel right now, we couldn't make anything but amazing memories. Relax. Let yourself go. I trust you."

He knew she was just talking about sex, but the rush of emotion her words gave him made him throb and burn. Her hands moved over his chest.

"Just one quick thing first," she said hesitantly. "I don't carry condoms around in my evening bag, so…"

"I have some," he assured her.

"Good. That's a relief. But since we're on the subject, let's just power through this part all at once. I got myself tested for everything under the sun a few weeks ago, after I found out that Rupert was cheating on me. Thank God he didn't give me anything. I'm in the clear, just so you know."

"Thanks for bringing it up. Me, too. Just got tested myself, and I'm all good."

"Excellent," she said, undoing another button, and then another, spreading his shirt and murmuring in approval at what she found. "In that case. I have a contraceptive implant. So... We could just dispense with the latex. If you'd like."

Liked? The idea of no latex with Jenna made him dizzy. "Dream come true."

"Great," she murmured, leaning forward to kiss his chest. "So... Do you mean to do the deed right here in your foyer? I wouldn't mind, since it's all so beautiful—"

He scooped her up into his arms. She made a startled sound. "Whoa! The hell?"

He carried her down the long corridor, toward his bedroom. "My bedroom."

She wound her fingers into the fabric of his shirt collar and tugged it. "Wow," she whispered. "How masterful and ravishing of you."

"Do you go for that?"

"Sure, if it's you."

Good. He nudged the door to the master bedroom open with his foot. His bedroom was very large and sparsely furnished, everything in it subservient to the view. Two enormous windows looked out over Lake Washington, the waving trees and garden. The light filtering in from outside was just enough to make the bamboo floor planks gleam and dimly illuminate the low, enormous bed.

Drew carried Jenna over to the bed and laid her down, climbing on top of her. Covering her slender body with his own.

She said she trusted him to let himself go, and he was taking her at her word.

Sixteen

She felt like a live flame. Pure and essential, like everything superfluous had gone up in smoke. She barely recognized the woman moving beneath Drew, making those helpless gasping sounds. Enthralled by him, and yet more marvelously free than she'd ever felt.

She loved his heat, his lithe, solid body on top of her. His bare chest pressed to her breasts. Then he slid farther down, kissing her throat, then her collarbone.

When he got to her breasts, she floated up to a new level of shining hyperawareness. She clutched his head, fingers slipping through his short hair, thighs squeezing together, just trying to breathe. She wanted to wrap her legs around him, but her thighs were clamped between his, leaving her writhing, gasping, struggling instinctively toward release as her excitement crested to terrifying heights—and crashed down on her.

The climax pulsed through her body. Deep throbs of pleasure wiped her out.

When she opened her eyes, Drew was poised over her, his eyes hot and fascinated.

"I'd call that a good beginning," he said. "I love watching you come."

She wanted to laugh, but she was so limp, her chest barely lifted against his weight. But he still felt it, rolling off her and pulling her tight against him, so they were on their sides facing each other.

She plucked at his shirt. "Get that off," she said. "I want the full effect."

Drew sat up, shrugging off the tux jacket, wrenching off the shirt. He tossed it away, prying off shoes and socks while he was at it.

Jenna sat up, too, with some effort, as relaxed as she felt, and sat on the bed, struggling with the ridiculously tiny buckles on the ankle straps of her shoes. It was almost impossible, with fingers that were still shaking.

Drew sank down to his knees on the floor in front of her. His big, warm hands pushed hers away. "Let me."

He undid the buckles swiftly, tossing the shoes behind him, and looked into her eyes as he slid his big, warm hands up the outside of her legs, all the way up to the bands of stretchy lace that held up her thigh-high stockings, and then onto the warm, bare skin above them. He began exploring, with his usual hypnotically slow, magical caresses.

"The dress has got to go," he said. "But leave the stockings on."

She stood up, grabbing his shoulder to steady herself, and almost couldn't get a good grip, it was so thick with muscle. "I just got all that fancy beading repaired," she murmured. "Don't want to tear out the seams."

Drew tugged the crumpled pale green fabric gently down over her hips, until it fell to the floor. He made a low, grinding sound deep in his throat as he swayed forward, pressing his face to her belly.

His breath was so hot, so tender. His lips trailed over her skin, and left a glowing trail of hyper-sensitized erogenous zone every place he touched.

She slid her fingers into his hair, caressing his ears, his cheekbone, his jaw. Savoring the texture of his faint rasp of beard shadow, squeezing the massive breadth of his powerful shoulders.

Drew hooked his thumbs into the pale lace of her panties and tugged them down. She shook them off her ankle, and sucked in a startled breath as he leaned to kiss her, his mouth moving skillfully over her sensitive flesh while his hands cupped her bottom. She vibrated like a plucked string.

"So good." Drew kissed his way around the swatch of hair adorning her mound.

Jenna wanted to respond somehow, but she was beyond words. She felt so vulnerable, so naked. Incredibly female. Tormented by longing as she wound her fingers into his hair, tugging wordlessly. Demanding more, more, more.

He responded eagerly, pressing his mouth to her, caressing her tender inner folds. He was bold and generous and tireless. So incredibly good at it. He went at her with ruthless skill until she was shaking wildly, head thrown back. Keening low in her throat, completely focused on the sensual swirl of his tongue, the delicate flick, the slow, suckling pull—and she came apart, as he unleashed another wave of shuddering pleasure.

Afterward, she found herself lying down with no clear memory of how she got there, but Drew was leaning over her, pulling the billowy, puffy comforter over her.

"Good?" he asked.

She licked her lips. "I never felt anything so fabulous in my life," she whispered.

"Excellent." She couldn't read his face in the dimness, but he sounded pleased.

She grabbed his belt. "The pants need to come off. I don't want to be naked alone."

"Oh, don't worry." He shucked his pants promptly. "I'll keep you company."

He worked his briefs down, and his erection sprang free. Jenna sat up with a murmur of approval. He was stiff, flushed, ready. She closed her hand around him, and Drew covered her hand with his own, moving it up and down his thick shaft. So hot and hard and sexy. Exciting her beyond belief. She stroked him, exploring him, teasing him, squeezing him. She loved making him shudder and gasp and moan.

Finally he stopped her hands, and stretched out next to her, sliding under the covers and into her arms.

The shock of contact with her whole body made her gasp. He was scorching hot. It was overwhelming. The buzz of intense awareness felt both brand-new and incredibly familiar, like she'd known him since eternity. Their connection was timeless, inevitable, in thrall to that kiss. Tongues dancing, arms clasping, legs twining. Struggling to get closer.

She didn't know what was up, what was down. He was her center of gravity, the only one that mattered. At some point, based on the fact that she was somewhat breathless, she realized that she was underneath, pinned by his solid weight. Her legs twined around his, pulling him closer. The heat of his erection throbbed against her belly.

"You ready?" he asked.

It was hard to respond, with her throat so soft and hot, her lips shaking. She nodded, pulling him closer. Insistently.

His grin flashed briefly in the dimness as he shifted on top of her, positioning himself as she arched and opened, stretching luxuriously.

"You're so soft," he murmured, parting her tender inner folds as he moved himself against her with small, teasing strokes.

She couldn't form words anymore, not in this state. She was stuck with nonverbal communication. She dug her nails into his chest and let out a low, breathless moan as he pushed himself slowly inside her exquisitely sensitized body. He filled her completely.

She could hardly move, but she was softer and slicker and hotter than she'd ever imagined being. They started slow, just rocking together, tiny surges, but soon it was just like all the other times he'd touched her. She felt possessed, out of control, writhing, making wild, demanding sounds, nails digging into his back. Demanding everything.

And he gave it to her. Deep, rhythmic thrusts that drove her wild, caressing all the new tender sweet spots that had suddenly come into being just for him. Every stroke was marvelous, perfect, poignant. She didn't want it to ever stop, but already the charge was building, bigger than ever before.

She had no idea what was on the other side of something so huge, just that it was unprecedented. She could burn to ash, disappear. But it didn't matter. There was no question of choice. She just let that wild power have its way. Like tumbling off a cliff.

And discovering, to her astonishment, that she could fly.

Drew lifted up onto his elbows, easing slowly and reluctantly out of her clinging depths. So hot and sweet. He hoped he'd read her cues right in his own frenzy, desperate for the next thrust before he finished the one he was doing. She was small and tight and perfect, and he hadn't kept it slow. The whole thing had gotten away from him.

He stretched out next to her, touching her body along its entire length, everywhere he could. Stroking her back and waiting. Holding his breath for the verdict.

He didn't have to wait long. Her beautiful eyes fluttered open, dazed and dilated. The smile she gave him was glowing. "Hey, you."

He pulled her hand up to his mouth, kissing her knuckles. "You good?"

"Great," she said. "I didn't know that was even possible."

"What?" He was cautiously hopeful. "Meaning...?"

"Feeling like that. Coming like that. It was... I never felt anything like it."

The tension inside him relented. "Ah. Okay. Good, then."

Her eyes went wide. "Wait," she said, rolling up to prop her head on her hand. "Were you actually worried?"

"Just wanted it to be perfect for you," he said, kissing her hand again.

"*Perfect* is the wrong word," she told him. "*Perfect* is careful and nervous and controlled. It wasn't like that. It was wild. Magic. But you know that. You were there."

He was grinning now, helplessly. "Still am. Not going anywhere."

He kissed her, and in a heartbeat, he was stone-hard again, as needy and aching as he was before.

Too soon. He had to hang back. Take it easy.

He rolled onto his belly, and tried to content himself by stroking her warm, lithe body under the covers. Studying the beautiful planes and curves and hollows of her face and throat in the shadowy dimness. So spectacularly pretty. So unique.

"I just don't get it," he said, almost to himself.

"What's that?"

"Your ex. I don't get how he could look at anyone else when he had you."

She snorted. "He didn't see me. He just expected to be the smack-dab center of my attention at all times. My job was to constantly make him feel a certain way about himself, and I couldn't keep up with it. It was exhausting."

"He works in your field, right?"

"He's an engineer, like me," she said. "He was on the team that developed the design for Cherise's arm. I'm not angry like I was before, though. Only my pride was hurt. Everything else is intact. All things considered, it was a near miss. He and Kayleigh did me a favor. A public, embarrassing, ego-crushing favor. Very generous of them. I'm grateful."

Drew shifted in the bed, rolling her over on top of him. "And I'm glad."

"About what?" Jenna positioned herself, and her sensual wiggling felt so good.

He adjusted their position so that she was settled right exactly where he needed her. She gasped as he pulsed his hips up against her. "I'm glad you're not hung up on him," he said. "Because I don't want to share."

She looked startled. "Um. Wow."

They stared at each other for a long moment, and Jenna's expression changed, as the ever-present heat between them surged.

She placed her hands against his chest and pushed herself until she was sitting up, straddling him. Tossing the cover back so it landed on his legs. Shoulders back. Eyes on his, full of fire. Full of invitation as she reached down, caressing his stiff, aching length.

She placed her other hand on his chest. "I can feel your heart. In both places."

Drew covered her hand with his own, pressing it. Then he seized her hips, lifting her up so he could position himself beneath her. She danced over him until they got the angle right, and she let out a low, wordless moan as she took him inside, sinking down with shivering slowness into her tight, clinging heat.

Together they found the perfect surging rhythm. He was desperate to explode inside her, and he also wanted this to last forever. Every point of contact was as sweet as a deliberate kiss. He went for all of them with deep, gliding strokes. Seeking out everything that made her melt and moan, the power building in her body.

She cried out, throwing her head back, convulsing over him, and just in time because his own climax was rumbling in his head, a landslide about to come down on him. Huge and inevitable.

It overtook him. Blotted out the world.

Some unmeasurable interval of time later, they drifted back to normal consciousness together. She was draped over his chest, kissing it.

"I knew it would be good with you," she murmured. "I just had no idea how good. My imagination didn't go that far."

"Same with me," he admitted.

He was taken aback when she looked up and laughed. "Oh, please," she said. "Seriously, Drew? With your history?"

"What history is that?"

"Come on," she scoffed. "With all the famous beauties that you swan around with on the red carpets and the luxurious yachts?"

He jerked up off the pillow. "What does that have to do with anything? A lot of women have been associated with me. That doesn't mean I had satisfying relationships with them. Or great sex. Or that I felt intimate with them. That's never come easy to me. Women complain that I can't open up. But with you, I can. It's different with you."

Jenna propped her head on her arms to study him. It was as if her beautiful eyes stared straight into his mind. All that sharp intelligence focused on him, trying to distinguish truth from bullshit. Trying to decide if he was for real. He was on trial.

He stared back. "I have never felt this way," he said. "Never. About anyone. That is not a slick, calculated line. I swear to God, I am being straight with you."

Jenna slowly reached out both hands, cupping his face, stroking it gently with her fingertips, from his cheekbones to his jaw. She gave him a misty smile, and nodded.

"Okay," she whispered. "I believe you."

It was as if the chains broke loose inside him, all at once. He pulled her close, and off they went again.

Like nothing on earth could hold them back.

Seventeen

Jenna drifted up from sleep, disoriented. She felt so good. Incredibly warm.

She opened her eyes. The two enormous windows showed the glow of sunrise on the lake and in the sky. Drew was behind her. One arm draped around her shoulders, the other curved around the pillow where she lay.

She stared at his powerful forearm, mere inches from her eyes, admiring the details. Trying to breathe. She couldn't believe this was real. It seemed like a dream, but her backside was pressed against his immense heat.

His bedroom was beautiful in the morning light. Soothing to the eye. Light reflected off the gleaming floorboards. Swaths of green and waving boughs set off the lake view. Mist rose in tendrils off the water. Tranquil and lovely.

Their hastily discarded clothing was strewn around the bed. She saw one of her shoes. Her dress, sadly crumpled. Sacrificed on the altar of lust, but she regretted nothing.

She really was here. Naked in Drew Maddox's bed. She'd spent the night in his luxurious bachelor lair. She'd been well and truly seduced.

Last night had been a revelation. Some time ago, after a series of romantic disappointments, she'd come to the conclusion that she was just one of those people for whom sex was just never going to be a big priority. She just didn't get what the fuss was about. She was a busy person. Everyone had to decide where to put their energy and attention. A family would have been nice, but all those songs about passion and obsession and need... She just didn't get it.

Well, damn. She got it now, like a wrecking ball. Roddy's song flashed through her mind.

In your deep and honest eyes, I find my reason why. Her own eyes overflowed.

No, no, no. Cool your jets, girl. Too much, too soon. She had to keep this light. She appreciated Drew's pronouncements about how special their connection was—that was all very sweet and lovely, and she meant to enjoy it to the fullest—but she wasn't diving into this headfirst. She was going to tiptoe. Eyes wide open.

She peered over at the digital clock with eyes that burned and stung from sleeping in her contacts. She had an early lunch with Bev and her friends from the Bricker Foundation. She barely had time to organize for it. And Smudge would be so hurt at being abandoned all night, he probably wouldn't speak to her for days.

She slid out of Drew's arms, trying not to disturb him, and slipped off the bed, gathering those of her things that she could find. The bathroom was in disarray, water and towels on the floor. She'd come in at some point to wash up, but Drew had joined her and turned her shower into another delicious erotic interlude. The memory made her face go hot.

After a quickie rinse in the shower, she dried off and put on her clothes, insofar as she could. The stockings were lost in Drew's bed somewhere. Her hairpins were scattered all over his entry hall. Her bra was missing in action. She pulled on the dress without it, hoping that her landlady and the other tenants wouldn't see her waltzing up the steps to her house in the morning in rumpled evening wear. Her first official walk of shame, whoo-hoo. Better late than never.

The makeup smears were alarming. A dab of lotion she found on Drew's shelf got off the worst of it, but nothing would dim that wild feverish flush on her face.

Or the glow of terrified happiness in her eyes.

He was still asleep, stretched out on the rumpled bed, the coverlet draped across his waist, when she tiptoed out of the bathroom. She moved closer to admire, and saw the scars on his lower back that she hadn't noticed in the dark the night before. The ragged path the bullet had made as it tore through him. The more regular surgical scars that surrounded it. Her muscles tightened in cringing sympathy, imagining all that pain.

She needed to call for a ride home, and for that, she needed her phone. The evening bag was probably still in the foyer somewhere, so she tiptoed out there barefoot. There it was, on the dining room table. She scooped up as many hairpins as she could find, and shoved them into her bag. She needed to know where she was to call for a pickup, so she poked around until she found an architectural magazine with a mailing label. She made the call and was heading back for her shoes when she heard him.

"Jenna? You here?"

"I'm here," she called back. "Just getting myself together."

Drew was sitting up and leaning back against his hands, the cover draped across his lap, hiding all his excellent masculine bounty. Probably just as well. She had to avoid temptation this morning, considering her time crunch. But oh, he was so gorgeous.

He looked dismayed to see her dressed. "You're leaving already?"

"I'm so sorry, but I have to go," she said apologetically, scooping up her shoes. She sat down on the bed next to him to put them on. "I have appointments today."

"Can't you reschedule? Say you're sick. Loll around

naked in bed with me here all day. I'm no master chef, but I can handle bacon, eggs and toast just fine."

It sounded so wonderful. She struggled with the stupidly tiny shoe buckle, fighting the overwhelming urge to give in and stay with him. "I'm sorry," she repeated. "It sounds great, and I'd love to, really, but I just can't. Not this time."

"Then I'll drive you home. Let me throw on some clothes."

"Oh, no, no," she said quickly. "The car service is on its way."

A guarded look came over his face. "You're not panicking on me, are you?"

"No way." She finished with the last buckle, and leaned to give him a slow, lingering kiss. "I am not blowing you off. By no means. I promise. I loved every second of last night. It was incredible."

"Then have lunch with me," he said. "After your thing."

"Lunch *is* the thing, I'm afraid. An early one, with Bev and her lady friends from the Bricker Foundation. Some of whom may have seen me wrapped around you in my bra last night, so I think I should change my clothes and freshen my makeup before I face them. Plus, I am desperate to get these contacts out and put my glasses back on."

He grinned. "I love your glasses."

She kissed him again. "Good," she said. "That is extremely lucky for you."

"Dinner, then?" he asked hopefully.

She was floating now, and couldn't even control the smile that seemed wrapped all the way around her head. "Dinner," she agreed. "We're on. Text me the details."

"Will do." He tugged the comforter off his lap, displaying his erection, in all its glory. "All the details," he agreed. "For your viewing pleasure. Nothing held back."

She looked him over appreciatively, biting her lip. "You're making this really hard, Drew," she murmured.

"I think that's my line," he said, and then cut off her giggles with a kiss that sent a fresh jolt of aching sexual hunger through her body. In no time, she was stretched out on the bed, feet dangling off, arms wound around him. Oh, that seductive bastard. Out of nowhere, she was a breath away from pulling her clothes off and leaping on him again.

But she pulled back, breath hitching, face red. *Play it cool. Keep it light.*

"You're so bad," she said, her voice unsteady. "Enticing me."

"I can't help myself. How am I supposed to make myself respectable for work with a hard-on like this?"

She shrugged. "Don't know, but I just heard my phone beep with a message, so the car is probably waiting out there. You're on your own with that dilemma. Poor you. Maybe I can help you brainstorm possible solutions for that problem tonight at dinner. If you're good."

"Cruel, heartless Jenna. I promise, I'll be good."

The car service SUV was waiting in the driveway, and the driver had a long-suffering look on his face, as if he'd been there for a while. When she got in, her phone started beeping almost immediately. Messages coming in, one after the other.

She pulled her phone out of the evening bag. From Drew.

miss you already

can't wait for dinner tonight

wasn't ready for the night to be over

It was a painful inward struggle to keep herself from telling the driver to turn right around and take her back. She could not make a fool of herself and get all goofy about him. Just. Could. Not.

She tapped in same but then the emoji menu beckoned. Should she add a smiley face, a kissy face, heart eyes, a throbbing heart? Fruits and vegetables? Damn.

Keep it restrained, she reminded herself. Dignified. Not goofy.

She finally went with it was a wonderful night. No emojis.

my pillows smell like your perfume he responded.

Oh, God, he was killing her. She scrolled down the emoticon menu again. Picked out a single flower emoji, and sent it. Restraint. Restraint was everything.

Then she sat there, face red, heart thudding. Toes curling in her shoes. Waiting like a lovesick ninny for his response. It didn't take long.

aloof and mysterious as always

The driver gave her a doubtful look in the rearview as she laughed out loud.

hardly she replied, and then added three flame emojis and a lipstick kiss.

After a moment, going for a run to burn off excess energy. text you after.

She wished she could see Drew Maddox running. That big, sleek, stunning body in motion, bounding along, radiating heat, all flushed and sweatily gorgeous.

Mmm. Yes, please.

sounds good. enjoy yourself she tapped in.

Excess energy, ha. They'd made love five times, counting the shower time, and slept hardly at all. But she was buzzing with plenty of excess energy herself. She was restless and fidgety, and wanted to break into a song-and-dance routine on the street. But she contained herself, with some effort.

When she got to her apartment, she was relieved not to

see her landlady or any of her neighbors. Smudge made his displeasure with her known the moment she walked in. She hastened to feed him and placate him, but he was having none of it, ignoring her frostily as he wolfed down his breakfast.

She plugged her phone in to charge and headed to the bedroom, picking out a burgundy wool dress suit with a short sixties-style skirt that made her feel like Audrey Hepburn. After a shower, she tried twisting her hair up into a tidy bun, but as usual, ended up looking like a burning bush. Sleek was just never going to be her thing.

As soon as she got her makeup on, she heard the rapid-fire beeping of text alerts. She lunged for the phone. It could be Drew.

It wasn't. Two missed calls from Ava, and a whole bunch of messages.

?? where are you?

didn't we have a coffee date at Ruby's to run over the Bricker Foundation stuff?

c'mon Jenna, I have things to tell you and a busy as hell day!

Oh, cripes. She'd asked Ava to give her feedback on the spiel she was going to give Bev's friends from the Bricker Foundation. All the drama had wiped that appointment completely out of her mind.

She tapped in a quick response.

sorry, running late. On my way. Hang tight.

A frowning emoji arrived and then, I'll order for you. cinnamon buns good today.

She gave Smudge an apologetic belly rub and got her thumb bitten, less gently than usual. Message received. She grabbed her car keys.

She got lucky with parking, and trotted into Ruby's panting and red-faced. Ava sat in her usual booth with her laptop out and a pair of severe black reading glasses perched on her nose that somehow only managed to accentuate how ridiculously pretty she was. Her honey-blond hair was loose and swirling down over her black sweater. She looked up at Jenna, and her eyebrow climbed.

She lifted a cup. "Vanilla latte, triple shot," she said. "Because I am a good friend."

"Thanks." Jenna slid into the booth and took a grateful sip of the hot beverage.

"So before we take a quick look at the Bricker Foundation stuff for today, let me just show you these stats," she started briskly. "Ernest and I were talking about the big picture for Arm's Reach last night, and it's fantastic, the progress we've made."

"Um, about that," Jenna said. "I appreciate everything you've done, Av, but I need to back off for a little while."

"Back off?" Ava looked horrified. "That's insane. Your visibility is through the roof. You show up first on every search. You're trending everywhere. You've been telling a juicy story, and everyone's paying attention to it. You can't stop now!"

"But that's just the thing, Av. You're a storyteller. I'm not. I'm a scientist. I like facts. Hard data. Not stories."

"Sure, but this is all in the service of science, Jenn. Oh, hey. Speaking of facts and hard data, where in the hell were you this morning?"

Jenna choked on her coffee and sputtered into a napkin. "Excuse me?"

"I went to your apartment, since I was up early," Ava

said. "You weren't there, but your car was, so I knew you hadn't gone to work. So what gives?"

Jenna almost blurted out the truth, but something stopped her. And she couldn't even lie and say she'd gone jogging, or to an early spin class. Her face got hotter. She couldn't meet Ava's eyes.

Ava took a bite of cinnamon bun, frowning in puzzlement. Then she stopped chewing, and just stared at Jenna's face, her eyes going wide.

"No way." Her voice was flat. "You didn't."

Jenna pressed her hands against her hot cheeks. She didn't bother to deny it. It seemed ridiculous to lie, after last night's huge, public scene. She tried to laugh it off. "It's so surprising to you? After what you saw last night?"

Ava swallowed her bite of pastry with evident difficulty. "I thought you were just, ah…you know. That it was all part of the, um…"

"Story? Good Lord, Ava, do you think I'd roll around half-dressed in front of the Board of Directors and your uncle just for a boost in my search engine optimization? How slutty and cynical do you think I am?"

"Not at all." Ava's voice was tight and colorless. "So you and Drew are…a thing now?"

Her friend sounded both incredulous and worried. Both reactions bugged the hell out of her. "It's so improbable to you?"

Ava didn't bother responding to that. "Since when has this been going on?"

"We've been circling around it since the very beginning," Jenna admitted. "But last night is the first time that we, uh…"

"Did the deed," Ava finished.

An appalled silence spread between them. The concerned look in Ava's eyes was driving Jenna nuts. "Don't look like that! Cripes, is it such a terrible development?"

Ava shook her head. "That's not it. I think you're wonderful. You know that. I just…it's just…" Ava's voice trailed off. She was uncharacteristically lost for words.

Icy clarity settled in, along with an ache of dread that threatened to completely dampen her buzz of excitement.

"You don't think I can hold his interest," she said flatly. "You don't think I can measure up to all his movie stars and models."

Ava dismissed the movie stars and models with a flap of her hand. "Not at all," she said impatiently. "They were a bunch of airheads, mostly. He was with them because they were cute and right there in front of him, so why not. Besides, he never wants to risk actually caring about somebody with substance, so I never thought that he would actually…"

"So you don't think we're believable as a couple," Jenna said. "Believable for the Maddox Hill Board of Directors, and your uncle, maybe, because playacting is fine. But not for real."

"Don't be mad," Ava pleaded. "When I proposed this to him, I never in a million years thought that—"

"That he could actually be interested in someone like me," Jenna finished.

"Don't put words in my mouth," Ava snapped. "It never occurred to me that this could have, you know, consequences. That I could set you up for disappointment, or hurt. You've had enough already. I didn't think it through, that's all. And that…scares me."

Well, great. That made two of them.

Jenna got up and grabbed her coffee. "Thanks for the vote of confidence. If you'll excuse me, I have a busy day ahead, so have a good one."

"Don't forget that tomorrow morning, you and Drew have that interview with the—"

"No," Jenna broke in. "Cancel the interview. Cancel

everything. Say I'm sick. Say anything you want. I can't handle any more PR events. I'm done playacting, I'm sick of being photographed. I appreciate your hard work and I think you're a genius, but the price is too high. As of today, Project Billionaire's Plaything is on indefinite hiatus."

"Jenn. Please." The tone in Ava's voice stopped her in her tracks. Her friend never sounded like that. Dead serious. Subdued.

"What?" she snapped.

"Just please. Be careful," Ava said.

That made her even more miserable. She'd spent weeks convinced that Drew could never be interested in her for real, and now look at her—all bent out of shape because Ava thought the exact same thing.

It was hypocritical and unfair.

She hurried toward her car. The text alert chirped as she got in. Then another. Two messages from Drew, responding to a picture she'd sent him of Smudge, glaring up at her over his chicken chunks.

Your cat fits my color scheme. He would look good in my living room.

Or I maybe I should say, my living room would look good on your cat.

Oh, man. Tears welled into her eyes.

All the feels. Floodgates open. His offhand remark unleashed wild fantasies of domestic bliss with Drew. Feeding chicken chunks to her kitty in his kitchen. Smudge curled up on his couch.

When he said things like that, how the hell was she supposed to stay careful?

Eighteen

The meeting about engineering problems in the Abu Dhabi project ran an extra hour over, but Drew was in too good a mood to be upset. Maybe he wasn't going to have to resign from his position after all. Which was a huge relief. Fingers crossed. For all of it, including Jenna.

He was on cloud nine after that night with her. He never allowed himself to look at his phone in meetings, but he could feel the phone vibrate in his pocket whenever she sent him a message. The constant buzz of anticipation kept his spirits sky-high, even with Harold giving him the fish-eye.

Eventually he was going to have to do something about his cousin's poisonous hostility, but today he couldn't be bothered to worry about it. He had better things to think about. Like Jenna's texts.

He usually felt annoyed and oppressed when his lovers texted him during a workday. He liked keeping things compartmentalized. Work was work, and he liked a hard focus.

Not an option with Jenna. She was interconnected with every thought in his head.

As they came out of the meeting, he already had his phone in his hand but was still talking to his VPs, including Harold. "Make sure you talk to Michaela and Loris about those budget details before you move forward," Drew said.

"Of course," his cousin drawled. "Look at you. In such a good mood today."

Drew gave him a wary look. "Why shouldn't I be?"

"I just expected you to look more hungover, considering the condition you were in last night," Harold said.

"I didn't drink last night," he said.

Harold snorted. "If you say so. Must be the health benefits of rolling around in bed with Jenna Somers. Guess I can't really blame you. She is red-hot."

Drew waited for a couple of breaths before he replied. "Don't say her name again," he said. "Don't even get near her. Or we will have a problem."

"Oh, yeah? You going to go all tough ex-Marine on me and rearrange my face?"

"If that's the only thing you understand," Drew replied. "Bring it."

"Break it up, boys." Ava's crisp voice came from behind them. "Harry, whatever your damn problem is, put it on ice and excuse us, please. I urgently need to speak to Drew. Alone."

Harold made a disgusted sound and stalked away.

Drew turned toward his sister. "Thanks for shutting him up. Uncle Malcolm wouldn't appreciate me breaking his jaw during working hours."

"Don't thank me yet," Ava said icily. "You're not going to be grateful when I'm done with you."

Tension gripped him. "Why? What have I done now?"

"Let's talk in your office, please."

Drew knew what this was about. He strode toward his office, Ava keeping pace beside him, and held the door for her. When the door closed behind them, he braced himself and turned. "Okay. Let me have it."

"What in holy hell do you think you're doing?" Ava burst out.

He sighed. "Help me out here, Av. Context, please."

"Don't you dare play dumb!" Ava said furiously. "I never meant for you to seduce her! That is self-indulgent and irresponsible!"

Drew let out a harsh laugh. "You threw her into my arms yourself."

"Is that what you think I did? That I just gave you license to amuse yourself?"

"Amuse myself?" Drew bristled. "What the hell, Av? She's a grown woman!"

"She's not like your usual type. You know. All the Lydia clones."

"Lydia is not my type," he snarled.

"Well, if Lydia herself was ever confused about that, I wouldn't blame her," Ava said. "I thought you understood. This was a little bit of theater to help you over a bad spot, and goose the stats for Jenna's company, and now you decide to have a taste? Of my best friend? What the hell were you thinking?"

Drew spoke through his teeth. "You're pissing me off."

"Yeah? Well, the feeling is mutual." Ava's voice was low and furious. "I love Jenna. And I mean, for real love her, get me? She's the kindest, most selfless, principled person I know. She is not a disposable squeeze toy for you to play around with!"

"What makes you think I'm playing?"

His sister laughed harshly. "Oh, I don't know." Her voice was heavy with irony. "Your track record? You bore easily, big brother. Don't think I or the rest of the world hasn't noticed. You've left a trail of high-profile, royally pissed-off women in your wake. If you do that to my girl Jenna, I will rip your head right off your neck."

"It's not that I bore easily," Drew said. "I've just been choosing badly."

"Seriously?" Ava shook her head in disbelief. "You just now realized, at the ripe old age of thirty-four, that you should maybe take something other than a pretty face and a hot body into consideration when choosing a lover? Wow, Drew! Boom! Blinding insight, huh? Congratulations! Better late than never, I guess!"

He turned his back on her and stared out at the view. "I don't get this," he said. "If you think she's so fabulous, what made you think I wouldn't notice?"

Ava made a frustrated sound. "I don't know. I just didn't think it through. I never would have imagined the two of you together, because you…" Her voice trailed off.

Drew stared her down. "You think I'm not good enough for her," he said.

Ava bit her lip. Her angry flush had faded. "No. I didn't say that."

But she'd hesitated too long for her denial to be convincing.

They were locked in an awful silence, unable to look away from each other.

Finally Ava shook it off. "Damn it, Drew. Just don't lead her on, okay? I don't want to be responsible for that. It would suck if she got hurt and it was all my fault."

He walked over to the door. "Get out." He opened it for her.

The crowd of people gathered outside suddenly turned away and wandered off with extreme nonchalance. Damn. So they'd been yelling loud enough to be heard through the expensively sealed soundproofed door. Ava stalked out, chin high, lips tight.

Drew closed the door after her, leaning against it. Stung.

He wondered if Jenna felt like Ava did. That he was faithless and irresponsible. Good for nothing but sex. A dog on the furniture, like his uncle said. He wondered if she was just amusing herself while keeping her shields up and her heart fully armored.

It didn't feel like that was the case, but it would serve him right if it was.

Ava and all the rest of them could all go to hell. He'd make this work. He could be a better man for her. He'd show her. If it took years. A lifetime.

This was the first time that the concept of spending a lifetime with one woman made sense to him.

Roddy's song ran through his head, along with a powerful sense memory of that soul-melding kiss they'd shared at the Wild Side. Roddy had nailed it with those lyrics.

He'd found his reason why. He was all hers. It was a done deal. On his part, at least.

All that was left was to convince her that he was for real.

"So, Jenna. Enough business. Let's dish a little. We're all so excited about your upcoming wedding!" Helen Sanderson said. "Give us some juicy details!"

Jenna looked around the table at the older ladies, all Bev's philanthropist friends from the Bricker Foundation, who were smiling at her expectantly.

"Um, we don't actually have firm plans yet," she hedged.

"Well, we certainly can help with that," Jayne Braithwaite said eagerly. "We have experience in these kinds of things. All of us have helped our kids get married."

"It was such a shock to hear that Drew Maddox finally got lassoed," Margot Kristoff confided. "That boy always was way too handsome. It's so satisfying when one of those types finally figures out what's good for him."

"Hendrick was like that, years ago," Bev mused with a nostalgic air.

The other ladies all chuckled. "He figured out what side his bread was buttered on quick enough," Helen said.

"Exactly," Bev said. "And that's what I hope for you, honey."

Jenna forced herself to smile. "Me, too."

"Did you ever see Drew in his dress uniform?" Gwen Hoyt asked, miming fanning herself. "Oh me, oh my."

"Only pictures, I'm afraid," she said. "I wish. I'm sure he looks stunning."

"My husband was in the air force, see," Gwen confided. "And that uniform just did something to me. I just love to see a man in a dress uniform."

"So, sweetie," Jayne said briskly. "The Wexler Prize Awards Banquet is coming up in just a few weeks. Are you shopping for the ultimate dress and writing your acceptance speech?"

"Oh, it's by no means a sure thing," Jenna said. "There are many excellent candidates. They're all fabulous projects."

"True, but I put my money on you," Bev said. "In any case, everyone wants to put money on you right now. The Maddox Hill Foundation is interested in partnering with Arm's Reach, and so is the Bricker Foundation. There's so much buzz about you! Seems like you can't turn around without seeing another photo of you and Drew, or hearing something about Arm's Reach. You're on everyone's lips!"

Jenna felt freshly guilty for being so angry with Ava at the coffee shop. "That's completely Ava's doing," she said. "She's a marketing genius."

"That she is," Bev agreed. "That girl is a live wire. But the magic was there to begin with, honey. She just shone a brighter light on it so everyone could see."

"Thank you." Jenna's face went hot.

Helen reached out and grabbed her hand. "So, you haven't set a date yet?"

"Not really," Jenna said. "We've just been kicking ideas around."

"If you're getting married close to home, your best bet is May through September," Gayle advised. "But always with an indoor option."

"My brother-in-law runs a gorgeous resort on the coast," Margot told her. "It's called Paradise Point. It's on this spit of land that juts out on the coast. Sea cliffs, beaches below, fields of wildflowers, crashing waves, stunning views. There's even a lighthouse and rock monoliths on the beach. And the resort itself is a gem. Drew designed the building, you know."

"No, I, uh, didn't know that."

"Here, look at this." Margot leaned over the table, showing Jenna her phone. "These are some of the pictures I took of my niece Brooke's wedding at Paradise Point last year. Enchanting place. And would you believe, it drizzled the whole time, but because of the way the building was designed, we never felt like we were trapped indoors. That's what I love about Drew's designs."

"Agreed," Jenna said. "His house is like that, too. It feels so soothing."

The older ladies exchanged delighted glances that she pretended not to see as she swiped through Margot's photos. "Isn't that just sweet?" Bev murmured. "He talks that way about her work, too. They're so proud of each other. I just love that."

"So next summer, then?" Jayne prompted. "Or did you want spring flowers?"

"Oh, good, I finally found it," Margot said, holding up her phone again. "This is my favorite. This is Brooke and her new husband, Matthias, the moment that the rain stopped and the sun came through. Look, how the photographer actually caught them framed in a rainbow. Isn't that just precious?"

Jenna looked at the picture. A pretty blonde held up the muddied hem of her wedding dress, gazing adoringly up into the face of a stocky, beaming young black-haired man. All around them, sunlight had broken through the clouds, highlighting the flowers.

And a rainbow arched over them. It was unbearably perfect. The couple looked so happy.

The feelings came over her too fast to fend off. She dove for a tissue. Margot pushed one into her hand before she found them. The older women clustered around murmuring in consternation.

Bev grabbed her hand. "Sweetie, are you okay?"

"I'm fine," she said. "These photos are so beautiful, and I'm just so damn emotional right now. Everything sets me off."

Bev pressed her hand. "You sure you're fine?"

Jenna dabbed carefully under her eyes. "I'm great. It's just that it's too new to talk about wedding venues. Seeing the pictures of Brooke and her husband—it's just too much. I'm so happy right now, but I'm still afraid of jinxing myself. Sorry."

"Don't apologize," Margot said gently. "That picture makes me cry, too, and I've been married for forty-two years. We're all just so happy for you. Sorry we pushed you, honey."

"We all know how risky it is," Bev said. "Loving someone, marrying him. You just have to cross your fingers and hope to God you don't crash and burn."

Jayne squeezed her shoulder. "We're rooting for you. You seem like a lovely girl."

Jenna looked around at their kindly faces, and her eyes got misty again. She wanted so badly for this relationship to be real, and worthy of all this benevolent well-wishing. But she wasn't even convinced herself yet. It was premature, to talk about wedding venues.

Too much, too soon. It was a recipe for disaster.

Nineteen

"Drew, will you do up these hooks for me?"

Drew finished buttoning his tux shirt and came up behind Jenna, who stood in front of the big standing mirror he'd gotten a couple of weeks ago for his bedroom. He'd never felt the need for one before, but now he had Jenna in his space, dressing for work, putting on her makeup, doing her hair. A beautiful woman like her needed a full-length mirror to put herself together.

He paused for a moment to admire her. The low-cut, midnight blue taffeta evening dress consisted of a tight-fitting strapless boned bodice of textured taffeta that showcased her elegant curves and narrow waist, billowing out into a big, full, rustling skirt.

The bodice was open over her back, showing the long, graceful curve of her spine and the delicate shadow of her shoulder blades, her fine-grained, flawless skin. The enticing shadow of her cleavage. Lust stabbed into him, predictably enough.

Jenna shot him a glance as he placed his hands on her waist and slid them up until he was cupping her breasts. "So fine." His voice was a sexy rasp.

She fluttered her lashes at him seductively. "Be that as it may, we can't be late. Don't be bad."

Her voice had that breathless catch that it got when he succeeded in tempting her.

"They'll wait for us." He bent down to press a hot kiss against the back of her neck, making a delicious shiver of sensual awareness vibrate through her body.

"Oh, no you don't," she murmured. "Don't make me all sweaty and damp and have to fix my makeup all over again."

"I'll make it worth your while," he coaxed.

"Save it," she said sternly. "You'll get what you want… but later."

He bowed to the inevitable, but took his own sweet time with the tiny hooks, relishing the opportunity to touch her hot, petal-smooth skin as he fastened them up. Admiring all the details. The shape of her spine, her elegant posture, the shape of her shoulder blades.

He'd liked the way his life felt, these last weeks. Liked it so much, it scared him.

Ava had eased off on the punishing PR schedule, thank God, so he and Jenna had been able to spend some free time together. He was greedy for all of it, so bit by bit, she'd started spending most of the time at his house— along with her cat.

Smudge wasn't quite sure about Drew yet. He kept trying to establish dominance. But even that couldn't put a damper on how much Drew loved having Jenna in his living space.

"One moment, for the full effect," she murmured, adjusting the cups of the bodice. Afterwards, her perfect high breasts spilled out of the top of the cups just enough to make Drew slightly uncomfortable.

"I could have adjusted that for you, too," he told her.

"And then we would have ended up being late. I know you." Her mouth was stern, but her eyes smiled.

"You look fantastic," he told her.

It was the stark truth. He couldn't stop staring. The deep

blue made her skin glow like it was lit from inside. The design hugged her stunning figure. Her blue satin spike-heeled shoes had delicate, glittering ankle straps. He ached to touch her.

"Which glasses today?" he asked. "The blue ones?"

"Contacts, for special occasions. The announcement of the Wexler Prize is a special occasion. I'm not wearing workaday specs for that."

"You know that your specs make me hot," he told her.

"No, Drew, you just exist in a generally overheated state, and the specs are incidental. Not that I'm complaining. I like having you perpetually ready for action."

"Always," he promised. "The dress looks great on you."

"It ought to, considering what it cost," she said, fastening her little diamond drop earrings into her ears with a secret smile. "I still think it was extravagant of you. My other dress would have been fine."

"I wanted you to get this dress because it looks good with this other thing I got you," he told her.

Her eyes filled with alarm. "Drew. We talked about this. Remember?"

"Yes, yes. I know. No billionaire's-plaything scenarios. Not even as fun, lighthearted bed-play. We're just two people enjoying each other's company. No mind games. No power plays. No expensive gifts. All of this is forbidden. Rules are rules."

"Good," she said cautiously. "Then… What did you do?"

"This." He pulled a teardrop sapphire pendant, ringed with smaller diamonds, out of his pocket and held it up in front of her. It settled right at the hollow of her throat as he fastened the clasp of the delicate, glittering white gold chain.

Jenna gasped. "Oh, my God, Drew. I can't accept this."

"I found it a couple weeks ago. I thought it would look

perfect with the ring. That was why I pushed for blue, even though the other dresses looked great on you, too."

"But… It's against the rules." Her hand went up to touch it delicately.

"Sometimes rules have to be broken. That nugget of wisdom brought to you by Michael Wu, who has finally kicked my underperforming ass up to level eight. He advised me to be bolder and risk harder, or else I'll just keep running around in the same circles."

She gazed at herself in the mirror, wide-eyed. "Very smooth," he said. "Video game wisdom, to manipulate me. You know that Michael is my soft spot."

"I love manipulating your soft spots," he whispered into her ear. "I'll use whatever works. But Michael's logic makes sense to me. Because I think we're ready."

She turned to look up at him. "For what?"

"The next level," he said.

They just gazed at each other. The air hummed with emotion. Endless possibilities.

He took her hand, and kept kissing it until he felt that subtle shift of energy, like the wind ruffling the grass. They were so attuned to each other. God, how he loved that.

Her eyes dropped. "This isn't a conversation to have when we're late to an important function," she said. "Let's, um, hit Pause. Pick this up later."

He let out a sigh. At least it wasn't a flat-out no. But he wanted so badly to nail this down and close the deal. "You will wear the necklace, though, right?" he wheedled.

She narrowed her eyes at him, fingering the pendant. "You are sneaky."

"Always," he assured her.

"Hmmph. This time," she conceded. "I have to go find my evening bag. I think I left it in the studio."

The skirt swooshed and rustled past his legs as she swept out, leaving him alone and secretly exulting. It was a huge deal that she was wearing jewelry he'd gotten her. She was so prickly about the billionaire-plaything vibe. Every little silly detail made her twitchy.

He looked around for his tux jacket and found it on the bed, with Smudge curled up on top of it, purring loudly.

As Drew approached, Smudge rolled onto his back and stretched luxuriously, flopping this way and that, making sure to cover the entire jacket. Then he flipped over and began digging his claws into the shiny black lapels, kneading them. His golden eyes fixed on Drew's face, waiting to see how he took it.

Drew sighed. "I need my tux jacket, cat."

He picked the cat up and dropped him on the floor. Smudge hissed and stalked away with his tail high to plot his next move.

The jacket was hot, creased and crumpled and covered with a layer of downy gray fluff. Drew got the lint roller, an item that now hung on the closet door for easy and constant access, and rolled the cat fluff carefully off from his jacket.

This was next-level stuff for sure.

The first part of the evening passed in a daze for Jenna. She had to hope that her mind was functioning on autopilot during the mix-and-mingle part of the evening, because she'd talked with what felt like hundreds of people and had not the slightest memory of what she'd said to them. She just kept touching the pendant at her throat and trying to keep herself from dancing with excitement.

Next level? What exactly did that mean, other than the screamingly obvious? She didn't dare get it wrong. Could she have misunderstood, projected, overshot his intentions? She was head over heels in love, and he kept luring her deeper into his life.

And it was so much fun. She slept at his house every night. Weekend mornings were coffee and sex and brunch, then more sex. Evenings they cooked dinner together, cuddled on the couch or on his terrace on the lake, sipping a glass of brandy under a cashmere blanket, legs wound together on the hassock. He'd dedicated a studio for her so she could work weekends from his house. He'd installed a cat door in his kitchen for Smudge. He'd designated a huge closet for her, as if she had a wardrobe vast enough to fill it.

And then, relentlessly, he was filling it. Like this gown, for instance. It was stunning, but it was total billionaire-plaything nonsense, the very kind she'd forbidden from the very beginning. Now the sapphire pendant, for God's sake. To match the ring.

He was getting bolder.

She wondered if she'd be required to spend obscene amounts of his money on dressing herself at the next level. Hmm.

She'd cross that bridge when she came to it.

At some point in the evening, Bev and her friends and colleagues from the Bricker Foundation ganged up on her and towed her away from Drew to introduce her to someone, and she quickly got embroiled in a lively discussion about partnership possibilities with a charity that helped the victims of land mines. Afterward, she strolled through the ballroom, scanning for Drew. It seldom took long to find him, even in a big crowd, he was so tall. And no one filled out a tux like that man.

"Jenna," said a familiar voice from behind her.

She spun around with a gasp and beheld Rupert, all dressed up in a tuxedo.

"What in the hell are you doing here?" she demanded.

"Way to make a guy feel welcome." Rupert sounded a little hurt.

Like he had any right to expect a welcome from her. But she suppressed a tart reply. There were people all around and she was tired of being the floor show.

"What are you doing here, Rupert?" she asked again.

"I was invited," he said huffily. "You do remember that I worked on these projects, right? The Wexler Foundation sent the invitation to the whole team." He tossed back the rest of his champagne and smacked it down with far too much force on the tray of a passing server, causing all the champagne flutes on the tray to totter and sway. By some miracle of coordination, the server managed not to drop them all, but Rupert didn't even notice.

"I knew they sent an invitation to the team, but I didn't expect to see you come," Jenna said. "I thought you were in Bali. Where's Kayleigh? Didn't she come with you?"

Rupert's face tightened. "Ah. Well, no. About that. It's over with Kayleigh. I came back early from Bali."

"It's over? You mean…"

"Finished," Rupert said glumly. "We broke up."

Jenna realized that her mouth was hanging open, and closed it. "Oh. That was quick."

He shrugged. "Can I speak with you?"

"You're speaking with me now, aren't you?"

"I mean in private. Please."

Jenna glanced around at the murmuring crowd filling the ballroom of the stunning Crane Convention Center, one of Maddox Hill's newest projects. "Rupert, I'm really busy tonight, and this isn't the time or place."

"Please," he urged. "Just a word. It won't take long. You owe me that."

Actually, she didn't owe him a damn thing. But she didn't want to make a scene and she also wanted to be done with this, whatever it was. That way, she didn't have to schedule another encounter. Things were always better dealt with hot and on the spot.

She sighed silently, and gestured for him to follow her. She led the way out of the ballroom and swiftly up the sweeping double staircase, to the luxury suite that Maddox Hill reserved for its own use. In this case, it had served as a headquarters for the event planners. It was deserted now, since all the event coordinators were downstairs, on the job.

"Okay, Rupert," she said crisply. "Dinner's about to be served. After that, they're going to award the Wexler Prize, and I'm really hoping to win it. So please, make it snappy."

"I see you're as career oriented as you ever were," he commented.

That got her goat, but she didn't rise to the bait. "You better believe it," she agreed, noting his peeling sunburn from too much beach in Bali and his affected little goatee. And the smug, superior expression on his face. Thank God, she'd stopped short of marrying that. She was so grateful. "Tell me."

"I'm not sure just how to say this to you, Jenna—"

"Figure it out fast."

He looked hurt. "You're being sharp."

She gave him a look. "Do you blame me?"

His expression softened. "No," he said earnestly. "I truly do not. Jenna, I've learned so much about myself in the past few weeks. That's what I wanted to tell you."

She stifled a groan. Just what her evening lacked. To hear what Rupert had learned about himself. "It's not a good time," she repeated, through her teeth.

"It was a mistake," Rupert said. "Getting involved with Kayleigh, I mean. I got carried away. It was an illusion. All lust and hormones. I just didn't realize who she really was."

It took all her self-control not to roll her eyes. "Really? What tipped you off?"

She immediately regretted the question, because Rupert didn't get the irony. "She had an affair," he said, his voice cracking with emotion. "Just days after our wedding. With the yoga instructor. At the honeymoon resort."

Jenna managed somehow not to laugh and tell him that karma was a bitch. "That's awful," she said. "How disappointing."

"I knew you'd understand." Rupert's eyes were soulful. "I have no right to say this, after what happened, but you are just…radiant tonight. I've never seen you look so beautiful."

Compliments from Rupert made her uneasy. She shifted back a step. "Um. Thanks."

"It's so strange. Almost as if it took that stupid, squalid adventure with Kayleigh to actually be able to see you clearly, for what you are. The contrast between you and her, you know? It's like, I never saw you… And now I'm dazzled. A veil has been lifted."

Jenna was horrified. "Rupert, don't."

"Please, let me finish. You're the only one for me. I'm sorry it took me so long to figure that out. I'm so sorry I ever let you down."

Jenna backed away from him. "I don't know if you've been paying attention, but I'm involved with someone else right now," she said cautiously. "I mean, seriously involved."

"Yes, and that's another thing." Rupert's voice took on that maddening tone it got when he decided to school her about something. "I know you might be dazzled by Drew Maddox. He's rich and famous, and all that. But I've heard stories—"

"Hold it right there. I'm not interested in hearing sleazy gossip about my boyfriend, and from you, of all people. Just don't."

"He'll be unfaithful to you," Rupert informed her.

Amazing, that he could say it with a straight face. "Are you listening to yourself?"

"Of course I am," he said huffily.

She realized, with a flash of understanding, that had been the problem all along. He listened to himself only.

That was the difference between him and Drew. One of the many. Drew actually heard what she said. Rupert never had.

"You cheated on me with Kayleigh, and you dare to preach to me?" she said.

"I learned from my mistakes," Rupert said loftily. "And I suffered for them. I doubt very much that Drew Maddox will. From what I read, he's not even capable of—"

"Shut up, Rupert," she said. "I don't want to hear about your mistakes, or your suffering. And don't say a word about Drew."

"I'm sorry to distress you, but you have to face the facts," Rupert said, in lofty tones. "Truth hurts, Jenna."

"So does a broken jaw."

Drew's voice sounded from behind them, low and soft with controlled rage.

Twenty

Jenna spun around, horrified. "Drew?"

Drew studied that son of a bitch looming over Jenna through a haze of red. His hands clenched. "What are you doing up here alone with this loser?"

"He wanted a word with me," Jenna said tartly. "And I didn't want to have an audience for this conversation. I'm tired of my life being public performance art."

Rupert shrank back as Drew strode over to stand behind Jenna, giving the man a stare that was calculated to make him squirm and sweat.

"Would you excuse us, Jenna?" he said. "I'd like to talk to this guy in private."

Rupert was now edging along the wall toward the door. *Good. Be afraid, jerkwad.*

"Why?" Jenna demanded. "You have nothing to say to him."

"I have plenty to say to a guy who's trying to move in on my fiancée." Drew kept his eyes fixed on the guy, tracking his every move. Rupert's forehead was getting shiny.

"The answer is no," Jenna said sharply. "I'm not going anywhere while you have that look on your face."

Rupert was almost at the door, still sliding along with his back to the wallpaper. "Come with me, Jenna!" he begged, holding out his hand to her as if to a drowning person. "We belong together! You deserve better than a…a degenerate playboy!"

Jenna sighed heavily. "Rupert, go. And I mean, right now. Leave the building."

"You had your chance, and you blew it." Drew's voice was low and menacing. "Stay the hell away from her. Or I will destroy you."

Rupert stumbled out the door and disappeared.

After a moment's stunned silence, Jenna turned to Drew, her eyes bright with outrage. "You'll destroy him? Did I really hear you say that?"

"I meant every word," Drew said. "That son of a bitch was making a move on you. Am I supposed to pretend I don't notice?"

"No!" she said sharply. "You're supposed to actually not notice! Rupert doesn't count! He's not your rival, he's just a silly, self-involved jerk. Nothing he says should be taken seriously!"

It took Drew a moment to work up the nerve to say it. "What about me?" he asked. "Do you take me seriously?"

Jenna looked startled at the question. She gazed at him for a moment.

"Yes," she said finally. "I do, absolutely. There is no comparison between you and him."

A sigh of relief came out of him. "So you don't still have feelings for him?"

She let out an incredulous laugh. "For Rupert? Oh, God, no. You were jealous?"

"Yes," he admitted. "I wanted to kill the guy."

"Oh, please. I never did have feelings for him, not really. I just convinced myself that I did, because I had nothing to compare it to."

"Meaning that now you do?"

Her face flushed. "Well, yes. As I'm sure you can guess."

"I could guess," he said. "But I don't want to. Not any-more. Spell it out for me."

Jenna let out a long, shaky breath. "I never felt for him what I feel for you."

He just kept on waiting. "So far, so good, but I'm still in suspense. What do you feel for me?"

She let out a shaky laugh. "Wow, you're relentless to-night."

"I just walked in here and found another man trying to steal my lady," Drew said. "I need some reassurance. So sue me."

"How's this for reassurance?" Jenna wound her arms around his neck and kissed him.

Reality shifted on its axis, like it always did when they touched. Desire flared up, hot and immediate. She wrapped her leg around his legs and braced herself, her breasts press-ing against his tux shirt. Melting for him, straining to get closer. Locked in a breathless kiss.

Jenna lifted her head when she felt cool air on her bare back. He'd undone some of the hooks of her dress. She pulled away, laughing and shaking her head. "Oh, no you don't! You're not getting my clothes off any place where people could burst in on us. Never again. I haven't even processed the trauma from the last time."

He looked around, and pulled her into the bathroom, flipping the door lock and switching on the light. Two soft-focus lights from wall sconces lit the flesh-toned marble of the bathroom. She was so beautiful, her eyes dazed, cheeks pink, red lips softly parted as he hoisted her up onto the wide sink, pushing up the big, rustling armfuls of midnight blue taffeta until he found her hot, smooth skin above the thigh-high stockings.

He slid his hands higher, to the tender, secret flesh. Stroking her with teasing fingertips, making her melt and writhe and press his hand against herself, demanding more.

He sank down to his knees, pushing taffeta out of his way and tugging her small blue satin thong panties down. He pressed his mouth to her tender secret folds.

Her hot, sweet taste was intoxicating. He could never get enough. The way she opened to him like a flower, and then melted into shivering pleasure, coming for him. A long, strong, lingering climax that made him feel like a god.

He held her there for a few minutes until the aftershocks gave way to the shimmering glow, and that was as much as he could stand. He needed her…right…now.

He rose up, unfastening his pants, and scooped up her legs, draping them over his arms. Her hands clutched at his shoulders, fingernails digging in as he eased himself slowly, insistently inside her.

She was exquisitely ready. She took him so deep. Every liquid, sliding stroke was unbearably perfect. She'd forgotten the rest of the world existed, and he was glad, because he loved those breathless whimpering sounds she made, until that deep, sensual pulsing rhythm of his thrusts made them shake apart.

He pulled slowly, reluctantly out of her, leaning his damp forehead against hers. Awestruck, like always.

He set her gently on the floor before he tucked his shirt back into his pants.

"Staking your claim much?" she asked shakily. But there was breathless laughter in her voice.

Drew took his time in responding, washing his face in the sink. "If that's what I was doing, expect me to keep doing it. I'll stake my claim every chance I get."

His phone buzzed in his pocket. A text from Zack.

Someone threw a rock through a window in the Azalea Room while they were setting up the dessert buffet. They're moving the buffet to the Rose Room.

"There's a situation downstairs," he said. "I need to check it out."

"I'll take a minute to put myself together," Jenna said. "See you back in the ballroom?"

"Yeah." He gave her a long, possessive kiss, then stepped back to watch as she smoothed and shook down her skirt. She started fixing her makeup. She was so damn gorgeous. It blew his mind.

Jenna slanted him an amused look. "Didn't you have someplace to be?"

Damn. "Yeah, guess so." He forced himself to back out. Closed the door after himself.

Kissing her had knocked Zack's message right out of his mind.

Being in love made it hard to concentrate.

Twenty-One

Jenna remained in the private suite for at least ten minutes before she could stand without wobbling. She washed up, freshened her makeup, adjusted her hair. She'd put her whole heart on the table for him. It made her giddy and scared.

She was as decent as she could make herself by the time she ventured out of that room, but her hot pink flush just wouldn't fade.

It would be all too easy to guess what she and Drew had been up to. All they had to do was look at her eyes, her cheeks, her hair. She was so sick of having her private life be everybody's entertainment.

"Jenna! I thought I might find you here."

She spun around with a squeak of alarm as a hand clamped her wrist. "Harold? What on earth—you scared me!"

"Just wanted a word." His eyes raked her up and down.

"Yeah, you and everyone else. Not now." She tugged at her wrist.

He didn't let go. "I just need a minute of your time. Could we slip into the suite to have a private—"

"Absolutely not," she said forcefully.

Harold shrugged. "Fine, but I have something to tell you and it's in your best interests to hear it behind closed doors. Trust me on this."

Trust him? *Ha.* "Right here is just fine," she said. "Make it quick."

Harold's eyes lingered on her flushed face, the smudges of makeup below her eyes, her cleavage. "I saw Drew strutting down the stairs like the cock of the walk," he said. "I can imagine what the two of you were up to in there. Fun, huh?"

"Get lost, Harold." She yanked again.

Harold held on, his fingers digging into her skin. "I'm trying to do you a favor."

"I'm doing just fine without any favors from you."

"Believe me, you'll be grateful." He held up his phone. "Have you seen this?"

Her eyes went to the screen, in spite of herself—and stiffened at what she saw.

The screen showed a photo of Drew, stretched out naked in a huge bed, apparently sleeping, and surrounded by naked women. And there was more—much more. Many women. The pictures flashed by, one after the other.

In all of them, Drew appeared to be unconscious.

Harold just watched her face avidly as she stared down at his screen. "Where did you get these photos?" she asked. "Who gave them to you?"

"Just what did Drew tell you about Sobel's party?" Harold asked.

"None of your business, Harold," she said.

"I know what he told my uncle," Harold said. "They knocked him down onto that couch and took compromising photos of him. Right? And that was all. He didn't tell you that he slunk out of that place the next morning after rolling around all night with a bunch of call girls. There's timed security footage of him walking out of that place at ten thirty-five. Word is, there are videos of the fun and games that happened during the night, too. Imagine how you'll feel when those videos drop."

She tried not to imagine it. There was a painful rock in her throat. "We are not having this conversation," she said. "Get the hell away from me."

"He's a liar, Jenna. Don't fall for it. You're smarter than that."

Jenna seized Harold's fingers, still clamped around her wrist, and pried them loose. She stepped back, rubbing her sore arm. There was a cold, sick weight in her belly. "I don't believe you," she said.

Harold's expression didn't change. "Those pictures don't care what you believe. Neither will anyone else who sees them. And they will see. They're viral already."

"All I saw was an unconscious man with some woman draped over him in bed," she said. "He told me he was ambushed. This doesn't disprove that."

Harold shook his head. "You are so far gone," he said, in a pitying tone. "What's it going to take to disillusion you?"

"A lot more than you've got," she told him.

Harold shrugged. "Your blind faith is touching but pathetic. Let Drew sort out his own garbage. You have a career and reputation to protect. The more distance you get from him, the better off you'll be. Believe me. I'm trying to help."

"No, you're not," she said. "I've had people help me before. It doesn't feel like this."

Harold walked away, and Jenna stood like she'd been turned to stone. Her euphoria had been transformed into a gut-churning cold sweat. If those pictures really were doing the rounds on the internet, then things were going to get ugly for Drew in a big, public way. Tonight. She had to warn him.

At the same time, she was furious at him. Had he been making a fool of her, telling her it had just been photos that evening at Sobel's party? He'd said nothing to her about staying the night in a bed full of naked women and leaving the next morning.

Not that it was any of her business. It all happened before she'd gotten involved with him at all, to be absolutely fair. Still, if they'd videotaped him in that state, his goose was cooked. At least at Maddox Hill.

Was that what she had to look forward to? Her lover's sex tapes, doled out online one by one, with lots of buzz and buildup to a gleeful, greedy viewing public? It would be so awful.

She stopped next to the window overlooking the garden, pressing her forehead against the cold glass. God, what was it about her and men? Was she destined for this? Did she have a sign on her back? Gullible Nitwit. Please Lie to Me.

In any case, she didn't want him taken by surprise. She texted him. where r u?

She hurried down the stairs and caught sight of Vann, Drew's CFO, muttering into a phone. He closed the call when he saw her.

"Vann, have you seen Drew?" she asked.

"Last I saw, he was heading over to the security station with Zack."

"Thanks." She stared down at her phone. Still nothing from Drew. She texted ?? and started trotting in that direction, tottering on those ridiculous heels. Then she stopped, and with a muttered obscenity, plucked the shoes off. She gathered up big armfuls of that huge skirt and ran in her stocking feet.

Zack gave her an odd look when she skidded into the security center sideways, pink and out of breath. "Jenna? What's up? Everything okay?"

"Fine," she said, panting. "But I need to find Drew. He's not answering my texts."

"I saw him heading back toward the ballroom a few minutes ago," Zack told her. He gestured toward the bank of security monitors. "Check those out. You might see him."

Jenna leaned over, peering at the images on various

screens, one after the other. Drew didn't show up in any of them. Damn.

She turned to hurry out, but something on the last screen caught her eye. She turned back, leaning closer. That camera showed part of the grounds and the parking lot, and a tall man walking toward...*wait*.

Was that Harold? What...?

A car pulled up, and a woman was getting out of the back seat. She was tall and slim with a big cloud of curly blond hair. In the orange-tinted gloom of the parking lot, her eyes were smudgy pools of shadow. Harold took her arm, and she stumbled back against the car.

Harold pulled the tottering woman sharply after him and out of the camera's range. They looked like they were heading toward the side lobby, which was currently not in use.

Harold was up to something. She had to find out what it was. She didn't need any more damn surprises tonight, thank you very much.

Jenna ignored the security staff's puzzled looks as she took off once again, shoes swinging by their straps as she ran to the side lobby. No time to explain anything to anyone.

The eastern lobby was deserted. It had a large number of large, bushy plants in the vaulted atrium around a decorative waterfall that wasn't in use yet.

The big revolving door was shut, but someone had propped open the door beside it. Jenna slunk back against the wall behind the bushiest foliage as Harold and the woman with him appeared through the glass door.

They burst through it, arguing. Jenna slid back along the wall and into the recessed entry to the women's bathroom, gathering her skirt into a tight bundle to keep it quiet.

"You had one job, Tina. One. I said not to be late. Timing is everything tonight."

"I told you! I had a problem with Lauretta's bonehead boyfriend, and he—"

"I don't want to hear about it," Harold snarled. "Hurry!"

"I gotta stop at the bathroom," Tina said, her voice sulky. "When you're pregnant, you gotta pee all the time. I came all the way from Lauretta's house and it's, like, an hour and a half from here. So I—"

"We don't have time!" Harold urged.

Jenna's heart thudded as she slunk backward through the bathroom door, hoping it wouldn't creak. She dived into one of the stalls, locking it and climbing up onto the toilet, her skirt wound into a ball in her lap. Her phone chirped with an incoming message. Oh, no, no, no... Drew was finally responding to her texts. Freaking spectacular timing.

Jenna jerked the phone out of her evening bag with trembling hands, silenced it, then clicked open the audio recording app. She crouched there, balanced on her toes. Afraid to move or breathe as she heard Tina's shoes clicking against the bathroom floor.

Harold followed her in, still scolding. "Hurry up! We're missing it!"

Tina banged open the door of one of the stalls. "Why do you have to be so mean?"

"Why do you have to be so dumb?" Harold shot back. "And speaking of dumb, did you check the bathroom stalls?"

"No," Tina said, her voice sulky.

Jenna's teeth clenched as Harold swept the line of stalls, peering under the doors for feet. He didn't try to open any of the doors, to her intense relief.

"I don't deserve to be treated like crap," Tina said.

"I paid you." Harold's voice was icy cold. "We had an agreement."

"Yeah, well we also have a baby," Tina said, sniffling.

Harold made an impatient sound. "You signed the documents. You took the money. Do what I ask and don't give me trouble. Have the baby or don't, whatever you want, just don't involve me. He'll give you more money not to bust his balls, or else my uncle will. So shut up and be grateful."

"Why do I always get sucked into your schemes?" Tina complained. The toilet flushed loudly. "It's gross," she went on, when the noise abated. "Having me spray ketamine in your cousin's face was a real psycho move, Harry, and it was a monster dose, too. Poor guy was sick as a dog. You coulda killed him. And now I gotta go in front of all those people and tell them he got me pregnant? Why do you hate this dude so much? Did he, like, kill your puppy?"

"Hurry up, Tina. It's too late for a crisis of conscience."

She banged the stall door open again. Her heels clicked on her way to the sink. "I don't see why you even have to be this big-shot CEO at all." The water hissed as she washed her hands. "You're doin' fine. I've seen your house, your car. You got money. More'n I ever had, that's for sure. Can't we just be happy? With the baby?"

"You really think that scenario could ever make me happy, Tina? Wake up."

Tina turned the water off, sniffling loudly.

"Oh, for God's sake, don't start crying," Harold said impatiently. "We don't have time for this. Put your lipstick on. Come on, hurry!"

The door sighed closed after them, and clicked shut. Their squabbling voices faded away.

Jenna finally dared to exhale, teetering. She caught herself on the side of the bathroom stall, stepped down onto the bathroom floor. Her legs felt like jelly.

She ran the recording back, with ice-cold, clammy fingers, and clicked Play.

...we're missing it.

Why do you have to be so mean?

Why do you have to be so dumb? And speaking of dumb, did you check the bathroom stalls?

The voices were faint, but clear, and turning the volume

up made Harold's nasal, drawling voice perfectly recognizable. Thank God.

She'd gotten it all, from the very beginning. But it wasn't going to do Drew a damn bit of good unless everyone heard it all at once, at the right moment, and before Harold's big fabricated bombshell.

Jenna edged out of the women's room and looked up the hall. Tina and Harold were just turning the corner, still snarking at each other as he dragged her along toward the ballroom. She couldn't go that way without overtaking them, and she wanted to get there first, without them knowing that she'd copped to their game.

The fastest alternative way back to the ballroom was outside, along the walkway skirting the building and back through the front entrance.

Jenna hurried out, barely feeling the frigid wind or the wooden planks beneath her feet as she ran. She hiked her skirt up and held her shoes with the other hand. They bounced against her leg with each step.

She stopped outside the lobby and stepped back into her shoes. A swift peek at her own reflection in the glass made her realize that at this point, there was just no way to salvage the up-do. Her hair needed to come down, once and for all. She plucked out the pins and shook her mane loose over her shoulders, finger-combing it as she hurried inside. She was flushed and her chest was heaving, but she was presentable.

She pushed through the double doors into the dimmed ballroom. All lights were trained on the dais where the master of ceremonies stood, about to award the Wexler Prize.

Vann stepped out of the shadows, looking alarmed. "Jenna? What's going on? They're announcing the prize! Get over there with your team, quick!"

Jenna grabbed his arm. "Vann, I need your help. Can you run an audio recording that's on my phone onto the sound system of this room, right now? It's for Drew. To save his bacon. Please, please, please help me. Time is of the essence."

Vann's eyes widened. "Yes," he said swiftly. "Of course. Where is it?"

She pulled up the file and handed him her phone. "Listen for my cue," she said. "It was recorded in a bathroom stall, so crank up the volume to the max."

"...and this year's Wexler Prize for Excellence in Biomedical Engineering is awarded to...the Arm's Reach Foundation!"

The room erupted in thunderous applause.

"Go!" Vann whispered into her ear. "I got this."

Her team, gathered at the table that had been assigned to them, had risen to their feet and were scanning the room for her with desperate eyes.

She waved at them and hurried up to the front of the room, hoping her hair wasn't too wild. She'd just throw her shoulders back, tilt up her chin, and act like she'd meant it all along. It was the only way to go.

Applause swelled as she climbed up onto the stage and joined her team. The master of ceremonies went on with his spiel. "We've just in the past few months had the immense pleasure of learning about the work of Jenna Somers and her amazing team at Arm's Reach. Now let's watch a video tribute to their passion and dedication that the talented Ava Maddox has prepared for us! Ladies and gentlemen...enjoy!"

The lights went down, the screen lit up and the video began to play.

Twenty-Two

Something was extremely wrong. Drew had been continually texting back to Jenna's frantic message, and she wasn't responding. She wasn't at her place for the dinner either, nor was she at the Arm's Reach table, and now everyone was giving him strange looks, as if they knew something that he didn't.

What the hell? The Wexler Prize was about to be presented, and Jenna was nowhere to be found. Screw this stupid ceremony. He was about to march up on the stage, grab the mic and tell everyone to leave what they were doing and start looking for Jenna when an excited murmur swept over the place.

There. It was her. A flash of light from the brighter corridor outside had spilled into the candlelit ballroom, lighting her up from behind. She'd let her hair down. It was a halo, rimmed with light from the door behind her like a cloud with the sun behind it. She looked wild and gorgeous and sexy. A celestial sky-being. The queen of the night. So damn hot.

Thank God she was okay. Now he could breathe.

She grabbed Vann by the arm, whispered something to him, pressing something into his hand. The murmuring of the crowd got louder.

"…Wexler Prize for Excellence in Biomedical Engineering is awarded to…the Arm's Reach Foundation!"

Drew pushed his way through the ballroom toward her, but Jenna didn't see him. On her trajectory, he wouldn't be able to intercept her before she got up to the dais.

Now she was up on stage with her team. She looked amazing. Her color was high and her eyes sparkled as she scanned the crowd.

The MC carried on with his presentation as Drew forced his way closer to the dais.

"…watch a video tribute to their passion and dedication that the talented Ava Maddox has prepared for us! Ladies and gentlemen…enjoy!"

The lights on the podium dimmed and the screen lit up, but it wasn't the montage of highlights that Ava had compiled from her video series that started to play.

It was a series of photos of him from Arnold Sobel's party. What the *hell*…?

There were gasps all around him. Drew fought the sinking feeling. Cold sweat broke out on his back. He suddenly had the stench of perfume in his nose. The pain of his throbbing head. He looked up at Jenna on the dais.

She wasn't even looking at the photos on the screen behind her. She was looking straight at him. There was no anger or blame or even surprise in her eyes, just a piercing urgency, as if she wanted him to do something, understand something.

He had no idea what, but he was horrified. Whoever was trying to mess with him had chosen the most public moment possible, and was humiliating Jenna in the process. This was her big night to be celebrated for all of her accomplishments, and somehow, Drew had managed to burn it to the ground.

Uncle Malcolm was yelling at him, of course, but Drew

couldn't bring himself to listen. He just stared up at the woman he loved, feeling it all slip away.

Uncle Malcolm's words started sinking in. "...turn that thing off, for the love of God! Turn it off!"

"I'm trying to, sir, but I don't know—"

There was a crash, followed by shrieking. Drew looked around. Uncle Malcolm had hurled the laptop down onto the marble tiles. Glass from the screen and letters from the keyboard were scattered all around.

"I've had enough!" his uncle roared. "No more!"

There was another flash of light from the back of the room, and another woman ran into the room, tottering on her high heels. She threw herself at Drew.

"You got me pregnant!" she shrieked.

She was close enough now for him to recognize her. It was the blond woman who had been pictured with him in the tabloid photos, and the ones he'd just seen. The same puffy lips, the same black-rimmed blue eyes, the same streams of mascara running down both her cheeks.

It was the perfume-squirting girl from Arnold Sobel's party.

Pandemonium. Everyone in the room was talking or yelling. Uncle Malcolm could be heard howling above them all. Jenna tried to catch Drew's eye, but now Tina was pounding her fists on Drew's chest. Drew caught her hands and immobilized them, leaning close to speak to her urgently. Whatever he said made her face crumple, and she started to ugly-cry, her mascara cascading down even faster.

"Get out!" Malcolm yelled. "Get this creature out of my sight! And you!" He rounded on Drew, pounding his cane on the floor, his face a dangerously dark red. "You think you can make a fool of me again? I am through with you! You are *done*!"

Drew didn't even respond to his uncle. He just turned his back, looking up at Jenna with a question in his eyes. She could tell that he thought he already knew the answer.

Jenna pulled the mic from the MC'S hand. The man was too startled to yank it back. "It's not his child, Malcolm," Jenna said into the mic. "She was paid to say that."

Malcolm swung around, eyes bulging. "Of course you would cover for him!" he sputtered. "You're in love with him, God help you."

"I have proof." Her voice rang out. "And I want you all to hear it."

Malcolm went still. He slowly turned toward her, his eyes sharpening. The room started quieting down. "What proof are you talking about?" he demanded.

"Vann?" Jenna called out. "Hit it."

There was a buzzy, staticky squeal in the speakers, and the recording began to play. Harold's voice blared out, grinding and nasal.

...we're missing it.

Why do you have to be so mean? Tina's voice, gratingly loud.

The room went silent to listen. The people in that room hung on every word of the bathroom conversation. Tina put her hands on her face, sobbing and shaking her head *no*.

Drew looked up at her, shaking his head. *How?* he mouthed.

Jenna shrugged, which was a very bad idea, considering the precarious state of her décolletage. She grabbed her bodice before it slid down to do a nip slip worthy of a Super Bowl halftime show, and tugged it up, willing it to stay put.

...put your lipstick on! Come on, hurry!"

The click of the bathroom door closing ended the recording. The crowd let out a collective sigh of wonder, and the excited conversation swelled again.

Jenna and Drew couldn't look away from each other. The MC was yelling at her excitedly but Jenna couldn't understand a word the man was saying.

"Harold?" Malcolm roared. "That was Harold on that tape?"

"Yes, it was Harold," Jenna said into the mic. "There he is, slithering away out the southeast door right now! Don't run off, Harold! Some people want a word with you!"

"Stop him!" Malcolm hollered. "That lying bastard has to answer to me!"

Once again, the room erupted into noisy madness. Jenna handed the mic back to the MC. Fortunately, the guy was an old pro, and good at crowd control. He got to work on trying to get the evening somehow back on track, but Jenna couldn't follow his patter. Not with Drew walking toward the dais, gazing up at her. His whole soul shining out of his eyes.

"…Ms. Somers? Ms. Somers?" The MC again.

"Jenna!" Charles, her team leader, stage-whispered from the back of the dais. "Hey! Jenna, he's calling you! Come and get the prize!"

Somehow, she got herself functioning again. She pasted on a big smile as she went over to receive the prize plaque, and held it up to thunderous applause.

It felt surreal. Far away, like a dream. She made some kind of an acceptance speech. God knows what she said, but the crowd seemed to love it.

So…great. She'd done it. Arm's Reach had the Wexler Prize, in spite of everything. She should feel triumphant, but she couldn't seem to breathe.

In front of the stage, Tina had crumpled to the floor in a dead faint. Pregnancy hormones, guilt, theatrics, who knew. Not Jenna's problem. All she cared about right now was Drew and the dazzled look in his eyes as he gazed up at her.

Afterwards, the rest of the team went back to their table,

but she didn't follow. She walked over to the edge of the dais where Drew stood.

He reached up, clasping her waist. She laid both hands on his shoulders as he lifted her and let her slide down his body into a tight, hot embrace. His arms tightened around her, and he put his mouth to her ear.

"That was incredible," he murmured. "Are you okay?"

"Fine," she murmured. "You?"

"Never mind me. I'm so sorry, Jenna. This was your moment to shine. And it got steamrolled."

She shrugged. "I'm fine. I got the prize, right? That's the important thing. And I kicked Harold's ass, which is very satisfying. So it's all good."

He shook his head, wonderingly. "How in holy hell did you pull that off?"

She wound her arms around him and squeezed. "I got lucky," she said. "Right time, right place."

Drew hugged her back, putting his mouth to her ear. "I want you to know this," he said quietly. "The only reason I was in that bed with those women was because I was drugged. That's not who I am."

She nodded. "Yes," she replied. "I know that."

He let out a sigh of relief. "Thanks," he whispered. "For believing in me."

They just swayed together like a single being, shaking with the intensity of their embrace. Drew looked up. "You know what this means, don't you?"

"It means a whole lot of things," she observed. "Where to even begin?"

"My uncle just fired me," he said. "And I'm fine with that. Finally, things between us are simple, like they should have been from the start. No putting on a show, ever again. I don't need you to save my reputation. I don't want anything except to love you. I don't have anything to offer you but myself."

She pressed her hand to her shaking mouth. "Drew," she whispered.

"Marry me," he said. "For real."

Jenna looked around them, at the crowd of people watching. She laughed out loud.

"You're proposing to me here? In front of everyone?"

Drew's laughter was so happy, she started laughing, too. "Sorry," he said. "I got overexcited and completely forgot they were there. You just have that effect on me."

Jenna wiped her eyes. "I…wow," she whispered.

"Take your time," he said. "As long as you need. I'm not going anywhere, Jenna. I want you to marry me, and I'll spend the rest of my life making damn sure you don't regret it."

"Oh, God, Drew."

Drew glanced around, as if suddenly noticing the ring of people around them, avidly listening. "Maybe some privacy, to talk it over?" he suggested. "We could skip town for a while. I'm a free man now, and your team can cover for you at Arm's Reach for a little while, right? We could blast out of here tonight."

"What?" Uncle Malcolm's voice cut through the murmuring buzz of voices around them. "Who said you were a free man? Who said you could blast out of town?"

"You just banished me, Uncle," Drew pointed out. "I think that means I can go."

"Oh, don't be childish," Malcolm said gruffly. "I wasn't myself. You're not going anywhere. You're my CEO!"

"Actually, you weren't invited into this conversation at all," Drew told him.

Ava stepped forward. She blew Jenna a kiss, her eyes shining, and then murmured into her uncle's ear in low, soothing tones, leading him firmly away.

Drew turned back to her, and when their eyes met, that

magical bubble reformed around them. They were surrounded by people, but they might as well have been alone.

Drew rested his forehead against hers. "Now, from the top," he said. "Shall we go find someplace private so I can try this whole marriage proposal thing again?"

Jenna laughed through her tears. "How about if I just save us some time and say hell yes right now, so we can skip ahead to the good part?"

His reply was a kiss of such molten intensity, neither of them even heard the appreciative roar of applause that shook the room. It could have been miles away.

All that mattered was the two of them together. The road ahead, to parts unknown.

And the love, lighting their way.

* * * * *

COMING SOON!

We really hope you enjoyed reading this book.
If you're looking for more romance, be sure to
head to the shops when new books are
available on

Thursday 4th March

LET'S TALK

Romance

For exclusive extracts, competitions
and special offers, find us online:

f facebook.com/millsandboon

🐦 @MillsandBoon

📷 @MillsandBoonUK

Get in touch on 01413 063232

MILLS & BOON

THE HEART OF ROMANCE

A ROMANCE FOR EVERY KIND OF READER

MODERN

Prepare to be swept off your feet by sophisticated, sexy and seductive heroes, in some of the world's most glamourous and romantic locations, where power and passion collide.
8 stories per month.

HISTORICAL

Escape with historical heroes from time gone by. Whether your passion is for wicked Regency Rakes, muscled Vikings or rugged Highlanders, awaken the romance of the past.
6 stories per month.

MEDICAL

Set your pulse racing with dedicated, delectable doctors in the high-pressure world of medicine, where emotions run high and passion, comfort and love are the best medicine.
6 stories per month.

True Love

Celebrate true love with tender stories of heartfelt romance, from the rush of falling in love to the joy a new baby can bring, and a focus on the emotional heart of a relationship.
8 stories per month.

Desire

Indulge in secrets and scandal, intense drama and plenty of sizzling hot action with powerful and passionate heroes who have it all: wealth, status, good looks...everything but the right woman.
6 stories per month.

HEROES

Experience all the excitement of a gripping thriller, with an intense romance at its heart. Resourceful, true-to-life women and strong, fearless men face danger and desire - a killer combination!
8 stories per month.

DARE

Sensual love stories featuring smart, sassy heroines you'd want as a best friend, and compelling intense heroes who are worthy of them.
4 stories per month.

To see which titles are coming soon, please visit

millsandboon.co.uk/nextmonth

JOIN US ON SOCIAL MEDIA!

Stay up to date with our latest releases, author
news and gossip, special offers and discounts, and
all the behind-the-scenes action
from Mills & Boon...

 millsandboon

 millsandboonuk

 millsandboon

It might just be true love...

MILLS & BOON

HISTORICAL

Awaken the romance of the past

Escape with historical heroes from time gone by. Whether your passion is for wicked Regency Rakes, muscled Viking warriors or rugged Highlanders, indulge your fantasies and awaken the romance of the past.

MILLS & BOON
MODERN
Power and Passion

Prepare to be swept off your feet by sophisticated, sexy and seductive heroes, in some of the world's most glamourous and romantic locations, where power and passion collide.

MILLS & BOON

HEROES

At Your Service

Experience all the excitement of a gripping thriller, with an intense romance at its heart. Resourceful, true-to-life women and strong, fearless men face danger and desire - a killer combination!